THE

DELUSION

THE
DELUSION

A THRILLER

T. O. PAINE

DARK
SWALLOW
BOOKS

Copyright © 2024 by T. O. Paine and Dark Swallow Books.
All rights reserved, including the right of reproduction in whole or in part in any form.

Published by Dark Swallow Books
www.darkswallowbooks.com

LCCN: 2023922088

Paperback ISBN-13: 978-0-9992183-8-9
Hardcover ISBN-13: 978-0-9992183-9-6
eBook ISBN-13: 979-8-9866958-3-9

"For this reason God will send upon them a deluding influence so that they will believe what is false, in order that they all may be judged who did not believe the truth, but took pleasure in wickedness."

—The Bible, *2 Thessalonians 2:11-12*

CHAPTER ONE

EMMA

A faded, metallic-gold car from the nineties pulls in behind me. I swear I've seen it before. Is it from the nineties? I'm not sure. It could be a decade newer than that. Or, like me, a decade older. An eighties baby. It's a plain, four-door sedan. Cheap and boxy. Tinted windows mask the person inside, giving off a desperate attempt at sophistication, smothering an otherwise dismal and run-down machine.

Like me.

I check my mascara in the rearview mirror. I'm not used to wearing makeup. My hair is already coming out of the bun, but it only needs to hold for a couple more hours until they announce the winners of this year's Tiberian Research Award in Psychology. Then, everything will change.

I can't be late for the banquet.

My thigh tenses as I hold the brake pedal to the floor, waiting for the light to change.

I'll shoot myself if I get stuck at a table with Wilson.

Wilson Sinclair doesn't deserve to win the award with us. He doesn't deserve to be there at all. Dr. Santan and I spent too many years working through to the dim light of dawn while Wilson slept. While he vacationed in Maui. While he eagerly put his name on our research papers, only occasionally cracking open a periodical or conducting an experimental study.

We deserve to win.

Wilson doesn't.

The doors to the hotel banquet hall opened over an hour ago, according to the schedule.

I'm going to be late. This isn't like me. I'm normally very punctual.

The traffic light turns green, and I accelerate through the intersection.

The golden sedan follows.

I consider turning right at the next light to see if it will follow me.

What a stupid thought.

It's not following me.

I'm imagining a stalker scenario only because I'm certain I've seen that car before. Of course, I've probably seen most of the cars on this road before. The difference is, I vividly remember the golden paint job. It sticks out amongst the newer black, white, and gray SUVs that have overtaken our majestic city of Baltimore.

Listen to me. *Overtaken our majestic city of Baltimore.* I sound like a news reporter.

My cell rings.

Alyssa. My best friend, confidant, and Queen of Bad Timing.

"What's up?" I ask.

"Tonight's the big night, right?"

"Yes."

"Congratulations. I'm so happy for you."

"It hasn't happened yet. I'm on my way there now."

"I'll be quick. Can you babysit for Vivian tomorrow?"

"Alyssa. Really?"

"Please. You know how much she loves it when you sit for her."

"I don't know what tomorrow looks like."

"It looks like a Saturday, but you wouldn't know what Saturdays look like, would you? Won't your research ever end? After you win the award, won't you get your life back?"

She has a point. When will I get my life back? We finished the research months ago, but the work hasn't stopped. I got caught up in circulating our findings. Conducting follow-on studies. Drafting potential proposals to fund the next phase. It hasn't ended, and it likely won't end soon.

I turn left at the light. When I wasn't looking, a large black SUV slipped between the golden sedan and my mini-SUV, but they're still back there. That nineties reject. Sitting in my lane.

"Can I call you later?"

"I wanted to tell Vivian you'd babysit before she went to bed tonight. She'll be so excited. Are you sure you won't have some time tomorrow? I only need you in the afternoon."

"I might have to work. I don't know."

"This wasn't your plan." Her voice has tensed. She sounds like my mother.

"I know."

She's so right. Working day and night on Dr. Santan's research—the psychology behind digital mass persuasion—for the rest of my life . . . that wasn't the plan. Working day and night until we were published, until my name was cemented in the field—*that* was the plan. And then we *were* published. Without my name. So, the carrot moved to tonight.

I need my name on that award to get recognition for my work and enter the next phase of my life.

I need it more than anything else in the world.

The hotel comes into view as I crest a hill and survey the parking lot for a spot.

The golden car is gone.

Alyssa's still at me. She's the dog, I'm the bone. "You always said you'd find someone and have kids once you made it. Right?"

"That was my mother's plan. Not mine."

"Sorry. I didn't mean to—"

"No, you're right. It was kinda my plan, too. I just don't know if it begins tomorrow."

"You're so great with Vivian. She loves you so much. You're going to be a great mother, just like your mom was."

"Thanks. I'm at the hotel. I've got to go."

"Good luck. Oh, wait—is your dad going to be there?"

"No. He couldn't make it."

"Oh well, I'm sure he's proud of you. I'm sure your mom would have been proud too."

I pull into a parking space and turn the engine off.

Sticking to the plan hasn't been easy since Mom died. Solidify my career and give her the grandchildren she always wanted. It can't happen now. It's too late for me to begin pumping out puppies. She's gone. Besides, the more I learn about the people in this world—how their brains work, how susceptible they are to misinformation—the less interested I am in contributing to the mess. My thinking has regressed back to my teenage years. Anti-corporate resolutions. Environmental activism. General angst. The world has enough people. We're all nothing but sheep, wandering aimlessly through life, consuming what each other makes, all the while destroying the environment.

Don't get me wrong. I'm not a granola-crunching, plant-based-meat-eating environmentalist. Those people are noble but too extreme for me. Besides, there's only so much a single person can do. I like to think I do my part. The problem is, the world is running out of time. There's never enough time.

"Emma? Are you still there? I'm sorry for bringing up your mom."

"It's okay. My head is just a little jumbled right now." I get out of my car and stride toward the front entrance. "It's been three years. You'd think I'd be over her by now."

"You know that's not how it works."

"I've got to go. I'm late."

"What do you want me to tell Vivian?"

"Tell her I'll be there. I'll come over around noon."

"Thanks. You're the best."

The hotel's automatic doors slide open, and I rush inside. A poster-size electronic screen directs me toward the main banquet hall. Lush green plants reach for the ceiling, their stems rising from blue and white ceramic pots placed along the walls, their leaves obscuring the windows. Dark wooden doors to the hall hang open ahead of me, and I quicken my pace down the long hallway.

Wilson will most likely have sat right next to D'Angelo. I should try to sit at the same table so we can accept the award as a team, but I secretly hope there are no seats left.

I do *not* want to sit next to Wilson.

A hotel attendant begins to close the doors before I can get there, but he stops when he sees me coming. I hate being late. Being last is so embarrassing. It's so—everyone always looks at you. I've tried to be fashionably late before, but I'm not the fashionable type.

Maybe I'm not the last one this time.

I glance back, hoping to see someone behind me, and my eyes are drawn to the big windows at the entrance.

The golden car pulls into the parking lot.

I slow down, watching as the nineties relic cruises to a stop near the automatic doors.

"Please, miss." The attendant waves me into the hall.

I crane my neck, hoping the driver will step out of the vehicle, but the door doesn't open.

Inside the hall, white tablecloths rest beneath polished silverware and spotless china, protecting round tables from drops of wine and breadcrumbs and pieces of cheese as the guests finish their entrees. Dr. Halsford, the master of ceremonies, takes the stage.

Far from the podium, two empty tables beckon me to end their loneliness, but it would be odd to sit that far away from Dr. Santan and my colleagues.

I walk softly toward the stage.

Heads turn to see the late-comer.

Me. They gawk at me.

There's one seat left near Dr. Santan in the front.

It's also next to Wilson.

His designer knock-off cologne smells like a nightclub bathroom.

I have no choice.

I take the seat next to him, and the awards ceremony begins.

CHAPTER TWO

TREY - *January 1998*

Trey Wilkes reached for his radio alarm clock when the buzzing sound erupted, but his fingers fell upon a cold, hard, empty surface. Nothing was where it should be. His throat ached. His eyes burned. He rolled over. The flowery yet soapy laundry detergent smell made his stomach convulse.

The buzzing threatened to split his head in two.

This is why he's always hated drinking.

He sat up, keeping his eyes closed. Fearful of letting the light into his pounding head. He sensed nothing but light in the room, and the light wasn't where it was supposed to be. Then he realized something.

He wasn't where he was supposed to be.

It wasn't the light that didn't belong.

It was him.

The buzzing stopped.

Sure enough, when he opened his eyes, a pain like no other shot into his head, and he was not where he was supposed to be. He was lying on the laundromat floor. No one else was there. He struggled to understand why he'd decided to do his laundry right after the party. He had no one to impress today. He didn't need his nice clothes today.

Not today.

What day was it?

He stood. Rubbed his head.

It was two weeks into the new year, and he hadn't found any investors yet.

A fog floated through his brain.

Somehow, he'd carried two black garbage bags of dirty clothes from his apartment to the laundromat in the wee morning hours and started a load. One bag lay empty, torn in half at his feet. The other leaned against a dryer across the aisle from the washing machines. He must have only slept an hour before the buzzing had come.

How much had he drunk?

Flashes of the dance club—violet LED strings, pink neon poster frames, black-lit lint exposing glowing skirts, short sleeves, silk button-down shirts—and then glimpses of Henrik's apartment with his European sound system pounding out Chumbawamba. Pounding it out. Pounding and pounding it out.

His head pounds it out.

He presses his temples.

No relief.

Had he made any connections last night? No.

Had any of Henrik's rich friends wanted a stake in his company? No.

None that he could remember.

He'd gone to the party hoping to network. Hoping to meet people to help with his business idea. Invest in him. Give him their time and money.

God knows his dad was never going to help. Rich penny

pincher.

After two years in college—okay, one and a half—he'd had enough. He was just like Bill Gates. Bill hadn't put up with this kind of crap. He dropped out of school and become the richest man in the world. He never tolerated boring classes and worthless assignments. Meaningless exams. Imbecilic professors. And things were worse now. Antiquated notions of business and technology flourished in the classrooms. Paleozoic, tenured professors going through the motions, teaching technology from books written in the sixties and seventies. Bill's era.

They didn't know anything about the internet.

Dinosaurs. Worthless dinosaurs. All of them.

He reached into his pocket and found a fist full of quarters. With classes starting this week, he needed his nicest clothes clean. Apparently, he'd been sober enough to remember to bring change for the laundry machines.

If only he'd stayed sober long enough to convince someone to invest. Like college, last night had been a major waste of time. He'd gotten wasted. He'd partied like it was 1999. It was his own fault he hadn't found an investor. If he was ever going to get out of here, he needed to stay on task. Take every opportunity to recruit the right people.

He tore open the other garbage bag and loaded his clothes into a washing machine.

The bells on the front door rang.

His head ached.

She came right up to him and put her laundry basket down next to his feet. "Are you using this one?" she asked, pointing at the washing machine beside his. Black dots curved beneath her lower lashes where her eye makeup had smudged. Her oversized sweatshirt hid the good parts, and the word

DONUTS ran in large pink letters down the thighs of her gray sweatpants.

"No, go ahead."

She opened the washing machine and emptied her basket into it. "What's your name?"

"Trey."

"I'm Meg." A gold bracelet adorned with diamonds slipped down her wrist. "Do you always do your laundry at four in the morning, Trey?"

"No. Do you?"

"This isn't my laundry. It's my sorority sister's."

Greek life. Hazing.

He closed the door to his machine. "What house are you in?"

"Alpha Tau Beta." She stood and closed the door to her machine.

The door slamming shut rang in Trey's ears.

Pain.

Along with four others, Alpha Tau Beta was on Trey's list. This was good. They were selective in their sisterhood. "Do you like that house?"

"Yeah, it's all right." She turned toward him, briefly made eye contact, then turned her gaze to the floor. "Are you in a frat?"

"No. I was my first year, but I'm my own now." He reached into his pocket and pulled out some quarters. His hand shook. He failed to slip the first one into the slot and dropped the rest.

"Oh, no," she said, kneeling to help.

He'd bent down also and, reaching for the coins, they hit heads.

The collision rocked Trey backward. Her hair smelled like

peaches and cigarettes. His guts revolted, but he held everything down. What had he eaten at Henrik's that was so fishy?

She leaped to her feet. "Sorry. Sorry. Here." She put a coin into his machine and then another. And then another. She hit the start button.

He stood. "Thanks."

The machine whirred to life.

"Are you okay?" she asked.

He rubbed his head. "It was a long night." There had been a green neon sign at the dance club hanging above the change machine. A dollar sign. Flashing. It had been flashing, and now, it was flashing in his head. He swallowed.

"Here's the rest of your change."

"No. You keep it. I have more."

The corners of her mouth curled up, and she averted her eyes. "Thanks."

"What's your major?"

"Anthropology."

More like anthro-*poverty*. Not good. There's no money in studies like that. But maybe she was a do-gooder. A Peace Corps idealist rebelling against her rich family's capitalist ways. But maybe someone in her family would like to invest.

"How about you?"

"Business."

"Oh." She ran her fingers through her hair and turned away. "What made you choose that?"

Something in his stomach made its presence known. Had he eaten sushi at Henrik's apartment? He swallowed hard, but the presence continued to push its way into his throat.

She picked up her laundry basket and placed it at the end of the seats.

"I don't know," he said. "I'm thinking of dropping or changing majors. I want to do something to help the world."

She turned back around. Looked at him with puppy brown eyes. "Like how?"

"I'm starting a business. With the internet. I have an idea for a website."

"It seems like everyone is doing that."

"Have you ever ordered anything online?"

"No. I only use it to look up things for school. I don't believe in credit cards, and you have to have one to buy anything on there."

"What do you mean you don't believe in credit cards?"

"Someone should blow up the credit card companies." She sat down. "They're ruining society. Everyone is going in debt and becoming slaves to those companies. Credit cards aren't even real. They're plastic."

"Hmm." She had a point. Building up debt was a fast track to a mediocre life—something Trey's father always pointed out—but credit cards weren't to blame. It was the credit card companies. Yet, where she was wrong was implying the companies were evil. All was fair in a free economy.

"Sorry," she said. "You don't want to hear my ranting on corporations. What does your website do?"

"Nothing, yet. That's my problem. I need someone to build it." He sat next to her. Glanced at the washing machines and looked away before the spinning motion could rile his insides.

"One of my sorority sisters is a computer science major. Sometimes they do projects for free. I mean, to get credit, they find people and do little projects for them."

"No offense, but I need someone good. Someone with

experience who won't just build my website, but join my company and help keep it going after it's launched."

"I hear you. She parties pretty hard. It probably wouldn't work out too well." She sniffed. "I love the smell in here."

"Oh yeah?"

"Yeah. I know it's from laundry detergent chemicals, but it works. It makes everything smell fresh."

"But it's not real."

"I know. It only smells that way. It's not as good as it pretends to be. Flowers and spring rain, or whatever. But I still like it. It's good enough."

"Hmm. Maybe your friend could help me. At least get me started."

"No, you're right. She's not very good. It sounds like you need—oh. What's his name?"

"Who?"

"This guy. He has a weird name. It's like a name for a bird. A big bird. A hawk or something."

"What year is he?"

"I think he's a junior. I don't know." She licked her upper lip and looked at the ceiling. "Oh, why can't I remember his name?"

"He's really good, though?"

"Yeah. The best in the school, I guess. My friend goes on and on about him, anyway. He made something that runs— no. It *crawls* over the internet, she said. Looking for things, going from computer to computer."

"Sounds like a search engine. There's already a lot of those."

She narrowed her eyes. "Yeah, but do you know how to make one? Maybe his is better."

"Better than something like Yahoo? I doubt it." Trey

tilted his head, and the room was slow to follow. His vision darkened.

His throat tightened.

Nausea gripped his stomach.

"Malcolm," she said. "That's it. His name is Malcolm."

"What's his last name?"

She shook her head. "I have no idea."

"Oh, no."

"What is it?"

Trey leaned forward, grabbed one of the empty garbage bags, and put it over his mouth.

He had eaten sushi last night, after all.

CHAPTER THREE

EMMA

The banquet hall attendants clear the plates and cutlery from the table, except for Wilson's. He grasps his plate with his free hand and twists his fork into a mound of pasta with the other, shooting a nasty glance at the poor attendant who reached for it a moment ago. Wilson is wearing one of his trademark turtle-neck sweaters with a gold neck chain. Most men here are dressed in suits and ties, but not Wilson.

"Glad you could join us," D'Angelo says—Dr. D'Angelo Santan, my boss—dressed to the nines in a black suit and tie. His trim white beard shows his distinguished years. "I was worried you wouldn't make it on time."

"Sorry." I take the empty seat between them. "Traffic held me up."

Our table is front row and center. The nearest to the stage. Dr. Halsford steps behind the lectern, announces an award for research on teen suicide in the age of social media, and everyone applauds. Three researchers at the back of the venue stand and make their way to the stage. It won't be long, and I'll be on my way to the stage. My name will be announced and forever linked faculty's minds, industry experts, and corporate profiteers seated throughout this place.

It's only moments away.

Nimisha, our clinical intern, sits across the table next to Dr. Judith Aimes, Professor Cal Beckman, and Tory, our office intern. We share a space in McConnell Hall, the psych wing at school. I wish I could have sat closer to Nimisha. She's been great. I'm not surprised she didn't sit in my seat. As open and bubbly as she is, even she avoids Wilson.

Wilson.

He forks another twine of pasta into his mouth and licks his lips. Right after the last attendant leaves the table, Wilson places his fork on his plate and wipes his face with a cloth napkin. "Oh, great. They're not going to take my plate?"

"This is so exciting," Nimisha says, beaming. "We're going to win. I can feel it."

"The odds *are* in our favor," D'Angelo says.

"You've done a great job." Dr. Aimes puts her elbows on the table and leans forward. Her red blazer has brown patches sewn over the elbows. It's something she would wear to school. Her team isn't up for an award, obviously. "I read your publication, and it wasn't what I expected. The results, I mean."

"That's the point of research," Wilson says. "To learn how things really are and record them for others."

"We know what research is," I say, turning toward him. "We're all researchers here. What did you learn?"

"Huh?"

"What would you say you found most surprising about our article?"

He throws a shocked glance at D'Angelo, then slowly smiles as if my question were a joke. "I'll let the psychological community decide that. I wasn't surprised by much. Nearly every hypothesis I presented held up."

I can't keep my eyes from rolling. "Oh, really? I wasn't aware you made any hypotheses. I wasn't aware you—"

D'Angelo puts his hand on my wrist. "Let's not do this here, Emma. We're a team."

"Some of us more than others," Wilson says.

I could kill him. He never did anything. Nothing. He sits there like he contributed as much as everyone else. The truth is, Nimisha deserves more credit than ten Wilsons. And she's only been with us for four months. We've been working on this project for three years. Seven, if you count the background studies we built up from our previous project.

Dr. Halsford announces another winner, this time for research into marijuana use disorder, and whoops and hollers come from the back of the room. From the winning team's table. They stand amid much applause, and one of the entrance doors begins to open.

I was late to the banquet, but I wasn't last after all.

On rare occasion, I'll see someone who appears to have been born with the genetic perfection of a futuristic, computer-generated being. The woman from the movie *Weird Science* pops into my head, followed by Data from *Star Trek*. It's not always about attraction, but often, it is. And this time . . . it is.

The latecomer entering the hall is a perfect specimen of male genetics. Older, early forties, but thin and upright. His square shoulders make the doors look askew by comparison, and his stride—he enters the room like he owns the hotel, smiling and nodding at people I presume he knows.

"Emma," Dr. Aimes says. "Move."

The marijuana research award winners are stuck behind

my chair, trying to reach the stage. I apologize and scoot forward.

"What are you staring at?" Nimisha turns in her chair and sees Mr. Handsome. "Oh."

"Who is that?" Tory asks.

"I believe that's Mr. Wilkes." Cal folds his napkin and places it on the table. "D'Angelo, did you meet with him?"

"No. I've never seen him before."

"He came to the university asking to talk to you the other day. Said his first name was Trey. I sent him to your office, but didn't think you were there. Guess I was right."

I've never liked Cal's Southern accent. I don't have anything against them. In fact, I often find their round vowels and slumbering drawls relaxing, but not Cal's. He lays it on with a trowel, exaggerates every enunciation, desperate to wave the flag of his heritage.

"I talked to him, too," Judith says. "His name *is* Trey. He's pretty impressive. He said he owns a computer company. He's looking to invest in artificial intelligence." She raises her eyebrows and gazes directly at D'Angelo. "You could probably make a lot of moola working with this guy."

"Our research isn't for sale," D'Angelo huffs.

The marijuana team thanks everyone for supporting their research. The dude on the left—the one with the dreads . . . he looks like he's stoned right now. What's that old saying? Love what you do for a living, and you'll never work a day in your life? I don't know when my work went from a love of learning to a tedious malaise of t-crossing and i-dotting proposal writing. But it was my choice. It will be worth it after tonight. I'll be able to write my own ticket. Kick back and get high like these guys if I want to. That's something I haven't done in years.

Relaxed, that is.

Mr. Handsome—Trey Wilkes, according to Cal and Judith—sits his genetic excellence down at a fringe table near the door. My mother would have loved his looks. We had the same taste in men. If she were here, she'd push me to talk to him afterward. Push me to have her grandchildren with him. And I'd tell her there'd be time for that after my career finally takes off. But, at thirty-six, I'm running out of time.

No. I ran out of time. She'll never see her grandchildren now, thanks to cancer.

I'm sorry, Mom.

Wilson claps loudly as the marijuana disorder researchers exit the stage. He leans close to me and breathes, "I helped them with their studies on my last trip to Barbados. You know what I mean, don't you?"

His breath smells like meatballs.

I lean away.

"Shh," D'Angelo says. "We're up."

"Our next award recognizes the single most innovative theoretical contribution to societal and personal psychology. The dedication, work, and imagination needed to obtain this award are among the highest, if not the highest, our institution has to recognize. Winners in the past have gone on to better the lives of millions by affecting change in personal treatment methodologies and mass communications practices." Dr. Halsford surveys the crowd. "There is a caveat to winning this award, however." He grins. "We ask the winners to remember us when they become rich and famous. Our new psychology facility isn't going to build itself."

A few people laugh.

Dr. Halsford lifts a card from the lectern.

My heart skips.

He pulls his reading glasses up the bridge of his nose. Squints. "And, the winner of this year's most innovative theoretical contribution is . . ."

I don't appreciate his dramatic pause.

"Dr. Santan."

The hall applauds, and D'Angelo stands.

I stand, but he puts a hand on my shoulder and shakes his head. Wilson also stands, and D'Angelo waves him away too.

"I'll accept this on everyone's behalf. I don't want to crowd the stage."

The stoners crowded the stage. There are only three of us who need to go. D'Angelo, Wilson, and me. It's not right. I reluctantly ease back into my seat. We should have talked about this beforehand. Oh well. It's not my face that people need to see. It's my name that they need to hear.

I scan the room. Nearly everyone's cheering. I sense some jealousy from the far side—and from Judith—but that's to be expected. It's only natural. Most faces are smiling. Congratulatory. I wonder which face will deliver my breakthrough. Who among them will seek me out after hearing my name? Offer me the path to a slew of profitable proposals. Side businesses. Financial freedom.

Several people near the back have stood up. Mr. Genetics, the gorgeous computer company owner, stands with them. It could be him. He already wanted to talk to D'Angelo about our work. After D'Angelo gives me credit, he'll want to talk to me.

D'Angelo accepts the plaque from Dr. Halsford, steps behind the lectern, and waves his hand to calm the attendees. "I'd like to say I'm surprised to be standing here before you, but I'm not. I've pictured this moment over and over for months. I knew if we worked hard and kept our minds open, gathered data, and blindly accepted the results for what they were, all the while ignoring our personal biases, the true nature of human behavior pressured by the onslaught of the modern communication channels under which we live would present itself. After that, it was simply a matter of recording our findings."

Mention me.

"I want to thank the institution for supporting our work, primarily over these last three years. I'm honored to have received this recognition. I could not have done it without my stellar team."

This is it. Thank me. Thank Wilson. I don't care. Just say my name.

"They've worked very hard and will continue to do so."

"You know we will," Wilson yells, standing. Rocking the table.

D'Angelo grins. "Thank you, Wilson, for everything you have done." He raises the plaque in the air. "And thank you, everyone, for bestowing us with the honor."

And with that, he turns and leaves the stage, tucking the plaque under his arm.

It takes everything I have to clap along with the crowd. Before sitting, D'Angelo raises the plaque in the air again, smiles, and pumps his fist like a man half his age.

It's good I missed dinner because I feel like throwing up.

How could he?

Nimisha beams from across the table, clapping her hands wildly. Then we make eye contact, and she knows what I'm thinking.

She stops clapping.

Dr. Halsford takes the stage and moves on to the next award.

CHAPTER FOUR

TREY - *February 1998*

The line to the checkout counter snaked around the corner, ran along the English composition books, and ended near the UBalt bookstore front door. Trey had been waiting for over thirty minutes. He, like everyone in line, needed his spring semester books today.

What a pain.

What an incredible pain.

It was like waiting for a block of government cheese in a third-world country. So demeaning. So unlike anything Trey should have to endure.

Only two people stood ahead of him now, but the guy currently at the counter was taking forever. Short. Longish brown hair. Shiny from grease, not conditioner. The guy wore a blue and black flannel shirt that hung loosely on his narrow shoulders. Probably a hand-me-down from an older grunge brother. He wasn't East Coast svelte like most well-off lemmings Trey often encountered on campus. On this side of Baltimore.

"Sorry, it's still coming back declined," the clerk said.

"Try it one more time?" The guy brushed his hair off his forehead, and it immediately fell back into place.

The clerk swiped the card once more and shook her head.

"I really need these for class."

The clerk waved her hand in Trey's direction and beyond. "Everybody here needs their books."

"Isn't there a way I can borrow these or something?"

His request brought to mind one of Trey's recurring business ideas. The situation here in the bookstore bordered on insanity. Why was everyone forced to buy books they would only read once, if at all, and why did they have to wait in line to do it? Why couldn't they go online, select the books they needed, have them shipped, and return the ones they didn't want to keep?

It seemed so simple.

The internet was just sitting there.

Idle.

Ideas like this came all the time. It was hard to choose just one.

Before coming to the bookstore, Trey had searched the internet for his books, and a website called *amazon.com* was the closest thing he could find, but they didn't have everything he needed, and he'd have to pay for shipping. It was worthless.

"Okay," the guy in the flannel said, "maybe I have enough for just this one?" He held up a book entitled, *Design and Analysis of Algorithms*.

That was a computer science book. He must be a computer science major.

"C'mon. What's the hold-up?" asked the guy behind Trey.

Something hit the back of Trey's neck.

He turned around.

A brutish, militaristic crew-cut guy stood there,

impatiently waving his hand. "Hurry up." When he spoke, he spewed spittle, and it hit Trey in the face.

He locked eyes with Trey, and Trey smiled in return. He smiled his biggest smile. You never knew who might invest in your business. Everyone was a customer. You didn't know who could have rich parents looking to get richer. As much as Trey wanted to stomp on the brute's foot and slap him in the face, he didn't. Instead, Trey wiped the spittle off and turned to face the front of the line.

The clerk took Flannel Guy's card and swiped it again. "Nope. You want to try a cheaper book?"

"Never mind." Flannel Guy lowered his chin and shoved his books to the counter's edge. He turned to go.

"Next," the clerk called.

Trey watched the guy head for the door. The hair and flannel shirt made more sense now. Computer geeks—the good ones, in Trey's experience—lacked hygiene and style. This guy might be just what Trey needed. An unkempt Wozniak to his Steve Jobs. His vision for the internet. His *can't-fail* business idea. The one that rose to the top of the heap.

The line moved forward.

The girl in front placed a pack of gum on the counter.

"Is that it?" the clerk asked.

"Yep."

Trey glanced over his shoulder. The front door to the bookstore swung closed behind Flannel Guy. The line had grown longer since Trey had arrived. There was no way he would leave now and lose his place in line, but he desperately wanted to talk to the guy.

"Can you believe that?" The crew-cut brute gazed down at Trey. "She waited all this time just to buy a pack of gum?

How stupid is that?"

Lunkhead. This guy was nothing but an arrogant lunkhead.

Trey nodded.

"Next," the clerk said.

Trey stepped forward. Placed his business books on the counter. "Hey, do you know that guy's name? The one whose credit card didn't work?"

The clerk scanned Trey's first book. "No."

"Are you sure? Didn't you see it on his credit card? It wasn't by any chance 'Malcolm,' was it?"

She scanned the next one. Then the next one. At over fifty dollars apiece, the total on the register broke a hundred. "No. It started with a 'K.' It was Keith or something. Or Kevin."

"What about his last name?"

"I don't know. I didn't see it," she said. "Will that be cash, check, or charge?"

"Wait." He reached over and slid the book pile Flannel Guy had left on the counter toward the register. "I'll get these also."

She shook her head and began scanning the books. "Whatever."

The brute grunted behind Trey.

"Okay." the clerk said. "Will that be cash, check, or charge?

"I'll get this too." He picked up a Snickers candy bar.

"Fine." She scanned the bar and put it on the counter. "Cash, check, or charge?"

"Check." Trey pulled his checkbook out.

"Aw, c'mon, man," the brute complained. "Why don't you use a credit card? It's so much faster."

"I don't believe in debt." He leaned over the counter and filled in the blanks.

"Just pay it off every month. You look like you could afford it. I'm sure you have one." He nudged Trey's shoulder and lowered his voice. "Use it."

Trey stopped writing. "Here. This is for you." He handed the Snickers to the brute, grinned, and spoke through his nose. "Not going anywhere for a while?"

"What?"

"You know," Trey said. "Those Snickers ads. 'Not going anywhere for a while?' Eat that while you wait for me."

"Oh." The anger drained from the guy's face. He put his books on the counter and tore the wrapper open.

Trey handed the check to the clerk and glanced at the brute's books. No surprise. Sports science and communications. Classes designed to help lunkhead athletes through college.

The clerk bagged Trey's books and handed them to him.

Outside, the clouds had cast the campus in a bone-chilling gray haze. The wintry air nipped at Trey's lips, and he licked them. He looked up and down the street and saw Flannel Guy waiting at a crosswalk two blocks away.

The books weighed him down, and he feared the plastic bags would burst, but he ran anyway.

The light changed before he could cross the street.

"Hey!" Trey shouted across the intersection.

The guy glanced back but must have decided Trey wasn't calling after him. He continued up the street.

Water splashed into the gutters as cars streamed across the intersection between Trey and Flannel Guy. Trey stood there, helpless, watching his opportunity move farther and farther away until the guy was out of sight. When the light changed, he ran to the other side, raced down the block, and rounded the corner. His business books weighed him down, but not as much as the guy's computer books. The plastic bag holding them began to tear.

Fighting to control his load, Trey ran down another block and rounded another corner.

Flannel Guy wasn't there.

He stopped, gasping for air. The bag holding his business books had now begun to give way, too. He re-bundled the books in his arms, holding them together against his chest. He let what was left of the bags drop to his feet.

"Hey," a voice said. "Were you yelling at me?"

Trey turned.

Flannel Guy wasn't only short. He was small in all ways. He'd sat down on a step in front of a Subway sandwich shop. His bird-like frame hunched over his short legs. His cheeks sunken in. Gaunt. Hungry. He ran his eyes up and down Trey. "What do you want?"

"I've got these for you." Trey dumped the books onto the wet sidewalk, relieved to be rid of the burden. "That pile is yours." His hands were freezing. He shoved one into his pocket and held the other out for a handshake. "I'm Trey."

"Oh my God." The guy picked up the algorithms book and looked to Trey. "Why?"

Trey moved his hand up and down as though they were shaking. "I'm Trey. And you are?"

"Kevin." He took Trey's hand and stood. "Why did you do this?"

"Because you couldn't afford them. You left them back at the bookstore, and when I saw your card get declined, I thought I'd help you out."

"Hey, thanks, but"—he tossed the book onto his pile—

"I've decided to sit this semester out. You can take these back."

"Are you sure?"

"Yeah."

"You're a computer science major, right?"

"Yeah."

"Have you learned much about the internet, or has it been all old stuff?"

"Mostly old stuff, but it's important. It's all a foundation for the internet."

"Oh." Trey looked down at the books. This might not be his guy.

"But," Kevin said, "I've spent loads of time making websites on my own. Are you a programmer?"

"No, I'm a business major, but I've read a lot. I know how the internet works."

"Cool." He bounced slightly, obviously happy to have someone to talk to. "The new HTTP specification is awesome, isn't it? It's so much better than 1.0. I'm so glad they added persistent connections."

Trey had no idea what Kevin was talking about, but he was sold. This was his guy. Anyone who'd read some dry technical specifications on their own had to be good. Dedicated. Maybe a genius.

Two co-eds sauntered up the sidewalk, their hips swaying, their voices chattering away about some party they'd attended last weekend. They paused to step over the books and gave Trey an annoyed look.

He smiled his salesman smile.

You never know.

Kevin looked away. Wiped his hair off his forehead.

The girls went into the sub shop.

"What year are you, Kevin?"

"Second, but I've been here for four." His voice fell weak, and he rubbed his neck. "I've got to graduate someday." He winced. "On second thought, can I keep the books? Maybe I can use them next semester."

"Absolutely. And I want you to use them this semester. Has money been your problem? Is that why you're still a sophomore?"

"Mostly. It's not like I'm failing classes or anything. Other than a couple of D's in some electives, I—"

"You're a computer genius, aren't you, Kevin?" Trey put his best Cheshire cat smile on display. "I can tell."

Kevin averted his eyes. "I wouldn't say that."

"Please, keep the books, and"—he pulled his checkbook out—"let me help pay for your classes. Room and board. Whatever."

"Wait."

"What?"

"What do you want?"

"Nothing. I just want to help you."

"No way." Kevin raised his hands. Took a step backward.

"Do you have a pen?"

"I'm not a charity case, man. I don't even know you. What do you want?"

"Like I said, I just want to help. That's all." Trey glanced inside the sub shop. He needed a pen to write the check. "And later, you can help me."

"No. I don't want your money."

"It's okay. You can pay me back."

"How?"

"I could make a payment plan for you, or . . . you could pay it back in other ways."

"No. Hell no."

"How much do you need for a semester? A thousand? Two?"

"Whatever you're into, man, I don't want it. I've been hit on before, and—I'm not bent that way."

"Oh, no." Trey stifled a laugh. "It's not like that. Let's go inside, get a table, and I'll explain everything. You look like you could use a sandwich." He stepped forward, motioning toward the door.

"Stop. You're creeping me out. "

"No. Wait."

Kevin jumped off the step and sprinted down the sidewalk.

"Wait," Trey yelled. "It's not what you think. I have this idea. A business idea—"

"No way."

"Come back."

Kevin vanished around the corner.

Damn.

He'd done it again. Gotten too excited before closing the deal. Pushed too hard, too fast. But how could he help himself? His idea gave him chills whenever he thought of it.

Today, the world mostly used the internet to sell products directly to consumers. There was no purpose to all those websites other than to make money. No higher calling. Trey's idea would use the internet to bring together the most advanced people in their fields. Help them solve the problems that have plagued mankind for centuries.

Imagine an oncologist in India discovering an abnormality in a cancer patient. The oncologist records the abnormality in the patient's file and moves on to the next patient. Years later, a scientist in the United Kingdom comes across the file. Synapses fire. He leverages the information to cure that particular form of cancer.

Thousands of people needlessly die between the two events.

Worse, imagine the scientist never sees the file.

With Trey's idea, the oncologist would have immediately shared the abnormality in a virtual community built by Trey's startup business.

And cancer research was just the tip of the iceberg. Eventually, Trey's business would host thousands of virtual communities designed to facilitate solutions across a limitless range of the world's problems. And with millions of brilliant eyes on his website, the opportunity to advertise and sell relevant products would be astronomical, all while serving a higher purpose.

He'd make more money than his father ever dreamed of making.

The door to the sub shop opened, and their signature baked bread aroma had a sweetness Trey'd never noticed before.

He scooped the books up and went inside to ask for a bag that wasn't torn.

CHAPTER FIVE

EMMA

Everyone has done something deplorable in their life. Everyone, except maybe D'Angelo. All he's ever done is show up to the university on time, work hard, and go home to his loving wife. Day after day. He's never been known to cheat on his taxes. He's never shown up to work drunk or hungover. The worst thing he ever did was call in sick one morning, then show up in the afternoon, spreading his cold to everyone else. He did that once and never again.

But now, he's done the worst possible thing I could have imagined.

He used me.

He took all my work on the project—years of work—and acted as if I didn't exist. He's destroyed my future.

I can't wait to tell Alyssa about this.

I sit at the table in the banquet hall, seething. Everyone congratulates him for winning the award. They all think he's perfect. He passes the plaque around the table. The plaque that doesn't have my name on it. I say nothing. That plaque is the summation of my career and doesn't even bear my name.

On the podium, Dr. Milford receives the last award. He's slightly bent from age, nearly bald save for a few gray strands floating over his brown, cobble-marked forehead. His award is for a lifetime devoted to behavioral studies. No doubt it has his name on it.

Before the old man can leave the stage, D'Angelo tucks our plaque under his arm, stands, and heads for the exit.

He's unbelievable. I can't let him get away with not giving credit where credit is due.

Everyone rises in a standing ovation, blocking my immediate path. I head the long way around the table, and Nimisha grasps my arm. "Wait. Where are you going? I was wondering if you wanted to—"

"Sorry. I've got to talk to D'Angelo." I jerk my arm free and push through the crowd.

The door clangs when I swing it open and march into the long hallway. He's already nearing the lobby past the windows looking over the parking lot. "Wait. D'Angelo."

He maintains his stride, acting like he can't hear me. All prim and proper. I gain on him as he bursts outside. The sun has set, and the air has grown cold. I glance up, fearing a chilling rain, and see nothing but darkness. The clouds have hidden the stars.

Across the way, the golden car from the nineties exits the parking lot. Curious. It was here the entire time.

"D'Angelo," I shout. "Stop. We need to talk."

I'm so close now. He can hear me, but he won't turn around.

He knows what he did.

Coward.

The headlights on his SUV flash once, and the monstrosity beeps.

He pulls on the door handle.

It opens, but I get there in time to block it with my hand. Now he turns around.

"What the hell was that?" I demand.

"Now listen, Emma. I can see you're upset."

"You're damned right I'm upset."

He stares at me with his analytical eyes. His evil, manipulative eyes.

"Well? Why didn't you mention me?" I want to smack that stoic, false concern off his face.

"You're a very important part of the team, but you're not the only contributor."

"You could have thanked me. You could have said my name."

"You know a lot of people worked on the project. I couldn't very well name everyone."

"You thanked Wilson!" I let my hand drop from the door. Angry tears well in my eyes, and I lower my head. "For God's sake. You thanked Wilson."

"I must leave now." He fully opens the driver's door to his SUV. "I'll see you in the office on Monday."

Glancing back at the hotel, I see the guests filing into the hall, passing by the windows. Wilson walks with Nimisha. They're all smiles.

I rip the awards plaque out of D'Angelo's hands and step backward. The inscription reads, "Dr. Santan and Team." My name still isn't there. And it never will be. Without some recognition—something—my future is over.

"Don't be childish," he says. "Hand that back to me."

"No. I want to know what you will do to make this right."

"What's done is done. We'll keep working. You know the project isn't over. In many ways, it's just beginning. We're entering the implementation phase. It's time to put our research into practice, and you're an integral part of that. Now, please, I want to beat the traffic. Hand me the plaque."

"You want me to work for peanuts. That's what you want. You want to keep using me for as long as possible, and I won't do it."

"Are you quitting? Right here? Right now?"

Wilson and Nimisha step outside the hotel and linger near the doors, watching us.

"No," I answer. "I . . . maybe. I want you to announce the award and give me some credit. I really need this."

"How would you suggest I give you credit now?"

"Add my name when you get it published in the *American Psychologist Journal*. I don't know. Post my name with it in your psychology Facebook groups. Host a party to celebrate the achievement and tell everyone you couldn't have done it without me. You couldn't have, you know. I did most of the work."

"That's debatable. Wilson did his fair share."

"The hell he did! Are you kidding me? How many vacations has he taken this year? Do you even keep track? He's never there." My arms shake with rage. "He didn't do anything."

"It's not the amount of time one puts into something. It's the impact they have."

"I had an impact, and you need to make it known."

"I greatly appreciate your work, and I know you'll continue to do great for me once you calm down and see the bigger picture. However, I won't tout our award just to appease your vanity. It's time to move on. Now, please." He slips into the front seat and holds out his hand. "Give me the plaque."

All around me, car security systems beep. Doors slam closed. Engines start.

"Please," D'Angelo says. "I want to beat the rush."

"No. I won't work for you anymore."

"Oh, I think you will."

It kills me, but he's right. I don't have a choice. I've come too far. But he will always treat me this way if I don't do something now. I'll work for free forever.

"Give me the plaque," he says.

"You want this?" I hold it high in the air.

"Yes, please."

My skin burns. I want to shove it down his throat. I want him to choke on my rage. My disappointment. Instead, I contain myself. I slowly lower the plaque toward his outstretched hand, and through my hot tears, a dark figure approaches to my left.

It's Nimisha.

She reaches in, grasps the plaque, and hands it to D'Angelo.

"Thank you," he says and pulls the door closed with a *thunk*.

"Don't thank her," I yell. "Thank me!"

He engages the transmission.

Nimisha's soft brown eyes engage mine. "Are you okay?"

"I hate him," I say. "I can't believe he didn't give us any credit."

Before she can respond, there's a hand on my shoulder.

I spin around, and there's Wilson.

Smarmy Wilson. Grinning.

"He gave me credit," he says.

"Get your hand off me."

CHAPTER SIX

TREY - *April 1998*

Malcolm.

The hot girl from the laundromat said his name was Malcolm. Her name was . . . it didn't matter. *His* name was Malcolm, and he was known as the best of the best. Trey had asked about him around campus. Trey had loitered outside the computer science building, eavesdropping on conversations. The name "Malcolm" floated through the air repeatedly like a number one hit that wouldn't leave the charts.

Malcolm.

Trey had to find him.

And he did. His face was glued to a computer screen in the engineering building study area, deep in the basement. Sitting in the darkest corner.

Trey waited.

He didn't want to disturb the delicate genius at work. At the same time, he wasn't leaving without a "Yes." So, he waited.

And waited.

After forty minutes, Trey's patience drew thin. He was about to give up and tap the brown-haired behemoth on the shoulder when Malcolm stood and headed for the vending machine.

Trey beat him to it. "Hey, you're Malcolm, right? I've heard a lot about you."

Confusion crossed the big guy's pockmarked face. "Do you mind?" Malcolm reached past Trey and put two quarters into the vending machine. The red decimals displayed the amount.

"You're the genius they call Malcolm, right? The 'Hawk?'"

"C'mon, man. I just want a candy bar. Will you get out of my way?"

Trey stepped to the side.

"Ugh." Malcolm took another dollar out of his wallet. "Everything is seventy-five cents."

"They're cheaper if you buy them at the student center, over the counter."

"What are you, a business major?" he sneered.

"Yes, actually." Trey smiled his salesman smile. "I am."

"I'm not interested." Malcolm fed the machine the dollar.

"Wait. Let me tell you about my—"

"About your business project? No. Save your breath. I already know what you want. You want me to write some lame-ass computer program so you can get credit in some lame-ass entrepreneur class without doing any work, and the answer is no. I'm not interested."

"It's not like that at all." Trey stepped in front of the vending machine, once again blocking Malcolm. If he got his candy bar now, he might leave, which would be unacceptable. "My entrepreneur class is taken care of. I don't need a computer program to pass it. All I needed was the idea, and I've got one. The best idea ever."

"Move."

"Hear me out. Wait. No." He raised his hands. "Don't hear me out now. Come to my class. We have mid-semester presentations soon, and anyone can come."

"Me? In the business building? No way. I took Econ 101 for a general ed elective, and I'm never going back there. I did my time. Now get out of my way."

Had Trey not known Malcolm was a sedentary computer geek, he might have been intimidated by the guy's size. Just over six foot tall and easily 260 pounds, Malcolm could crush most people by sitting on them.

But he'd have to catch them first, and Trey wasn't afraid. Time to play hardball.

Trey pushed him in the chest to get his attention. He rocked backward. "Listen, my idea is bigger than getting credit in some stupid business class. It's going to change the world. I—we. We're going to use the internet to change the world."

At first, Malcolm looked like he was about to cry, but Trey had misread him. The geek had an upside-down smile that made his cheeks cradle his eyes like egg saucers whenever he found something amusing. "Out of the way, business boy."

With one hand, Malcolm knocked Trey off-balance, and he fell to the floor.

Malcolm made his selection and bent over to retrieve the Snickers bar.

"Heh, heh." Trey stood up. "Nice one. I wasn't sure you had it in you."

"I was hungry. I didn't hurt you, did I?"

"No, no, not at all." A twinge in Trey's back begged to differ. "Please. You've got to come to my presentation. I could tell you about my idea now, but I can see you want to eat and get back to what you were doing, or . . . can you talk now? Could you tell me about the web crawler you developed?"

He narrowed his eyes. "How do you know about that?"

"You don't know how famous you are, do you? Everyone talks about you whenever the internet comes up. That's why I had to find you. Do you have a purpose for your crawler? A business plan?"

"That's the problem." He took a bite out of his candy. "Everything with you guys is about money. Business. It blows."

"No, not with me. Really. My idea is going to revolutionize the way people interact. It's going to help them solve big problems. The world's problems. Things like collaborating to cure cancer. End world hunger."

"Oh, yeah?"

"Yeah. Having something like your web crawler that can go from computer to computer—it's just a part of the bigger picture. Seriously, I'm not in this for the money. I mean, not just the money. But, if you need money—"

"I've got class in ten minutes. Sorry."

"Wait." Malcolm headed for the stairs, and Trey followed close behind. "Stop."

"No can do."

Malcolm breathed heavily as he climbed the steps and exited on the first floor.

"At least come to my presentation and see what I'm talking about."

"No." He reached his classroom, gazed down at Trey, and raised a finger. "I've got my own plans for the internet."

"Five hundred dollars."

"What? You're crazy."

"No. Really. I'll give you five hundred dollars right now." Malcolm turned and went inside.

Trey walked across the hall and sat on a bench. This wasn't over. Other students went inside, and soon, the professor closed the door.

Trey waited.

After scaring that other geek away—Kevin—he wasn't about to lose Malcolm. Mid-semester was only a week away, and his sophomore year would soon end. Two years wasted when he could have been working on his business. He could have been making money hand-over-fist by now. He needed that special partner. His Wozniak.

He needed Malcolm.

He waited.

He took out his checkbook.

He licked his pen's tip to ensure the ink would flow freely.

He made a check out to Malcolm Schmidt.

One thousand dollars.

The door to the classroom opened, and when Malcolm appeared, Trey pushed his way into the throng of students and trailed behind the big guy.

"Get away from me," Malcolm said. "I told you. I'm not interested."

"Here. Take this." Trey tapped Malcolm's shoulder, check in hand. "All I want you to do is come to my presentation, and you can have this."

Malcolm turned abruptly.

A small, wiry kid glanced off him and stumbled toward the front door, nearly dropping his books.

Malcolm looked at the check. His expression went from fire to ash. "A thousand dollars? Just to sit through a lame-ass business class?"

"Yes."

He took the check in his hand. "No strings?"

"Nothing." Trey took the check back. "Just show up, and the money's yours."

"And you're not in this to make money?"

"When we get rich, I'll donate to your favorite charity. How's that? In fact, if you come to the class, I'll donate this money anywhere you'd like, right now."

"No," Malcolm blurted. "You don't need to do that." He pulled the check out of Trey's hand. "I'll come to your stupid thing, but I'm not working on your project." He pocketed the check, opened his binder, and scribbled his email address on a paper scrap. "Here. Email me the place."

"Thanks, I'll see you there. This is going to be great."

Malcolm walked outside and paused at the top of the steps. The sun shone around him, and providence played a song inside Trey's head.

Malcolm turned around and eyed Trey. "Don't get your hopes too high. I might change my mind." The wind tried but failed to lift the oily brown hair off Malcolm's forehead.

"But you took the check," Trey said.

"Don't worry. If I don't show, I'll rip it up." He raised his arms and looked out over the campus. "I love this place. I'm not here for the money, either."

CHAPTER SEVEN

EMMA

I've yet to recover from last night. Had I known D'Angelo planned to take all the credit and, worse, continue to enslave me for the foreseeable future, I'd never have agreed to babysit for Alyssa today.

Little Vivian yells something from the living room.

I'm popping Ibuprofen pills in the bathroom and looking at my crow's feet in the mirror.

"I'm hungry," Vivian shouts.

She's outside the bathroom door now. She knocks.

I love her, but sometimes . . . "You just had lunch. An early lunch."

"I want dessert. I want ice cream."

I open the door, and there she is with that perma-smile cemented to her face. She can be crying, and I swear, she still looks like she's smiling. In my studies, I've learned individuals with positive attitudes have fewer emotional problems. They live longer, happier lives. Vivian might live forever. Even on the heels of her parents' divorce last summer and with the new year of fourth-grade bullying Alyssa told me about,

Vivian has every reason *not* to smile.

Yet, there she is. Lit up like a firefly.

I wish the only thing I wanted in life was ice cream. The thought of returning to work on Monday as if nothing happened at last night's banquet has me twisted in knots. When I woke this morning, an empty feeling made my stomach want to collapse. Like my future. Empty.

"Can we?" Vivian says. "Can we go?"

My head says *no*, but my heart says *yes*. I'd rather lay on the couch and stew over the awards ceremony, but the path of least resistance ends at Baskin Robbins. I am "The Babysitter Extraordinaire." I consider myself Aunt Emma to Vivian, though she never calls me that. Besides, if I remember right, ice cream can be soothing. I wonder how often Alyssa, and all other mothers for that matter, go on jaunts to get ice cream. Or play in the park. Or watch kid's movies. Or have a life worth living.

I never do things like that.

I only ever work.

"Yes, get your coat. Let's go."

It's only five minutes from Alyssa's suburban domicile to the nearest strip mall. So far, she's keeping the house in the divorce, but she can't possibly afford it for long. I don't know the details. I do know Jeremy has a one-bedroom apartment somewhere across town. He's had it for a while, since before he filed for divorce. She didn't know about his little hideaway, but it's not what you think. He wasn't using it as a secret hideaway for cheating on her. He supposedly leased it to have a place to go whenever living with her became too intense.

Alyssa is my best friend. She can be intense, but he's a wimp, and her intensity is what I love about her.

I park, and we walk across the parking lot. If I'd slowed

down and thought about it, I would have made Vivian wear a thicker coat. It's unseasonably cool for October in Baltimore. I hope the clouds lift soon.

"Her name is Jordan," Vivian is saying. "She's in my class, and we're going to be best friends."

"That's great."

She glances up at me. "Best friends like you and Mom."

"That's great."

"Do you have more friends like my mom?"

"Yes."

No.

I really don't. I have friends I haven't seen in years, but because of that, they don't count. I seldom go on Facebook. My only other friends are at the university, and they're work friends. Compared to Alyssa, they don't count. I wouldn't spend time with them if I didn't have to.

I do have my dad, however. Over the years, he's become more and more of a friend.

Especially since Mom died.

I face the parking lot while holding the door open to Baskin Robbins for Alyssa. At the distant end of the long commercial block, a golden car passes through the intersection. It's a car, and it's golden, but I can't tell if it's the one that followed me to the banquet last night. Probably not. Odds are, my brain is attempting to spot every golden vehicle to fulfill my primordial protection mechanisms. My lizard brain is on alert.

"I want a sundae," Vivian says.

"Why don't you just have an ice cream cone. The sundaes are expensive here."

"But, I want chocolate syrup, and whipped cream, and nuts—no. Chocolate chips, and—"

"Okay. Get the sundae."

I order a single-scoop cone, and we sit by a window. The sun peers in through the clouds and shines on our table. Vivian dives into her sundae with reckless abandon, and I lick my ice cream cone. My shoulders relax. My eyes close.

This is nice.

Maybe this is all I need.

I imagine a routine. Saturdays like this, sitting in peace. Sometimes, ice cream. Other times, pie. I could routinely relax in a pie shop with my own daughter. Or my own son. No research papers. No proposals. No late nights wondering why Wilson isn't at the university while I'm trapped, listening to the great Dr. D'Angelo Santan's endless theories on how social media affects our brains.

No pressure. No deadlines.

Just a nice life like my mother always wanted for me.

"Is it good?" I ask.

"Yeah." Chocolate syrup runs down Vivian's chin. She spoons another dollop into her mouth. Her frizzy hair shakes with every bite, and she licks her lips, failing to keep the syrup from running through her smile. She's a beautiful child. Messy but beautiful. "It tastes real good."

"Good."

I ought to call it quits. I ought to dump the project and start a family. The next time a millionaire entrepreneur with the godlike genetics walks into a room, I should at least introduce myself. The man at the banquet last night, Mr. Handsome—he had it all. But, the sad truth is, I can't call it quits. D'Angelo still owns me. I've come too far on the project to quit now. I need to find a way to force him into giving me the opportunities I deserve.

Halfway through my ice cream cone, my shoulders have

tensed up again. I can't stop it.

"Are you almost done?" I ask. "We should go. Your mom will be home soon."

Vivian slurps a swirling blend of melted ice cream and syrup from her spoon. "My mom says you're always in a rush."

"Is that so?"

"She said you're like a one-way train with no stops." She licks her fingers. "What does that mean?"

"I'm not sure."

"She also said your caboose is bigger than hers." Vivian tries, but she can't keep from giggling.

"No. She didn't say that."

I glance out the window.

The sun glints off a car's windshield as it exits the parking lot, forcing me to squint. When the car turns onto the road, its metallic golden paint sparkles in the sunlight.

It's the car from last night. From last week. There's no doubt about it.

My cell phone buzzes. "Hi, Dad."

"Hey, sweetheart. How'd it go last night? You didn't call."

"I'm sorry. It's a mess."

"What happened?" he asks. "You lost?"

"No, we won, but"—the golden car waits at a stoplight, but it's too far away to see the driver—"I shouldn't have wasted my time going. Dr. Santan took all the credit."

"What?"

"He didn't thank me or anything."

"That jerk."

"It's okay. I talked to him afterward and threatened to quit. I think he heard me."

"I know how much you were looking forward to this,

sweetie. I'm sorry he did that. It was low, even for him."

Picturing D'Angelo holding that plaque burns me all over again. He didn't only hurt me. He hurt my dad. He hurt my future.

"Why don't you come over tomorrow and have lunch with me? Get your mind off it."

The light turns green, but the golden car doesn't move. My eyes moisten, and I blink.

Is that car watching me? Did it follow me to Alyssa's house, then here? Vivian doesn't notice it, but she wouldn't. The car hasn't been following her for days, or—shivers course through my body. What if I'm wrong? What if they've been waiting for an opportunity to kidnap Vivian? What if they've been following us both?

"Emma? Are you still there?"

"Yes. Sorry, Dad. What did you say?"

"Come over for lunch tomorrow. Let's talk about it."

Vivian drinks the remains of her sundae straight from the bowl. Ice cream seeps from the corners of her mouth and drips onto the table. Syrup trickles down her arm. I grab a napkin and wipe her face, pressing the phone to my ear with my shoulder. "Here, let me get that."

Emma Petranova. Babysitter extraordinaire.

"Stop it," she says.

"What are you doing?" Confusion creeps into my dad's voice. "Are you okay?"

"Yes, Dad. I'm fine. I'll see you tomorrow."

The light changes, the golden car turns right, and it disappears into the city. But it will be back. I'm certain of that.

My shoulder cramps, and the phone slips, hits the floor, and slides under the chair.

I want to slide under there with it.

CHAPTER EIGHT

EMMA

The house I grew up in lies at the end of a cul-de-sac between two other red brick ranches, all three trimmed in white. I park against the curb to avoid blocking my dad's car and his spare utility truck. Mom wanted him to sell that truck because he rarely used it, but he swore it paid for itself whenever he needed to haul something, which was almost never.

I don't want to get too deep into my dilemmas at lunch. Over the years, I've spent too much time complaining to him about the injustices at work. About D'Angelo. My dad has developed a strong dislike for the man. I didn't mean for it to happen, but after so many one-sided conversations, it was only natural. Now, he's probably livid I didn't get credit for the award, and I'm tired of thinking about it.

I step onto the front porch and slip my hand into my pocket. I caress the rusted metal ring around my magnifying glass. My mom's magnifying glass. Actually, I don't know if it was hers, but I like to believe it was. I found it by the farmhouse she grew up in the day we spread her ashes under the weeping cherry tree. It's a small child's toy, and I don't know for sure, but it must have belonged to her once upon a time. It has her energy.

I can't believe three years have passed since the funeral.

I crack the door open. "Dad? I'm here."

I'm in my thirties and still don't know whether to knock or walk inside, so I split the difference.

He doesn't respond.

"Dad?"

He's not in his chair in the living room, watching his flat-screen, "smart" television. What a waste. Not having cut the cord, he still subscribes to cable. Streaming Netflix is beyond his technical capabilities. I'd take it off his hands, but there isn't a wall in my apartment large enough for a TV like that.

"Dad, where are you?"

"Down here," he calls from the basement.

His model train makes a *woo, woo* as I reach the bottom of the stairs. He's wearing one of his old, corn-flower blue, button-down work shirts. It's not tucked in and hangs over his denim shorts. And he's wearing sandals with socks. Every time I visit, I consider the psychological correlation between years-retired and the diminishing fashion sense plaguing our older generations.

He checks his watch. "Is it noon already? I was just giving this guy a little test run." He flips a switch, and the train stops.

"It's past noon," I say. "Sorry I'm late."

He moves in, and we embrace. "I'm so glad you're here."

"Me too."

"I'm late too. Time got away from me. I'm afraid there's no lunch made."

"That's all right. I'm not hungry." I sit down on the couch in the corner. Model train tracks run around the room, clinging to the walls, crisscrossing onto three separate tables.

An urban city, a rural city, and the countryside are all modeled to represent areas in Maryland. His obsession with this hobby has taken over the entire basement. Besides the couch, there's nothing but a cabinet filled with train parts, a display case of train engines, cars, and cabooses, and a quaint desk where he sits and paints his miniatures. In the rural town, a liquor store sits across from the church next to a post office, a fire station, a police station, grocery stores—it's his little world, and it continues to grow.

Mom isn't around to keep it under control anymore.

He walks to the far corner of the room, and that's when I realize he's added a fourth, smaller table. "What have you done now, Dad?"

"I'm adding onto this part. You won't believe it. I built the entire countryside and forgot to put the most important part on it, so I had to add more land. I just need to connect it now."

"Won't a train track there block the way to the bathroom?"

"No one uses the bathroom down here." The track sags. "Hm. That's not going to hold." He turns toward me, his face like a child's beneath his gray hair. "I believe you're right. I should put in a drawbridge to hold up the trains, and we could raise it if someone wanted to use the bathroom."

He's such a goof. "What will you do when you run out of room?"

"You sound like your mother." He grins. "I guess I'll have to add onto the house." He puts the track down. "You can't stop progress." The new table is covered with a blanket of long grass, and it bends in the back, rising up the wall. It's an empty slate.

"I'm not so sure about that," I say.

"It's going to be okay, sweetheart." He goes to the cabinet and opens the doors. "Hey, did I tell you I sent in pictures of my train set for a competition?"

"No."

"I got third place and a mention in *Model Railroader* magazine."

"That's great, Dad."

"I know." He pulls a few miniature trees out of the cabinet and begins gluing them to the part of the table that rises up the wall. He's making a mountain. "But that's nothing compared to the award you won."

"I didn't win."

"Why do you say that? Just because Jerk Face didn't give you credit? You and I know the truth. You've been carrying him and everyone else over there for years, and you finally won. That's the truth. No one can take that away from you."

"I suppose, but no one important knows about it."

He puts the last tree on the table and looks up, his laugh lines deepening by the second. "What? I'm not important?"

"You know what I meant. It's just that I don't know if I can keep working on *his* project for nothing more than self-satisfaction. I'm tired, Dad. I hate my apartment. I wanted to have a house by now."

"If you don't want to work for him anymore, quit."

I know what he's doing. He's playing my pity-party attitude against me. Quitting has always been a bad word in the Petranova household. He made it that way by finishing everything he ever started. "I can't do that."

"Your mother always wanted you to quit."

"She also wanted you to stop expanding your train set."

"But if I had, I would never have gotten into *Model Railroader* magazine."

I reach into my pocket and grasp the magnifying glass. "I don't know what to do. I feel like I'm running out of time."

"Are you dating anyone?"

"No."

"Anyone on the line?"

"There was this guy at the awards banquet, but I'll probably never see him again. Besides, D'Angelo has a ton of work for me. Now that we won, he wants a new grant proposal finished by Friday. We need to tout the accomplishment. It'd be a waste not to."

"So you'll keep working on *his* project until you die?"

"No. I—you don't have to be so morbid, do you?"

"Your mother and I always wanted to go to Costa Rica and pet the sloths."

"I know."

"But it never happened."

"I know."

"Can you bring me that box from the cabinet? The blue shoebox?"

"Here." I hand him the box.

He opens the lid. "At first, we didn't go because of money. It was too expensive for us back then. Years later, when retirement closed in, it became a logistical problem. We couldn't take you out of high school for any trips, and I couldn't afford to take time off from work. We needed to save every penny."

"Maybe if you'd spent less on your trains . . ."

He puts the box down and lightly raps his fingers on the table, smiling. "I built most of these trains after she passed away. I love it down here."

"I know."

His eyes comb the room. "But, you're right. I would

rather have spent this money on a trip to Costa Rica with her."

"Why there? Why sloths?"

He pulls a large tree from the box. "I'm not sure. Maybe because sloths are accused of being lazy. Back then, your mother and I had fantasies about laying on beaches and doing nothing, but over time, I learned something about myself. I hate doing nothing. I've got to stay busy to be happy."

"That makes sense."

"In some ways," he presses the large tree onto the table, ensuring the glue takes hold, "I envy those little creatures. Those sloths really know how to relax and enjoy life."

I picture ice cream running down Vivian's chin. The peace I felt sitting in the ice cream shop yesterday, doing nothing. Her jokes. Her giggling. My shoulders dropping. Pure relaxation . . . until the golden car came.

He says, "You need to discover what makes you happy, then do it. I know it's easier said than done, but it's important. It took me fifty-five years and losing your mother to breast cancer to find out what was important to me, and some days, I'm still not sure."

"What's important to you?" I take a step back. "Wasn't Mom important to you?"

"Yes, but she's gone now. She's been gone a long time, and I've found happiness without her. I love it down here."

"Really?" He averts his eyes. Gazes upon the table. "Working on this thing day after day makes you happy?"

"It's not all, but it helps. There's more to happiness than this. They say happiness is only real when it's shared." He straightens one of the large tree's branches. "Like right now. I'm sharing all this with you, and I'm pretty happy." He turns. Puts his hand on my shoulder. Looks me in the eyes. "I think it's why your mother constantly asked when you would give her grandchildren. It wasn't so much for her. It was for you. She didn't want you to grow old and alone."

"I know. I just wanted to get my career going first."

"Then maybe working for Dr. Santan is a means to an end, but it doesn't look like it's ever going to end, does it? Like you said, you're running out of time. Maybe you should demand a date for when he gives you what you want, and if he doesn't make it by then, you leave. There is always a way to get what you want."

"Maybe."

He walks to the cabinet.

I glance inside the shoe box. Among the dozens of little statues, there's a sloth. I understand now. He's building the trip to Costa Rica on the fourth table. He's right. There is always a way to get what you want. Tomorrow, I'll demand D'Angelo have my name shared with every publication mentioning the award. If not, he won't get that proposal on Friday.

Easier said than done.

I always end up working on whatever he tells me.

But not this time. This time, I mean it.

I will quit. I will walk away.

My dad returns with a miniature farmhouse. "Do you recognize this?"

"It looks familiar."

"I thought you might." He places it on the table opposite the large tree. "This is how I imagined the farmhouse back when your mom was a child. I can picture her running from it down to this weeping cherry tree. You know this tree, right? It's where we spread her ashes." He closes his eyes. Wipes his forehead. "I miss her so much. I wish we'd had more time together."

CHAPTER NINE

TREY - *May 1998*

Excessive nervousness shows you care. And, if you care, others will care.

Trey needed Malcolm to care.

Standing at the head of the classroom, facing his fellow business students, Trey was all nerves. He took a deep breath, smiled his salesman smile, and the tension drained from his shoulders.

He had this.

He put his floppy disk in the class computer and loaded his PowerPoint presentation. "Can everyone see that?"

Roughly half the class nodded. The other half feigned interest.

Malcolm didn't move. He sat at the back of the room, wearing an old Guns-n-Roses T-shirt and a scowl. He looked like he wanted to kill everyone there, but at least he'd showed up. He'd taken the check Trey gave him and honored his word.

Now, it was all up to Trey. He wasn't worried. After this, there would be no way Malcolm wouldn't partner with him.

"In only a few short years," Trey began, "the internet has dramatically changed the world. This is the beginning of a new era." He advanced his presentation to the next slide. "Imagine what it will be like in ten years. In twenty." He paused for dramatic effect. "I can tell you, the internet will be so much more than it is now. It won't just be a place to share boring research papers—no offense, professor—or order books or compare real estate prices. The internet will become a virtual world of new thoughts and ideas, and my business will become the universe for that world. A place where solutions to tomorrow's problems will grow like wildflowers."

Professor Scaulding sat behind his desk, leaning back in his chair. When Trey glanced over, the professor checked his wristwatch as if he was late to pick up his dry cleaning. The rest of the class appeared to be paying attention, but it was hard to tell if they were really listening.

Malcolm sat motionless at the back, a dead stare on his face.

"In the 1800s and a little later, people in small western towns worked together to survive. If someone needed a barn, everyone in the town would help out. They'd have a barn-raising. This is where we are now with the internet. It's the Wild West." Trey was especially proud of his Wild West slide where he'd substituted Billy the Kid's face with Bill Gates's. "Like the railroads connecting the towns and cities across North America, the internet is growing rapidly, connecting people like never before. Instead of transporting items in rail cars, the internet can transport ideas. Instead of rural farming communities, the internet can foster vibrant thought communities where exchanging ideas will occur way faster than trains ever delivered coal."

Dr. Scaulding yawned. He wasn't interested.

But Malcolm had his eyes on the screen. He seemed . . . awake. At least he was awake.

"Think of virtual communities as the barns in the Old West on an immediate, intellectual scale. Each virtual community raised up to solve a specific problem, like finding a cure for a specific type of cancer or reducing congestion on inner-city roads, or bringing third-world countries into the fold. We won't need to wait for scholars while they spend years writing and publishing periodicals for other scholars to read, refine, and dispute. The exchange of ideas will happen in minutes."

"It sounds a lot like newsgroups," Dr. Scaulding said. "We've been using those for years to exchange ideas."

"Yes." Trey motioned toward the professor. "You have been using newsgroups for years. College students, the government, and some businesses have posted limited, text-based articles and messages to newsgroups, but compared to the internet's capabilities, and the plans I have for my company, newsgroups are nothing more than scribbles on a caveman's wall."

Trey swore he saw a flicker of a smile cross Malcolm's lips.

"Your company?" Dr. Scaulding asked.

"Yes, my company." He didn't want to skip ahead in the presentation, but Scaulding was forcing his hand. Trey advanced the slide deck. "My company will provide the places and tools to build virtual 'barns.' More like virtual communities. Instead of providing land, wood, and nails to build towns, I'll make it so people can post text, pictures, and short videos. They will use the content to build solutions to the world's problems. One person will upload an engineering schematic for an innovative heart monitor, and someone else will build a prototype. No more waiting for snail mail to share complex designs."

Dr. Scaulding looked at his watch again.

Trey's forehead heated up. He glanced at the clock. Time was running out.

The next presenter had his floppy disk in hand, ready to go.

"My company will also build software to allow people to instantly work together, sending messages to each other in real-time and automatically discovering like-minded individuals." He advanced to the next slide. "The first step is connecting like-minded scholars and giving them the tools to build their virtual communities. To do this, my software will crawl the internet, looking for—"

"No scholar will throw their hard-earned research onto the internet without going through the traditional publication channels." Dr. Scaulding sat up. He put his elbows on his desk and held his hands out. "And they're certainly not going to pay for something like that. Get to the point, Mr. Wilkes. How do you intend to make money with this? How much do you plan to charge for a virtual community?"

"Nothing. But after thousands of people have joined, they will naturally recommend products and services to each other. They'll recommend the things they need to solve problems."

"Like what?"

Trey hadn't prepared for an interrogation. This wasn't fair. "Like test tubes and weather balloons. I don't know."

"So, you're going to sell test tubes and weather balloons?" Professor Scaulding stood and made his way over to Trey. "I'm sorry, but you're out of time. I'd work on your profit model if I were you. For the finals, focus on the product you're selling and your return on investment. This goes for everyone. Financials are everything, people."

"But, I didn't get to—"

"Jake. You're next."

Jake rushed to the head of the classroom, ejected Trey's floppy disk, and inserted his own.

Trey watched as Malcolm took the opportunity to sneak out the back.

"Mr. Wilkes." Professor Scaulding raised his voice. "Where are you going?"

"I have to talk to someone." Trey headed for the door. "I'll be right back."

But Trey was lying.

He was never coming back.

CHAPTER TEN

EMMA

It's exactly nine o'clock when I hit the UBalt campus, heading for McConnell Hall. No stopping for coffee. No bagel. Nothing but the aching desire to make things right.

D'Angelo, I refuse to work for free. You want that proposal by Friday? Then do what I say. Put my name on it.

I've been practicing my speech since leaving Dad's house yesterday. It's driving me crazy. Seeing Dad recreate Mom's childhood home in his little train world, setting up the farmhouse and the giant weeping cherry tree—it lit my heart on fire. I was certain he was building out Costa Rica, home of the sloths. I thought he was building himself a new future, but he wasn't. He was lamenting the past. Something I've done too much lately.

D'Angelo, I've waited years for this. You owe me.

Cars stream down Pratt Street. I wait for the crosswalk light to change.

And, thinking of Dad, I kick myself while I wait. I should have recognized the model cherry tree when he pulled it from the shoe box. He doesn't know it, but I've driven up to the farmhouse several times since Mom passed away. We talk, her and I, beneath the cherry tree. The place where we spread her ashes. It's where I found the magnifying glass. It's where I go when I need her strength. Her advice. Depending on how D'Angelo reacts to my ultimatum, I want to go there later today.

No. I don't just want to. No matter what happens, I'm leaving early and going for a visit.

The light changes. I march across the street and pass by the community outreach police station. It's tiny compared to the psychology building. The old red bricks of McConnell Hall rise five stories high. It's a bastion of academic research. I remember the first time I entered this place. I was a frog falling off a lily pad into a huge pond. That was before the dark nights. The endless hours sitting behind a computer screen, writing papers. Wishing D'Angelo wouldn't work so hard.

The proposed psychology building will have eight stories and cover twice the land if they acquire funding. I'm not holding my breath.

With my hand on the front door, I stop. That sinking feeling I'm being watched hits me. I look up and down the street, but the golden car is nowhere to be found. I didn't see it yesterday, either. That creepy old car followed me when Vivian and I went for ice cream Saturday, and I haven't seen it since. Maybe they lost interest in me. Or, I lost them.

This is something I need to talk to Mom about.

Nimisha steps into the hall, blocking my way to D'Angelo's office. She's wearing one of her career jackets: a white two-button cotton blazer with a notched collar. She may only be an intern, but she dresses and behaves like someone with years of experience. She took to swimming in the huge pond quickly when she joined us a couple of months ago, but today, her face has a reddish tint shining through her makeup. Something's up. "Hi, Emma. I'm glad you're here."

"Sorry, I don't have time to talk. Is D'Angelo in his office?"

"No. That's the problem. He hasn't come in yet."

It's after nine. D'Angelo has never missed a day of work in his life. He's also never arrived after eight except for the one time he was sick. That was three years ago.

The door to his office at the end of the hall is closed. He's nowhere to be seen in the halls.

"I was hoping you knew where he was," Nimisha says.

"I don't."

"We have a conference room full of counselors he promised to meet with. Could you—"

"I'm not ready. I didn't—I don't have anything prepared."

"What should we do?"

"Where's Wilson?"

"He's . . . you know. He's not here." She covers her eyes and shakes her head. "This is bad. Very bad."

"Okay. I'll take care of it. Stall them a little longer."

The door to D'Angelo's office isn't locked. I vaguely recall him talking about this meeting last week. It was something about using our research to spread Emotional Positivity throughout a clinical facility, easing the patients' reluctance to accept help. Sure enough, a stack of papers titled "Emotional Positivity" lay on this desk.

In a rush, I open the door to the conference room and startle the counselors. Their eyes widen and focus on me. "Sorry, I—my name is Emma Petranova, and I'll be covering for Dr. Santan today." I take a standing position at the head of the table.

The eldest woman in the room glances at her watch. She's the only person wearing one. Everyone else looks at me with excited anticipation. A bunch of tadpoles sitting on a lily pad in my pond.

I introduce myself, then dive into the papers I pulled from D'Angelo's desk. It's horrible. I read a line or two from each paragraph to myself, then attempt to paraphrase and explain it to the group. I'm not familiar with this part of the research. It makes me wonder how much other work D'Angelo did without me knowing.

"Could you repeat that part?" the older woman asks.

No. I can't. I'm barely getting through this as it is.

The door opens, and Wilson charges into the room. "Greetings, everyone. I apologize for being late."

"Are you Dr. Santan?" one of the counselors asks.

"No, he's not," I say. "He's—"

"I'm Wilson Sinclair." He moves in next to me and takes the papers from my hands. "Expert on Emotional Positivity."

The room fills with smiles that match his.

He gestures for me to sit.

I want to smack him, but I'm also relieved.

"I don't know if Emma here mentioned this, but this is what you've got to do."

I sit, doing my best to act interested, like we're the best of friends.

"You must encourage your patients to throw away their first thoughts. Studies show over ninety percent of the first thoughts people experience in reaction to an external circumstance are negative. For example, you open your mailbox and see a letter from the tax authority. Your first thought is, 'Oh, no. I'm being audited.'" Wilson is making this up. I didn't see anything like this in D'Angelo's papers. "Throw away that thought. Let's say your manager wants to speak with you in his office later. You think, 'Oh, no. He's firing me.' Throw away that thought. Replace it with, 'Maybe I'm getting a raise.' Replace the tax authority thought with, 'Maybe I'm getting a refund.'"

The watch woman shakes her head. "You're so right. I do this all the time. I always assume the worst."

Everyone else nods in agreement.

I feel sick.

Wilson carries on, spouting out whatever his mind comes up with, completely devoid of any real academic substance, and they eat it up. They applaud him at the end, and I overhear the watch woman asking if he does speaking engagements outside the university.

I've got to find D'Angelo.

"Hey, Emma. Wait up." Wilson treads down the hall behind me.

I whip around. "What?"

"Aren't you going to thank me for saving your butt back there?"

I roll my eyes. A habit I'm not fond of. I blame my mother for it, but most of the time, my dad deserved it. Him and his overblown train set. Wilson deserves worse. Much worse. "I don't have time for this. I've got to find D'Angelo."

"Okay." He hands me the papers I took from D'Angelo's office. "Let me know how that goes. See you later."

"Where are you going?"

"Wouldn't you like to know?" He heads toward the elevators.

"You can't leave. We have a proposal to work on. It's due Friday."

He steps into the elevator and hits a button.

I reach out to stop the doors from closing, but I'm too late.

He's not doing this. I won't allow it.

I race down the stairs. When the elevator doors open on the ground floor, I'm there.

"Emma? Really?" He struts past me, rolling his eyes.

God I hate eye-rolling.

I turn and follow him inside. "Stop."

The elevator dings, and the doors close behind us.

"If I'd known he wasn't here, I wouldn't have come in at all today." He heads for the front door. "Let me know when D'Angelo comes back. Hasta la vista, baby."

"No." I hustle after him and grab his arm. "You're staying. We're working on that proposal. We only have four days."

"Unhand me, woman," he says, sporting a half-grin and pulling his arm away. "I won't be treated as such."

Now he's mocking D'Angelo's speech patterns. I don't know why, and I don't care. "The fact that Dr. Santan didn't come in today is all the more reason for you to stay. I need your help."

"I think I helped you quite a lot already. You should have seen yourself floundering in front of that group."

"If you don't stay and help, I'll make sure D'Angelo and the department head know, especially if we don't get the grant."

"Do your worst. D'Angelo loves me."

The elevator dings behind us, the doors rattle open, and someone gets off.

He turns to go.

I grasp his arm again. "No." I can't keep my voice down.

"You're staying. So help me, God. You're not going anywhere this time." I tug on his shirt sleeve.

"Is everything okay?" Nimisha walks up next to me.

Wilson aggressively pulls his arm away, his face twisting in disgust. "Get a life, Emma."

"Wait," Nimisha says to him, "are we still on for lunch?"

"Of course," Wilson says. "I'll see you there. Noon, right?"

"Yes." She sweeps her hair off her shoulder. "See you there."

And with that, he exits the building.

I'm fuming.

I wonder if his boyfriend knows about his lunch date.

"What was that all about?" she asks.

"I hate how he always skips out when we have tons of work to do." The words fly out of my mouth. My tongue feels dry. "I hate—I hate him."

"Hate's a strong word, Emma, but I understand." She heads for the elevator. "But, you know, he has this thing about him. Charisma, I think."

My cell phone rings.

Balt PD.

I've never seen this caller id before. It's probably a scammer, but if . . . if it's a scammer, I'll hang up. "Hello?"

"Who am I speaking with?" a gruff voice asks.

"Who did you call?"

"This is Detective Galen with the Baltimore police. I'm trying to reach Emma Petranova. Is this her?"

My first thought is, *Oh, no.* The police want to arrest me for something.

I throw the thought away. Not because of Wilson's speech, but because—okay. I admit it. Damn him. He got into my head. Now, because of his interpretation of Emotional Positivity, I think the police have called with good news. Maybe I won a raffle to the Policeman's Ball. "Yes, this is her. How can I help you?"

"You work with a Dr. D'Angelo Santan. Is that correct?"

"Yes."

"When was the last time you spoke with him?"

"Why?" The last time I spoke with him, I yelled at him. D'Angelo's smug face taunting me. Telling me he'd see me Monday. Telling me I'd continue to do great work for him. The last time I saw him, I wanted to shove the award plaque down his throat.

"He's been reported as a missing person. I need to know if you or anyone else has seen him recently."

"I haven't seen him since Friday night. When did he go missing?"

"Friday night." There's a pause as if the officer is writing something down. "If it's okay with you, I'd like to talk to you this afternoon. Can you meet me around three?"

If ever I needed to head out of the city and visit my mom's farmhouse, today's the day. I have no interest in spending my afternoon at a police station. "I'm sorry, but I'm busy. How about tomorrow?"

"You've attended the University of Baltimore since graduating high school. Is that correct?"

"I'm faculty now, but yes. That's right."

"And you've worked with Dr. Santan the majority of that time, correct?"

"Yes."

"Are you on good terms with him?"

"Of course I am."

"Then it seems like you'd want to help me find him. His

wife is worried sick."

I do not like D'Angelo, and I do not like his wife. A few years ago, D'Angelo consoled me immediately after the doctors diagnosed Mom with breast cancer. It was the only time we ever saw each other outside school. Marjorie decided we were having an affair—which was ludicrous—and put a stop to it. I've avoided her ever since.

"I do want to help, but—"

"Great. I'll see you at three. Here's the address."

CHAPTER ELEVEN

TREY - *May 1998*

Malcolm can move fast for a big guy. When Trey stepped into the hallway, Malcolm was already on the stairs, descending toward the back of the business building. He'd chosen the nearest exit.

"Hey, wait up," Trey called.

He didn't.

Trey sprinted and caught him before he could open the door to the parking lot. "What did you think?"

"I've got class."

"Classes don't start for another twenty minutes. C'mon, what did you think of my presentation?"

"I think PowerPoint is lame."

"My project. What do you think about my project? Will you help me?"

"You're not wrong about the internet." He glanced up the stairs. "Your professor's a Luddite."

"I know. You see what I'm dealing with here. Won't you help me? If I could just show him, or if I had something to show investors—"

"I ought to help you just to show him how dumb he is."

"That'd be great."

"But if you really want to make the world a better place"—he narrowed his eyes, and the life behind them drained away—"you ought to come up with a way to rid the world of people like him. Investors." He cleared his throat and leaned forward, lowering his chin. "Businessmen."

"Do you . . . you don't mean that, do you?"

He straightened up. Lifted his chin. "I came and saw your pony show, so thanks for the money. My next class is all the way across campus." He turned. "I don't have time to drive there now and find a place to park." He headed outside. Stepped into the business building parking lot.

"Wait. You drove here? I didn't know you had a car."

"My parents gave me one for college, but I hate it. It doesn't matter. I've got to walk now."

The brisk air disagreed with the sun. It looked warmer than it was. Filled from dawn 'til dusk, the parking lot held onto several cars parked illegally along its edges.

"Wait." Trey followed, walking inside Malcolm's shadow. "You'll help me, right? You see the potential, right?"

"Your idea isn't bad, but it won't work."

"Why not?"

"Your first phase. Collecting data on your users to connect the—what did you call them? Little-minded people?"

"Like-minded."

"Right. Like-minded. There's no good way of doing that."

"But, your web crawler software. Can't you use it somehow?"

"Unless your little-minded people host their own websites, it can't do anything. It goes from website to website, scraping pages, not computer to computer, reading private information."

"Couldn't you make it do that? There must be some way."

"There's a way. I know a way, but that's not my point."

"I thought you were the best. But I guess if you can't do it—"

Malcolm stopped walking and turned around. "I can do it. I know how. Cookies. Third-party cookies. But that's not the problem. Besides, what you're saying—it might be illegal."

"Illegal? Are you sure? I doubt there are any laws on this. The internet is the Wild West."

"Yeah, and you want me to build your barn." He waved me away and started walking again.

Trey rushed up behind him and put his hand on Malcolm's shoulder. "Exactly."

Malcolm dropped his shoulder and twisted away. "Don't do that."

"Please, won't you build *our* barn? Let's show Professor Scaulding how wrong he is." This struck a nerve. Trey averted his eyes. Giving him space. "Unless you don't know how to do it. Or you're afraid."

Oh, that did it.

Malcolm stepped forward, leaned down, and met Trey eye to eye. "I told you, I know how." His breath smelled like burnt lunch meat.

Trey took a step back.

Malcolm stood up straight and raised his chin. "The problem is getting started. We'd need to put code on a lot of websites to get it to work, but only each website owner can do that because of security."

"But you said your crawler goes from website to website."

"It's more complicated than that. You'd need to persuade a lot of people to help you. Who do you have? Anyone?"

"I've got you."

Malcolm shook his head. "You're going to need a lot more than me."

"Look." Trey let his salesman smile takes over. "I don't have to understand how it works. I just need to get this thing off the ground. You're the smart one. Anything you want, just tell me what you want me to do. If we need people, I'll get people."

"Yeah, you need people. You need to get as many people as possible to host code on their website."

"Okay, what else?"

"You should also start gathering information about your little-minded people, but they'll have to volunteer it. Like I said, I can't—I won't hack into their computers and steal it."

"How do I get them to volunteer it?"

"I don't know. Have them fill out a questionnaire. Poll them."

"Do you know how to do that? I mean, how to get a poll in front of someone?"

He sneered at this. "Uh. Yeah."

"Great. That's great."

"But it's a lot of work."

"Don't you have some computer friends who could help?"

He turned and headed for the street. "No."

Trey wasn't surprised. Malcolm left that burnt lunch meat smell in his wake, but that wasn't the big guy's only social problem. Something strange flickered in his eyes, a felonious trickster darting behind trees, hiding in the bushes. His distaste for anything to do with businesses or making money was so off-putting. Everyone needed money. Everyone needed businesses.

Trey caught up with him at the crosswalk. "You're going to work on this, right?"

"Sorry. It's a no-go."

"But you said it was a good idea overall, right?"

"I said it wasn't a bad idea." He kept his eyes on the Don't Walk signal. "Using the internet for something other than selling stuff *is* a good idea."

"Then help me."

The crosswalk light changed.

Malcolm stepped into the street.

Trey checked his watch.

He had two minutes until his next class, but it was in the other direction, back inside the business building.

"Are you going to do it?" Trey shouted.

"No way, business boy. I don't have time."

"When will you have time?"

"Call me next century, after I've graduated."

He couldn't be serious. This wasn't happening. That was too long.

By the year two-thousand, Trey planned on having made millions with this idea. That's how it worked with dot-com companies. Get the idea, make a prototype, and pull in cash from opportunistic investors. Malcolm was making the biggest mistake of his life. Professor Scaulding was a moron. Even Trey's dad, an entrepreneur at heart, was short-sighted, insisting Trey finish his degree first.

The main business building loomed over Trey as he walked across the parking lot. He was going to be late for class.

His hair felt out of place.

He was going to be late for everything.

Something had to be done.

Giving up was not an option.

He stopped next to an elegant car. A four-door Acura Integra with tinted windows. The car's golden metallic paint twinkled in the sun. It reminded him of his father's car. One of his father's many cars. Someday, Trey would have cars. Plural. More cars than his father. More cars than Bill Gates. More money than both of them.

This wasn't over.

He walked away from the car.

Away from the business building. The classrooms.

Away from the short-sighted stupidity.

CHAPTER TWELVE

EMMA

My fingers won't move. I've read the research papers three times, but I can't get myself to type out the proposal due Friday. My office is stuffy, but I don't want to open the door. Hallway traffic always distracts me.

Right now, everything distracts me. The photo of my mother and father on my file cabinet. The dirt peaking out from under my bookshelves. My fingernails.

Everything.

I close my eyes and concentrate.

I have four days to write this thing, but it's a mountain of work, especially by myself.

Wilson has gone home, and D'Angelo has disappeared.

That's the problem.

D'Angelo has disappeared, and no one knows why. Not even the police.

I've got to focus on the proposal, or it'll never get done.

A door slams shut in the hallway, and I leap from my chair. I peer into the hall, but no one's there. It's almost noon, and I've already checked D'Angelo's office three times.

I check it again.

He's still not there.

The psychology wing is strange today. It's hollow.

Back at my desk, I finally strike the keyboard.

Over time, institutions have published hundreds of protocols for treating people wrongfully persuaded on an individual level. These protocols helped clinicians treat individuals whose beliefs departed from reality when an influential person in their life lied to them. This is commonly known as "gaslighting."

While cults employ gaslighting on a societal level, their influence has always been limited to a few hundred people. Institutions have published protocols for deprogramming at the societal level, addressing the nuances of influence from a leader versus that of a close friend or relative, but these protocols do not scale. We now live in a world, because of social media, where the abusive power of gaslighting can affect millions of people overnight.

And . . . so what?

I don't know. I do know, and I don't know, but my fingers freeze, and I don't know where to take the proposal next. At this point, I'd normally talk to D'Angelo, but—

Where the hell is he?

Our preliminary research shows the protocols for treating individuals will never—

I can't do this. Not now. I have to get out of here.

Alyssa answers her phone on the first ring.

"Can you meet me for lunch?" I ask.

"Who is this?" she says jokingly.

"You know who it is."

"If this is one of those companies selling glow-in-the-dark condoms, I'm not interested. I already have a flashlight in the shape of a—"

"Alyssa, stop it. Listen. I need to get away from work."

"Now I know it's not my friend Emma. She never leaves work. Certainly not in the middle of the day."

"Something's happened. Dr. Santan has disappeared."

"What do you mean?"

"He disappeared. His wife reported him missing."

"This is great. How long has he been gone?"

"Since Friday, but it's not great."

"Sorry. You're right. But you have to admit it's super exciting. Renowned psychology dude goes missing, and Emma Petranova is on the case."

I was afraid of this. Alyssa watches too many crime shows. She's especially obsessed with true crime. Since her divorce, she's done nothing but tell stories about murderers, rapists, and robbers in the Baltimore area.

"Can I help?" she asks.

"I'm not on any case. I just wanted to know if you could meet me for lunch."

"With bells on. Vivian is at her father's, so we can discuss the gory details of the case."

"There is no case, and there are no gory details." Lunch might not be a good idea. "He could show up any minute."

"I hope not. That'd ruin everything. How about Marley's in an hour?"

"Sure."

I put my phone down and stare at the computer screen.

Simply put, we want a grant to further our research into the treatment of millions of people who've fallen victim to criminal mass persuasion. More accurately, we want to help those duped into believing lies they found on social media. The question is, who would want to pay for this research? Certainly, not any companies that depend on advertising.

Nimisha appears in my doorway and checks the polish on her fingernails. "I'm heading out for lunch."

"Tell Wilson 'Hi' for me." That was snarky, but I couldn't help it.

"Sure." She bounces, then tips her head to the side. "Are you all right?"

My screen saver kicks in.

"It's Dr. Santan, isn't it?" she asks.

"It's this proposal." I stand. "I don't think there's any way I can get it done in time."

"You can do it, Emma. You're the best. I haven't been here long, but it's obvious who's carrying this place."

"Thanks." I pick up my phone and my wallet. "You're right. I'm worried about Dr. Santan. I need his help with this. Let me walk with you." We head for the elevators. "If he doesn't return soon, the project could be jeopardized."

"My brother says worry is like watching a horror movie. You sit there, constantly preparing yourself for the jump scares, but when they don't come, you realize you were watching a rom-com the entire time."

"That's deep."

"I know, right?"

She pulls out her phone and taps the screen.

The elevator doors open.

We get on and begin our descent to the ground floor.

"Where are you having lunch?" I ask.

"This little bistro kind of place. It's our favorite."

"I'm sorry, Nimisha, but I've got to ask. You know Wilson is taken, right?"

She laughs. We exit the elevators, and she puts her hand on my arm. "I know. He's gay. We're just friends."

"Whew."

Her phone buzzes. "Oh, no. I'm late. Let's catch up later." She hustles through the lobby doors.

I step outside and look both ways. No golden car. I haven't seen it since Saturday. I need to stop looking for it. Whoever it was, they stopped following me.

They must have gotten what they wanted.

CHAPTER THIRTEEN

EMMA

The sun made a strong appearance today. It's still cold outside, but it's warmer than usual. When I pull up to the cafe, Alyssa waves to me from an outdoor table. They've blocked off half the sidewalk for extra seating. Her frizzy blonde hair resists the tender wind, and she's holding a spiral-bound notebook. I hop over the wrought iron railing and take a seat.

"Here's what we're going to do," she says, opening the notebook. "We need to list everyone who knows your boss best, then interrogate them."

"Put that away. We're not interrogating anyone."

The door to the cafe opens, and a waitress approaches us. "What can I get you?" She looks annoyed. We're the only people sitting outside, and she's wearing a sleeveless uniform. This place is going for some kind of retro '60s style, but the menu is all over the place. American. Italian. A choice of two Asian noodle bowls. The waitress is hiding a white skirt beneath an orange apron, and her light blue top matches the highlights in her hair, all done up in a single bun. There's a pencil sticking out of her bun, but she's holding a pen and paper.

"I'll have the Caesar salad with chicken," I say.

She turns toward Alyssa. "And you?"

"I'll have the pepperoni panini. With extra *panini*, if you know what I mean."

"You mean you want extra bread?" the waitress asks.

"No," I say. "She's joking. She thinks the word panini sounds like 'penis.'"

"Yeah." Alyssa grins. "I want extra penis."

"Oh." The waitress forces a smile. "Okay . . . I'll be right back with your orders."

"You're thirty-six years old," I tell Alyssa. "Why do you always have to do that?"

"I'm thirty-four, and do what?"

"Embarrass me like that."

"Whatever." She readies her pen. Looks down at the notebook. "You're only as old as you feel."

"I guess."

"Let's get started. Who saw him last?"

"No. We're not doing this. I just want to have lunch."

"But what if he's gone for good? You were so upset about the awards. I thought you were going to make him start giving you credit."

"I was—I mean. I am."

"Then we've got to find him. Just let me ask you these questions. Please? I downloaded them from this awesome forensics website."

"If I play along for a while, will you drop it?"

"Question one. When did the deceased first go missing?"

"He's not deceased."

She gives me her deadpan stare, pen in hand. "Okay, let's call him the victim. When did the victim first go missing?"

"No one has seen the *victim* since Friday night."

"Okay. Can you give me a list of people he was closest to?"

"Why?"

"The website said ninety percent of the time the culprit in child abduction cases is a family member or close friend."

"D'Angelo isn't a child, and we don't know he was abducted."

"That's debatable. Let's see if we can find out. He has a wife, right? She'd be the closest to him. What's her name?"

"Marjorie."

"Okay. Who's the next closest?" She writes in the notebook. "Does he have any children? Friends?"

"No. Neither. He spends all his time at work."

"Coworkers, then. In order of closeness, please."

I don't know how *close* I am to D'Angelo, and I'd rather no one consider me close to him at all, but over the last several years, he's probably spent more time with me than anyone else.

"Me, I suppose. Then Wilson, Nimisha, Tory, Dr. Aimes, and Dr. Beckman. It's hard to tell after that."

She scribbles the names down.

"Wait," I say. "I forgot. He does have some friends outside work. Once a week, he meets with these old cronies at some coffee place downtown, but I don't know who they are."

"Okay. Got it." She taps her cheek with the pen. "Victim profile. I already know some of this." She writes some more. "He's a workaholic, right? Most workaholics have a strict daily routine. Does he?"

"Yes, I'd say he does. He comes into work early, the same time every day, and he leaves late, around the same time every night."

"But the awards banquet—that was out of the ordinary."

"I'd say he goes to things like that about once or twice a year. He'll probably go to more now that our research has been recognized."

"But Friday was out of the usual for him."

"Yes."

"So, if it wasn't someone close to him, it was someone close enough to know where he'd be."

"I suppose so. Are we almost done with this?"

The waitress places our meals on the table. "Here you are. Can I get you anything else?"

"We're good," I say, but Alyssa frowns.

"Is everything all right?" the waitress asks her.

"Where's my extra penis?"

"We're good," I repeat. "You can ignore her."

Alyssa dives into her sandwich.

I dab at my salad, thinking about the people in D'Angelo's life. We've all had issues with him, but that's expected when you work with someone day in and day out. Frustrations mount. Conflicts occur.

"One thing's for sure," Alyssa says between bites, "he didn't kill himself. With that award, he had too much to live for to commit suicide."

"Don't be ridiculous. He's not dead. We just don't know where he went."

"I disagree. The way you talk about him, he'd rather be dead than miss work." She licks tomato sauce off her fingertips. "Yeah. I think we can assume he's dead. It's so cool."

"No, it's not."

"Yeah, it is. We're like Holmes and Watson."

"Which one of us is Watson?"

"No. Wait. We're more like Mulder and Scully. Do you think aliens might have taken him?"

"Stop it."

"I got it." She licks her lips and swallows. "We're Cagney and Lacey."

All those nights spent watching TV with her when she was pregnant with Vivian—binging on crime shows from the '70s, '80s, and '90s—come rushing back to me. She's going to mention Columbo next. "Really? You think we're Cagney and Lacey?"

"Hear me out. It's perfect. You're Cagney, and I'm Lacey."

"Why am I Cagney?"

"Because you're a single, career-driven woman caught up in an unsolvable mystery."

Career-driven—my mother pleads to me from beyond the grave: *Stop working all the time and give me grandchildren*. But it's like my father said, she didn't want the children for her. She wanted them for me.

I put my fork down.

"What's the matter?" Alyssa asks. "Don't you want to be Cagney?"

"I'm not going to be anyone. You said you'd drop it if I answered your questions for a while."

"I'm not done." She pushes her panini to the side. "We need the motive. What did Dr. Santan have that someone else would want?"

"I don't know. He's got money."

"That's boring. What else?"

"Nothing, really. Other than his brain, nothing is appealing about the man."

"Hm. Maybe we should be Mulder and Scully, after all. I can see where aliens might want to steal his brain, replicate it, and build an army of overachievers."

I take one more bite and push my salad aside, half-eaten. "Can we be done now?"

"Not yet. You're on to something. It's not his brain someone would want. It's his work. If you guys won an award or whatever, it must be valuable."

"Alyssa, I know you're really into this, but what's the point?"

"My list of suspects here—they all work with him, right?"

"Yes."

"So, they would already have access to his research. None of them would need to hold him hostage to get it. Right?"

"That sounds right."

"Okay. So someone else wants it, and they kidnapped him. Or, like I thought: He was murdered." A cool breeze tickles my neck hair. "He was murdered by someone on that list."

"Hey, I'm on that list."

"I know." She narrows her eyes and circles my name.

"Okay." I fold my napkin and place it on the table. "I'm done."

"Was it good? You didn't finish."

"It was okay."

"Awesome. Now we can go start the real investigation. I've already interrogated you. We need to talk to everyone on this list."

"No, we don't. We're done."

"But, we've got to determine their motives. One of them killed him."

"You don't know that."

"Please, Emma? I only have until Friday before Jeremy brings Vivian back. Just take me to your office and introduce me to everyone."

"No. You'll embarrass me."

"Me? Embarrass you?"

"Yes."

"No, really. Take me with you. I can do this."

"You're serious."

"Yes. I've got nothing else to do. Please?"

"Absolutely not. You're blowing everything way out of proportion. The police will find him any minute, if they haven't already."

"The police? How do you know they're even looking for him yet?"

"Because they called me."

"What?" Her body trembles with excitement. "You didn't tell me that. This is so great. We've got to find him before they do."

"Why?"

"Because that's how it is in every show. The scrappy outsiders always have to band together and solve the crime themselves because the police are lame, or corrupt, or they— what if the police killed him?"

"I'm staying out of it, and so are you."

"You're on my list of suspects, Emma."

"So?"

"So, if you're on my list, then you're on their list."

It's past noon. The detective I spoke with this morning coerced me into meeting him at three o'clock today. He said he just wanted to talk.

"In fact"—Alyssa scans her notes—"if it were me, you'd be the prime suspect. Other than his wife, you knew him the best. You knew where he would be and when he'd be there. And, the worst part . . ."

"What?"

"You have a super strong motive."

"Huh? No, I don't."

"Yes. You do." She leans over the table. Gives me her deadpan stare. "He angered you when he took all the credit for your work. You said he ruined your career. You said he ruined your *life*. You followed him last Friday night and made him disappear after the awards banquet so you could take the reins. So you could take what was rightfully yours. You murdered him."

"No, I didn't. I—"

She sits back. Laughs. "I know."

Her fascination with true crime borders on insanity. We both know I had nothing to do with D'Angelo's disappearance. Yet, my heart is pounding.

She's not wrong.

My nerves are on fire.

If I'm on her list, then I'm on their list.

CHAPTER FOURTEEN

TREY - *October 1998*

Trey knew the carpet would eventually wear away. He'd traversed the same path for the past hour, pacing back and forth. Thinking. He was on the cusp of a solution to his funding problem. Money. The pervasive problem kept his business from launching. He needed money to hire computer programmers, and he didn't have it.

So, he paced.

Back and forth.

Back and forth.

After months of work, countless emails and meetings, he'd done what Malcolm suggested. It took quitting school last spring and networking with online business owners all summer, but now he had a list of people with websites a mile long. All of them agreed to host his code snippets in exchange for increased traffic to their websites. He'd also written and tested nearly a hundred polling questions to identify common interests and connect like-minded people. The foundation of his virtual communities.

He'd spent the summer right here in his apartment. His

parents believed him when he told them he had a summer job, and why wouldn't they? It was true. His summer job was building the foundation for his business.

His parents were clueless.

He paced.

He needed funding.

Every venture capitalist he'd met with over the summer loved his idea, except for one part. The making money part. They were all like Professor Scaulding when it came to monetizing a product—Luddites with the technology, ancient merchants with simplistic brains. They wanted Trey to charge people for access to his virtual communities like his business professor had suggested. Sell the spaces like shoes. Maybe Scaulding was right, but Trey couldn't go down that path.

It's not how the internet worked. It's not how it should work.

Luddites.

Trey didn't want to sell space on the internet to a few thousand people. He wanted to connect millions for free. What no one understood was, with millions of eyes on his website, the money would come in. It would come in droves. In high school, he'd had a vision the first time he saw a web page load inside the Mosaic browser.

But no investor had believed in him or his vision.

He had one chance left. Calimico Venture Partners. He had one week left.

His last chance presentation.

How could he convince Calimico to give him money when he'd failed to convince all the others? Everyone insisted he productize his virtual communities and charge a monthly fee.

He couldn't do it.

Trey slumped down on the couch, and it came to him. He didn't want to lie, but there was no other way. He would tell Calimico that he would sell subscriptions. He'd need to write a new business plan. Then, months later, after his business had launched, he'd change his mind. Once they saw the results, they'd follow along. They'd have no choice.

He was sure of it.

A knock came at the door.

"Dad," Trey said. "What are you doing here?"

"I was in the neighborhood."

"You live in New York."

"I know," he said, winking.

Trey held the door and kept his eyes on his dad. He tried to remember if he'd left any college textbooks lying around. Had he left any notebooks, notes, pens, papers, flyers to parties, anything to show he was attending classes this fall?

No. He had not.

His studio apartment was organized in corners. One corner had a TV, a coffee table, and a couch. Another had a computer desk and an office chair. The kitchen held down the other corner, and the bathroom crowned the fourth. He'd lived here since his second year of school. It sucked, but his father had said, *You need to live like all starving college students. Eat Smack Ramen and learn how to follow a budget.*

"Are you going to let me in?" His dad flashed his famous salesman smile. He was wearing a dark blue suit with a muted golden tie. His thinning hair was unnaturally black and shiny.

"You picked a great day to come." Trey stepped aside. "I just finished cleaning."

His dad glanced at the couch. A laundry pile lay at one end.

"Let me get that." Trey quickly put the clothes on the

floor to clear a spot, but his dad grabbed the desk chair and pulled it over to the coffee table. He unbuttoned his suit jacket and sat down.

Trey sat on the couch. "So when did you get here? To Baltimore."

"I flew in this morning. I would have warned you, but I wasn't planning on coming by until they canceled my connecting flight. Then I thought, hey. I should go see how school is going for Trey."

Nothing good came to Trey's mind. He didn't know what to say. The sink was full of dishes, and an odd stench emanated from the bathroom. Glossy venture capitalist folders and brochures sat on the floor next to his computer desk. The rejection pile. A single red and white folder lay next to the computer keyboard on the desk. Calimico Venture Partners. His last chance. Notes from his meetings with venture capitalists were strewn across the coffee table.

The place was a mess.

He gathered his thoughts.

"School's great." He nonchalantly scooped the papers off the coffee table and coerced them into a neat pile.

"Less than two years left. I can't believe how time is moving. Do you have all your classes planned out until graduation?"

"Yes, sir." Trey put the papers down. He smiled his salesman smile. "From now until the very end." This was not a lie. Trey had his classes planned out. He planned on taking zero classes between now and spring 2000. And beyond.

"Great. You know, looking around here reminds me of when I went to college, except I couldn't afford to live on my own, and I wasn't so messy. My roommates would never have allowed this." He glanced at the sink. "I didn't get to have an apartment until my senior year, and even then, I had to share it to make ends meet."

"I won't lie, Dad. I miss my room at home and the swimming pool, but it's not so bad here. There's a pool in the rec center."

"Good for you. Things are better for kids these days. You know, I didn't even have a credit card back then. They weren't as popular as they are now."

"Everyone's got one."

"Back then, we could only spend the money we had in our bank accounts. Our money, not someone else's."

"Times change, I guess."

"What's this?" He picked the notes up off the coffee table. "'Panacea. Finally, a place where we can come together and solve the world's problems.'"

"It's a project for one of my business classes." Trey shuddered. The top sheet contained a list of pitches for his business. *Panacea, the answers await you. Panacea, the key to unlocking the power of intellectual communities. Panacea, a virtual utopia, making the dreams of tomorrow happen today.* Trey held out his hand, but his dad didn't give him the papers.

"It looks interesting." He flipped to the next page, skimmed it, then to the next.

"It is. Actually, I might try to make a real business out of it."

"Is that so?" his dad muttered. "It takes a lot of money to start a business."

"I know."

"I worked for years after college before I started mine. I don't think I could have gotten it off the ground if I hadn't funded most of it myself. All these dot-com startups these days"—he shook his head—"they're going to crash. Mark my words. It's only a matter of time."

"I don't know. The internet is the real deal. A lot of them are doing really well."

"It only looks that way. Most of them spend other people's money on marketing and fancy-looking websites. They're not actually selling any real products. It's going to catch up with them."

Trey'd had this conversation with his dad before. It never went anywhere, but he couldn't help getting sucked in. "There's Amazon. They sell books. Those are real products."

"Books. Ha." He kicked back in his chair. Crossed his legs. "They're not going to get very far with that. You can get books for free at the library."

"How's Mom doing?"

"She's in Europe. You know, traveling with her coven." He uncrossed his legs, leaned forward, and put the papers on the coffee table. "There is something I wanted to talk to you about."

"What's that?"

"Your credit card."

"Oh?"

"I helped you get it for convenience and to learn how to manage money." A pained grin curled his lips. "I wanted you to make your own mistakes and learn from them. That's why I never checked the charges. But a couple of weeks ago, they sent a notice saying you'd exceeded your limit."

"It's okay. I paid it with the allowance from my trust fund."

"I know, but then I accidentally saw the charges."

"Oh."

"Why did you spend so much at The Men's Warehouse over the summer?"

Trey had written a paper on the importance of appearance in his second-year marketing class. At one point, he'd blamed his failure to acquire funding on his attire. "I needed some clothes."

"Suits?"

"I *am* a business major."

"And there are several cash-out transfers. You're not buying drugs, are you?"

The bribes to computer geeks like Malcolm and Kevin had been paid in cash, but no one had taken the bait. Trey had thrown good money after bad before he finally decided to focus on getting a *lot* of funding. Once he'd done that, he would hire a *lot* of geeks. But now, his dad was accusing him of buying drugs. No worries, though. It wasn't for real. His dad was just trying to get a rise out of him. "I needed some cash. Not everyone takes credit cards."

His dad glanced at the venture capital folders on the desk. "That's true. It's a good thing for you cash is still an acceptable form of payment."

"What do you mean?"

"I haven't spent as much time teaching you how to manage money as I'd planned. I'm sorry I didn't do more."

"Dad? What are you saying?"

"I don't want you to become dependent on your credit card. The money from it belongs to the bank, and you can't learn how to budget by spending other people's money." He cleared his throat. "I'm paying off your credit card and canceling it."

"What?" Trey stood. "You can't do that."

His dad stood. "I've deposited enough money in your checking account to get you through next month. You can use your debit card from now on to make withdrawals. Every month, I'll make another deposit."

"Why?"

"Think of the deposits as your paycheck. It will get you used to working a real job."

"But, I—"

"I know you didn't work over the summer, but don't worry. I'm not mad."

"Did you tell Mom you're doing this?"

"She's got nothing to do with it."

"What about my trust fund?"

"I can see you're upset." His dad fastened the bottom button on his suit jacket and turned toward the door. "I won't be doling out any more of your trust fund until you graduate and get a paying job."

"I'm calling Mom."

"Go ahead. She doesn't care." He reached the door, opened it, and stepped into the hall. "The trust fund came from my father, and I'm the executor."

"But I need money now. For my project. My business."

"I know." He faced Trey from the hallway. "I see you've been busy trying to get your hands on other people's money." He gestured toward the folders on the desk. "And it's obvious you haven't been taking classes this semester. You're probably not graduating in 2000 after all, and that's okay. I'm not mad. I only want you to learn from your mistakes."

"Wait."

"Goodbye, son."

CHAPTER FIFTEEN

EMMA

To go to the Baltimore City Police Department, I have to take two one-way roads and double back twice to find a parking spot. Then, I step off the elevator one floor too soon and have to climb the stairs. When I exit the stairwell, a heavy police officer shoving a skeletal addict knocks me into the wall. He did this to avoid an officer shoving a young woman who had put on way too much makeup today.

Business is good down at the station.

I weave my way to the front desk, following a sign for accidents and missing persons. The smells range from aftershave to overly sweet marijuana to vomit. Mostly vomit. The place is a cross between a bus station and a typical office. Police officers and detectives rush in all directions, and if they're not rushing, they're seated at a desk talking on the phone or addressing the person in front of them.

The officer behind the lobby desk speaks into his headset.

I don't want to be here, and I don't want to wait. "Excuse me. I'm here to—"

He raises one finger without glancing up and swivels away

from me.

I wait.

"Emma Petranova?" a man asks.

I turn around. "Yes."

"I'm Detective Galen. We spoke on the phone." Amid the station bustle, he stands straight and tall, like a lighthouse in a sea storm. He's wearing a flannel-lined leather jacket over a dark, button-down blue shirt. I can't immediately see his eye color because of what appears to be a permanent squint. They're dark brown, I think. His lips are thin and straight, and he doesn't have laugh lines. It's not that he's too young to have them—he must be in his mid-forties—it's that he probably hasn't had much to smile about working in this place.

A police officer bumps into the detective from behind, knocking him into me. My heel hits the officer's desk when I try to keep my balance, sending shock waves up my leg. Detective Galen grasps my wrist and holds me up.

"Thanks," I say.

He glances around. "Would you be willing to walk with me? I'd love to get away for a while. It's so crowded right now, and the interrogation rooms are full."

"Interrogation?"

"Not that this is an interrogation. It's not at all." He wipes his forehead. "I just want to talk with you. Can we go?"

"Sure."

We head for the elevator. Once inside, I keep my head down. I'm glad to leave the crowded station, but I'm worried about being alone with him. What is he going to ask me? At least this way, it won't be a good-cop, bad-cop situation. I only hope he is a good cop. I wonder if he's a Cagney or a Lacey, but I don't even remember which one is the good one.

He marches off the elevator and exits the building. When I make it outside, he's standing there stretching, holding his arms out wide.

"It's a beautiful day," he says.

I agree. The sun shines through the wispy clouds on what would normally be a cold autumn day.

The light for the crosswalk changes, and he steps into the street. "Let's go down by the docks. Do you want to walk by the water?"

"Sure."

"So, what do you do for fun, Emma?"

"Excuse me?"

"Fun. You know, hobbies."

"I thought you wanted to talk about Dr. Santan?"

"I took up calligraphy a couple of weeks ago."

This is not what I expected.

"I know what you're thinking," he says. "What's a tough guy like me doing with a little quill pen and a bottle of ink?"

"I wasn't thinking that."

"The thing is, I enjoy it a lot. It relieves my tension. I didn't want to do it at first, but the doctor said I needed to do something. How about you? What do you do to relieve your tension?"

"Not much. I spend most of my time working. I run to stay in shape whenever I can, but I don't get to very often."

The breeze picks up across the water and blows over the red brick walkway. Benches, streetlamps, and a single row of trees separate the walkway from the harbor. I zip my jacket up.

"The guys at the station don't know I'm a calligraphist."

"I see."

"It's all in how you hold your pen. You've got to keep it

at a steady angle to get the letters to look right."

The more he talks, the less time I'll have to go to the farmhouse. I need to go there and tell Mom everything that's happened. Visiting her is my true way of relieving tension. I doubt I'd ever tell Detective Galen that. In fact, as nice as he's being, I don't want to tell him anything.

"Then there's the pressure," he goes on. "If you push too hard, the nib will bend. I ruined two pens before I figured that out."

"I'm sorry, but when you said you wanted to talk to me, I didn't think it would be about calligraphy."

"So, work keeps you busy, huh? Too busy to exercise?"

"Yes."

He veers off the walkway and stops at the waterfront's edge. Gazes at the ships in the harbor. "I want you to know that I already knew that."

"Excuse me?"

"I've already done everything possible to learn about you. I just wanted you to know that. It's part of the investigation into Dr. Santan's disappearance. I think it's better you know I've read your files and scoured the internet to create your profile. I know about your schooling, the university, the work you've done with Dr. Santan. In missing persons cases, we act fast, but there's a limit to your digital footprints." He turns to face me. "At this point, I need your personal help."

He says digital footprint, but I wonder if there's been more. Has he followed me? Was he lurking outside my dad's home when I visited yesterday?

"I understand," I say. "I have nothing to hide, but I don't think I'll be much help."

"You don't seem too worried. That's good."

"I think Dr. Santan will return on his own pretty soon."

"Let's sit." He chooses one of the cleaner benches and sits down.

A ferry blows its horn in the distance. A few seagulls cross the sky.

I sit beside him, and he pulls out a notepad and pen.

He catches me trying to read his notes and shields the notepad. "This isn't my calligraphy, but I'll show you some later if you want."

"Sorry, I wasn't trying to—"

"It's fine." He puts his pen to the paper. Holds it there. "Why do you think Dr. Santan will come back soon?"

"He hasn't been gone very long, and he loves his work. He loves it more than anything. I can't imagine he'd stay away much longer."

"Last Friday night, you attended an awards ceremony with him and others. Is that correct?"

"Yes. How did you know that?"

"I've talked at length with his wife about the days leading up to his disappearance."

A seagull separates from the flock, and I imagine what it must be like for him up there, looking down on the harbor. Looking down on Detective Galen and me.

"Was your entire team at the event?"

"Yes."

"And, can you tell me their names?"

"Sure." I give him the same list I gave Alyssa. As much as her questioning during lunch annoyed me, I appreciate it now.

"How would you characterize your relationship with Dr. Santan?"

"We work together well."

"Would you say you've become friends?"

"He's not that type of person. He's very professional."

"If I'm not mistaken, you've been on his team longer than anyone."

"That sounds right."

"It's odd you're not closer to him. Is your relationship adversarial?"

"No. Not at all." I'm flustered. "I would have gotten closer to him, but he's not that type of person. It's not me. It's him."

He writes something on his notepad. "Do you know anyone who would want to harm Dr. Santan?"

"No. I don't even think he's in danger. I think he is probably taking a break after years of overworking himself."

"Interesting. Tell me about his work. Not the details, but—how important is it?"

"It's very important to us. To the university."

"I see. So, you'd say it's valuable. Is it under lock and key?"

"We've published most of it, but not everything."

"Why not?"

"We have research data saved for future publications, and there's always confidential information." He's barking up the same tree as Alyssa did earlier. Our research is valuable, but it's not worth kidnapping someone. They're both blowing this entire situation out of proportion.

"To your knowledge, in the time you worked on the project, did anyone express an extreme interest in it? Anything out of the ordinary?"

"Not that I know of."

Galen makes a lengthy entry on his notepad.

The seagull circles and flies away.

"Where did you go after the banquet?"

"I went home. Why?"

"Did you talk to Dr. Santan or anyone else after the ceremony?"

I replay the argument with D'Angelo in the hotel parking lot. The things I said . . . I wish I could take it back now. "We congratulated each other because we won the award and went our separate ways."

"Exactly where were you when you parted ways?"

"At the banquet."

"Please be specific. Were you in the hotel? In the hallway? The lobby? Where?"

"We were in the parking lot."

"Were you the last to see him?"

"No. Nimisha, his intern, and Wilson Sinclair were there right before he left."

"So, the three of you saw him last."

"Yes."

Galen checks his watch. "Is there anything in that final moment about Dr. Santan that might have seemed off? Did he say he was going anywhere other than home?"

"No. He seemed normal."

But did he? I can't recall. I was so infuriated at the time that I don't remember how he behaved, let alone anything he might have said. All I remember is his threat to make me continue working for him.

The narrow canyons of Galen's dark brown eyes narrow further. He's studying me. He's looking for something specific in my response.

"Did you leave on good terms with him that night?" he asks.

"I—hold on. There is something else. There was this golden car in the parking lot."

"A what?"

"An old car with metallic gold paint. I only mention it because you asked if there was anything off about Dr. Santan."

"Was it his car?"

"No. I don't think he noticed it, but it made everything seem off."

"Why?"

"Because I'd seen it earlier in the week, and at the time, I thought it might have followed me to the hotel."

"Are you sure it wasn't a coincidence?"

"I saw it again the next day, but I haven't seen it since, so yeah. It might have been a coincidence."

"Hmm. Did anyone else say anything about the car that night?"

"No."

"Okay. I put it in my notes, but it doesn't sound like anything. I'll remember to ask the others about it."

"The others?"

"Yes. I'll be talking to everyone you told me about. Standard procedure." He glances at his watch again. "I need to get back to the precinct, but I really appreciate your time." He stands.

I check my phone. It's too late to make the trip to the farmhouse and talk to Mom. The sun has held up all day, thwarting the clouds' attempts to dampen the sky, but it will probably rain before I can leave town.

I take in the ocean air. "I think I'll stay here for a while."

"Okay. Thanks for bearing with me. I know meeting with a detective can be stressful."

"It wasn't bad."

"Thanks. I look forward to seeing you again."

"Again?"

"More than likely, I'll need to clarify some things after I speak with your colleagues. You weren't planning on leaving the city anytime soon, were you?"

"Are you telling me not to leave town? Am I a suspect?"

"No, no. Not at all." He stows his notepad. Gazes up the walkway. "But, you were the last to see Dr. Santan alive."

"No, I wasn't. I told you. Nimisha and Wilson were there."

"Just stay in town, okay? It might make things easier later on, after I talk to them."

CHAPTER SIXTEEN

TREY - *November 1998*

The Savior's name was Brad Hollins. Trey believed Brad was the one person who could help him fund his startup business. Immediately after Trey's father had taken away his livelihood—his credit card, his trust fund—Trey wasted no time calling Calimico Venture Partners. After dropping the names of people his father had worked with in the past, and his father's name, the receptionist on the other end transferred him to Brad.

Brad the Savior.

Trey was overjoyed when Brad actually listened to his idea. After only ten minutes, he could tell Brad wasn't like Professor Scaulding. He wasn't like his father. Brad asked pertinent questions. He understood the power of attracting millions of people to a website first, then making money with targeted products and advertising.

But—and there's always a big but—Brad needed to sell Trey's idea to his partners. He assured Trey they'd be interested but also told him it would take a while for him to call back because the Thanksgiving holiday was coming in a few days.

Trey waited.

He paced a hole in his carpet.

Then he took action.

He told his father he couldn't come home for the holiday because he didn't have enough money now. Instead, he spent Thanksgiving refining his business plan. He prepared for the worst by adding a section on optionally charging for virtual communities. Though Brad had understood Trey's vision, Trey couldn't be sure Brad's partners would. Too many venture capitalists had turned Trey down over the summer for this very reason. Of course, Trey would never actually charge subscribers. He'd obtain the funding, then follow his vision. They'd forgive him when it worked.

The week after the holiday passed, and Brad didn't call.

Trey called Calimico and left a message for him.

Another week passed.

He left another message, walking the line between showing continued interest and becoming annoying.

Trey spent hours lying on his bed, staring at the ceiling. Campus had become a strange place. Because he hadn't registered for classes this fall, he wasn't allowed in places like the recreation center. He couldn't swim in the pool. He'd barely left his apartment in weeks, and that was okay. It was what he needed to do. When he wasn't lying on his bed, he sat at his desk by the phone, waiting for the Savior to call.

Four days before Christmas, the phone rang.

"They love it," Brad said.

Trey's heart fluttered like he was a schoolgirl in love for the first time.

He closed his eyes and muttered, "Yes."

"What was that?"

"Yes," Trey said. "That's great news."

"When we spoke before, you said you had a polished business plan. Mail it to us, and I'll get back to you next year."

Next year? Trey needed money. Now. He'd drained his checking account, and the next deposit from his dad wasn't until next month. "Could I email it to you?"

"I'm as excited to get moving on this as you are, but some of my partners are old-fashioned and already on vacation."

"No problem. I'll put it in the mail today."

"I'm looking forward to working with you, Trey."

"You don't know how much this means to me, Brad. Thank you."

Trey made the mail cut-off by five minutes. After hearing the dreadful term "old-fashioned" come out of Brad's mouth, he spent the afternoon rewriting the virtual community monetization section. He removed the "optional" part. He doubled down on the lie that he'd ever do it. When the plan hit the bottom of the outgoing mailbox, the waiting for Brad to call began again.

Trey ate Tombstone frozen pizza—on sale for $3.99 a box—and bowl after bowl of Smack Ramen noodles—three for a dollar. He awoke on his floor next to his desk chair some days. He spent his nights discovering online business owners whose websites would eventually host his polling questions. Once started, once he had funding, his business would take off like wildfire.

Standing in his boxers with the water running, Trey was about to hop in the shower when his phone rang. He ran to his desk.

"We're all here, Trey, and we're excited to talk about your business plan. Do you have a moment?"

"For you, Brad, I have eons. Thanks so much for calling."

"Like I said, I've got everyone in the conference room with me. I hope you can hear us okay."

"Everyone except Jack," an older voice hissed over the line.

"I can hear you all just fine," Trey said.

"Great," Brad said. "We like what you've got here, but we have a few questions. First, have you secured funding with any other firms or banks? Are we competing with anyone?"

Trey hesitated. If Calimico thought competition existed, it might push them to act faster than they had, but leading them in that direction would be dishonest. "No. I've talked to other firms. I've been most impressed with Calimico. You are the guys for me."

"Great. That'll make things smoother," Brad said. "According to your plan, and depending on multiple factors, you'll see revenue within three months by selling the virtual community spaces."

"We're very excited about your profit model for those," chimed a mature female voice.

"Me too." Trey's throat tightened.

"Why three months?" Brad asked.

"I have everything ready except for the backend systems needed for the polls and virtual community spaces."

"I see. How many software developers do you have working on this now?"

Trey suddenly became acutely aware of the temperature in his apartment. He'd lowered the thermostat to save money, but right now, his boxers did nothing to keep his upper body warm. The shivers began at his elbow and ran to the receiver.

He switched hands. "None, at the moment. There's a staffing plan documented—"

"Yes, yes." The female voice sounded oddly rough now.

"We reviewed that, but we assumed you'd already obtained some resources."

"He doesn't have anybody working on this?" another voice asked.

"Hey, Trey," Brad said. "I'm going to put you on hold for a moment. We'll be right back."

They didn't come right back.

Trey pulled on a dirty sweater and sat at his desk, pressing the receiver to his ear. Minutes took days. What could they be talking about? The plan was clear. Obtain the funding, hire the geeks, build the software, and change the world.

"Sorry that took so long," Brad said. "So you know, it's just me in the conference room now."

"Oh. Okay."

"We still love the idea and want to work with you."

Trey exhaled, not realizing he'd been holding his breath.

"However, we need to see a fully functioning prototype before we can move ahead. Do you think you can do that?"

"Absolutely. I know a great software developer. He's the best on campus, graduating next year. A real wiz."

"Great. If everything works out, we have connections in the tech community, and we can help with staffing later on, but first, you've got to show us something. It sounds like you can be ready by the end of March."

"Absolutely. No problem."

"Great."

It wasn't great.

Trey had no software developer. He had no Malcolm. He had no Kevin.

He had no money.

The Savior had spoken, and the Savior had done his part, but things weren't *great*.

CHAPTER SEVENTEEN

EMMA

"Mom. If you can hear me, I'd like to know what to do."

This is all wrong. Mom's not here. She's at the farmhouse. Her spirit is beneath the weeping cherry tree, and I don't have her magnifying glass with me. The dark clouds rolling in over the harbor aren't helping either. They appeared on the horizon right after Detective Galen left me sitting alone on this bench. I can't believe he insinuated I am a suspect.

Me. A suspect in a crime. That's all I need.

Right before he left, Galen acted like D'Angelo had been murdered or something. No one even knows if D'Angelo disappeared on his own or not. No one is considering his wife. It is mean to think this, but if I were him, I'd have left Marjorie long ago. The woman is wicked.

The wind coming over the water picks up, and I wrap my arms around my chest.

I close my eyes.

Footsteps sound on the red brick pavers somewhere up the walkway. A jogger, probably.

Galen does calligraphy to relax.

I talk to Mom.

But she's not here.

The footsteps get louder. And louder. Coming closer.

The possibility that someone watched me come here and talk to the police crosses my mind. Maybe a crime *has* been committed. The golden car has been gone for two days, but what if I've just missed seeing it? What if I'm being watched right now?

The footsteps are so loud.

What if the car followed me here, and someone is coming to kidnap me?

I try willing myself to relax.

My thinking is ridiculous, but the footsteps—I open my eyes. Turn my head.

I was right.

A middle-aged man with a long-sleeve running shirt and headband that reads "NYC Marathon 2016" jogs down the walkway behind me. He's a little too close for comfort, but he's not paying any attention. He's wearing headphones, and he's focused on the distance.

Dark gray clouds move over me, and the wind dies down.

I'm not ready to leave. Not until I think things through.

I close my eyes again and pull the salty air through my nose. I exhale out my mouth.

Detective Galen and his interrogation.

He got into my head.

Alyssa and her interrogation.

She got into my head.

The golden car coincidence.

It's all in my head. I know how this psychology works. This irrational paranoia. The mind fills in the blanks between coincidental events, making them suspicious and bigger than they really are. This especially occurs when someone has been put through a high degree of stress. I blame D'Angelo for that. Nothing has seemed right since he took credit for *our* work.

More footsteps.

I refuse to panic again.

If D'Angelo decided to leave his wife, why would he do it right after the awards banquet?

How could he abandon the project like this?

The footsteps come closer. They're evenly paced and slower than the jogger's.

I tell myself, *I'm not being watched.*

But I am.

The footsteps stop.

Someone is standing right behind me. I can feel it.

I wheel around without standing up.

"Ahh!" a man shouts and jumps back.

It's him. It's Mr. Handsome from the banquet.

"Why'd you whip around like that?" he asks. "You scared me." He pulls a white earbud from his ear.

"I scared you?" I stand. "I scared you? You're the one sneaking up on people."

He pulls out the other earbud and stows both in his pocket. "No, I'm not. I mean, I'm sorry. It's just that I saw you from over there and—you're Emma Petranova, right?"

He's wearing a thin leather jacket only zipped part way up, exposing a light blue dress shirt with the top two buttons unbuttoned. He has a flawlessly groomed beard, and he's built like a Ferrari. Blessed with perfect genetics. "Do I know you?"

"I'm Trey Wilkes." He extends his hand and we shake. "I thought it was you." He flashes a smile like I've never seen.

"How do you know me?"

"You work with Dr. Santan, right? I saw you at the Hilton

last week. Your team won the award for the most innovative theoretical contribution. That *was* you, wasn't it?"

"Yes."

"Do you mind if I sit?"

"Actually, I was just leaving." I turn my back and step onto the walkway. "Nice to meet you."

"Wait." He comes up behind me. "I need to ask you a favor?"

"What's that?"

"I intended to talk to Dr. Santan at the banquet, but he rushed out of there so fast, I didn't get a chance. His office hasn't returned my calls, and I really need to talk with him. Do you think you can help me get in touch?"

"And why would I do that?"

"I've been following your research, and I think it would benefit my company. I don't know how these things usually work between businesses and universities, but I'd be willing to donate to your school or whatever."

That's right. I remember now. Judith said his name was Trey, and he owned a startup computer company specializing in artificial intelligence. He seemed on the up-and-up. Yet, this random meeting suddenly doesn't feel so random. "I'm sure they'll call you when he comes back."

"I can't wait. Isn't there something you can do?"

Walking in lockstep at my side, I can tell he isn't the type of person to take "no" for an answer. I don't want him to know what type of car I drive, so I've got to get rid of him.

I stop and pull my phone out. "Give me your number, and I'll pass it on to him."

"Here."

"A business card?"

"Yes. I guess you could say I'm old school."

His body says early thirties, but his face has the distinguished look of a man in his mid-forties. That's not too old. I stick his card in my phone case.

"When do you think he'll call?" Trey asks. "My project has a pretty aggressive deadline."

"It was nice meeting you." Hint. Hint. *Leave me alone now.*

"Wait. Can I have your number?"

No one's asked for my number in a long time, but he doesn't want me. He wants D'Angelo. But he has such a strong smile. Trusting eyes. I need to get my irrational paranoia in check. He came to the awards banquet. He came to the university before that and talked with Judith. He knows I work with her. A stalker wouldn't put themselves out in the open like that, then follow me to the harbor, would they?

I don't think so.

"Okay." I tell him my number.

He types it into his cell phone.

I wait for him to leave, but he just stands there.

"Well," he says.

"Well, what?"

"Aren't you going to ask for my number?"

"Sure." I enter it into my contacts.

A raindrop splatters on my cell phone's screen. "It's starting to rain. I've really got to go." I turn and walk away. If he follows, I'll walk past my car until he gives up. I still don't want him to know what I drive. I'm not being paranoid. I'm being safe.

"If you had to guess"—he jogs up next to me again—"when do you think Dr. Santan will call?"

This is getting tiring. "I don't know. I can't promise that he will."

More rain begins to fall.

I quicken my pace, and so does Trey.

"Look," he says, "just give me a ballpark figure."

"I don't know. A day. A week. A month."

"A month?"

"Yes, a month." I stop. Face him. "I don't know when. Dr. Santan is missing."

"What?"

"Well, not really." Now I've done it. "I mean, people *think* he's missing. I can't promise you anything, and I want to get out of the rain now."

"Is he missing, missing? Like, the police are looking for him?"

"Yes, but he'll turn up on his own."

He wipes his forehead. Rivulets of rain run through his beard. He turns toward downtown and gazes at the buildings. "I can't wait for the police to find him. What about you?"

"What about me?"

"I'm sure you must be worried. I know you've worked with him for years. You've probably already tried to find him."

"I'm letting the police handle it. Like I said, he'll return on his own."

"What if he doesn't? Do they have any suspects?"

The question hits me like a sledgehammer. Detective Galen suggested I was a suspect. He said not to leave town. It doesn't matter what I think. If D'Angelo doesn't return on his own, the police will continue to take up my time. Or worse. If they find any false evidence, if Wilson tells them something stupid about the banquet, I could be arrested. I was visibly angry at D'Angelo that night.

Trey pulls his earbuds out of his pocket, glances at the rain, then puts them back. "Emma," he says, gently touching my shoulder, "what if Dr. Santan doesn't come back?"

CHAPTER EIGHTEEN

TREY - *January 1999*

Trey followed Malcolm into the student center half an hour ago. Malcolm had gone straight to the game room and plunked a quarter into the oldest machine. Joust. The ostriches on the game squawked, and their feet sounded like snapping rubber bands. Malcolm wore an Aerosmith T-shirt and a pair of jeans so large, they barely clung to his hulking hips. Trey stayed out of sight, lurking around the corner near the pool tables, watching the big guy battle the birds.

He watched, and he waited.

After twenty minutes, Trey was confident Malcolm wouldn't abandon the game. He'd played that entire time on a single quarter.

Trey moved across the carpet slowly. Quietly. The balls on the pool tables beyond cracked loudly. Bright lights hung over the tables, but the video games were left to illuminate themselves along the far wall. He stayed out of Malcolm's peripheral vision until the last second, then leaned in and viewed the screen. "Going for the high score, huh?"

"What do you want?" Malcolm keeps his eyes fixed on

the game.

"I just want to talk."

"How much do you want to pay me this time?" His ostrich flew high on the screen, knocking the rider off an opposing bird.

"Can't we just talk?"

"Last time, you paid me a thousand dollars. How much this time?"

"That was to attend my presentation."

"Go away, business boy."

"I'll make it quick. Do you remember my presentation last year?"

"Some. Not that I want to."

"You were right about how to start my business. Your polling idea. You still have your web crawler, right?"

The game's glow made the grease in Malcolm's pockmarks glisten. Craters of oil. Playing the game made the big guy sweat, but he also smelled like he hadn't showered in days. Some of that grease had lived there a long time. Same with his flat brown hair.

"I'm not working on your project."

"I'll be able to give you way more than a thousand dollars. I've sold my idea to a major investment firm. All I need is a solid prototype, and I'll pay you a salary. A very high salary."

A screeching pterodactyl flew across the screen and killed Malcolm's jouster. "Dammit. Go away."

"No."

"Please?"

"No."

"We'll be rolling in money. I just need your help for a couple of months."

"I thought you wanted to make the world a better place.

Why is it always about money with you business guys?"

Trey wanted to say, *Uh, because we're business guys? Duh.* "I do want to make it a better place. That's the whole goal. Don't you want to do that?"

Malcolm glanced at Trey. His eyes narrowed. "Can we start with ridding the world of guys like you? Business guys?"

Trey had seen this before. There was nothing behind Malcolm's eyes except a cold, dark place devoid of emotion. It gave Trey the chills. "No, we can do worse to them. We can take their money."

"What do you mean?"

"I told the investment firm I'd sell access to my website per person, but I'll never do that. I'm going to take all the investment firm's money and spend it to make the world—"

"Yeah, yeah. A better place." He tapped the flap-your-wings button with vigor. His ostrich took to the sky and killed the pterodactyl. "That's interesting, though. I like the idea of hitting them where it hurts. Their wallets."

"I'm telling you, once this thing takes off, we can pay them back with money from advertising and do whatever we want. I've been thinking even bigger."

"Oh yeah? How's that?"

"While millions are working together in our virtual communities, we can secretly display motivational messages."

"You mean subliminal messages?"

"Yeah. Something like that. The messages will accelerate their work. They'll work harder to solve the right problems for the right reasons without knowing it."

"That sounds suspicious. What stops someone from convincing them to cause problems rather than solve them? What if some greedy business guy uses it to sell them things they don't need?"

"I won't let that happen. Our communities will only help the world."

"*Our* communities?" Malcolm loses the battle with the next pterodactyl. Game over.

"You got the high score," Trey said. "That's amazing."

Malcolm entered the letters "HWK" into the machine. "It's not the first time." He turned to face Trey. If ever someone needed a Mentos or a Tic-Tac, it was him. "I maxed my credit card last month, and if my parents find out, they'll kill me. How about that hundred dollars?"

"Will you build my prototype?"

"Sure. I'll see what I can do."

"That's terrific!" Trey left his feet and held out his hand, but Malcolm didn't shake it.

"But things will be on my terms. If I need equipment, you'll get it for me. If I need more time, I'm taking more time. With classes, I can't have deadlines for this."

"The sooner we demonstrate it to the firm, the sooner we can get the money."

"No deadlines."

"But—"

"I'll do it as soon as possible, but no deadlines. That's been my problem with school. They'd rather I half-ass my assignments than put in the time to make my code perfect."

"I understand. No hard deadlines. But, they're going to want to know when we can show it."

"Fine." He headed toward the pool tables. "Tell them April. That way, when I finish early, they'll be happy." He stopped and turned around. "Then we'll take their money."

"That's right. I'll demonstrate it to them in April."

"No. I will." He looked Trey up and down. "You won't be able to handle it if something goes wrong."

The thought of introducing Malcolm to Calimico made Trey's neck tighten. He knew a lot of entrepreneurial types accepted the lack of professionalism exhibited by today's geeks, but he wasn't sure about Brad's "old-fashioned" colleagues. Malcolm wasn't merely unkempt in a pizza-eating, shut-in geek way. He was disgusting and a little scary.

A pool ball skipped off the table and rolled between Malcolm and Trey. The orange five ball. Trey put his attention back on Malcolm and heard the ball bounce off the wall.

"You can present the prototype," Trey said. "But you've got to clean up."

"Clean up what?"

Trey waved his hand. "This. You." His face felt hot. "You can't give a presentation looking like this."

"Looking like what?" Malcolm leaned forward.

"I think you look fine, but the management at—"

"No one runs my software but me. I'm not changing anything just to impress a bunch of pretty boys."

"Actually"—Trey stepped back—"at least one of them is a woman."

"The deal's off. I'm not a sell-out."

Trey took another step back, and his heel landed on the pool ball. He went down, his lower back hitting the floor first.

Malcolm's lifeless eyes hung in their sockets above him. "Smooth move, Ex-lax."

"You're right." Trey stood. "We can't sell out. That's not our style. Anything you want. Please, let's just do this."

"On my terms?"

"On your terms."

"Okay. I'll do it."

Trey instinctively held his hand out to shake on their accord, and Malcolm left him hanging.

CHAPTER NINETEEN

EMMA

The proposal is due in less than eighteen hours. Friday at 9 a.m. I want to sleep tonight, but I'll probably need to pull an all-nighter. I have an entire section left, and my brain has stopped working.

It didn't have to be this way.

All week, I've been working alone. D'Angelo didn't come back. Worthless Wilson kept true to his departing words Monday morning: *Let me know when D'Angelo comes back. Hasta la vista, baby.*

I haven't seen him since.

Sitting at my desk, I watch the clock tick past three in the afternoon. My computer screen stares at me. The proposal waits inside for me to finish it. Everyone has their own way of dealing with the stress of not knowing what happened to D'Angelo. Nimisha has been a champ this week, pulling together interesting articles and giving me ideas based on the grant committee's profile, but she's done all she can do as an intern. Everyone else, including D'Angelo's primary assistant, Tory, has kicked back in his absence. We're all worried, but no one talks about it.

The remaining section of the proposal is arguably the most important and complicated. I've saved it for last, hoping for D'Angelo's return. He'd knock it out quickly with my help.

Instead, the page is blank, like my mind. I need a nap.

But, the project needs this grant.

I can't give up now.

I know: I'll crank out whatever comes to mind for the next two hours, then get some sleep and wake up super early to rewrite it. It's the only way.

My fingers fly over the keyboard, but after only two sentences, my phone rings.

Balt PD.

Not now.

I haven't heard from the police all week, which has been both a blessing and curse. I've wanted to hear that they've found D'Angelo, and at the same time, I've been glad I haven't had to talk to Detective Galen. I didn't like him telling me not to leave town.

"Hello, this is Ms. Petranova."

"Hi Emma, it's Detective Galen." *Ugh.* "Do you have a few minutes?"

"I . . ." The proposal stares me in the face. "How can I help you?"

"I really enjoyed our talk on Monday. How's the exercise been going?"

"Exercise?"

"Your running."

"Oh. It hasn't. Did you find Dr. Santan?"

"Okay. Get to the chase. I get it. We're still searching for him, and like I said Monday, I have some follow-up questions for you. We were able to talk to all of your colleagues except for Wilson Sinclair. Have you been in touch with him this week?"

"No. Once he found out D'Angelo wasn't coming into work, he decided he didn't need to either."

"Did you call him? Talk to him on the phone at any point since you last saw him?"

"No."

"When was the last time you saw him, exactly?"

"Monday morning."

"Where?"

"In the office. Why are you so interested in Wilson?"

"Be specific. Was it in the lobby? His office? Where?"

"The lobby downstairs. I was trying to convince him to stay."

Silence. He's probably writing in that little notepad of his.

"Were you angry with him?" Galen asks.

"Yes. He always does stuff like this, and with D'Angelo gone, I really needed help this week."

"Did you assault him?"

"What? No. Of course not. What are you saying?"

"Did you threaten him in any way?"

"No, not really. I mean, not physically. I just let him know if he didn't stay and help me, I'd make sure Dr. Santan knew about it when he came back. We've had this kind of discussion in the past. It's normal for us."

"Hmm." He pauses. "So, you and Wilson have a history of altercations?"

"Altercations? What is going on?"

"Do you know a Mr. Travis Bluthe?"

"Yes. That's Wilson's partner."

"Mr. Bluthe reported Mr. Sinclair missing yesterday."

"Excuse me?"

"After returning home on Monday morning, your Wilson left his domicile and has not been seen since, if what you told me is true. You haven't seen him this week, correct?"

"Yes." I'm both fuming and running on fumes. My eyes want to close. "If you knew he was gone, why'd you ask me all of these questions?"

"It's my job to see if your story matches everyone else's, and you were close. That's good for you, but I'd still like to meet face-to-face again to continue this discussion."

"Close? What do you mean I was close?"

"After talking with your colleagues, I learned you did indeed have an altercation immediately before Mr. Sinclair left the psychology building. The description in my notes borders on assault."

"But, I didn't—"

"Is there anything else you want to tell me right now?"

"Are you implying I had something to do with Wilson disappearing?"

"I'm not implying anything. This investigation has just begun, but it's most likely related to Dr. Santan, given his workplace relationships. This is why we need to meet again."

"No. I—I can't." I put my head down on my desk. "Wilson is always taking trips to the tropics and other places. Did you check the airlines?"

"Yes, we did. Does he take these trips without his partner?"

"I don't know. I never thought about it."

"Can you meet me this evening?"

"No."

"Emma, you have a habit of threatening your coworkers right before they go missing. I strongly suggest you meet with me as soon as possible."

"I didn't kidnap anyone."

"I'm not saying you did."

"Do I need a lawyer?"

"You and I need to meet."

I sit up.

The screen saver kicks in, and my screen goes black.

This is all so preposterous. It's insane. I need to sleep.

"Emma, when can you meet me?"

"I don't have anything to say that will help you."

"This is serious."

"I've told you everything I know. I'm sure there's a logical explanation, but I don't know what that might be. D'Angelo and Wilson are going to show up. I promise."

"Are you refusing to help me?"

"No." I tilt my head back against my chair as far as it will go and close my eyes. Why did I think I had the energy to work on the proposal for the next two hours? "Isn't your job to find them?"

"Emma. Don't go there. You're making a mistake. It will only hurt you long-term if you don't cooperate."

"Stop trying to scare me. I know my rights. You can't make me meet you tonight."

"Not without an arrest warrant."

"What are you saying?"

"I'm saying I can get one. You were the last person to see each man alive, and you threatened both of them."

"That's not true. Nimisha and Wilson were in the parking lot when I last saw Dr. Santan, and Nimisha was there when Wilson left."

"This is the other part of the story that doesn't line up. In both cases, Ms. Shaan said she walked away before either of the men left."

I think back, and I can't remember exactly what Nimisha did. It's possible she turned her back and walked away before D'Angelo drove off. It's possible she got in the elevator, and the doors closed before Wilson left the building. It's possible, and she's not the type of person to lie.

"I can't meet you tonight. I need to sleep. I'm going to hang up now."

"You do sound tired. Okay. Let's meet first thing in the morning."

"No, I—I don't know what I'm going to do."

"Don't drag this out, Emma. If you don't come to me, I'll be forced to come to you."

At some point in the night, I awaken to discover that I've moved to the break room and crashed on the couch. It's not like me to sleepwalk.

I check the time.

It's 1 a.m.

I return to my desk and stare at the proposal.

It stares back at me.

An hour passes, and I make no progress.

Another hour goes by.

With all that sleep, I'm able to focus, but not on the proposal. My conversation with Galen keeps replaying in my head. He said it was serious, and he was right. I'm on the hook for two missing persons. Those idiots. They've got to come back so this nightmare will end. If I found them, I could end it. Though I'd rather just quit.

I don't mean that. I've put too much work in. Haven't I?

I switch the monitor off.

Will that guy, Trey, call me?

With his perfect genetics, we could make great-grandchildren for Mom. I must still be light-headed from my messed-up sleep schedule, but it's true. If I quit my work, and things went well with him, or someone else, I could move on with my life. Follow my original plan. Build a career, then start a family. It's just that I wanted more from my career than I have now.

It might not matter.

Without D'Angelo, the project might be over anyway. I'm too old to start a new project with a different professor.

And I'm not finishing this proposal.

I give up and head for the elevator.

CHAPTER TWENTY

EMMA

I'd never tell Alyssa this, but my mom was always my best friend. We had problems like mothers and daughters do, but I was fortunate. She never judged me. She always listened.

"I miss you, Mom."

The wind gusts and blows a cluster of leaves toward the farmhouse. They fly up the wooden steps the way I imagine my mom and uncle did when they were children. Running inside to play checkers. The house must have seemed huge to them back then, but it's not. A single-story ranch with only two bedrooms, a bath, and one large room holding both the kitchen and a living area. It's mostly empty inside. Nothing but a kitchen table and some broken chairs. No one has lived here in years. On the outside, raw wooden planks peek through the peeling red paint. Half the shake shingles are missing. The forest behind the house stretches up a hill and down the other side, running on for several miles. I never venture over the hill. Instead, I always kneel in the front yard, where we put Mom's ashes.

I kneel here beneath the giant weeping cherry tree.

I didn't go to work today. The proposal went unfinished. I hate to admit it, but the project could die without D'Angelo.

"What should I do, Mom?"

I pull the toy magnifying glass out of my pocket and hold it the way a priest holds a rosary. There's a quote by a famous author—I can't remember who—that goes, "Sometimes a change of perspective is all it takes to see the light."

I want to see the light. I want to know whether I should search for D'Angelo or walk away. Leave school and meet somebody and start a family.

The wind gusts again. Soon, the sun will set, the temperature will drop, and I'll know what to do. I hope. When I hold the magnifying glass at the right distance from the tree, the bark turns upside down, just like my life.

It's a different perspective.

From my perspective, I still think Dr. Santan might have left on his own. Gone out on a high note, taken the award, and disappeared to escape his wicked wife. Wilson takes ten trips a year, visiting islands or Vegas. He probably forgot to tell his partner about this one, or more likely, he and Travis had a fight, and Wilson is getting even by "disappearing."

"Mom. What should I do?"

I look through the magnifying glass and see things from Detective Galen's perspective. Through his eyes, I'm Emma Petranova. Someone who argued with both missing persons the last time they were seen. Her motive? To take over the most important research project the University of Baltimore has ever known and profit from the notoriety. She's a suspect. She must not leave Baltimore.

His perspective is wrong, of course. Ridiculous, but there it is. I must accept it. As a suspect, if I were to quit working on the project, red alerts would ring throughout the Baltimore

PD. Galen would be on me in a heartbeat.

I've got to act like everything is normal.

"I know you still want me to have children someday, Mom. For me, not you. And, I want to, too. But I can't leave the university until D'Angelo and Wilson are found."

The grasses around me bend with the wind. They point toward the farmhouse. The front door rattles and the shingles shake. I could go inside and hide. Pretend the outside world doesn't exist. But how long could I make that last? The fact is, I can't move on with my life until I find my colleagues.

"Right, Mom? Do you agree?"

I return the magnifying glass to my pocket.

The cherry tree's branches sway.

It's not up to her. I have no other logical choice.

The cold wind blows my hair in my face. I rush to the car, jump inside, and start the engine. If I find D'Angelo, he can clear everything up. Then, I can leave the project and the university on clear terms.

I'll let the police worry about Wilson.

The road winds through the woods.

Detective Galen wants to meet me face-to-face. He wanted to meet earlier today, but I didn't answer my phone. I don't know how much longer I can put him off. He seemed like a decent guy the first time we talked—the proverbial "good cop"—but then he accused me of foul play and attempted to trap me in a lie. I don't trust him. He said D'Angelo didn't go home after the awards banquet, but it was D'Angelo's wife who told Galen that, and I don't trust her.

The last thing I want to do is talk to that wicked woman.

She probably still thinks we' are having an affair.

But what choice do I have?

She might be the last person to have seen D'Angelo alive.

CHAPTER TWENTY-ONE

TREY - *February 1999*

Trey's apartment sucked, but the dorms blew. He never had to live in a dorm because of his father's connections, and most students moved out after their freshmen or sophomore year.

But not Malcolm.

Malcolm seemed like a lifer. He was set to graduate the same year as Trey, 2000, but now, they wouldn't graduate together. At this point, Trey had officially dropped out. The thought made him smile. He told himself he was living the dream. Like Bill Gates, he wouldn't be graduating next year or any year.

Trey was just like Bill Gates.

It was hard to believe spring 2000 was less than a year and a half away. By then, he would have a thriving business, with or without Malcolm. But for now, everything depended on the big guy.

The sunny day had no way of entering the windowless hallway, and most of the lights were off. The dorm was a cave. Trey couldn't tell for sure, but he thought he saw cobwebs on the ceiling. Didn't they ever clean this place? The lack of light made it difficult to see anything. Some guy opened the door to his room, and a fearful light escaped into the hall. The guy was young, a freshman, perhaps. His pale skin and bloodshot eyes screamed hangover.

"Can you tell me which room is Malcolm Schmidt's?" Trey asked.

The guy pointed to the last door at the end of the hall. He touched his temple and squinted.

"Thanks."

Knock, knock.

The door opened.

Malcolm filled the doorway.

No light escaped his room. It was actually darker in there. "Oh," Malcolm said. "It's you."

He turned and walked to his computer. Sat behind a large, glowing monitor.

One wall held cabinets above a countertop over a set of drawers. The opposite wall hosted a sink and a bunk bed. The far wall had a window, but Malcolm had blacked it out. That was it. Trey could have spit and hit the window from the doorway. The place was more like a prison cell than a dorm room.

"You can come in," Malcolm said without turning around. "Close the door. You're letting the light in."

Trey did as he was told.

The cabinet doors had corkboard exteriors with papers pinned to them. The papers overlapped each other and hung crooked. Loose notes and worn notebooks littered the counter and spilled onto the floor. Every note Malcolm had taken over the past two years was dumped here. Trey didn't bother looking at the sink. He could smell it, and that was enough for him.

"How's it going?" Trey asked.

Malcolm typed something into the computer. "It's going."

"That's great." Trey waited for more from him, but Malcolm said nothing. He kept typing. "Where's your roommate?"

"I don't have a roommate anymore."

That made sense. Who would want to live in this room with him? In this squalor. An electric guitar with a broken neck leaned against the wall behind him. Trey wondered how long it would take before staring at a bright screen in a dark room would drive someone mad.

"Do you play guitar?"

"No." Malcolm glanced at the guitar. "That was my roommate's. We didn't get along."

"I see."

Trey stepped closer and noticed things other than papers on the counter. Various knick-knacks surrounded the monitor. A Panic Pete with bulging rubber eyes. A Koosh ball. Concert ticket stubs. Bent paper clips and thumbtacks. A throwing star embossed with yin and yang.

"So, can we present the prototype next month, sometime in March?"

Malcolm said nothing.

Tucked behind the monitor, a picture of an old woman peeked out from between the wires. Malcolm's mother, maybe.

"What's left to be done?"

Malcolm swiveled his chair around. His lifeless eyes looked like they hadn't blinked in hours. "It'll be done before April."

"Sure, got it. Does any of it work now?"

"Almost everything. I ran an end-to-end test, and it worked, but it was in my development environment. There's a lot I need to do to cover edge cases and test it for real."

Trey couldn't believe it. He had struggled for more than two years to get this far, and now—he would have a prototype. In only a month, Malcolm had made something work. Malcolm *was* brilliant. "Edge cases?"

"Things like when a user does something stupid answering the poll questions, or when things about the host's website break my code. I haven't put error checking in yet."

"This is great news. I'm so excited."

"Don't be. It only works on my computer, and I simulated capturing the end user's information. The real deal would be to show how we can capture a few users' data in real time."

"A few? Don't you mean a few thousand?"

Malcolm laughed. Turned back to his screen. "No. It would take weeks for the application to capture that many."

"But, that's what we have to show them. The entire basis of the business plan depends on pulling in thousands of users in a short time. How many can it do now?"

"It takes a minute or two for each—it can do about twenty to thirty an hour. It'll be slower over the internet."

"Slower?" Trey searched the gray tile floors for an answer. "It needs to do three thousand an hour."

"Never going to happen."

And Trey's pacing began.

Brad and his people at Calimico might be okay with the slowness as long as each new user paid for an account, but this went against everything. "There must be something we can do?"

"I might be able to get it up to fifty or a hundred, but not with this." He waved his hand over the keyboard.

"How about five hundred in thirty minutes? I'm not sure they'll give us more than half an hour for the demo."

"I don't know. To convince five hundred users on a new website, we might need to expose the poll to several hundred thousand. I just don't know."

"Why don't you know? Don't you think you can do it?"

Malcolm stood up and grabbed the throwing star off the counter. He began flipping it over the knuckles in his left hand, making it tumble from his pinky to his index and back again. "I can do it. I need more equipment, is all."

"How much?"

"At least five Pentiums with 64MB SDRAM, a router, cables, high-speed NICs—"

"No, not how much in geek speak. How much money?"

Malcolm brushed aside some papers and lifted a super thick magazine with the words *Computer Shopper* emblazoned across the top. "You figure it out." He tossed the book to Trey with his right hand. He continued to flip the throwing star back and forth with his left.

Trey missed the catch, and the catalog thudded onto the floor. "There must be five hundred pages in that thing. Can't you just give me a ballpark figure?"

"You business guys and your ballpark figures. You think geek speak is bad. I hate how you talk."

The star tumbled. An uneasiness settled inside Trey. The dark room seemed darker now.

"Give me five thousand and another month," Malcolm said, "and I'll make this thing scream."

Trey looked away. He paced. He could only take three steps before reaching the door, but paced anyway. He had to find a solution. Calimico was *the* last chance. The demo had to be impressive. It had to be like nothing they'd ever seen. "Couldn't you use the university's computers?"

"No." Malcolm had raised his voice. "That's against school policy for a reason. We have morons abusing the campus network all the time, ruining it for everyone else. No. I won't be one of those guys." He stopped flipping the star and held it in his hand. He squeezed it.

"Okay. I understand." Trey picked up the catalog. "If it takes that much to obtain five hundred users, how much would it take to reach fifty thousand?"

"I think you can figure that out yourself, business boy."

A lot. Way more money than he'd built into the business plan. "We'll ask for more, but it won't matter if we can't show them significant numbers. I'm not sure they'll go for it."

"So, is that it? Can I stop working on this now? If we're not going to get the money, then—"

"No. No. It's going to be okay. I'll find a way."

Malcolm stopped fiddling with the throwing star and put it down. "Fine, then let me finish what I was doing." He sat behind the monitor. Began typing.

"It's a good thing you told me to tell them we'd be done in April now that we need more time."

"It's a bad thing you didn't give me good requirements. I don't know about April. It depends on when I get the new computers."

Trey flipped through the computer catalog. "I have an idea. If it works, I'll order them tomorrow. Is that enough time for you?"

"Yeah. It should be." A red message flashed on his screen. He hit some keys in rapid succession, and it disappeared. "Goodbye."

The hallway was brighter now.

Outside was absolutely blinding.

Trey's apartment was the Ritz Carlton compared to Malcolm's squalor.

His answering machine light flashed red.

Brad from Calimico.

I hate to leave this on your machine, but I've called a couple of times already. My team has looked at the last startup for funding for this year, other than yours, and they want to pull the trigger on that one. We can't wait until April. I fought for you, but is there any chance you could show us what you have by mid-March—in, say, two or three weeks?

CHAPTER TWENTY-TWO

EMMA

D'Angelo's wife opens the door to their colonial suburban home at the end of a tree-lined street. Lit up by the morning sun, it's the kind of home I've always wanted. Quiet, peaceful, and inviting. Everything that Marjorie is not.

The look on the woman's face says it all. She hates me. She must still think D'Angelo and I had a thing. She keeps her hand on the door, ready to close it at any time. Her frilly white blouse and peacock blue cigarette pants scream all dressed up and nowhere to go.

"Do you know where he is?" Marjorie says as her upper lip curls.

"No, I was hoping you—"

"Then why are you here?"

"I was hoping you could tell me about the last time you saw him."

"The police told me *you* saw him last." She plants her hands on her hips. "Why don't you tell *me*?"

"I saw him at the awards banquet. Didn't he come home after that?"

"No, and I already told the police everything. Haven't they talked to you? I told them to talk to you." She's pointing her scrawny finger at me.

"Yes, they did, but they didn't tell me what you said. I'm trying to find your husband, and I need your help. Our project depends on it."

"You mean *his* project." She fakes a smile. "All you people ever care about is his project. Glomming onto my husband's brilliance. I wouldn't be surprised if you had something to do with all this."

"What are you implying?"

She just glares at me.

"I'm sorry. I know you're upset. Believe me, I'm truly more worried about him than the project. Please, isn't there something you can tell me about the night he didn't return home? Why didn't you attend the awards ceremony?"

"I was sick. He didn't come back, and I reported him missing. That's all I've got to tell you." She begins to close the door.

I believe her. On the few occasions over the past couple of years, she never attended any of the university functions that I could remember. She may not have been sick last week, but now that I thought about it, it wasn't abnormal for her to stay home.

I grab the door handle. "Why do you think he didn't come back?"

"If I knew that, I wouldn't have reported him missing, would I?"

"Is there anywhere else he usually went? Maybe I wasn't the last to see him."

"The only place he ever went," her upper lip curls again, baring her teeth, "other than the university with you, was down at the Royale to drink coffee with his buddies, but that was a morning habit. Goodbye." She closes the door hard, making it rattle in its frame. The deadbolt *clanks* into place.

I get into my car.

Café Royale.

Situated on a gently sloping hill, sandwiched between several other shops, D'Angelo's hangout is covered in cascading ivy leaves. I drive past and park two blocks down from the red brick buildings defining this quaint area of Baltimore. At 10 a.m. on a Saturday, I hope D'Angelo's old cronies are still hanging out together.

My phone rings.

It's Nimisha. "Hey, Emma. Is everything okay?"

"Yes."

"Why didn't you come into the office yesterday? We had that proposal due. They were expecting it."

"Did you reschedule the meeting?"

"Yes. I had to. What's up with you?"

"Well, you can cancel it. The project is on hold until Dr. Santan comes back. I couldn't do the proposal without him."

"Oh, okay. I'll do that. Will I see you Monday?"

"No, probably not." Down the street, an elderly man exits the coffee shop. "Hey, I've got to go, but promise me you'll call if you hear from Dr. Santan or Wilson, okay?"

"Sure. I still have a pile of research he left me to work on, so I'll be there if they return. I'll call immediately if they do."

"You're the best, Nimisha."

Potted plants hang from the ceiling in the corners of the Café Royale. The walls are the same inside and out. Red brick with white residue blemishes. A band of old men sit at the largest table toward the back. I recognize Dr. Mancini and one other. Mancini retired a few years ago, and the other's black and white portrait hangs in the psychology wing along with several esteemed professors of yesteryear. I'm fairly certain his name is Lorenzo.

One of the other men, the only one with a beard, glances up at me when I reach their table. "Could you bring me another nonfat latte, miss?"

"I'm sorry, I don't work here," I say.

Everyone's side conversations come to a halt. They all look at me. The two men at the end of the table are both balding, wrinkled, and have the posture of a buzzard. If Alyssa were here, she'd make a joke about Statler and Waldorf from *The Muppet Show*.

"Can we help you?" Dr. Mancini asks.

"I work with Dr. Santan."

"Oh," says the bearded one. He turns away from me, clearly disappointed I'm not an employee.

"He hasn't been here," Lorenzo says.

"Yes." Dr. Mancini cocks his head. "You must be aware of what happened."

"No. What happened?"

"He's gone. Certainly, you knew that or you wouldn't be here asking about him." Lorenzo downs the last of his coffee.

"I know he's gone, but—" I steel my nerves in their presence. I'm both honored and annoyed to speak with them. "Do you know where he might have gone?"

Statler and Waldorf resume their conversation at the other end of the table.

Dr. Mancini raises a tiny coffee cup to his lips and sips slowly.

Lorenzo waves at the barista. This isn't the type of place that waits on tables, but someone from behind the coffee comes around.

"So, I was saying," the bearded man directs his attention at Lorenzo, "my wife has these orchids she hasn't watered in three years."

"Dr. Mancini," I say. "Please. When was the last time Dr. Santan was here?"

"How do you know my name?"

"I remember you."

"Well, I'm sorry, but I don't remember you."

"Dr. Santan has disappeared, and I'm trying to find him. Isn't there anything you can tell me?"

"We don't have to talk to her." Lorenzo raises his cup toward the wait person as she approaches the table. "Could I get another nonfat latte?"

"Sure thing."

"You're that Petranova girl," Dr. Mancini says. "I remember you now. He talked about you, but only on occasion. My understanding is you spend more time with him than anyone."

"More than his wife," the bearded man says with a smile.

Someone touches my shoulder from behind. "Excuse me, Emma?"

I turn.

Mr. Handsome himself gazes into my eyes.

Mr. Trey Wilkes. Entrepreneur extraordinaire.

"Oh, hi," I say. "What are you—"

"I was walking by and saw you through the window." He points to the front of the shop. "Thought I'd say hello."

"Hello."

"Those damn flowers won't die," the bearded man says. "Those orchids are possessed, I tell you."

I turn back around.

"I don't know, James," Dr. Mancini says. "Maybe they're

magical orchids."

It's obvious these men don't care about me. They don't seem to care about D'Angelo much, either. Maybe they're stuck in denial like I was, thinking he will return on his own. Either way, I'm getting nowhere.

"Emma," Trey says. "I'm so glad I ran into you. You're just the person I needed to see."

"Yeah?"

"Can we talk outside? It's noisy in here."

"I hadn't noticed." It didn't seem that noisy to me.

"It is noisy in here." He waves toward the coffee bar just as the barista fires up the milk steamer. "It's noisy in here."

"Okay, okay." I follow him outside. The pleasant aroma of freshly ground coffee is replaced by Baltimore's dank, brackish air.

"Dr. Santan hasn't called me," he says. "I take it he's still missing."

"That's right, but I'm trying to find him now."

"Gave up on waiting for the police to do it?"

"You could say that."

"I can help." He puts on that amazing smile. "I have reason to think an old acquaintance from my college days contacted Dr. Santan recently."

"Acquaintance?"

"Actually, we were more than that. We worked on a big project together, but things didn't end well. That's why I'm so glad I ran into you. I'm very concerned for Dr. Santan." He averts his eyes. "I'm afraid his disappearance may have had something to do with me."

"What do you mean?"

"My old friend is trying to sabotage my work. There's no other reason he would have tried to talk to Dr. Santan."

"Do you think he might have done something bad?"

"That's exactly what I'm afraid of." He puts his hands in his pockets. "If any harm came to your friend, I'd be sick."

D'Angelo isn't exactly my friend, but I know what Trey is saying. He seems to genuinely care about D'Angelo's well-being. He hasn't mentioned wanting access to our research, like last time we met. But beyond that, the last time we met was eerily similar to this time. Twice now, he's *coincidentally* run into me.

His phone buzzes, and he swipes the screen. "I'm sorry. I've got to make a call. Can we meet later? I want to help you."

"How?"

"I don't have enough on my old friend to go to the police, but if he's involved, he might lead us in the right direction." His phone buzzes again. "I've really got to go. It's an investor. I'll call you later, okay?"

"You don't have my—"

He walks away briskly. "We exchanged numbers at the harbor, remember?"

He's right. I forgot about that. I trusted him that day, so I should trust him now. Besides—those old men, Marjorie—I've got nothing else to go on.

I follow behind him, watching as he holds his phone to his ear. He walks with purpose. His stride is confident, and his posture is perfect, and he'll call me later. It's not a date, but who knows. It could be the start of something.

He turns at the first intersection, and I continue straight ahead to my car. I unlock the door, and . . . there it is.

Directly across the street sits a golden car.

The golden car.

I look both ways, then race across the street.

Casually, I circle the vehicle, pretending to be captivated

by my cell phone. The four-door is an Acura. It's old. I stop on the sidewalk and type the license plate number into my phone. A couple stroll hand-in-hand across the street. There's no one else around. No one who notices what I'm doing. Still, I pretend to drop something on the ground and lean close to the passenger-side window. The tint is dark, but I can see inside. A laptop bag sits on the floor, and a pair of white earbuds rest on the seat.

Trey was wearing white earbuds when we met at the harbor. I remember thinking his ears might get shocked when it started to rain, but he kept the buds in his pocket. That's probably a myth, anyway.

I back away from the car.

A lot of people own white earbuds.

Trey walked in the other direction when we parted.

This can't be his.

I wait across the street for an hour. Then two. The car is still there. I only have so many games on my phone. Around one o'clock, I give up. My paranoia gives way to common sense. Whoever it is, they're not after me or they would have returned by now. I can't spend the rest of my life here, waiting for some stranger, and what would I do if they came?

I start my car and put the transmission in drive and—

A black SUV with tinted windows pulls in between me and the golden sedan. A car door slams. Then another. When the SUV continues down the street, I can't see who is behind the Acura's steering wheel. It peels out of its parking spot.

I pull in behind it like I'm going to give chase, and I do . . . until the first stoplight. The sedan runs the red light, barely making it across without hitting a Jeep Cherokee wagon filled with children, their faces glued to the windows.

I can't get across, and the golden mystery gets away.

CHAPTER TWENTY-THREE

TREY - *March 1999*

Trey stood in the parking lot outside Malcolm's dormitory. They needed to talk. A neutral place to talk without the gloom, the broken guitar, and the throwing star. Malcolm came out and got into his car. Trey ran to his car, started his engine, paused, then began following Malcolm at a distance. He kept two cars between him and the golden treasure. Malcolm's '96 Acura Integra with tinted windows and metallic paint. It screamed, *Look at me—I'm a shooting star.*

It was a really nice car.

Malcolm had once said he hated it. His parents gave it to him for college, so he had to drive it. Trey thought Malcolm was crazy. He loved that car because, like him, it was a shooting star.

Malcolm drove to an area near downtown Baltimore and parked along the street.

Trey hid his face as he passed by and found his own parking spot. He got out and ran up the sidewalk.

Malcolm walked to the front of a tobacco shop and paused outside the door.

"Hey," Trey yelled. "Malcolm. What a coincidence, huh? Wait up."

Malcolm opened the door, glanced back at Trey, then went inside.

It had been a week and a half since Trey ordered the computer equipment and sent it to Malcolm. The company he chose to order from in *Computer Shopper* magazine accepted orders on invoice. Order now, pay later. He didn't have a plan for the pay later part. His allowance appeared in his checking account each month, but it barely paid his living expenses.

He crossed the street. The corner tobacco shop's jagged gray bricks clung to the cracking mortar. Trey found Malcolm inside leaning over a glass case.

"Which one do you want?" the clerk asked. A small, round man with a face like a grapefruit and hair to match the bricks outside. "You got that one last time, I remember?"

Trey gazed into the case. "You chew tobacco?"

"No." Malcolm pointed to a box at the end of the case. "I'll take that one."

"Buying it for a friend?" Trey asked.

The clerk retrieved the box and put it on the counter. "Eight dollars and ninety-nine cents."

"No," Malcolm said to Trey, picking the box up and putting it in his pocket. He'd yet to look at him directly. "It's for me."

"But, you said didn't you chew tobacco."

"I don't." Malcolm paid with cash and headed for the door.

"Hey, anyway—" Trey ran up behind him. "How are things going with the project? Did you get the computers?"

Cars hummed down Charles St.

Malcolm stopped at the crosswalk. "One computer and

148

some other stuff came last week, but the rest was on backorder. It might come tomorrow."

"Oh, no. Is it enough for you to do everything?"

Malcolm turned to Trey. Those lifeless eyes. "No. If it was, I wouldn't have told you to get five computers, would I?"

"No. It's just that—"

"Don't get your panties in a bunch. The other stuff will come." He lifted his chin. Gazed at the crosswalk signal. "We have time."

"No, we don't." Trey tried but failed to keep the tension out of his voice.

"What? What do you mean?"

"The venture capitalists called. They want the demo in two weeks."

"Tell them no. I said April. Two weeks from now is still March."

"I can't. They will go with another company if we don't show them something by then. We can't let that happen. Brad, the guy I talk to, said they wouldn't look at us again until next year if we didn't present before the other company."

The walk signal changed, and Malcolm trounced a puddle on his way across the street, splashing the windshield of a stopped car. Trey took a wide path around the puddle, then jogged to catch up with Malcolm. "Where are you going?"

Malcolm walked past a kitschy cafe, a bar, and a hair salon before turning down an alley surrounded by early-century townhouses. He stopped near a dumpster, pulled the tobacco box out, opened it, and dumped some on his wrist. It came out in a fine brown powder.

"What is that?" Trey asked.

Malcolm snorted the powder. "It's snuff. It works faster

than chew. The nicotine goes straight to your brain."

"Oh—wow. Why do you—"

"It helps me stay awake. It's better than NoDoz."

"It's noon."

"What's your point?"

"Never mind. Can you get the prototype done by the fifteenth?"

"I told you, no deadlines." Malcolm looked both ways, up and down the alley. He dropped more snuff onto his wrist and snorted it. "My aunt lives near here. She doesn't know I do this."

"I didn't know anyone still did that. It's like something from the 1920s. Honestly, it's kind of weird."

"Don't call me weird." Malcolm stowed the box and headed back toward Charles Street.

Trey followed.

A bare skin island had formed on the back of Malcolm's head. His greasy brown hair wasn't long for the world. The dates for the '97 Kiss Alive Worldwide Tour jerked up and down on the back of the big guy's T-shirt as he hoofed it to the street. Trey couldn't believe he'd agreed to let Malcolm present at the demo.

But, he had agreed.

In desperation, Trey had agreed to all of Malcolm's terms, including no deadlines.

Malcolm turned around in front of the hair salon. "Are you going to follow me all the way back to the dorms?"

"If I have to."

"I said, no deadlines."

"If the equipment comes tomorrow, can you have the prototype done by the fifteenth?"

A car drove too close to the curb and splashed Malcolm's

jeans. "Wooh!" Malcolm thrust his chest out. "That's a rush." He turned toward Trey. Those steely eyes. "The snuff, not the water."

"Just put me at ease and tell me you can finish the prototype. Please?"

"Right now"— tobacco snot trickled onto Malcolm's upper lip—"I could do anything."

And yet, the big guy's eyes still had no fire behind them. He walked away, heading for his golden car. He was a passionless giant, hopped up on snuff, and brilliant all the same.

And he held Trey's future in his hands.

CHAPTER TWENTY-FOUR

EMMA

I step out of the shower and wrap a towel around my body. Alyssa always says I'm lucky. She thinks it's easy for me to stay slim. Maybe she's right. I rarely go to the gym and mostly eat whatever I want. It's the stress that keeps the weight off. At times, I've been so engrossed in my work I've forgotten to eat. Last summer, we took Vivian to the beach, and I wore a bikini. Alyssa told me I could have any man I wanted. Again, she said I was lucky. She said she didn't know where her stretch marks started or where they ended.

I'm not so lucky. I don't have a Vivian.

I should call Alyssa. She was so excited when D'Angelo went missing. It did nothing but fuel her True Crime love affair. She was desperate to put her Sherlock hat on and help me find him. Cagney and Lacey hit the streets. I could use her help.

My phone rings. I barely hear it over the hairdryer.

The screen reads, *Mr. Handsome*. I put the dryer down.

"Hi, Emma? It's Trey."

In the living room, I plop down on the couch, my hair

still wet. "Hi."

"Sorry, I had to bail on you before. I didn't get to tell you how happy I was to run into you."

"I think you told me that."

"But, I'm still sorry. All I did was talk about Dr. Santan. I wanted to warn you about my friend, but I also wanted to tell you . . ."

"Yes?"

"I've just been thinking about you a lot since we met. That's all. When I saw you in that coffee shop, it was—oh God, this is going to sound corny."

"What is it?"

"Do you believe in fate?"

He likes me. I can't believe where this conversation is going. "I want to believe in fate, but I also think it's something that can be controlled."

"Me too. I think your research work with Dr. Santan has brought us together for a bigger purpose than my business. I couldn't believe it when I saw you in the coffee shop. I think I'm supposed to help you find him. Not only because my business needs his expertise, but because I need you. Uh, I mean, because I need to help you."

"Are you hitting on me?"

"Will you let me help you?"

"Yes." The word escapes my mouth before I can hold it back.

"Great. The more I think about it, the more I think my friend from college has finally snapped. I think he may have taken Dr. Santan, or worse."

"Who is he? Why?"

"His name is Malcolm Schmidt. We worked together on a project a long time ago, but it failed. Actually, it was more than a project. We started a business together. When the stock market crashed, I had to part ways with him. He has resented my success ever since. Over the years, he showed up and tried to sabotage me a couple times. Nothing big to start with. First, he trolled my businesses on review websites, but later, he hung outside my offices and taunted my employees. I had to have him removed more than once."

"I don't understand. Why would anyone waste their time like that? Why didn't he move on?"

"I don't know. He was always strange. He had a real thing for holding onto the past. He used to wear these T-Shirts with eighties bands on them. They barely fit him. He was over six feet tall and must have weighed over three hundred pounds. Anyway, he loved that old retro stuff, but that wasn't the strange part. Even when we worked hard together, sitting side-by-side, he'd make these little comments about how much he hated corporations. I was a business major at the time, but he'd still talk about how much he'd like to—how did he say it? Eradicate the world of all businessmen. Something like that. It used to give me the creeps. For a time, I thought he might shoot up the school. Especially after Columbine happened."

"Why did you work with him?"

"He was a computer science major, and he was the best. I needed someone to build a website."

"And you fired him?"

"When the dot-coms crashed, I had to make some hard choices. Everything went under, including him. I've always felt bad about it."

"It doesn't sound like it was your fault."

"It doesn't matter. A few weeks ago, I got a strange email warning me not to continue with my latest business venture.

The return address had the word 'hawk' in it. Malcolm's nickname in college was 'The Hawk.' I ignored it, and now your professor is missing."

"So you think he's still trying to get even with you after all this time?"

"Yes. Maybe. I don't know for sure, but I know he hates me. He threatened my life the last time I saw him, and I was only a few steps away from getting a restraining order when he stopped stalking me. He just disappeared. I thought he'd finally given up."

"When was that?"

"About four years ago." He breathes into the phone. Lowers his voice. "Malcolm is smart. Very smart. I've probably said too much already. Can you meet me in person?"

"Do you think he's listening to us?"

"It's entirely possible. He's a technical genius. I don't think hacking into a cell tower would be problematic for someone like him. When can we get together? I have a plan to find out if he's behind all this or not."

"I'm not sure." I stand, and my towel falls to the floor. I leave it there. Being naked in the living room is one of the few perks of living alone. Trey said he wanted to help me find Dr. Santan, but now it sounds like he wants me to help him stop an old enemy. Maybe it's both, or maybe he just wants to see me. I decide to test him a little. If he wants only me, then he won't want Alyssa to come. "Can I bring a friend? She really wants to help me, too."

"I don't know if that's a good idea. I don't want to scare you, but this situation with Malcolm could be dangerous. Based on that email trying to scare me off, he knows I'm interested in Dr. Santan's research, so he might know about you and everyone you work with. Is your friend part of the project?"

"No, but if what you're saying is true, I'd want her to come even more. There's safety in numbers."

"How long have you known her? Can she be trusted with information about your project? About my business?"

Beginning in middle school, Alyssa could always do the gutsy things I couldn't. Protest injustices. Walk away from bad situations. Disarm pushy salesmen with the sheer force of her personality. I need her with me. "I've known her all my life. There's no one I trust more."

"I see."

"Did you report that email to the police?"

"No. I've been through this before. We live in a world flooded with spam. The police won't take some random email seriously. I need more."

"Do you think your old buddy would kidnap more than one person?"

"Do you mean you?"

"No. It's just that another of my colleagues hasn't been coming into the office, and the police are looking for him also. Personally, I don't care if he ever comes back, but—"

"See, Emma? This is dangerous. Malcolm is dangerous. You should listen to my plan before bringing your friend or anyone else into this. What's your colleague's name?"

"Wilson Sinclair."

"Okay. That sounds familiar. I've got meetings all day tomorrow, but we could get together the next day to discuss my plan. Do you like shopping?"

"Why?"

"I thought we'd meet at a mall. If Malcolm has started stalking me again, we could make it hard for him to follow us from store to store. If he doesn't know about you, we will look like any other couple shopping together, and he might stay focused on Dr. Santan and me."

I can't hold back. "Are we going to be a shopping couple, then? Is this going to be a date?"

"Do you want it to be a date?"

I gaze at the ceiling. I want it to be a date, but what kind of a first date consists of plotting to stop a kidnapper? The whole situation is off. Trey could be the dangerous one. Then again, what do I have to lose? A mall with lots of people around—sounds safe enough. If he's right, I might be able to find Dr. Santan sooner than later and move on with my life. "I'll meet you."

"Great." The excitement in his voice rings true. "We're going to have an awesome time."

"You're going to tell me your plan."

"That's right, and I'll probably buy you something. Do you like diamonds?"

CHAPTER TWENTY-FIVE

TREY - *March 1999*

Rome wasn't built in a day. But, the Calimico investment firm would be. Trey believed that day was today. He put on his jacket and headed for the door. To his relief, Malcolm had actually answered his phone an hour ago. The prototype was finished. The demo was in an hour, and Malcolm was on his way over.

And this morning was destined to be a major milestone in the history of Trey's new business. He grabbed a disposable camera on the way out the door. He waited downstairs until Malcolm pulled up in his car. The sun glinted off the car's golden paint, and it was beautiful. Gold is beautiful, and Trey had nothing but gold in his future. He held the floppy disk in the air as he approached and waved for Malcolm to get out. "Stop right there." He handed the disk to Malcolm. "Let me take a picture."

The car, the disk, and Malcolm. Pure gold.

The beginning of an era.

Despite Trey's previous pleadings, Malcolm wore an old Mötley Crüe T-shirt, hadn't combed his hair, and a red boil threatened to overtake one of his grease-filled, pockmarked face craters. At least they arrived on time.

The receptionist at Calimico Venture Partners guided Trey and Malcolm to a conference room. A lone desktop computer sat on the far end of a polished hardwood table in front of a pull-down screen. Black leather chairs with plenty of padding surrounded the table. The receptionist showed them how to project the computer's screen onto the big screen, and Malcolm rolled his eyes.

"I'll let everyone know you're here," the receptionist said on his way out.

"Nice chairs, huh?" Trey asked.

Malcolm sat at the head of the table behind the computer and inserted the floppy disk. In minutes, a web page appeared on the screen behind him. It simply showed the number of people exposed to the poll and the number of people who had answered the questions. Both values began at zero.

Trey sat at the end near Malcolm.

"All set?"

Malcolm nodded. He pressed his lips together and cracked his knuckles. He kept repositioning the browser window, trying to center it on the screen.

"Trey Wilkes?" A man entered the conference room, his hand extended. "I'm Brad. We spoke on the phone."

Trey stood. "Yes." He shook Brad's hand—he shook *The Savior's* hand. "I'm so happy to meet you."

"Me, too. Here, before I forget, take my card."

Brad Braxton, Partner. Calimico Venture Partners.

"Thank you."

Brad's tan khakis and white button-down shirt put Trey at ease. Trey had worn his best suit—dark blue with a power red tie—but he'd hoped the environment would be more casual than that.

"And this must be your developer?" Brad asked.

"Yes. This is Malcolm Schmidt."

"Hi, Malcolm," Brad said.

"Hi." Malcolm kept his eyes on the computer monitor.

Others filed into the conference room. Three men and a woman, all in business attire. They introduced themselves briefly and took seats around the table. The woman fixed her gaze on Malcolm. Her graying black hair fit her head like an ancient Roman helmet. Unlike the men, she hadn't smiled cordially during the introductions. She stared at Malcolm until he glanced away from the computer monitor and caught her eye.

She pulled out a leather-bound notebook and wrote something down.

Two of the men, the older ones, told Trey they had helped found the firm. Peter and—dammit. Trey couldn't remember the other one's name. The introductions happened so fast. The third man's name was Jessop, which was easy to remember because he looked like a Jessop, and Trey had never known anyone named that before. Jessop had a blond beard and an easy look in his eyes, like nothing could get him down.

The woman's name was Annie Wilkes. This name was unforgettable. Sharing the same last name with Trey and the same full name as the woman from Stephen King's *Misery*, Trey would never forget Annie's name. He loved Stephen King, but he had never read the book. He'd only seen the movie.

"Let's get started," Brad said.

"Go ahead, show them the poll, Malcolm."

Malcolm pulled up one of the websites whose owner had

agreed to host a poll. "These three questions appear on over one hundred business websites right now. When a user answers the questions, a new browser window opens and prompts them to create a user account on my virtual community website." Trey paused. "Malcolm, show them one of the communities."

Annie glanced at Malcolm again and wrote in her notebook.

Malcolm pulled up a virtual community web page and clicked to open a member's profile.

"After filling out their profile information, the application suggests a list of virtual communities based on their interests and, more importantly, their skills." Trey put on his salesman smile. "They're going to love joining these communities. They'll get a charge interacting with like-minded individuals to tackle major world problems. Curing diseases, or—"

"It sounds complicated," the nameless older man said.

"I agree," said the older man's counterpart, Peter.

"It will be seamless to the user." Trey leaned over to Malcolm. "Did you start polling yet?"

"No." Malcolm loaded the original page with the number of users exposed to the poll and the number of users who had answered the questions, both still at zero.

"Malcolm is going to start collecting users' answers now. The way it works—"

"Why don't you let him explain it?" Annie asked.

"Okay. Sure."

Malcolm leaned around the monitor so everyone could see his face. "The top number is how many people saw the poll. The bottom number is how many people answered the questions." He returned his head behind the monitor and hit a button. The web page refreshed, still showing zeros.

"That's it?" Annie asked.

"I'm sure there's more," Jessop said.

"Yes." Trey had to recover quickly. Malcolm was messing everything up. "We're going to let this run for thirty minutes and demonstrate the massive scale at which we can build the communities with real people."

"How many do you think you'll get?" Brad asked.

"I've updated the business plan to indicate our future numbers will attract over a million people in a very short time, but we have limited resources for now. Today we intend to pull in five hundred people before our presentation ends."

"That sounds good." Brad directed his attention at the two older men. "Yes?"

"I agree," Jessop said. "More power to you."

"I wish Jack could have been here for this." Peter leaned back in his chair. "He understands the technical stuff better than I do. When does the website charge the user?"

There it was.

The hated question.

The question that had led to every failed venture capitalist meeting last summer. But Trey was ready this time. He explained how users would have a month to interact for free, then get hit with a pay-to-keep-playing proposition. Something Trey would never actually do.

Everyone in the room bought it. Smiles—except for Annie.

After a while, Malcolm refreshed the page.

"Look at that," Trey said. "We've got over two hundred people already." He glanced at his watch. Fifteen minutes gone. The demo was on track.

"That's excellent," Brad said. "This is going well."

"Refresh it again," Trey said.

Malcolm hit a button.

500 - Internal Server Error

Peter squinted at the screen. "Five hundred. It did it."

"No." Annie sounded as if she were speaking entirely through her nose. "It crashed."

Trey touched Malcolm's wrist and whispered, "Fix it. Hurry."

Malcolm pulled his arm away.

"What's wrong?" Brad asked.

Malcolm typed desperately.

"He'll get it back," Trey said. "It'll just take a moment."

But Malcolm didn't get it back. He worked for the remaining fifteen minutes while Trey attempted to make small talk. The weather. Sports.

"Well, we're done here." Peter and the other founder stood. Shook hands with Trey.

"I'm so sorry it didn't work out this time," Jessop said. "It's a great idea."

"Wait," Brad said. "Should we have them come back when it's fixed?"

"Next year," Peter said.

"I disagree." Annie stopped in the doorway. "Just look at him." She motioned toward Malcolm. "He's not someone with the professionalism I can trust. I knew the moment I came in here this was a flop."

Malcolm closed the browser window, ejected the floppy, and towered over the conference room table.

Annie walked out.

Jessop, Peter, and the other man followed.

"Hey," Brad said. "I'm sorry about them." He directed his attention to Malcolm. Cocked his head. "Are you all right?"

Malcolm ignored him and marched out of the room.

"Thanks for everything, Brad." Trey headed for the door. "I've got to go after him."

"Wait." Brad grabbed Trey's arm. "Here's my *other* business card. Get this fixed and contact me in a few months, okay?"

Brad the Savior.

"Thanks. I'll definitely call you." Trey pocketed the card and raced to the parking lot. He didn't know what Malcolm was going to do. He didn't know what Malcolm was capable of when angry. He pictured the broken electric guitar in Malcolm's dorm room. He pictured Malcolm breaking it over the head of his former roommate. He pictured the yin-yang throwing star.

Malcolm was already sitting behind the wheel, ramrod straight.

"Unlock the door." Trey repeatedly pulled on the passenger door handle. "Now."

Malcolm reached over and unlocked Trey's door.

"What happened in there?" Trey asked.

Malcolm took out his tobacco and snorted some. "I don't want to talk about it."

"It's okay. Brad gave me another business card. We can try again."

"No. I'm done." Malcolm put the car in gear and took off toward campus.

"What?"

"I'm never doing that again."

"I didn't want you to come to begin with, but you insisted. You said if something went wrong, you'd be there to fix it."

"It wasn't my fault. I couldn't connect to one of the computers in my room over their pathetic network." He slammed his hand on the steering wheel.

"Calm down." Trey held his tongue for a while. Eventually, some of the color drained from Malcolm's face. He turned onto a one-way street. For a moment, Trey imagined Malcolm driving him out of the city, into the forest, and beheading him. "Go that way," Trey pointed. "It's faster."

Malcolm did as he said, but his silence was threatening.

"Hey, let's talk about all this later, after we've had a chance to calm down."

"I don't want to talk to you ever again."

"Why? What did I do?"

"I told you. I don't work well with deadlines. This was your fault. You business guys—you ruin everything."

Trey bit his cheek, but it wasn't enough. "Without us, you geeks wouldn't have jobs. Bill Gates was a businessman first and a geek second."

"I wish Bill Gates were dead." He pulled into Trey's parking lot.

"Wait," Trey said. "You're really quitting? Just like that?"

"Get bent." Malcolm parked the car.

"Can I at least have the prototype? Is everything on there?"

"Get out."

Trey opened his door and stepped onto the asphalt. He extended his hand back inside. "Please, can I have it?"

Malcolm tossed the floppy disk at him.

It bounced off Trey's fingers and tumbled beneath the seat.

While he was trying to reach it, Malcolm revved the engine.

His Acura purred like an angry cat.

CHAPTER TWENTY-SIX

EMMA

Emma, you have a habit of threatening your coworkers right before they go missing.

Those were Detective Galen's exact words. They turn over in my head like a cement mixer trying to keep the concrete loose until it's time to pour. I didn't do anything wrong. I don't know where D'Angelo disappeared to, and I don't care about Wilson. But I must wait until tomorrow to meet with Trey and discuss his plan for finding D'Angelo, so today, my only option is to find Wilson.

Finding Wilson is a means to an end, I say to myself. *I've got to knock on this door.*

My internal pep talk isn't working.

I don't want to be here.

I turn around and gaze at the other townhomes. This modest community was built in the nineties. The light beige three-story townhomes have wrap-around porches and windows behind dark, wooden shutters. The way Wilson always talked about trips to exotic places, I though he was rich. Lived in a mansion. But now I realize he spends his college stipend on experiences instead of extravagant living spaces. This is a nice place, but it's no MTV crib.

Dread fills me as I turn back toward the door. I fear Wilson will open it, and I'll be forced to confront him about D'Angelo's disappearance. I hate talking to Wilson. I also fear Wilson will *not* answer the door, and he really *has* gone missing. His partner, Travis, might accuse me of foul play like Detective Galen did. I don't want to go through that, either.

It's a lose-lose.

Then, another possibility dawns on me. Nearly every reason Detective Galen gave for suspecting me could be applied to Wilson. Galen thinks I would profit more from the research if D'Angelo were out of the picture. It's not true, but what if Wilson was stupid enough to think the same thing? What if he did do something to D'Angelo after the awards banquet, then came into the office on Monday, acting like his usual jerk self to throw off the police?

No.

Is it possible?

I've never trusted Wilson, but he's not a murderer. He doesn't have it in him. He's not a kidnapper either, or . . . could he be?

There's only one way to find out.

I knock.

Travis opens the door. We've only met a few times. Wilson started dating Travis a few years ago. I didn't know they had moved in together until recently because Wilson rarely talks about his personal life, and I rarely listen. Travis has grown a thick, puffy beard and gained some weight around the middle since I last saw him. I remember being impressed with his eyebrows and lashes, so black, he always looks like he's wearing mascara.

"Hi . . ." He shakes his head subtly and searches the sky for my name.

"It's Emma." We shake hands. "From the university."

"Oh, I know. I just blanked for a second." His eyes are a little bloodshot. "Sorry about that."

"It's all right."

He glances over his shoulder. "I'd invite you in, but the place is a mess." He's wearing a soft teal terry cloth robe, and his slippers don't match. "There's laundry everywhere."

"That's okay. I won't take much of your time. I just wanted to ask you about Wilson."

"Have you seen him?"

"No. Is he still gone?"

"Yes." His eyes dart back and forth, searching my face. "Do you know where he might have gone?"

"No, I'm trying to find him. The police told me you reported him missing. Haven't they found anything?"

"They're not trying very hard. I told them everything I knew, but they always steered the conversation toward Dr. Santan whenever I asked about the investigation."

"When did you see Wilson last?"

"Uh, a week ago Monday. I didn't report him missing until Wednesday, though. That was so stupid." He bit his upper lip. "I'd always heard the police wouldn't do anything until someone was missing for two days." He closes his eyes and shakes his head. "Apparently, that's a myth. I should have done something sooner."

"Monday was the last time I saw him, too. I remember he was planning to meet Nimisha for lunch that day. Did he return after that?"

"He was, was he? Lunch with that intern again?" He swallows hard.

"Yeah. So, you know her?"

"I know of her. I know Wilson was spending a lot of time with her when he should have been here, and now . . ."

"What?"

He covers his eyes. "You came at a bad time. I just started going through his things."

"I'm sorry. I'll leave. Just tell me if you saw him on that Monday night."

"I did. He came home, but I didn't know he'd been with her again. I thought everything was fine but, when I woke up the next day, he was gone."

"Did he take any of his things?"

"I don't know. It's like I told the police—I don't keep track of his stuff. I'm not his mother. When I looked around afterward, it didn't seem like anything was missing except him."

"Are you sure? Are you sure he didn't pack a day bag and go on one of his fancy trips without you?"

He shook his head slightly and pursed his lips. "What do you mean?"

"You know. Barbados. Puerto Vallarta. Vegas. All those places he's constantly running off to."

"He's never been to those places. Sometimes he goes down to Virginia and stays with his mother because of her dementia, but he always tells me when he goes there."

I shouldn't be surprised. Wilson is a liar. Always has been, always will be, but this is—wow. "Have you spoken with her since he left?"

"Yes. He's not there. That's the one place the police did check, you know, because you can't believe what she says over the phone."

Like mother, like son.

CHAPTER TWENTY-SEVEN

TREY - *May 1999*

The song "Du Hast" blared so loud over Henrik's European sound system Trey could barely hear what the girls were saying. One of them said something about what a great end-of-semester blowout party this was and how she's spending the summer on her "witch brother's sock."

Or, did she say, her *rich uncle's yacht*?

Du hast.

The other girl leaned close to Trey, beer dripping onto his shoes, and shouted, "Yacht. We're going on a yacht."

Trey nodded. "Sounds like fun."

Both girls flashed him love eyes and attempted to make him laugh with lame jokes. When they weren't doing that, they tried to impress him by talking about their vacation plans, their cars, and what it was like to have parents who are politicians in Washington, D.C.

Trey's patience had worn thin. He wasn't looking to hook up with anyone. His friend, Henrik, threw this end-of-school party complete with two kegs, disco lights, sushi, and these weird turkey sausages the size of Trey's pinky. All the most affluent students were here. Some of the most imbecilic ones as well. Trey knew Henrik from high school, but they weren't really friends. More like strong acquaintances with a common past.

"I got this tan in Bali during Spring Break," the bleach blonde on the left yelled.

"Do you know anyone who can write software?" Trey shouted.

The girls shook their heads.

A tall guy in a concert T-shirt caught Trey's eye. The guy was out of place in Henrik's apartment. Most everyone there had dressed as if they were at a dance club. Trey took another look, thinking it was Malcolm, but it wasn't. He hadn't seen Malcolm since he repossessed the computer equipment. Malcolm was scary that day. Scarier than usual. After verifying the floppy disk had the demo and code on it, and the five computers still worked, Trey decided to find someone else to take over the development work.

"My cousin made a website," said the brunette. "She put pictures of cats on it."

"Really," her friend said. "That's sooooo interesting."

They laughed. Beer fell from their red Solo cups as they playfully pushed each other.

Trey turned away, and there he was. Kevin.

Kevin, the homeless computer programmer. The guy who wouldn't take Trey's money outside the Subway over a year ago. Kevin didn't look homeless anymore. He wore a white, long-sleeved shirt and black slacks, barely held up by a brown belt. His brown shoes were a shade too dark but not overly worn out. He had shaved his face and cut his hair. Trey did double-take to verify it was him, and Kevin nodded.

Trey returned the nod.

The blonde girl put her hand on Trey's shoulder to get his attention, but before she could speak, she snorted and coughed. Beer shot out her nose. The song changed, and Henrik's disco lights faded to a soft pink and green, making the ceiling look like cotton candy mixed with seaweed. Trey waved Kevin over, but the geek took one look at the two girls and shook his head, so Trey went to him. "Hey, do you remember me?"

"Of course I do," Kevin said. "I always wanted to thank you." He'd nearly finished his cup of beer, and Trey wondered how much he'd had to drink as he swayed with the music.

"What?" Trey asked.

"You were trying to give me money. Buy me lunch. I shouldn't have run off."

"No, I'm sorry. I was too pushy. I—"

"No, you weren't. You weren't pushy enough. Don't you remember?"

Trey had wanted so badly to recruit Kevin's help on his project he'd thrown himself and his money at the homeless geek, thinking he could buy him. He hadn't only been pushy. After Kevin had gotten the wrong idea, Trey had pushed harder until Kevin ran away. "Are you sure?"

"Absolutely," he slurred. "You mentioned a project you were working on, but you wouldn't tell me about it. I kept asking you questions, and you just tried to give me money for nothing. Like the song." He swayed again and put his hand on Trey's shoulder. "Who sang that? Dire Straits?"

"I think I told you about my project."

"Nope."

"You look like you're doing better now."

The music blared.

"Huh?"

"You look better. Have you been going to classes?"

"I missed last spring, but I got lucky and went all this year. All computer classes, too. One of the loans I applied for came through—these idiots actually gave me a loan." He finished off his beer. "I wish I'd taken your money, though. I'm in deep again. I would have helped you with your web stuff if you'd only told me about it."

"I did."

"Nope. I kept asking you to tell me about it, but you wouldn't talk."

"I'm pretty sure I told you about it."

"Nope. I kept asking you about it, but you only wanted to give me those books and buy me a sandwich. You're such a great guy. Thanks for trying to help."

"Sure, but—again. I told you all about it. I was so insistent you help me, I scared you away."

"Nope. I asked how I could help, but you wouldn't talk."

This was not how Trey remembered things, but it didn't matter. No sense in arguing over the past.

The floor vibrated to the beat of the bass notes. "Everybody Dance Now."

"Hey, let's go outside where we can talk," Trey said.

Kevin nodded, hit the keg, and filled his cup. He put it down and filled a second one. Whatever beer Henrik had bought tasted like flowers, but Trey accepted the second cup anyway and thanked Kevin as he descended from the second-floor apartment and strode into the night.

Overcast as usual, the downtown Baltimore skyline faded into the heavens. Antennas with red and blue flashing lights jutted from atop the largest buildings and jabbed the darkness above.

Kevin sat down on the curb. Slurped his beer. "What did

you want to talk about?"

"My business idea. The one I wouldn't tell you about. I'm still working on it."

"Oh, so you'll talk about it now?"

"Yes. I—look, this other guy wrote an application, but it crashes. Do you think you could fix it?"

"What's it written in?"

"Java. Do you know that?"

He stood. "Do I know it? I love it. It's all I've been using outside of class. It's too new for this school, but everyone is using it. Who was the guy?"

"Malcolm Schmidt. Do you know him?"

Kevin dropped his beer and hugged Trey. "The Hawk. Yeah, I know him. Thank you. Thank you." He jumped back suddenly. "You'll show it to me, won't you? The Hawk's code? I can fix it. I promise. You're not going to keep all this a secret from me again, are you?"

"I didn't keep it a secret last time, did I?"

"I kept asking you about it, but you wouldn't talk, remember?"

That's not how it was. Not how Trey remembered the conversation, but it didn't matter now. "I have no secrets."

"Hey," Kevin said, pointing at Trey's cup, "are you going to finish that?"

"No. Here. Take it."

Kevin chugged it down.

"I can't pay you, but if you can fix it—I have investors interested. They almost gave me a lot of money. If you can fix it—"

"I'll do it for free just to see his code, but"—he averted his eyes—"I need money and . . . I don't know if I can fix it. Malcolm is the best. It might take me a while to understand what he wrote."

"I can show you right now. My place is only a few blocks away."

"Yeah. You got beer there?"

"Yeah," Trey lied. Kevin didn't need any more beer. The skinny little geek walked like a marionette in the wind. His bird-like frame twisted with each step, but his posture was straighter than before, and he often raised his chin when making a point. The change in him from last year was miraculous. He had really gotten himself together. "Where do you live now?"

"Nowhere." Kevin swerved to avoid tripping over a jag in the sidewalk. "Moved out yesterday."

"To where?"

Kevin didn't answer.

"To where?" Trey repeated.

The look in Kevin's eyes reminded Trey of Bentley, the giant show poodle he'd grown up with in Connecticut. The shame in that dog's eyes the day Trey's father scolded him for digging a hole in the yard was forever burned in Trey's memory.

The grass grew back, but the dog was never the same.

"I've got money problems, too," Trey said. "Here's my place. This is it." His apartment building stretched toward the sky with others, dwarfed by the taller downtown structures only blocks away. This late at night, most windows were dark. Lifeless.

Trey sighed.

One more year, and he'd be out of here. Sooner, if Kevin could fix Malcolm's code.

"Here's the computer equipment I bought for the project." Trey pointed to the five computers he'd repossessed from Malcolm. They sat on the floor near the glass sliding door to the balcony. Wires lay in a heap in the corner.

"That's awesome." Kevin licked his lips and belched.

Trey went to his desk, opened a drawer, and pulled out the floppy disk. "Here's the code." When he turned around, Kevin had laid down on the couch. "It should have everything you need on it."

Kevin closed his eyes and folded his arms over his chest.

"Kevin." Trey waved the disk in the air. "Here. Don't you want to see what's on it?"

The geek snored and didn't open his eyes until morning.

While Kevin slept, Trey got busy. He hooked up the computers and backed up the floppy in case Kevin wanted to work with the original. He reviewed his business plan and updated the timelines. He made sure he hadn't lost the second business card Brad The Savior had given him.

And, he hadn't.

The morning light pierced the blinds, but not enough to wake Kevin, so Trey pulled them open. "Hey, are you all right?" The light shone on Kevin's face.

"What?" Kevin asked, squinting. "Where am I?"

"How's the hangover?" Trey asked. "You passed out on the couch."

Kevin sat up. Wiped his face. "Oh, yeah. Sorry."

"Don't be." Trey beamed. "Here, have some water." He handed Kevin a glass, then retrieved the floppy disk from the desk drawer.

Kevin drank.

"Look," Trey said. "I plugged everything in."

"What are those for?" Kevin asked, waving toward the computers.

"The project. Remember?"

Kevin drank more water. Licked his lips. "What's wrong with this?"

"I put salt in it. It helps with hangovers."

"Oh." He drank more. "I don't feel good. I should go."

"Wait. You wanted to see Malcolm's code." Trey held out the disk. "Just take a look. You don't have to get started today, but—"

"What are you talking about?"

"The project. You said you'd try to fix this. It's written in Java? Remember what we said last night?"

"No." He stumbled toward the door. "I don't know what you're talking about."

"You—"

"Where's my backpack?"

"What?"

"Oh, no." Trey watched panic grip him. "Everything I own is in my backpack. It's at the party. I left it there." He opened the door. "I've got to go."

Trey grabbed his arm. "You said you'd help me. Here. Take the disk."

He pulled away, stepped into the hall, and threw up on the floor. His yellow expulsion looked like Henrik's flowery beer but with white clouds instead of bubbles floating in it. Trey waited until Kevin's convulsions dried up. "Come back inside. I'll get you more water."

"No way. I'm sick." He looked up at Trey. His eyes went wild. "Hey, you're that guy. Leave me alone." He turned away. "Leave me alone, you pervert." He scurried down the hall, bending at the waist and holding his stomach. "Leave me alone."

Trey slowly closed the door, lowered his head, and returned the floppy disk to the drawer.

CHAPTER TWENTY-EIGHT

EMMA

When I return home from Wilson's, a tall man in a long gray coat stands across the street from my apartment building. He's got his hands in his pockets, and he's wearing a black knit cap pulled down over his ears. I've never seen him before, but it's not so unusual. What is unusual is how he's standing there. He's built like a brick wall. Not thin and not round, but thick and perfectly proportioned, like a bodybuilder. I watch him from the intersection, waiting for the light to turn green. He's not standing at a crosswalk, and he's not waiting outside someone else's apartment.

He's standing across the street, staring up at my second-floor windows.

I consider driving past him, parking farther away, and sneaking into my apartment from the other side, but I rarely get the spot right in front of my building. It's that damn paranoia again. I'm not going to let it control me. I pull forward and slip into the parking space without hesitation.

Quickly, I get out and walk around the front of my car, but before I make it to the stoop, he calls out. "Excuse me."

I pretend I can't hear him.

His shoes pound the pavement behind me.

I take the steps two at a time, reach the door, and glance over my shoulder.

He's already on the sidewalk at the bottom. "Are you Miss Petranova?"

"Whatever you're selling, I'm not buying. Sorry." I grasp the doorknob.

"Wait." He raises his voice. "Are you Emma Petranova? Do you work with a Dr. Santan?"

A silver minivan drives down the street behind him. Several teenagers wait to cross at the intersection I drove through moments ago. There's no one in the other direction. As far as I can tell, there is no golden Acura anywhere.

"I have some information you might want if you will give me a minute," he says.

"How do you know me?"

He wipes his face and pulls his hat off. Holds it to his chest. His bald head glistens as though running across the street made him break a sweat, but his pockmarks show a history of oily skin. Maybe he's always sweating.

He puts his foot on the bottom step, and I press my back against the door.

"You are Emma Petranova, right? You work at the university with Dr. Santan."

"I don't know who you are"—I pull my phone out and swipe the screen with my thumb—"but you'd better stay right there."

"Don't be afraid. I'm here to help you." He raises his hands and takes a step back.

"Who are you?"

"My name is Malcolm Schmidt." My heart leaps into my

throat. It's him. The one Trey warned me about. "I think I know what may have happened to your professor. Have you been seeing a 'Trey Wilkes'?"

"That depends. Have you been spying on me?" I open the dialer app on my phone and hover my finger over the nine. One wrong move, and I'm dialing the police.

"Trey Wilkes is a dangerous man. You can't trust him."

"Oh, and I suppose I can trust you? A stalker? Trey told me about you."

"I haven't been stalking you, honest."

"Where's your car?"

He tilts his head and points across the street to a boxy green SUV with scratched paint and a dented fender. It's so old I wonder if the term "SUV" was even a thing when it was built. "It's right there. Why?"

"Prove it."

"Will you listen to me then?"

"Yes," I say. "But keep your distance."

This is Malcolm Schmidt. Trey's enemy. He knows all about me, and he knows about Dr. Santan's disappearance. He's clearly been stalking me. I look up and down the street again. He's got to have hidden that golden car somewhere.

He puts his cap back on and whips across the street to beat an oncoming car. He's surprisingly fast for someone his size. He puts a key in the SUV's door, unlocks it, gets in, and starts the engine without closing the door.

"See?" he yells.

I nod, but this doesn't prove a lot. He might own two cars—this SUV and the Acura. But so far, he hasn't given me a reason to think he's here to hurt me. Only to talk to me. He's done everything I've asked, and we're in broad daylight. Yet, I believe Trey's warning. How Malcolm has trolled his businesses online. Threatened his workers. This man could be here to do the same to me.

He returns to my side of the street, and this time, he stops on the sidewalk. "Hear me out, and I'll go."

"You've got one minute." I switch apps on my phone and start the clock timer.

"Trey Wilkes is not who you think he is. Whatever he's told you, it's lies. All lies." He takes a breath. "He's up to something, something big, and I need you to help me stop him."

"Is that so? What's he up to that's so big?"

"I'm not sure exactly, but I know you can't believe what he says. He'll tell you he's a successful entrepreneur and take all your money. Or, in this case, your research. He's not successful. Everything he's ever done has gone up in flames."

I glance at my phone.

"Listen to me," he says. "You can't see him again."

"Yes, I can. He told me all about you. He said you trolled his businesses, and now you're trolling me. He said you've been trying to get even with him for years. Why should I believe you?"

"Because I'm not a gaslighter!" He scrunches his face. Closes his eyes. When his body shakes, the street shakes with him. "Ahh. I *hate* businessmen. They're so convincing."

"Your minute is up."

"No, it's not."

"I'm going inside, and if you're still here when I get upstairs, I'm calling the police."

I can feel his eyes on my back as I open the door and walk inside.

By the time I get to the second-floor window, he's gone.

CHAPTER TWENTY-NINE

TREY - *May 1999*

If Trey lowers the price of lemonade, he'll sell more cups but make less money.

Or will he?

He rolls over. Pulls his pillow close to his chest. Keeps his eyes shut tight.

The classic computer game, Lemonade Stand, appears before him. He's dreaming, and he knows it, but he doesn't want it to stop. Sometimes, he's playing the game. Other times, he's watching his dad play. His dad must buy more lemons so he doesn't run out, but he's almost out of money. A crate of lemons crashes to the floor with a *bang*.

Something *bangs* outside Trey's apartment.

He doesn't want to get up. He rolls over again.

His dad yells at him to sell more lemonade, but Trey needs more lemons. He needs money.

You can't make money by spending other people's money.

The banging outside Trey's apartment gets louder.

Bang. Bang. Bang.

He sits up. Stretches. Gets out of bed.

Knock. Knock. Knock.

It's eight o'clock on a Sunday morning. No one has ever come here at this time.

Trey puts on a sweatshirt and shorts and goes to the door.

"Hi, roomy." Kevin stands in the hallway. Skinny little Kevin, his puny biceps flexed to the max, holding a box. "Wanna help me with these?" Three matching boxes with the word "U-Haul" stamped on the side surround his feet. He's wearing the same stained shirt he wore to Henrik's party and an overstuffed backpack. A dark spot from where he vomited still graces the hallway floor.

"What are you doing here?" Trey asked.

"Moving in. Remember our deal?" Kevin hands his box to Trey.

"Thanks, but no. I don't remember. What deal?"

Kevin picks up another box and pushes his way into the apartment. "The deal. You let me stay here, and I fix your website."

"I didn't say you could stay here." Trey puts the box down inside the door.

"You said I could stay here if I fixed your website. Remember our deal?"

Trey did not remember any deal. In fact, when Kevin woke up in Trey's apartment yesterday, it was Kevin who didn't remember anything. But before that, he said he would fix Trey's website. Malcolm's broken code. "My place is pretty small. I don't think I would have offered to let you move in."

"You said you didn't have any money to pay me, but you'd let me stay here if I helped you." He waved toward the hallway. "Can you help me with those?"

"I don't—"

"C'mon. Remember our deal?" Kevin went into the

hallway and picked up a box.

"I suppose I might have said you could come here."

"You did."

Trey picked up the last box and brought it inside.

"You said I could sleep on your couch. Remember our deal?"

"Okay. Sure. I remember, but it's going to be tight."

"I can't wait." He put the box down by the couch, and Trey put his next to it.

"And you promise to fix the website?"

"Absolutely. I can't wait to see The Hawk's code."

"The Hawk. Right." An odor came off Kevin. Rotten milk. "Do you know Malcolm? You've had classes with him?"

"I've never talked to him. He hides out a lot. Honestly, he's kind of big and creepy."

"Like a serial killer, right?"

Kevin laughed. "Yeah, I never thought of that, but I could see it. Maybe he's the real Zodiac Killer."

"Maybe." It was funny because it might be true. Malcolm had scared off the investors, but Kevin had potential. He was the opposite of Malcolm, especially physically. He'd do better presenting a prototype to investors. All he needed was a shower, a laundromat, and a gallon of cologne.

"Can I use this corner?" Kevin pointed to the space at the end of the couch near the balcony door.

"Sure."

Kevin popped open a box and unloaded his things into the corner. The five computers and cables Malcolm had used sat against the wall opposite the couch. Trey retrieved the project disk from his desk drawer and put it on the coffee table. "I hooked everything up yesterday. Have at it."

"I need a desk."

Kevin was serious. Trey finally had someone to work on his project, and the best part? Trey could watch over Kevin while he worked on it. "Okay, then let's get you one." They went to a thrift store and bought a used desk. Trey bought Kevin a chair. He bought him lunch. He invested in Kevin, and that night, Kevin went to work, reading the Java code.

But, after a week, it became obvious Kevin would need more time. While he didn't spend every waking moment on the computer, he did sit there a lot, mostly at night. He often disappeared during the day, occasionally returning with change ringing in his pockets. Trey bought all the groceries, but he'd seen Kevin inside a convenience store a few times. He wondered if Kevin was still panhandling.

A month passed, and Kevin had not fixed the website, but he was still trying. Trey exhibited patience. He didn't have a lot of choice. He always kept the second business card Brad had given him in his wallet. He needed the website to run flawlessly. No exceptions. He had to give Kevin as much time as needed. And he did.

He also gave Kevin a lot of space.

Like, a *lot* of space.

Trey didn't know if Kevin had become accustomed to homelessness, only showering every week or two, or if Kevin had an unnaturally strong aversion to water. The dirty laundry in Kevin's corner stung Trey's nose. Sometimes, Kevin wore a tank top, exposing his bird-like frame, sitting at the desk in the sweltering heat, fumes coming from his armpits like gases from a paper mill. As the summer wore on, Trey spent more and more time at Starbucks.

He gave Kevin his space.

And time.

But, time went on and on—and on, and summer ended.

Trey had to do something, or the misery would never end. He went to the balcony and pulled the curtains back. Gazed at the late August sky. The full moon burned orange. Brad's business card burned in his wallet. Time was running out. He turned toward Kevin. The geek's keystrokes sounded like someone stomping on bubble wrap, except louder. This did not help Trey's headache.

The sound.

The stench.

"Hey, look," Kevin said, pointing at the screen.

Trey went to the desk and leaned over his shoulder. The web page displaying the number of people who'd answered poll questions showed one thousand sixty-three. Malcolm had failed to reach five hundred during the demonstration last spring. "Wow. Over a thousand. That's promising."

Kevin swiveled his chair and blocked the computer screen. "Over ten thousand."

"I saw one thousand sixty-three."

"It's at *ten* thousand sixty-three."

Trey leaned to his left. The screen clearly read one thousand sixty-three. "Are you sure?"

"It's at ten thousand sixty-three. I think I've finally optimized it. If we can add more computer power, it will go much higher."

"Do you think we can show it to Brad soon?"

"There's still a couple of gremlins running around in there. It sometimes crashes when I loop the requests through the school's network to simulate increased network traffic."

"That's not good. It can't crash again. But I'm glad you have such a high user count."

"It's great, isn't it? It's at ten thousand sixty-three."

"Yeah. Sure it is."

CHAPTER THIRTY

EMMA

A song by Coldplay hisses over the speakers as I enter the mall. Trey said he'd meet me at the bottom of the spiral staircase near the fountain in the center, and he didn't lie. I see him first, pacing back and forth, his phone in hand, his earbuds in his ears. He's talking to someone.

He's early for our date.

Is it a date?

He's wearing the same thin leather jacket, taut over his shoulders. He sees me coming, pulls his earbuds out of his ears, and waves me over.

My pocket vibrates. It's Nimisha calling me back. Why is it that no one ever answers the first time I call them? They never answer when I have time to talk. Instead, they always call back at the worst possible time.

I raise my finger and put the phone to my ear.

Trey nods from a distance.

I head toward a corner of the mall near the Foot Locker for privacy. "Hey, thanks for calling me back."

"No problem. Where have you been? We miss you here."

Trey finds a bench and sits down. The aquamarine water from the fountain bursts into the air behind him, pulsing to a beat totally out of sync with Coldplay. He clasps his hands and lowers his head.

"I don't have time to talk about the project right now. Do you remember the last day Wilson came to the office?"

"Yes."

"It was the Monday after the awards, right?"

"That's right."

"You said you were going to have lunch together that day. Did you?"

"That was the last time I saw him. Have you talked to him? Is he back?"

"No, but I talked to his partner, Travis."

"Oh, I see."

"What's wrong?"

"I shouldn't be telling you this, but—Wilson and Travis have been having problems lately. He called me that night, and I could tell they'd been arguing."

"Travis didn't say anything about that."

"He wouldn't have. I've been helping Wilson through some things, and I—I *was* helping him. Now he's gone. Oh, Emma. I'm so worried."

"Me too." Not for the same reasons as her. Not because I miss Wilson, but because he's truly missing. If I knew where he went, it would be easier to find D'Angelo. If nothing else, finding Wilson might eliminate him as a suspect.

Or confirm it.

Trey crosses his legs, folds his arms, and gazes in my direction with a wolfish stare. If this is a first date, I'm screwing it up by spending it on the phone with Nimisha.

"Thanks again for calling back. It's a bad time right now,

but I'll call you later tonight, okay?"

"Sure. Don't forget."

Trey sees me coming and stands. He has one of the best smiles I've ever seen.

Now that Nimisha confirmed she last saw Wilson at lunch that Monday, it means Travis was the last to see Wilson. And she said they were having relationship problems. Maybe Wilson walked out on Travis, or maybe Wilson decided to run and hide because of something he did to D'Angelo. It's so frustrating. I'm no closer to knowing what really happened.

"Sorry," I say. "I had to take that call."

"It's fine." He spreads his arms as if he's about to hug me but stops short by grasping each of my elbows instead. "It happens to me all the time."

I put my hand on his wrist, and he lets his arms drop. "How long have you been here?"

"Not long." He glances up at the mall clock. The massive white face with Roman numerals hangs from the upper floor. We can see most of the first and second-floor shops from here. Two jewelry stores compete for customers in the lower corner. I haven't forgotten what Trey said about buying diamonds. "I was early because a friend dropped me off, and he needed to be somewhere at four o'clock also."

That's strange. A millionaire entrepreneur without a car? Actually, now that I think about it, it might be strange for a millionaire entrepreneur *to* have a car. He ought to be riding around in a limo. "What happened to your car?"

"Don't laugh, but it's kind of special, and I don't really like to drive anything else. It's in the shop having the engine rebuilt."

"What's so special about it?"

"It's almost as young as you are." He grins and glances at

my waist. "And every bit as sleek."

Blushing is not something I normally do, but . . . I avert my eyes and watch the fountain spray. "Stop it."

"And, if you must know, my friend is more of a coworker." Now, he averts *his* eyes.

"Uh huh."

"Okay. He's more of an employee. I guess you could call him my driver. I came in a limousine." I knew it. "Please don't think I'm spoiled. I either ride with him or drive my Acura. It's not like I own a hundred sports cars."

"Your Acura? Is it—is it a gold with metallic paint?"

"Yes, how did you know?"

I take a step back. "It was you." I picture the earbuds. The white earbuds he wore the first time I saw him. The ones he wore when I entered the mall today. The ones on the front seat of the car that's been—"You've been following me."

"What are you talking about?"

"You. It's you. I've been seeing a car like that everywhere I go."

"Calm down. I'm sure it's a coincidence. When did it start?"

I have to think for a moment. "The night of the awards banquet. It—*you*—followed me to the awards banquet."

He titters. His smile is annoying now. I can't tell if he's taking me seriously.

"I didn't follow you there. I was there for the ceremony. We must have crossed paths on the way. I remember seeing you sitting with Dr. Santan. Did you see me?"

"Yes."

"So, of course, you saw my car. It doesn't mean I was following you. We went to the same place. That's all."

"But I saw that car again the next day, outside an ice

cream shop. Then it followed me to the Café Royale the next week."

"Emma. I was near the Café Royale to meet with an investor. Think about it. My car sticks out like a sore thumb, and I pass at least five ice cream places between my house and work every day. If you see it, you're going to notice it. That's part of why I like it so much."

He's right. The age and paint. It's a unique vehicle, just like him. I remember from my undergrad classes how the human brain builds callouses to repeated experiences like skin does to repeated abrasions. I've seen millions of white, black, and gray SUVs, and they all blend in my memory, but that golden Acura from the nineties—it's like a bad bra, the underwire rubbing against my sides.

I let my shoulders relax.

"Trust me," he says. "I haven't been following you. It was all a coincidence."

"You're right."

He winks. "Or maybe . . . it's fate."

"I feel so stupid."

"Don't. It makes sense. With everything that's happened recently, it's perfectly understandable why you'd be on edge."

I'm glad that's over. Mystery solved, and I wasn't going crazy. Those *were* his white earbuds. Thinking I was being followed had me and my paranoia looking for that car everywhere I went, constantly reminding me of it. But I actually saw it far fewer times than I spent time thinking about it. That's another brain thing. Imagination becoming a reality.

"Hey." He grasps my elbow. "Do you want to go in there? Smell the candles?"

"Sure."

The shop's called Candle Carver Ltd, and the overbearing

scent inside is a cross between lavender and birthday cake.

"I had a chain of places like this once," he says as we make our way to the back of the store, "but they didn't do well. I had to close them down in the recession of 2008."

"That's too bad."

"Not really. It was a great lesson." He picks up a candle, sniffs it, then waves it under my nose. "What do you think?"

"I like it. Kind of earthy."

He leans forward. "Okay, about my old college friend, Malcolm. We need to lure him into a safe place and record him saying or doing something incriminating. The more I think about it, the more I think he's behind your professor's disappearance. Maybe your colleague's, as well. We need to get him to make an appearance."

"I think he already has."

"What?"

"He came to my apartment building yesterday."

Trey jerks his head back. "When? Are you sure?"

"He said it was him. Malcolm Schmidt. He told me not to listen to you."

Trey hurriedly scans the store. He takes me by the arm. "C'mon." We flee the store, not stopping until we're near the hallway by the bathrooms. "This is a good vantage point. Do you see him anywhere?"

The typical crowd meanders throughout the mall on both levels. Mothers with small children. Teens with nothing better to do. Flamboyant twenty-somethings with money and also nothing better to do. "No. I'd have noticed him earlier if he were here. He's really tall and built like a muscular tank. Not your typical mall rat. More ominous."

"I don't see him either." Trey's eyes meet mine. "Wait. What did he look like? I wouldn't describe him as ominous."

"He had a long gray coat on. Like a trench coat, but made of wool."

"Could you see what he had on under his coat? Was it a T-shirt?"

"No. I think it had a collar." I close my eyes and picture the man. "He had a black cap, and when he took it off, he was bald."

"Hm. I don't know. Was he big around? You know, fat?"

"No."

"It doesn't sound like him."

"He knew about you and Dr. Santan and me. He could have changed since college. Lost weight."

"Not the Malcolm I know. It's been a few years since I saw him last, but he'd hardly changed. He was balding, but not bald. He wore an old concert T-shirt like always, and he was heavier than ever. He definitely wasn't a muscular tank."

"If it wasn't him, then who was it?"

"Mommy, Mommy. I want a pretzel." A woman pushing a stroller with a child much too old for it passes by.

Trey straightens his back and leans away from me casually. Waits for the mother to pass.

"It'll ruin your dinner," she says. "No pretzels."

"I should have warned you," Trey whispers. "My businesses are often the victims of corporate espionage. We've generated a lot of intellectual property over the years, and my competitors want it. Patents are worthless and give everything away, so we don't file them. Sometimes, spies pose as acquaintances and attempt to steal information from people in my circles. It's entirely possible someone was pretending to be Malcolm to trick you into telling them why my business is interested in Dr. Santan's research. That man might have been phishing."

I don't know what Trey means by "phishing," but I don't care. I understand his point. "That man was very convincing then. He acted exactly like you described Malcolm. A troll."

"If it is Malcolm, you're in danger."

"What should we do?"

"I want you to send a message to that email address from 'The Hawk' I received a few weeks ago. Ask him to meet you somewhere, and we'll record the rendezvous for the police. I'll hide out nearby in case he tries to do something."

"I don't know. Isn't there some other way?"

"None I can think of. I tried talking to the police already, and they won't do anything without some proof. We need to get on this ASAP. Can we go to your place and do it tonight?"

At the outset, I take him literally. "Excuse me? My place? Do it?"

"Yes. Send the email." He pulls a thumb drive out of his pocket. "I have a program that will mask the location of your computer, but it's best if we send it from a machine with your digital footprint on it. Malcolm will know I'm behind this if I use any of my devices."

"Okay. I'm in, but I want my friend Alyssa to know we're doing this." She will love me for pulling her in, and I need her help. The danger for her is inevitable. If Malcolm or the corporate spy—or whoever the man standing outside my apartment was—can find me, he can find her. Our Facebook pages are filled with pictures of us sitting together, laughing.

"Why do you want to involve her?" he asks. "It could be dangerous. Remember?"

"I just feel like someone else ought to know what's going on in case something happens. I'm sorry, but I just met you."

He doesn't flinch. "I understand. Do you trust her?"

"Yes. I trust her with my life."

CHAPTER THIRTY-ONE

TREY - *Fall 1999*

"Are we taking it back to the apartment?" Kevin asked.

"No." Trey gazed at the menu hanging over the sub sandwich makings. He thought he could smell the apartment from here, but it was only Kevin's body odor. "Let's eat here."

Kevin nodded and ordered the meatball sub sandwich.

Trey got the chicken club.

They sat near the window at the front. A fresh breeze blew in every time a customer opened the door. Eating out, even at this dinky place, had become a luxury. Anything besides Smack Ramen and frozen pizza was a luxury, but it was time for a little celebration. The software could pull in more than five hundred users in thirty minutes without fail. No "500" errors. Trey had made Kevin prove this to him by running it at least twenty times in twenty different ways.

Their meeting with Brad was in an hour.

"I'll do all the talking, okay?"

"Sure." Kevin chewed with his mouth open. He always ate fast like a starving dog.

"And if it fails, what are you going to do?"

He swallowed and took another bite. "It's not going to fail." He licked his lips. "This tastes so good."

"But what if it does?"

"Then I'll restart it at a lower number and explain why it failed."

"Okay. That sounds like a good plan. We're not leaving until Brad sees it working end-to-end."

The mayonnaise on Trey's sandwich tasted extra sour. Maybe it was normal. He hadn't eaten mayonnaise in a while. He also hadn't had any ketchup. He missed putting ketchup on french fries. He missed french fries. They should have gone to a hamburger place instead.

"How long will it be before this Brad guy gives us the money for your business?"

"Let's get through the demonstration first. Are you ready to go?"

Kevin sucked down his last bite and wiped the marinara sauce from his chin. "Yep."

They met Brad at a small office not far from Calimico's building. The sign read HERO CAPITAL GROUP, but Trey doubted a group existed. It appeared Brad was trying to build his own company. Brad was the only person there when Trey and Kevin arrived. He sat them down at a table in the front, complete with a Gateway desktop computer.

Only one door led deeper into the office next to a tall reception desk. The place seemed better suited for an insurance salesman or a therapist.

Kevin loaded the client software onto the computer and pulled up the application.

Trey and Brad gathered around him and watched as the number of users climbed.

It surpassed five hundred in a matter of minutes without

196

fail.

Success at last.

"That's impressive," Brad said.

When the total surpassed one thousand, Kevin stood and raised his hand. "We did it."

Trey high-fived him just to make him sit back down.

"Very, very impressive," Brad said. "What would it take to get it to one hundred thousand?"

"It's at one hundred thousand," Kevin said. He turned, blocking the screen.

"Don't," Trey muttered.

"It's at one hundred thousand," Kevin repeated.

Trey got up from his chair. "He means it can hit that number with more work." Kevin began to open his mouth, and Trey nudged his chair. "We would need to buy a few more computers, is all. We have five in our server farm right now."

"Did I say 'one hundred thousand?'" Kevin turned back to the screen. "No, I read it wrong. It's only a thousand. I don't think one hundred thousand is possible."

Brad glanced back and forth between Trey and Kevin. "Why not?"

Trey struggled to keep his salesman smile steady. "Of course it is."

"No," Kevin said. "It will crash if I add more threads. It's a concurrency issue."

"We can fix it." Trey's jaw muscles tightened.

Brad stood. "Well, I love what I've seen so far." He held out his hand.

Trey shook it. "Great. What's the next step?"

"Because you're not charging per user, which I totally agree with, you'll need to pull in tens of thousands of people quickly and refresh the list at least once a month. At the rate it's running now, that's not possible. I've invested in too many dot-coms that would have been successful if they'd only been able to handle the load. You need to scale. Come back to me when you can pull in more than one hundred thousand an hour."

Trey put his hand on Kevin's shoulder.

Kevin stared at the screen. Shook his head.

"We'll fix it and call you as soon as possible," Trey said.

"I look forward to it. Keep in touch."

In the car, Trey couldn't hold back. "What the hell was that?"

"What?"

"Why did you act like we couldn't fix it?"

"It's not broken. It didn't break." Kevin squirmed in his seat. "There's nothing to fix."

"But you told him it would break. We were so close." Trey slammed his hand on the steering wheel.

"He wanted it to handle a hundred times more than it can, and by the way, I tried to convince him it *was* handling more, but you hit me."

"Don't be so dramatic. I pushed your chair a little."

"Whatever. There's no way it can do a hundred thousand an hour. I've never got it to go over two thousand."

"What if I got more computers?"

"It doesn't matter. The problem is deep in Malcolm's web crawler code. I haven't taken a class on multi-threading yet, and I don't understand it very well."

"Multi-threading. What's that?"

"To make the system do more at once, you can send and retrieve multiple polls simultaneously, like having multiple train tracks with multiple trains racing toward the same place. The problem is, when there are too many trains arriving at once, the computer crashes trying to sort it all out. That's what I think is happening. Adding more computers only makes the crashes happen faster."

Trey realized he was going twice the speed limit and backed off the gas. "How long will it take to fix it?"

"I don't know. I need to buy a book on concurrency or something." He gazed out the side window. "It could be a while."

"How long is awhile?"

"A month or two."

His voice was way too calm. The year 2000 was right around the corner. Based on some conspiracy theories, the world might catch fire because of the Y2K bug. The internet might go down forever because those brilliant geeks only stored the last two digits of the year everywhere, making it so computers couldn't tell the difference between 2000 and 1900. Kevin was way too nonchalant about fixing the code. And, if he hadn't fixed it by now, he probably couldn't.

Trey looked at the skinny geek out of the corner of his eye.

Either the freeloader was dragging things out, or he couldn't fix it. Either way, Brad wasn't going to wait forever.

There was only one way to get it done and get it done fast.

Malcolm.

CHAPTER THIRTY-TWO

EMMA

The door to my apartment has a door lock and a deadbolt. I turn the deadbolt while Trey steps past me.

"Nice place," he says.

"You can take your jacket off and throw it on the couch if you want."

It's past time when I've normally eaten dinner. I hope he doesn't expect anything to eat. I can't remember what's in the fridge, but I'm sure it's not much.

I step up next to him.

"I like that print," he says, pointing to my Escher of two faces connected by a single, fleshy ribbon. It hangs above the couch.

"Thanks."

"And what's this?" He picks up the magnifying glass off the coffee table. "Oh, just an old toy." I take it from him. "It was my mother's when she was little." I don't want to discuss my trips to the farmhouse or talking to my deceased mother. What a buzz kill that would be. I stow the magnifying glass in my pocket.

He gazes toward the open kitchen.

"It's small, but I like it here," I say. "The rents are high this close to campus, but I spend most of my time in the office anyway." I point toward the kitchen table. "My laptop is over there."

His cologne is a combination of sandalwood and cedar. It reminds me of waking up on a crisp autumn morning. I shift my weight, and the backs of our hands touch. We're here to send an email to Malcolm. To trap that goliath and send him to the police. But I turn, and Trey's eyes meet mine. A surge of energy rushes through my core.

He leans down.

I put my hands on his cheeks, and we kiss.

Our lips touch gently for an instant, then we turn into ravenous animals. Together, we move across the room, our lips locked, until I back into the couch. He unzips his jacket and lets it fall to the floor. Something hard hits my foot and makes a *thud*, but I don't care. I pull him onto the couch with me as I fall backward. He straddles my waist and sits up.

I begin unbuttoning my blouse.

My cell phone rings.

He stops moving. The lines on his face go slack.

It's hard to stop, but I've got to know who's calling. I pull out my phone, and it's the police.

Detective Galen.

Trey pushes my phone away and leans down to kiss me.

"Stop," I say. "I—" My heavy breathing catches up with me. I swallow. Arch my back. "Don't."

He sits up.

"I've got to answer this," I say. "I'm so sorry."

"To be continued?" he asks, making a playful grin.

"You can bet your life on it."

He slides off me, and I head for the kitchen, tapping the answer button. "Detective Galen, this is *not* a good time to talk." The receiver is cold on my lips.

"We've uncovered some vital information, and I need to speak with you immediately. It would be best if we talked in person."

"Did you hear me? Now is not a good time."

"Are you alone?"

"No, as a matter of fact, I'm not."

"Who is with you?"

"That's none of your business. Look, if you have something to tell me, then do it." I glance at Trey sitting on the couch, waiting for me.

My laptop is closed on the kitchen table. We'll send that email later. Until then—until we prove Malcolm is behind this—I'm still one of Galen's suspects. I can't forget that.

"I need to meet with you," Galen says. "Now."

"I can't meet tonight. How about tomorrow? What's so urgent?"

"Have you been in contact with a Trey Wilkes or Malcolm Schmidt?"

He knows about Malcolm. That's good, but I don't like how he mentioned Trey. It's bad enough that I've been falsely accused. Trey is innocent in all this. Trey is Malcolm's victim. "I don't feel comfortable answering that."

"Have you?" His voice drums in my ear. "You've got to tell me now."

"Why?"

"Just tell me if you've seen either of them. You could be in trouble."

"Are you saying you'll arrest me if I've been associating with known criminals?"

"No. Not that kind of trouble. Not by me."

"I think I need to talk to a lawyer."

"Listen."

Trey stands. Tucks his shirt into his pants.

"I'll call you tomorrow," I say to Galen. "I need time to think."

"Wait—"

I hang up.

"Who was that?" Trey asks.

"No one." I stride toward him.

"Did I hear you say, 'Detective Galen?'"

"Yes, but it's nothing. Let's—"

He grabs his jacket off the floor.

"What's wrong?" I ask.

"Sorry, Emma. I've got to go." He heads for the door.

"Why?" I grasp his arm. "Is it me?"

"No, not at all."

I search his eyes. "Then what is it?"

"Remember when I said the police wouldn't listen to me about Malcolm?"

"Yes."

"It was Detective Galen I talked to. He seemed helpful at first, but then he began interrogating me. He made me feel like a suspect."

"Oh, my God. Me too."

"The thing is, I can't have that happen. If word got out I was implicated in Dr. Santan's disappearance, it would affect my business and everyone who works for me." He slips an arm into his jacket sleeve. "I should never have told him about Malcolm."

"Wait." He slips his other arm in and pulls the collar up in the back. "Don't leave. I know exactly what you're talking about with Galen. You don't have to go."

"It sounded like he really wanted to talk to you. If he's coming here, I can't be here." He undoes the deadbolt and opens the door.

"He's not coming. I promise."

Trey turns and kisses me on the cheek. "I'll call you tomorrow." He stares into my eyes. "To be continued."

"Don't go."

He charges into the hallway.

I hang onto the door and watch as he walks away. "What about the email?"

"Tomorrow."

"Let me at least give you a ride. You don't have a car."

He yells something in return, but he's already halfway down the stairs.

The hallway swallows his words.

I close the door, and throw the deadbolt.

CHAPTER THIRTY-THREE

TREY - *December 1999*

A desk lamp sat on the corner of the computer lab help desk, but it wasn't on. Trey watched Malcolm sitting behind the desk from outside the computer lab. He practiced what he would say to Malcolm to make him fix the web crawler code. Trey had spent part of last week waiting outside Malcolm's dormitory, trying to catch him, but it hadn't worked out. Today, when the big guy hustled across campus to the computer lab, he followed. It appeared as though Malcolm had gotten a job running the help desk for the lab.

Trey stood in the hallway, watching through the windows. All the desks in the lab shimmered beneath the overhead lights, but Malcolm's desk sat against the wall. He sat in darkness. A student approached Malcolm, presumably to ask for help, and Malcolm snarled. After a moment, Malcolm waved the student away and returned to whatever he was doing on the computer. He didn't look happy in this job. That could be a good thing. Maybe he needed money.

Trey walked into the lab just as an old dot matrix printer with green bar paper began to rattle and print. The lab wasn't full of students, but it wasn't empty either. Malcolm had his head buried in the screen and didn't look up when Trey reached him.

"Excuse me," Trey said, "but I need some help."

Malcolm sighed and continued to type on the keyboard without looking up. "Welcome to the computer science department computer lab. How may I help you," he droned.

"You can make the web crawler code pull in one hundred thousand users."

That got Malcolm's attention.

His eyes met Trey's. "Oh. It's you."

"How have you been?"

He went back to typing. "Fine."

"I see you got a job. Everything okay?"

"What do you mean by that?"

"Well, this is new, right? You weren't working last spring."

"That's right. I needed some extra cash this fall. Speaking of which, if you want help with any of these computers, I'll help you. If you're here to discuss your project again, you'll have to pay me."

"I didn't think you were about money. I thought you were all about using the internet to make the world a better place."

He stopped typing. "That's you. Not me. After what you did to me last time . . ." He shook his head. "All those stupid business people. Are you going to pay me?"

"Sure. Fix your code, and I'll pay you whatever you want after I get funding. You don't have to demonstrate it again or meet with 'business' people. I only need you to fix it."

"My code's not broken. You're just a moron."

"Hey," said a guy standing behind Trey. "How much longer are you going to be?" The guy wore a coarse, multicolored baja hoodie and reeked of weed. His half-opened eyes confirmed Trey's suspicions.

"Can you move out of the way?" Malcolm said to me. "I have someone who actually deserves my help." Trey stepped aside. "Welcome to the computer science department computer lab. How may I help you?"

The guy held up a mouse. "How do you make this work, man?"

"Are you serious?" Malcolm asked.

"Yeah, man. Here, plug it in."

Malcolm grabbed the mouse and turned it over. "Where's the ball?"

"The ball?"

"Yeah. The mouse ball. See? Like this one." Malcolm held his mouse up and turned it over.

"Oh." The guy started looking around the room. "I don't know."

"Just go get another mouse off that desk."

"Cool. Thanks, man." He walked away.

"See what I have to put up with?" Malcolm's voice quaked. "The only thing worse than business majors are hippies."

"That's good to know," Trey said. "I thought the College of Business was at the top of your hit list."

Malcolm leaned back in his chair. His soulless eyes rotated toward the ceiling. "I have more than one hit list."

Trey didn't know what to say to that.

Malcolm sat up. "I'm busy, so if you aren't going to pay me, get bent."

"You're busy doing what? Writing more crappy code that breaks whenever someone tries to show it off?"

"It was the network and lack of computing power." He

stood up and leaned forward. Put both hands on the desk. "Your business boys had a horrible ISP. It wasn't my code."

Trey didn't back down. Without a doubt, he was at the top of one of Malcolm's lists, but without Malcolm's help, he might as well be dead. The future of his business certainly was. "My new programmer says it has nothing to do with the network or needing more computers. He says your code has multiple threads and doesn't work. It's a real train wreck."

"Your new programmer is wrong."

A girl in a torn UBalt sweatshirt and gray sweatpants stepped up. "Is everything okay?"

Malcolm rotated his eyes toward her, keeping his face pointed at Trey. "Everything's fine. Welcome to the computer science department computer lab. How can I help you?"

She held up a mouse. "This doesn't work."

Malcolm picked a backpack up off the floor. Shoved a book into it and slung it over his shoulder. "I'm out of here."

"But what about me?" the girl asked.

"It's missing a ball," Trey said calmly.

She turned the mouse over. "Oh."

Malcolm walked past Trey toward the door.

He ran after him. "Are you saying your web crawler code works?"

Malcolm didn't stop.

"Hey, I'm talking to you." Trey followed him into the hall. "Stop."

"No money. No talk."

Trey grabbed a fistful of concert dates printed on the back of Malcolm's shirt and pulled.

Malcolm spun around. "Touch me again and die."

"If you think nothing is wrong with your code, prove it. I'll pay you to prove it." Trey had no idea how he would do that, but without Malcolm, he had nothing.

"How much?"

"One hundred."

"Two."

"Okay. When can you—"

"Let's do this now."

"Fine."

Once again, Trey was impressed with the speed at which Malcolm walked. They crossed campus in no time and in complete silence. Trey flung the door to his apartment open and motioned for Malcolm to enter.

"What's that smell?" Malcolm said.

Kevin startled. He stood up from the computer desk and gazed at Malcolm with big eyes.

"Malcolm, this is my programmer, Kevin." Trey wiped his nose.

"Hi," Kevin said.

"Kevin, can you show Malcolm where the code is broken?"

Kevin stood there, starstruck. "Huh?"

"You told me the problem was deep in his code. Can you show him where that is?"

Malcolm took Kevin's seat.

"Sure," Kevin said. "I—I think it's in that file." He pointed at the screen.

"It wouldn't be there." Malcolm moved the mouse. Clicked the button. He searched for something, opening and closing windows.

Kevin watched over Malcolm's shoulder. "Why are you—"

"Shut up," Malcolm said. He began typing on the keyboard. "This thing is networked with all these computers here, right Trey?"

"I think so." Trey stepped closer so he could see better. The screen was filled with gibberish.

"Yes," Kevin said. "I made sure the network was configured correctly."

"I told you to shut up." Malcolm pulled up the status web page and clicked the start button. The number of users the application pulled in from the internet went from zero to one hundred almost instantaneously. It hit one thousand a minute later. Then two thousand.

Then three.

Kevin turned toward Trey. "It's loaded three *hundred* so far."

"Not this time, Kevin," Trey said. "I can see that it's loaded over three thousand."

"No. It's loaded three hundred so far," Kevin repeated.

Trey put his hand on Kevin's shoulder. "Get your things and get out. You and I are done."

CHAPTER THIRTY-FOUR

EMMA

Trey told me he would call tomorrow. Now, I just have to make it that long. The ice cream isn't helping. He's only been gone a few minutes, and I'm already on the couch, eating out of the carton. Why did I get raspberry swirl? I don't like raspberry. I like strawberry and chocolate, and—I wish I had chocolate.

My thoughts spin. Trey didn't leave because of me. It wasn't anything I did. He left because of Detective Galen. They say you are innocent until proven guilty, but it's really you're guilty until you prove you're not. The sentence for not proving you're innocent to the police is arrest. The sentence for not proving your innocence to the court is time served, or worse. It's a flawed system.

Knock, knock, knock.

He's back.

Trey came back.

I rush to the kitchen, throw the ice cream in the freezer, and go to the door.

He's back.

The deadbolt sticks a little when I twist it, and my fingers slip off. I try again, and this time it gives and makes a satisfying *clank*.

Detective Galen stands in the hallway. He immediately looks past me. "Who's with you?" he asks.

"No one, now."

He pushes past me.

"Hey. You can't come in here." I follow him, not bothering to close the door. He's going the need it open so he can leave.

"You're sure no one else is here?"

"Yes. What's your problem?"

He circles my apartment, enters the kitchen, and returns to the living room. "Who were you with this evening?"

"I already told you. That's none of your business."

He goes to the door. Closes it carefully.

"If I'm not under arrest," I say, "then I want you to leave."

"I think you were with Trey Wilkes."

I say nothing.

"We began a background check on him last week, but I only saw it today. It's very troubling." He searches my face.

I don't react.

"Were you with him tonight?"

"I want a lawyer."

"You don't need one unless you plan on lying to me."

I say nothing.

"Fine. Just listen to what I have to say. Trey Wilkes is a high-profile con artist. He's started and bankrupted more businesses than Donald Trump. He has countless pending lawsuits tied to several criminal activities, though no charges have ever been brought against him."

"I don't believe you. You're trying to scare me into saying something incriminating about him. Or me."

He takes a deep breath. "No, Emma. I'm trying to warn you. Trey is a very dangerous man. After reading his background report, we did some more checking this afternoon. He has a strong interest in your research project. Very strong."

"I already know that. Since when is having an interest in someone a crime?"

"So, you *have* spoken to him? Did you tell him anything about your project? About Dr. Santan?"

Dammit. I press my lips together.

"Emma, I don't suspect you anymore. You can talk to me. We're far more interested in Trey."

"How did you find out about his new business venture?"

"That's not important."

Trey said the man outside my apartment yesterday might not have been Malcolm. Now, I think it may have been an undercover policeman. "Does the Baltimore PD engage in corporate espionage?"

Galen furrows his brow. "What?"

"You asked me before if I'd talked to Trey or a man named Malcolm Schmidt. Here's what I think. Malcolm Schmidt came to you and spread lies about Trey, and you believed him. Then, you sent out a bunch of little spies to dig up dirt on Trey's businesses. You've been following me."

"Not as much as Trey has been following you. We found out about that golden car you mentioned. It belongs to him."

"I already know that, too. It was a coincidence. What about my missing colleague? Wilson Sinclair. I bet you haven't done a thing about him. What if he did something to Dr. Santan? Would you even know?"

"Yes. We checked into him. Everyone is a suspect. However," he holds his hand out, palm up, "in missing person cases, we act fast and follow the strongest leads first before they go cold and die. Everything points to Mr. Wilkes, so you need to tell me what you know. Now."

"I bet you told Trey the same thing about me."

"Are you going to cooperate or not?"

I say nothing.

He glances around the apartment. "Don't make me get a warrant."

"You said I wasn't a suspect anymore."

"You're not. You're . . ."

"What?"

"Okay. It's obvious you're not only trying to protect someone I suspect"—he focuses his attention on my laptop in the kitchen—"you're working with him."

"Get out." I put my hand on the door.

"For your own good," he says as he leaves. "Stay away from Trey Wilkes. There's only so much my department can do to protect you."

I slam the door behind him. Turn the deadbolt.

Clank.

CHAPTER THIRTY-FIVE

TREY - *December 1999*

Kevin packed his things and moved out of Trey's apartment before the pizza came. Trey had splurged and ordered not one but two pizzas. It was a desperate attempt to keep Malcolm seated at the desk, working on the code. He'd already fixed the major scaling problem in less than twenty minutes. Something Kevin hadn't been able to do in four months.

Good riddance, Kevin.

Malcolm updated the code on Trey's computers, patching it with changes he'd made to his web crawler software over the last summer and fall. The performance improved, but it wasn't good enough. The pizza came, he ate it, and he worked. Night came. He wanted to stop and leave, but new ideas kept bursting inside his head. Two-in-the-morning arrived, and he finally left.

But he came back the next day.

And the next.

Trey scrounged and paid Malcolm one hundred dollars to gain his confidence. Malcolm kept coming back. By the weekend, he declared victory and demonstrated the application to Trey.

It was mind-boggling. Fast, friendly, and efficient.

They had a viable product.

Trey drafted a working agreement with Malcolm containing, among other things, the words "no deadlines" in bold and all caps. He promised he would never force Malcolm to work directly with business people. For three straight days, Trey woke up at noon, sat next to Malcolm, learned everything he could about the application, and hit the hay at three in the morning. Sometimes later. It was pizza, all day, every day.

Brad said he couldn't schedule a meeting between Trey and Calimico Venture Partners. The same as last year but worse. The partners' schedules were jam-packed ahead of Christmas and the millennial New Year's Day. The world was jam-packed. Calimico and other firms had invested in dot-com companies heavily throughout 1999, but many of them had shown signs of failure. Brad said even if the Y2K problem didn't destroy the internet, Calimico might not want to revisit Trey's project. The competition was thick.

Trey was running out of money. He couldn't wait until January. Too much pizza.

After what could only be called outright begging, Brad agreed to let Trey show him the results of Malcolm's efforts. Brad's little investment firm, Hero Capital Management, didn't have a large bankroll like Calimico, but Trey couldn't risk waiting any longer.

Brad loved it.

Like a miracle, like the savior Trey had believed Brad to be, Hero Capital Management funded Trey's business right before Christmas. After explaining his personal finance problems, Brad gave Trey a sizable advance. A very sizable advance. Trey gave half of it to Malcolm, and neither enrolled for the spring semester.

*Thought*Fluence was born.

Trey awoke on the couch the morning of January 1st, 2000, and the world hadn't exploded. The internet hadn't shut down.

And so, it began.

Wake up. Greet Malcolm at the door on the way out. Drive to Brad's capital management office. Drink coffee. Order equipment. Interview software developers, quality assurance testers, and project managers. Turn down anyone who couldn't pass Malcolm's technical tests while the big guy sat alone in Trey's apartment, working on the application. Working the way he liked. Away from the business people.

Malcolm truly was amazing. The application improved daily.

Trey wore suits to Brad's office. He ate lunch wherever he wanted. Brad gave him a cell phone. He signed a lease for a large business space, and Malcolm worked from there. He gave Malcolm his own office.

On day one, Trey stood before his inaugural employees. A group of eight. Trey introduced Malcolm as Chief Technical Officer and told everyone that every day was casual day. Malcolm had gone to see a Black Crowes concert the night before and wore the concert T-shirt. The minute Trey finished his speech, Malcolm vanished into his office and shut the door. Everyone else got to work, also.

Trey sat in his office. Put his feet on his desk. He couldn't stop smiling. He'd done it.

He'd finally done it.

He pulled his cell phone out. His answering machine at home contained an annoying number of messages from his father. It was time.

"I didn't think you'd ever call me back," his father said. "You must be busy with school."

"No, not really. I'm sorry I didn't call sooner. You're right. I have been busy."

"Where are you calling from? I just got this Caller ID thing on my phone. This isn't your number."

"I'm calling from a cell phone."

"Oh." Trey imagined the gears turning in his dad's head. "Well, I'm glad you called back. I have bad news."

"What's that?"

His father groaned. He'd never heard that noise come out of his dad's mouth before.

"Dad, are you okay?"

"I have a lot of bad news." He cleared his throat. "Your mother left for Europe before New Year's again this year, but she's not coming back this time. Apparently, she spent this past year building a new life with someone else. We're divorcing."

Trey sat up. He hadn't seen her since the summer before last. He wasn't surprised, but he wasn't *not* surprised, either. He'd thought his parents would divorce when he left for college. They never spent time together like a normal couple. He hadn't seen her in over a year, and with everything going on, starting his business, he hadn't missed her. But the pain in his dad's voice made him nervous. Uncomfortable. "I don't know what to say. I'm sorry?"

"There's more. It's been in the works for a while, but with the divorce—no, I can't blame her. Dammit."

"What?"

"They thought my personal life was too much of a distraction. The board let me go from the company."

"Oh, no. They can't do that."

"They can, and they did. Don't worry, I'll be okay. We disagreed on a lot of things recently, and I never told you, but we also lost a lot of money over the last couple of years." He sighed. "It's probably for the best."

"How did you lose money?"

"They told me we missed too many opportunities to modernize. It would have cost us millions to upgrade our operations, and we didn't have millions, so I didn't do it. You know how I feel about borrowing. They're going to be sorry. All these website companies—our snot-nosed competitors . . . they're a flash in the pan. Our customers will come running back when it all collapses."

"I'm so sorry, Dad." Outside Trey's office window, his facilities manager and one of his software developers carried a desk across the open space. "What are you going to do?"

"Your mother is taking me to the cleaners. She wants everything I have left in the divorce. I just need to know if you're on track to graduate this spring. It will help when I don't have to pay your tuition anymore."

"You can stop now."

"What do you mean?"

"I did it. I started my own business, and it's doing really well."

"What?" he shrieked. Like the groaning before, Trey had never heard anything like that come out of his dad's mouth.

"Right after the New Year, I formed a business with my idea. Remember it? I showed you last summer. I have an office near downtown now, eight employees, and plenty of seed funding to get me through, so you can stop paying tuition and depositing my allowance now if that helps."

Dead air.

"Dad?"

"You don't have a business. You have seed funding. You have something bought with someone else's money."

"I have a solid business plan. My investor will get all his money back plus tons more when it takes off."

"I told you not to borrow. I told you to graduate, get a job, and save up your own money for a business."

"I know, but that's not how the world works now. It's all about leverage. Startup companies don't have time to save cash. Because of the internet, things are moving fast. You have to borrow money to get ahead of technology."

"No, you don't. Mark my words. It's all going to come crashing down."

"I don't think so."

"You sound like my CTO." It was like someone had poured gravel into his father's voice box. "He wasted millions trying to outsource our operations to these dot-coms, fly-by-night shams, and I'm the one they ousted."

"I can help, Dad."

"No. Don't call me again."

"What do you mean?"

"You're cut off, and I don't want to talk to you again. I did everything I could to help you, and you didn't listen. I'm done with you. If you want something, call your mother."

The phone went dead.

Trey didn't need him anyway.

Brad had funded *Thought*Fluence through the end of 2000. Brad understood the long-term vision of collecting millions of users on the website by offering free access to virtual communities. After a year or so, Trey would monetize his technical assets and his giant consumer base. Advertising. Product placement. All targeted to provide his virtual communities the information and products they would need to solve the world's problems. To make the world a better place.

He didn't need his father's money anymore.

He didn't need his mother's love. He couldn't remember having it to begin with.

Their divorce was their problem.

Trey had to focus on *Thought*Fluence.

He was the new Bill Gates.

The new millennium had started, and nothing could stop him now.

CHAPTER THIRTY-SIX

EMMA

Most nights, I unplug. My cell phone and laptop sleep in the kitchen, and I sleep in my bed. Brains work best with plenty of sleep, but I kept my phone within reaching distance last night. Trey said he wouldn't call until today, but I had hoped he would in the middle of the night. I'd hoped he spent the night unable to sleep, thinking about me the same way I had been thinking about him.

I check the time and shut my alarm off thirty minutes early. The sun hasn't risen yet, but it won't be long. My eyes don't want to stay open. Sleep finally came to me around two in the morning, so I only got a couple of hours.

My phone has no missed calls.

No new text messages.

Time to get moving. There's no point in lying in bed, doing nothing. I get up, scoop my dirty clothes off the floor, and throw them in my laundry basket. My magnifying glass falls out of my pants and bounces on the carpet. That was close. The washing machine would have destroyed it. Perhaps I'll take a trip to the farmhouse later today. I could use the peace and quiet and tell Mom about Mr. Handsome. It would make her happy to know I might have found someone.

Two hours later, my clothes are clean, and Trey still hasn't called. It's early, but I want to talk to him. Concern dominates my thoughts. With the laundry done, I have nothing else to distract me. My apartment is already clean. I wonder if Detective Galen went from my place to Trey's. The way that nasty detective talked, he wanted to arrest Trey. Maybe that's why I don't have any messages. I'd like to be honored as the recipient of Trey's one phone call from jail, but that's ridiculous and vain.

We've barely started dating.

I find myself sitting on the couch, scrolling through old Facebook posts on my phone, traveling into the past. Pictures of Alyssa, Vivian, and me at the beach a couple of years ago. The post shows Vivian shoveling sand into a plastic pail, her bright pink swimsuit adorned with pictures of SpongeBob SquarePants. I scroll the posts up until about a month ago when Dr. Santan's stoic face catches my eye. This picture shows my colleagues and me holding the nomination for the award. Wilson, Tory, Dr. Santan, Nimisha, and me—all smiles. The beginning of the end.

I owe Nimisha a phone call. I forgot to call her last night.

"Hey," she says. "I waited up, but you didn't call."

"I'm sorry. I meant to, but I got busy and forgot."

"Do you know where D'Angelo keeps his research files on mass persuasion? I can't find them."

"They're in his office, but I don't understand. Almost everything for the project is on mass persuasion. Are *all* his files gone?"

"No, I have the approach and definitions, but the studies citing the success rates for behavioral pattern changes among large groups are missing. He must have kept them somewhere else, or I was wondering, did you take them?"

"No. I haven't seen them. They weren't part of the proposal I was working on."

"Okay. I'll keep looking. Do you think Wilson would have had them?"

"I doubt it. Did you check his office?"

"I can't get in there."

"How did you get into Dr. Santan's office?"

"It was unlocked. I hope it's okay. He wanted me to do this research before he left." She pauses, and when she speaks again her voice trembles. "When do you think he's coming back?"

"Don't worry. I'm going to find him. Everything is going to be okay."

"Okay. We miss you."

"I miss you too."

Call Ended 10:07 a.m.

It will be wonderful when everything returns to normal. When D'Angelo comes back. When we promote the project and receive the attention we deserve. Trey and I can—

I can't wait any longer. I type "Mr. Handsome" into my contacts search bar, his entry comes up, and I hit the call button.

It rings once.

Nothing.

C'mon, answer.

It rings again, and my couch hums.

Ring. Hum.

Ring. Hum.

I'm on the floor in an instant, searching under the couch. The phone call goes to voice mail.

I sweep my arm under the couch and retrieve a mass of hair, a plume of dust, a receipt for take-out food, a white earbud, and a cell phone. The screen on the phone I found reads, "Missed Call," then goes black.

I take the earbud and phone to the kitchen table. The screen is locked, and I don't recognize the brand. Kyivfone. The small text embossed on the back is hieroglyphics to me. The magnifying glass doesn't help. It only makes the confusing characters bigger. Some characters are in English, but the others are completely foreign. I swipe the screen and guess at the four-letter pin, randomly hitting the buttons, but it won't let me in.

Incoming call.

The number looks familiar, but the answer button doesn't work.

Quickly, I pop the earbud in my ear.

"Are you there?" a man asks. He has a deep voice and a strong European accent, but I can't place the origin. For some reason, pictures of pancakes come to mind. "Mr. Wilkes?"

I lower my voice as far as it will go. "Mm, hm."

"I had to let him out. He was pissing all over the cage. Mr. Sohlmann is not answering, and the man won't be coming out of the—" A toilet flushes in the background. "Come out. Wait." There's a loud *crash,* and the voice shouts, "Ah, neh!" Another loud noise bursts through the receiver—more of a *thump* this time—followed by static.

I momentarily pull the phone away from my ear, then listen again.

"Hello?" says a different man. His voice is ragged but familiar. "You can't keep me here forever."

"Where?" I ask.

"Who is this?" he screams. "Who is this?"

CHAPTER THIRTY-SEVEN

TREY - *January 2007*

Between the interstate highway and the UBalt Academic Center stood a line of thick trees and bushes, their leaves black and green, fluttering in the night. Trey had put on his best suit and shoes and now he combed his hair by shining a flashlight on his pocket mirror. He still looked good, even after all these years. He switched the light off and stowed it in his backpack. He'd need a fresh set of batteries soon.

As expected, the light to Kevin's office on the fourth floor of the Academic Center was on. The geek had worked late each of the last two Thursdays. Probably grading papers for Friday classes.

Trey walked across the street with a stabbing pain in his foot. He had a rock in his shoe. The tape covering the hole had fallen off somewhere. He stood right outside the front door for a moment, then decided better of it. He didn't want to be too obvious, and he didn't want to scare Kevin away, so he walked around the corner and waited near the parking garage.

He pulled his shoe off and dumped the rock onto the

sidewalk.

His heart beat heavily.

With his fist, he pounded his chest one time. His heart beat back against his sternum in retaliation. It wouldn't slow down. Trey had pitched business ideas to countless investors over the last seven years. He'd stood in countless conference rooms, smiled his salesman smile countless times, and shaken hands with some of the richest people in the world. And, with some of the slimiest. But even after all that, his nerves were getting the better of him. His heart refused to slow down.

And he was nervous for who? Kevin? That emaciated little stink-boy from back in the day?

Twice, after abandoning his original idea, he'd sold investors on a new idea, but that one flopped, too. He couldn't let it happen again.

He didn't want his heart to stop beating. He just wanted it to slow down and stop *pounding*. He just didn't want to feel it anymore. The knuckles in his hand cracked when he beat on his chest a second time.

Kevin came around the corner.

Trey put on his salesman smile.

Underneath Kevin's long-sleeved dress shirt and khaki slacks, his spindly arms and legs hadn't gained any discernible weight since college. He had grown a thin mustache, though. It was not becoming. His laptop bag tugged on his shoulder as he strolled toward the parking garage.

"Hey, Kevin." Trey stood in the shadows of the parking garage. "I can't believe it's you."

Kevin stopped cold. His grip tightened on his laptop bag. "I'm sorry, do I—"

"It's me." Trey strode forward, holding his hand out. "Trey Wilkes. From college." He glanced up at the building.

"From here. Remember me?"

Kevin's face went white, but he recovered with a forced smile. "Right. Trey, it's you."

They shook hands.

Trey leaned his head back to avoid the odor out of habit, but Kevin didn't smell bad. He smelled like Irish Spring. "You're looking good."

"Sorry, I didn't recognize you at first. I guess it's the beard."

Trey stroked his beard. "Nice, isn't it? I like your mustache."

Kevin rubbed the back of his neck. "What are you doing here?"

"No, the question is, what are you doing here? You're not still trying to finish your degree, are you?"

"No. I'm a professor now. I more than finished my undergrad."

"That's great. Congratulations."

"Thank you. You look—" He glanced down at Trey's shoes, then at his suit. "Hey, it's late." He pulled his bag to his chest. "I need to go home. We should have coffee sometime."

Trey had taken his suit out of his backpack only a few times over the past two years. He'd tried to keep it as nice as possible. The pant legs were frayed, but Kevin couldn't possibly see that in the dark. "Coffee. Yes, let's do that."

Kevin took a wide path around Trey.

Coffee?

Not likely. Kevin was blowing him off. Kevin was never going to have coffee with him.

"Wait," Trey yelled as Kevin entered the garage. "Don't you have a few minutes to catch up now?" He ran to him. Yellow lights in cages hung from the corners of the concrete ceiling on both sides.

"Sorry, no. I really must go home. It was great seeing you."

Impossibly, yet true, a fresh rock had slipped into Trey's shoe and gouged his arch. He stumbled to his left. "Let me walk with you to your car."

Kevin pulled his keys out. "Are you drunk?"

"No, no. I've got a rock in my shoe." He tittered, trying to make a joke of it.

Kevin walked up to a late-model luxury sedan.

"Nice car," Trey said. "Hey, please, I have something to tell you."

Kevin raised his wrist. Looked at his watch. "Make it fast. I've really got to go."

"I know things didn't end well with us. I hope you can see past that. I've changed. I've learned a lot since school." Kevin's eyes narrowed. "I was young. I thought you were using me, and all I wanted was to start my business. I'm sorry I kicked you out, but I had no choice. I had to go with Malcolm."

"You had a choice. I could have solved your scaling problem." He bared his teeth. Small and scraggly, like the rest of him. "From the looks of it, you made the wrong choice."

"I did. I did. You're right, but it's not too late."

"Oh, no. No way." He pressed his key fob. His car went *boop, boop.*

"Please, hear me out. You're right, I made the wrong choice, and the timing—I didn't know the dot-com crash was coming. It wasn't your fault or Malcolm's. People weren't ready for my idea then, but now—"

"Your idea?" He opened the car door and faced Trey. "You're still trying to find someone to work on your stupid project? Now? Where have you been? Haven't you heard of MySpace? Facebook?"

Trey *had* heard of those websites. In fact, he'd spent some time in Palo Alto, California, where it was warmer. Before returning to Baltimore a few weeks ago, he'd tried to connect with Malcolm again. Malcolm was a Senior Software engineer at Facebook. He'd joined right after college. After the collapse. After Brad and Hero Capital Management abandoned Trey.

After the world abandoned common sense.

The thought had crossed Trey's mind that Malcolm stole the best parts of *Thought*Fluence and gave them to Zuckerberg, but Trey knew in his heart of hearts that wasn't true. Malcolm had always had a frustrating inclination to follow the rules. A destructive sense of morality. Yet, it wasn't fair. Malcolm drove an expensive car and lived in the world's most expensive city. Without working at *Thought*Fluence, he would never have acquired the social skills needed to get a job at Facebook.

He owed Trey for that experience. Because of Trey, Malcolm had a great life now, and the big lummox didn't even give him the time of day out there.

But Kevin would. He had to.

"My idea wasn't the same as Facebook," Trey said. "Similar, but not the same. I don't want to connect the world to sell advertising. I want to connect people to solve problems."

"Yes, I remember. You thought you could help them cure cancer and stuff, but I can't believe you'd come here and try to make me help you after what you did. And you're not exactly—wait. I've seen you around. That beard. How long have you been stalking me?"

"I haven't. I wasn't." Trey's heart finally stopped its incessant pounding, but his lips started shaking. His face tightened. "Kevin, without you, I have nothing."

"I've heard that before."

"Please, don't make me beg."

"What happened to you?"

Trey cast his eyes down. His fraying pant legs were much worse than he thought. "When the dot-coms crashed, I missed the warning signs. Pets.com was the first to go. The others fell like dominoes. I thought my business was immune, but we ran out of money. Fast. I borrowed and borrowed to keep it going because I believed—I still believe in making the world a better place. Please, listen to me. I've learned so much since then. It will work this time."

Kevin closed his eyes. Tipped his head forward. "Listen. I know what it's like to have nothing."

"I remember."

"But your idea, it's too late. You can't take on those big guys."

"Please."

"No, I can't help you. I like working in academia. It's safe."

"But, I've got nowhere to turn."

"You should find a safe job and work toward building a new business. Get a better idea. That's the best I can do for you, Trey."

"No! I don't work for other people." His heart started up again. He pounded his chest. "I'm a businessman. An entrepreneur."

Kevin got in his car and shut the door. The rat-faced freak sounded like Trey's father. Trey slammed his hand against the glass. He was glad his father's business collapsed, just like his.

He was glad his father was dead.

Kevin started the engine.

"I took you in when no one else would," he called through the driver's side window. "I helped you. Now, you have to help me."

Kevin cracked the window. "Move out of the way. I don't have to do anything."

"You owe me."

"Move out of the way." He scrunched his eyes shut. "I don't have to do anything."

Trey stepped back.

"I don't have to do anything." Kevin roared out of the parking garage. The fumes from his exhaust pipes hung in the air.

Kevin was right. Trey was too late. His idea was better than Facebook, but the world was moving on. It didn't want to make itself a better place. The world didn't want to use the internet to solve its problems. It wanted to use it to watch funny cat videos.

Trey awoke the next day, lying on his back with dew dripping down his cheek. Cold and wet, the bushes blocking out the sun. His body ached like an eighty-year-old's. He was only thirty-two. Kevin had been his last chance, and though he'd vowed to never give up—to never have a job working on someone else's dream—something had to change.

His dream had to change.

He'd wasted years dreaming the internet could be used for the greater good, and it had landed him here. Homeless and hungry. He would have been better off if the internet had never existed.

The wind moved the leaves, and the sunlight broke through. It blinded him, and he realized shutting his eyes to the light wouldn't work. They burned. He couldn't make the sun stop shining or make the world follow his dream. He had to listen to the light. To the light of this world.

This world.

This technology-riddled wasteland.

Nothing but people staring at computer screens, day in and day out. No one knew what they wanted. No one knew why they were alive. Their purpose. Filled with chaos and confusion, everyone lived their lives like robotic arms on an assembly line. Constantly scrolling and clicking on "likes" on their social media websites. Forever seeking those dumps of dopamine when someone new follows them. They'd squandered the internet's power and lost contact with the physical world. With each other. Day by day, everyone had become more isolated and more insane.

They needed Trey's help.

They needed him to tell them what to do.

How to live.

The internet was no longer part of the solution to the world's problems.

It *was* the world's problem.

CHAPTER THIRTY-EIGHT

EMMA

"Who is this?" the ragged voice screams. "Who *is* this?"

He sounds older. Definitely male. Raspy, like he's got a severe cold or laryngitis. He screams his question again, and I pull my phone away from my ear until he stops.

"Hold on," I say.

"Emma? Is that you?"

Now, it's my turn. "Who *is* this?"

"It's me, D'Angelo. Oh, thank God."

I grip the kitchen table with my other hand. This can't be happening. D'Angelo is calling Trey's phone. I have Trey's phone in my hand. It must have fallen out of his jacket before we started making out last night. He hasn't called me this morning because he couldn't.

I have his phone.

"Emma. You have to help me."

"Where are you?"

"I don't know."

His voice is so ragged, for a moment, it doesn't sound like him.

My paranoia kicks in.

Trey said corporate spies often try to steal information from people in his circles. He suggested the big body-builder guy who surprised me outside my apartment was a spy. The one claiming to be Malcolm Schmidt. This could be a spy calling Trey directly.

"How do I know it's you?"

"They're coming back. Please. It's me. D'Angelo."

I think of something only he and I would know. "Why didn't your wife go to the awards banquet?"

"What does that matter? They've got me locked in a cage."

"Just answer me."

"She was feeling under the weather that night."

"What's the real reason?"

"She hates my work. Always has. She's jealous of the time I spend on it." He pauses. "She's jealous of you."

That's Marjorie. No spy could know that about her. I doubt anyone on the project knows that about her. A flood of emotion makes my throat tighten. "Are you okay?"

"No. They're torturing me."

"*What?*"

"They're torturing me. I think they're going to kill me."

"Did you call 911?"

"No. All I could on this phone was hit redial."

"Okay. Where are you? Who took you?"

"I'm in a room upstairs somewhere. I've heard noises above and below. Some men threw a hood over my head, and I woke up here. I'm not sure what day it is, but—it was that man from the banquet. The investor everyone talked about. He had me kidnapped."

It can't be.

Not Trey.

My lips are still warm from his kiss. "Trey? Trey Wilkes?"

"Yes. Everyone here calls him Mr. Wilkes. He's been asking about our work, and when I don't talk—please, you have to help me."

No. Not Trey. It can't be him.

"Someone's coming." A door slams. "Emma, I'm—"

"What are you doing?" A woman's voice collides with his, shrill and panicked, sounding like a banshee. "Put that down."

Click.

"D'Angelo? D'Angelo?"

He's gone.

I put the strange phone down on the table.

Kyivfone.

Call Ended 10:49 a.m.

I work everything backward through my brain, hitting each instance of denial and paranoia like speed bumps in a hospital parking garage. Trey came here, and we got busy on the couch, but did he come here for me or my research? He said it was so we could send an email to protect me from his old friend, Malcolm.

He always referred to him as an *old friend*.

Never as an enemy.

He saw me at Café Royale when I attempted to question D'Angelo's buddies. That was a convenient interruption. He also happened to spot me after my first meeting with Detective Galen at the harbor. Both times, I was engaged in a discussion about D'Angelo's disappearance.

I take the earbud out of my ear. One of Trey's white earbuds.

The golden car belongs to Trey, and he *was* following me. He followed me to the banquet and elsewhere, then lied about it.

And I believed him.

It feels like I've been working out.

My heart races.

I stand and gaze at the couch. A cold sweat forms on my forehead. I pick up Trey's phone, but it's still locked. I need to call the police, but I can't. Detective Galen tried to warn me about Trey. He said Trey was dangerous. I didn't believe him. By defending Trey, Galen will think I lied, but I didn't mean to. Galen accused me of working with Trey. He accused me of working with Malcolm Schmidt. He still thinks I have something to do with D'Angelo's disappearance, but I don't.

Do I?

What's the truth?

Am I an unwilling accomplice?

One by one, I throw every emotion I have for Trey in the trash and hold onto the facts. The man in the gray coat outside my building. Was he trolling Trey, like Trey said, trying to gaslight me into believing Trey was dangerous? Or was he actually Malcolm Schmidt? He called Trey a gaslighter.

Trey is a gaslighter.

That man was trying to warn me, just like Galen.

I'm innocent, but from Galen's point of view, I am very guilty. Guilty until proven innocent.

I'm sick to my stomach. I haven't eaten yet this morning, and nothing sounds good. Not even the ice cream.

I pace the kitchen.

The worst part is Trey has a strong motive. He wants the research from D'Angelo's project for his business, and D'Angelo sounded like he wasn't giving it to him. Despite being tortured. So he came after me.

Galen said Trey was up to something big, whatever that

meant. Regardless, Trey is a kidnapper. A torturer.

I must move past my denial and accept these facts.

Now.

I wonder if Trey had Wilson kidnapped also. If so, the joke's on him. Wilson knows the least of anyone on the project. But maybe Wilson went willingly. Maybe they've been working together for a while. Not likely. Trey seems too smart to work with him.

I rush to my bedroom and get dressed. Amid these revelations, my heart has broken. I haven't felt this kind of hollowness since Mom died. I allowed myself to fantasize a future with Trey, and now it's all gone. What a delusion. My paranoia was right all along.

I'm sorry, Mom. I'm going to make everything right. I'll find someone someday, but first, I will get D'Angelo back. I'm going to get my life back.

I take Trey's weirdo cell phone and earbud, and I put on a jacket.

To get my life back, I'll need help.

There's only one person I can trust now.

I step into the hall and twist the knob.

The deadbolt *clanks* into place, and I head for my car.

CHAPTER THIRTY-NINE

EMMA

Alyssa and I met in middle school. The first time I saw her, the principal removed her from the cafeteria for blowing milk bubbles out of her nose at Melanie Johnson. Melanie was evil, always putting everyone down because of their appearance. She couldn't do that to Alyssa. Nothing ever fazed Alyssa.

After I was caught cheating on a test, Alyssa and I bonded in detention. We've been friends ever since. She's my sister from another mister, and I'm hers. We're family. From the day she gave birth to Vivian, I've been known as Aunt Emma in her house.

I ring the doorbell and peer at the little glass lens above the button. "Alyssa? Can you hear me?"

Alyssa's doorbell has a camera. When someone rings it, her cell phone displays the front porch. She's always been a gadget person. Her ex-husband, Jeremy, not so much. Talk about a mismatch. Alyssa is vibrant, funny, and full of life. Jeremy is dull and serious. She got the house in the divorce, and it's way more than she needs. Four bedrooms, a three-car garage, situated in one of Baltimore's nicer neighborhoods.

She has a camera in her doorbell for security but doesn't need it. This area is as low crime as it gets.

I ring the bell again and hold the button down. "If you can hear me, let me in."

The leaves on the trees in her front yard flutter in the wind. Someday, I'll have a place like this.

I reach into my pocket to pull out Trey's weirdo phone but get mine instead. I have a missed text from Nimisha. She still can't find the research papers she asked me about before. She's a workaholic. God love her.

I ring the doorbell one more time and send Alyssa a text. *I'm here. Let me in.*

She returns my text. *Just woke up. On my way.*

The door opens. She's wearing a pink silk robe with fluffy white trim and a pair of slippers adorned with two stuffed animal heads. Two cartoonish pigs. The breeze isn't powerful enough to move her curly blonde hair, especially the side matted to her head.

"What's up, player?" she says before turning around and heading for the living room. "Come on in."

"Is Vivian here?"

"Yeah." She lies on the couch and kicks her feet up on the armrest. "She's asleep in her room."

I sit in the recliner, not sure how to begin. Alyssa knows I was interested in Trey, but everything has changed. I feel so stupid for believing his lies. Rescuing D'Angelo has become the number one priority in my life, but I'm still grappling with the reality that Trey was using me.

"You know," Alyssa says, "I love her, but I can't wait for her to go to her father's condo this week. Does that make me a bad mother?"

"No. I—"

"She can be such a little SNP."

I take the bait. "What's an SNP?"

"All little kids are SNPs. Sticky Narcissistic Parasites. If it's not peanut butter under their fingernails, it's jelly. They only talk about themselves, and if it weren't for their parents cooking for them, they'd die of starvation. Dirty little parasites."

"Right. Poor you." I glance at the Gauguin print of a Tahitian mother and child hanging above the couch. It's four times the size of my Escher. "You're the epitome of a struggling mother."

She laughs. "What's going on, Emma? Why'd you come over?"

"Seen any good crime dramas lately?"

"You know I have. I just finished watching a documentary on the Golden State Killer. It was good. Not great."

"I want you to help me find Dr. Santan."

She swings her legs off the couch and sits up. One of her slippers falls onto the floor and makes an *oinking* sound. "Really?"

"Yes."

"That's awesome sauce."

"Calm down."

"But, you said he would return on his own. What about the police? Did you talk to them again?"

I tell her what happened with Trey and Detective Galen last night and about the man in the gray coat spying outside my apartment. She listens carefully, occasionally cracking a smile in excitement. Investigating a real crime is her dream come true.

"Wait," she says. "Was he a corporate spy, or Trey's

friend from college?"

"I don't know. Here, take a look at this." I pull out the weirdo cell phone and hand it to her.

"It's heavy." She turns it over in her hands a couple of times.

"That's the phone D'Angelo called me on. It's Trey's."

"Who knows you have this?"

"Only you. Trey might realize it's gone and assume he left it at my place, but it fell out of his pocket. He didn't take it out, so from his perspective, he could have lost it anywhere."

"That's good. If he doesn't know where he lost it, then he might not know you know he kidnapped D'Angelo."

I untwist her words. "Right. Even if he does think he left it at my place, he doesn't necessarily know D'Angelo called me. What do you think about the writing on his phone?"

"It looks like Russian. It's weird." She swipes the screen and taps it a few times. "Hm. Sixty-nine isn't the code." She glances up at me. "That's the one I always use."

"Of course it is."

She types in another code. "Uh, oh."

"What?"

"The screen dimmed." She tries another code. Then another.

"Stop it. You're not going to be able to unlock it."

She hands the phone back to me. "You're right. It's dead."

Sure enough, the screen won't come on anymore. "Thanks."

"When D'Angelo called you, did it show the Caller ID, or was it 'Unknown' or something?"

"It was a number, but I don't remember it. I think it had a Baltimore area code."

"And you have no idea where he was calling from?"

"Nope. He thought he was upstairs somewhere, but that's all." I put my head in my hands. Remembering the conversation hurts. "He said Trey had someone kidnap him. They were torturing him. His voice sounded horrible. I can't believe how foolish I was."

"Don't. It's always hard to see the truth when attracted to someone. Plus, it sounds like Trey is a major con artist. That detective said he's been conning people for years, right? If so, he's got a lot of practice. You shouldn't beat yourself up."

"I know." This is why I need Alyssa. She's always defended me, even when it's been me attacking me.

She beams. "This is so great." She stands. "We'll find clues, put them together, and find him. I know how to do this. You and me. Lacey and Cagney."

"Yeah, sure, but how?"

"Let's start with that spy. That Malcolm guy." She pinches her chin. "You saw his car, right?"

"Yes, it was an old dark green Ford Explorer, but we don't even know who he was."

"It doesn't matter. He knows about you, and he knows about Trey. If we can find him, he might be able to help us."

"He might kill us."

"I don't think so." She slides her hands over her hips. "You think he'd want to kill all this? No way. If anything, we'll woo him with our womanly charms like in every Double-O-Seven movie. He's the spy, but we're the temptresses. The love interests."

"Be serious. How do you suggest we find him?"

"We drive around and look for his car. We can look for Trey's car also. Maybe we'll get lucky and find both of them." She turns away. "Let me get dressed, and we'll go."

I follow her down the hall and stand outside her bedroom. She won't be able to afford this place much longer. She wasn't specific, but she and Jeremy were fairly house poor before the divorce, and she doesn't work. The heating bill alone would cripple me.

"Mommy?" Vivian calls from her room.

Alyssa opens the door to her bedroom.

"Come here," Vivian calls from inside hers.

"The SNP has awoken," Alyssa whispers.

"Are we taking her with us?"

"Yes, but we can drop her off at Jeremy's before we start our search. It's his week."

"Okay."

"Honey," Alyssa calls out, "get dressed. We're going to your father's early."

"Why?"

"Because Mommy's got to help Aunt Emma find a murderer."

"Holy—" I cover my mouth. "Why do you tell her things like that?"

Alyssa's phone vibrates and plays the intro to *Mission Impossible*. "Someone's at the door." She gazes at the screen.

"Can I see?"

She turns the phone toward me. A man wearing a long gray coat blocks out the driveway. "That's him," I say. "That's Malcolm, or the spy, or—he followed me here."

"Great." Alyssa charges down the hallway toward the door. "We don't have to go looking for that old Ford after all."

CHAPTER FORTY

TREY - *Now*

Trey strides down the hall, passing through *Thought*Fluence's data science department. The air buzzes with activity. The data analysts type with urgency. Spreadsheets appear on screens. Numbers, charts, and graphs scroll at high speed. Everything here is as it should be. Bright and sterile. Plain white walls. White desks arranged in straight lines across an open floor. No distractions. Nothing to stand in the way of optimizing Trey's reach throughout the internet.

Nothing except Malcolm.

But he has a plan for Malcolm.

He'll call Emma and arrange another "date" later today. Together, they'll lure Malcolm out of hiding. It's only a matter of time before Trey's influence on the world takes hold.

Work and time.

Then Malcolm won't matter.

He is hopeful the penetration numbers are up today as he strides into the executive conference room. When he leased this place last year, he spared no expense on the conference rooms. A large screen monitor hangs on the far wall connected to a sophisticated conferencing system with sound-activated cameras located throughout the room. Luxurious leather-bound chairs surround a black marble conference table. Seats for eighteen. A wet bar by the door.

Sverker is already there, but that's not a surprise. Sverker Sohlmann is the most reliable associate Trey has ever employed. He stands with his back straight and chin up, towering over a security guard seated at the table. Sverker may be getting on in years—his black mustache fading into his bristly gray beard, his war-torn cheeks showing the depth of youthful contests—but he's the best. Age has only made him wiser. It's made him better at using his tools to extract information from resistant individuals. Few have looked into his cold eyes beneath those devilishly arched eyebrows in that penultimate, life-or-death moment and not spilled the beans.

The guard stands when Trey enters the room.

Sverker gently puts his hand on the guard's shoulder and urges him to sit back down.

He does.

"Is this him?" Trey closes the door.

"Yes," Sverker says. "Pradeep Kushagra."

The guard is one of the darker-skinned ones. An independent contractor with a military history, like most of Trey's security staff. "What happened?"

"I am being so sorry," Pradeep says. "He attacked me." He rubs his head.

"Start at the beginning. Why did you let him out of the cage?"

"I told you. He urinated everywhere. I couldn't be letting him do that."

"You never told me that," Trey says.

Sverker backhands Pradeep in the mouth. "Don't lie."

Trey loves how Sverker's Swedish accent always gives his commands a comical intonation. The irony is delicious.

"He wouldn't come out of the toilet stall." Pradeep gazes up at Sverker. "You always said to call before using force with him, but you did not answer."

Sverker raises his hand.

Pradeep covers his face. "It is truth."

"Then what happened?" Trey asks.

"Then he came out of the stall and attacked me. I am being so sorry."

"The bathroom was torn up," Sverker says. "The mirror was broken, and there was a toilet seat on the floor."

"We can't let this happen again," Trey says. "Take care of him, Sverker."

Sverker reaches inside his suit jacket.

"No." Pradeep leans away, raising his hands.

Sverker pulls out his cell phone.

"What will you be doing with me?" Pradeep asks.

Trey snaps his fingers to get the guard's attention. "Listen. You no longer work here, and if you violate the confidentiality agreement in your contract, you won't be working anywhere ever again. Ever. Am I clear?"

Pradeep nods.

"Rasmus," Sverker says into his phone. "I'm in the executive conference room on the second floor. I need you to escort someone out of the building."

Trey takes a seat at the conference table and flips his laptop open. "Have you seen the numbers for today?"

"Some," Sverker says.

"Are they good?"

"Some."

Trey opens his internet browser and loads the operations

dashboard. Sixteen graphs fill the screen, and like Sverker said, some trend up, and some trend down. "Get Lessard in here."

Sverker taps on his phone.

Trey clicks the link for the Kandour city statistics. The people of Kandour don't know it, but they're the first step in *Thought*Fluence's thousand-mile journey.

The door opens, and Rasmus slinks into the room.

Sverker checks his watch, then jerks on Pradeep's collar. "Go with him."

Rasmus sneers at Pradeep as he escorts him out of the room and closes the door.

"Come, take a look at this," Trey says.

Sverker steps behind him and looks over his shoulder. "What do you think this means?"

"I don't know," Sverker mumbles. "The penetration significantly declines there. Perhaps because of firewalls? Maybe virus blockers?"

The door to the conference room opens. Jack Lessard, head of data science, walks inside, his gait quick and even. His laptop open. His eyes fixed on the screen. How he doesn't walk into walls all the time Trey has never understood. His short-sleeved, button-down shirts always add color to the office. Today's is crimson with a gray lattice pattern.

He sits next to Trey and adjusts his black-rimmed glasses.

"What's this?" Trey asks, pointing at a chart on his laptop. "See this decline? Is something blocking the message?"

"No," Lessard says. "They simply stopped clicking on it during that time."

"Maybe something kicked in and blocked entry into the poll or hid it from the web pages."

Lessard opens a terminal window and types in a few commands. "The logs don't show any fatal errors on the partner sites." He turns to Trey. "They simply aren't attracted to your message. Furthermore, they're not sharing it with others, or we'd have a much higher organic conversion rate."

Trey closes his laptop. "Where are we at overall with Kandour?"

"Around thirteen percent," Lessard says, "but it has slowed down."

"It's taking too long." Trey stands. "We need a better message."

Sverker nods.

Lessard rises from his seat. He lifts his laptop and keeps his eyes on the screen. "I'll be at my desk if you need me."

Trey waits until Lessard leaves. "How much longer before our guest in 2B cooperates?"

"He's strong," Sverker says. "Pradeep was one of our smarter guards, and the doctor fooled him."

Trey paces, looking down at the floor. "We don't have time. If the beta test in Kandour doesn't succeed soon, the whole thing might unravel."

"I understand. Don't worry, the doctor will break. I'll increase the intensity of my visits."

"Okay, and from now on, I want two guards, watching him *and* each other. That old man's mind games will have a harder time fooling two people at once."

"Understood."

Trey instinctively reaches into his pocket and comes up empty. He has been so busy today, making his rounds through all the departments, he forgot his phone was gone. "Oh, and one other thing, Sverker. I lost my phone. Do you think you could have someone try and locate it for me?"

"We can do a trace. If it's still on, we should be able to find it in no time."

CHAPTER FORTY-ONE

EMMA

I reach out to stop Alyssa, but she escapes my grasp, heading for the front door of her house.

The man in the long gray coat waits on the other side.

"Don't open it," I shout.

"Mommy?" Vivian steps into the hallway behind me. She's in pajamas, her curly brown hair matted to the side of her head like her mother's. Do they always sleep in this late? I tell her to go back inside her bedroom. Having heard the theme to *Mission Impossible* play on her mom's phone, she asks who's here, and I tell her I don't have time to explain.

"Alyssa." I break into a run. "Stop. He—"

I'm too late.

She opens the door.

The man stands on the porch, as large as life, wearing his black, knit cap over his bald head. His pockmarked skin is draped over his cheekbones.

"Can I help you?" Alyssa asks.

"I don't mean to bother you, but I—" He sees me coming. I grabbed one of Alyssa's crime fiction books off a side table as I walked past the living room. I don't know what I plan on doing with it, but it feels good to have it in my hand.

"Back off," I shout. "Get off the porch." I raise the book in the air.

"What are you going to do?" Alyssa laughs. "Throw the book at him? You're not a cop."

The man raises both hands and steps backward.

I keep the book raised and step outside. "Close the door, Alyssa."

She falls in behind me and shuts the door. Her morning breath is raw.

"Don't be afraid," he says.

"You're the one who should be afraid," I say. "Who are you?"

"I told you. My name is Malcolm Schmidt." He reaches inside his coat and pulls out his wallet. "For real. Take a look at my ID."

I keep the book raised with one hand and take the card with the other. The picture resembles him. The ID looks like any other Maryland ID I've ever seen. "Alyssa, what do you think?"

When I hand it to her, I notice Vivian standing in the living room window. She's moved the curtains to the side and watches us with her big brown eyes.

Alyssa scrutinizes the ID. "It looks real to me." She bites it and checks for teeth marks. "I don't think it's fake."

I believe her. She worked in a bar for a long time and checked a lot of IDs. This man isn't exactly like Trey described, but Trey is a liar. The man isn't wearing a concert T-shirt under his coat, and he isn't overweight, but those pockmarks are something he couldn't change. Not without major surgery.

A garage door rumbles open two houses away.

Malcolm glances down the street. "Can we talk inside?"

"No, way," I say.

"Look," Malcolm says, "I understand why you didn't believe me about Trey Wilkes. He's very convincing. But you've got to understand I'm not trying to troll him. Whatever he told you isn't true."

"We know," Alyssa says.

Malcolm tilts his head back. "You do?"

"Yeah, he kidnapped—"

I grab her arm. "Shh."

"I knew it." Malcolm bends his knees slightly. "You've got to help me find him. I've got to stop him."

"Stop him from doing what?" I ask.

Alyssa's neighbor two doors down drags a garbage can overflowing with collapsed Amazon boxes out of his garage. He watches us as he goes.

"It's a long story." Malcolm glances at the neighbor. "Are you sure we can't go inside?"

Alyssa and I glance at the living room window. Vivian hasn't moved.

"No," I say. "Just give us the gist."

"Trey and I worked on a project in college together. It relates to the research you've been doing, but I'm not exactly sure how. I think he's trying to revive the project, and if he does . . ." He shakes his head.

"If he does, what?"

"I'm not sure, but it could be bad. Like, epic bad."

"What is he going to do," Alyssa says, "make a better porn site than Pornhub? How bad could his plans be?"

"It's not like that. It's not a website." He takes his cap off and wipes his forehead. "I'm not exactly sure what it is, but he has the power to hurt everyone. It could be a major virus unlike the world has ever seen."

Alyssa whispers in my ear, "He's pretty dramatic for a nerd."

"Okay," I say. "We need to find him too. He's taken Dr. Santan and locked him up somewhere. Actually, he had someone else take Dr. Santan." I quickly tell Malcolm the other details. The phone call from D'Angelo. The cage. Trey's weirdo phone. "He has help."

The neighbor puts his garbage can on the curb.

"Hi, Mr. Milson." Alyssa waves to him.

He waves back, keeping his eyes on us as he walks up his driveway.

"We can't talk here," Malcolm says. "Listen, Trey came into a lot of money when his father passed away a couple of years ago. He doesn't only have help. He has teams of people working for him. Mostly computer people. We have to find out where they're operating from and stop them."

"We need to find D'Angelo," I say.

"That too." He puts his cap back on.

Mr. Milson stops inside his garage and pulls out a cell phone.

"What's he doing?" Malcolm asks.

"Using his cell phone," Alyssa says. "You do know about cell phones, right?"

Malcolm frowns. Shakes his head. "Do you have any idea where Trey's office is?"

"No," I say. "I don't even know where he lives. We only had one date."

"If we could find him, we could follow him," Alyssa says. "It's sort of bad we have his phone." She turns toward me. "He can't call you. If he could, you could have set up another date, and we could have ambushed him."

"We're not ambushing anybody," I say.

"I mean, we could have followed him."

"I've tried following him," Malcolm says, "but it didn't work. I always stay so far back that I lose him. If he caught me, I'm afraid of what he might do." Malcolm looks up at the sky. "I swear, he bought that golden car just to mock me." The neighbor catches Malcolm's eye. "Trey has the power to listen in on that man's phone call right now." He looks down the street in the other direction. "Let's meet later today and make a plan. Somewhere safer."

"Yes." Alyssa puts her hand on my shoulder. "Let's do this, Emma. Cagney and Lacey and—who do you want to be?"

"What's she talking about?" Malcolm asks.

"Nothing. She just gets excited sometimes."

"Give me your phone number," Alyssa says. "I'll text you so you'll have mine, and we can send each other the coordinates of our first rendezvous point."

I roll my eyes.

"Don't give this number out," Malcolm insists, then rattles off his digits.

CHAPTER FORTY-TWO

EMMA

We chose to meet Malcolm on the north side of town, far away from the university and the Café Royale. Actually, Alyssa chose the place. Whole Foods. She insisted Malcolm enter ten minutes before us, pretend to grocery shop, then sit in one of the booths near the deli.

Alyssa and I went inside, bought two buffalo chicken wraps, and sat in the booth next to his, facing away from him. The earthy scent of raw vegetables mixed with organic bulk foods—nuts and oatmeal—and homemade soap hovered above the checkout stations across the way. My chicken wrap was suffocating in its plastic wrap, but I didn't let it out.

"We're here," Alyssa says.

"I know," Malcolm murmurs.

"What?" she says. "I can't hear you."

I look at her. "This is stupid." I get up and sit across from him at his table.

She follows.

"Do you want anything?" I ask him.

"No." Malcolm folds his hands over the table. His thick

fingers match his bulging shoulders. The booth is small for him. "I don't know what Trey told you, but I'm sure he lied about everything. He's incredibly delusional, so let me set some things straight."

Alyssa leans forward, all ears.

"Okay," I say. "Shoot."

"In college, we formed a computer company together. This was back in the nineties. We wanted to use the internet to make the world a better place. At least, that's what Trey told me. He actually convinced me to quit school to work with him." He winces. "Anyway, it went bust when the dot-coms failed, and so did we. Trey didn't take it well. I returned to school, graduated, moved to California, and started working at Facebook. He just disappeared."

"Wow," Alyssa gasps. "Did you meet Zuckerberg? Is he as creepy as he seems?"

"I—"

"Don't answer that," I say. "Go on."

"Around 2007, Trey showed up outside my office in California. He tried to make me help him with his business again. He'd started a couple of others in the previous years, but they'd failed, so he was back on his original idea. I wanted nothing to do with him, but he kept at me until I agreed to discuss it. We met at a coffee cart by the pier. I think he'd been sleeping under the pier. He insisted the problem with our first business was infrastructure, claiming the internet couldn't support his idea back in the nineties. But now, he'd said, some companies had built giant fiber optic cables beneath the Atlantic, fixing the infrastructure problem. Now, he could spread the word to the entire world. In his words, he could make the world a better place."

"That sounds like crazy talk," Alyssa says. "Culty."

"It was." Malcolm glances around. He eyes the checkout stations. "And he only got crazier. Listen, his businesses didn't fail because of technical infrastructure. They failed because of him. He always blamed technology, like every businessman *ever*." He gazes out the front windows into the parking lot. "I wish I'd never met him."

"Then what did he do?" Alyssa asks.

"I thought I was his last resort at the time. My job at Facebook was awesome, so I turned him down. He tried contacting me several times that week, but I ghosted him. About a month later, he was still calling and leaving notes on my car, so I had to answer. I was going to threaten him with a restraining order, but he was really nice. He told me he was going back to Baltimore to find someone else to help him, that he'd never give up, and when I changed my mind, he'd take me in. It was hard not to laugh at that last part. I wished him the best, and we didn't talk again for several years."

Alyssa rips the plastic off her chicken wrap and shoves the drippy end into her mouth.

"During that time, I wondered how things had gone for him. I hoped he had learned from his failed businesses and found success, but that didn't happen. Instead, he inherited a ton of money when his father died and started pouring it into his business. The one based on our original idea, except . . ."

"Except what?" I ask.

"Except, his approach to changing the world for the better had changed. It went from creating a place where like-minded people could solve the world's problems in online communities to something else. More like a place where he could send messages to the world, his personalized messages, with or without anyone realizing it. He'd told me about someday using subliminal messages back in college, but I never thought he'd actually do it. If he's using them now, I don't know what they are, but I'm sure they're not good."

"Wow," Alyssa says. "That's scary. Why'd he change?"

"Let me backtrack a little. I left Facebook and returned to Baltimore in 2016. Homesick, I guess. One night, I was working out in the gym late, and when I left, these two guys pushed me into an alley. Trey was there. He was a full-on businessman—fancy suit and tie, his hair slicked back. He told me—for like the millionth time in my life—he wanted my help with his project. He said we were thinking too small back in the nineties. With the prototypes his new team of software developers had created, he said he could infiltrate every computer in the world. The work I had done on my web crawler back in college had helped him make progress twenty years later, and he said he had, like, a moral obligation to include me in his new plans, whether I wanted to help or not."

Redness crept up Malcolm's neck.

"What did you do?" I pressed him.

"I'm not a violent person, but I didn't like those guys. I— I decided to leave, and when they tried to stop me, I stopped them." A vacant look entered his eyes. "I got out of there but couldn't stop thinking about it. If what Trey had said was true, he had the power to do something awful to the world."

"You're right," Alyssa says. "It doesn't sound like he was trying to make a better Pornhub."

"What exactly do you think he's trying to do?" I ask.

"I don't know for sure, but I've thought of several scenarios. Imagine if you could control everyone's computer. You could create a virus that secretly funnels tiny amounts of money from everyone's bank accounts into yours, like in *Office Space*. Or, you could hold millions of people's bank accounts hostage, collecting ransoms the way e-commerce sites collect taxes. Or, you could threaten to turn off every computer in the world, which would be, like, just turning off the internet. That would be a nightmare."

Alyssa chews, enthralled with Malcolm's story.

I haven't opened my wrap yet, and I'm not going to.

"Whatever he's thinking," Malcolm continues, "it could be horrible, and because of my past with him, no scenario for me ends well, either. I'll go to jail for sure if he's still using any of my web crawler code. Engineers always get blamed when business people do bad things."

Alyssa finishes eating her wrap. "He's like Dr. Evil. He wants to take over the world for one billion dollars."

"I don't care what he wants. I want my life back," I say. "Whatever he's doing, he needs Dr. Santan, or he wouldn't have kidnapped him. If we can get D'Angelo back, then the police can step in and stop all this nonsense. Right?"

"It wouldn't hurt," Malcolm says. "Either way, we need to find out where Trey operates from. He's probably holding your professor there."

I get Alyssa's attention. "Well, Lacey, what do you think we should do?"

She leans over the table toward Malcolm. "When you were in California, he told you he was going back to Baltimore to get help with his business from someone else, right?"

"Yes."

"Who would he have talked to?"

"I'm not sure." Malcolm rubs his chin.

"Would there still have been people here from his first company?" she asks. "I mean, computer people?"

"No. I was really the only developer he ever had, but—wait. There was this one guy. He never worked at our company, but he did help Trey out before me."

"Who?" I ask.

"Yes, definitely." Malcolm glances up as the memories come to him. "I remember now. Trey said he was going back to get help from this one guy."

"Who?"

"He was this skinny little—I can't remember his name. He wasn't a very good programmer."

"And he went to college at UBalt?"

"Yes. I remember seeing him around campus. He kind of stuck out."

"Emma." Alyssa puts her hand on my wrist. I pull it away and wipe the Buffalo sauce off. "Can you look him up in the school records? He'd be an alumnus, right?"

"I can't find him without a name. Malcolm, are you sure you can't remember it?"

He closes his eyes. "I got nothing."

"Would you know him if you saw him?"

"I think so. If he hasn't changed too much."

Alyssa stands, puts her hands on her hips, and speaks with a deep, commanding voice. "All right, men. It's a long shot, but we've got to find this guy." The customers at the checkout stations look in our direction. "If he's still working with our perp, he can lead us to him. We've got to find him, find out what he knows, and take the bastard down."

Some of the checkers turn to see who is talking so loud.

I grab Alyssa's wrist, my face feeling flush. "Sit down."

She ignores me.

"Emma. You locate every photo of every computer major from UBalt during the late nineties, show them to Malcolm, and let's go get this guy." She waves her hand like she's shooing a black fly away from a glass of chardonnay. "You've got your orders, men. Now, be careful out there."

CHAPTER FORTY-THREE

TREY

The door leading to the "interrogation" room has no handle. The door's border is obvious, and people can see it clearly on their way to the second-floor stairs. It resembles the entrance to an ordinary maintenance room with nothing but a security scanner on the outside. One would assume the room contains electrical panels, and it does indeed. The room houses eight, floor-to-ceiling panels, concealing its true purpose.

One of the panels leads to the interrogation room. The one labeled "2B."

Trey had wanted to completely conceal the outer door. No outline or cracks or security keypad. But Sverker talked him out of it. Sverker said it was better to hide the door in plain sight, disguising it as a maintenance room, and he was right. People would notice a flaw in the paint of a completely concealed door and raise suspicions. They'd never suspect a simple maintenance room.

Trey glances at Sverker as they approach the door. He's proud of himself for hiring Sverker years ago. That trip to Sweden will live fondly in his memory forever, and it has paid back tenfold. Disguising the door rather than concealing it . . . Sverker is the best.

"Have your men located my cell phone yet?" Trey asks.

"No, but we'll keep trying. It appears to have been shut off."

"The battery probably went dead."

"It's okay. We pulled data from the cell towers close by. The last time your phone was near was yesterday morning." Sverker glances up and down the hall, then waves his badge over the card scanner to the interrogation room.

"So, I could have lost it anywhere I went yesterday."

The maintenance room door pops open.

"That's correct."

They enter, and Sverker pulls the door closed. This part always reminds Trey of *The Lion, the Witch, and the Wardrobe.* They open the third panel on the right and step inside it like an entryway into a magical world. The false backing opens when they close the panel door, and a narrow hall leads them to the interrogation room.

Dr. Santan's eyes lock on Trey the moment Sverker switches the light on. The doctor sits on the floor in the far corner of a black metal cage. He sits next to an aging pee stain. He sits with his hands peacefully folded across his lap, his legs slightly bent at the knee. He sits motionless. His back is straight, and the look on his face is creepy. Trey hates it. Creepier now, even, with that gash across his forehead and the cuts along his jawline. His trim white beard is mangled like a used S.O.S. pad.

The man disgusts Trey.

The room smells like an overflowing toilet. Pungent urine and bitter feces.

Next to the cage, Sverker's tools are arranged upon a

black card table, just beyond Dr. Santan's reach through the cage bars. A bucket of water rests on the floor next to a microwave stand, and a collection of liquid cleansers and towels line the wall. The microwave is plugged in. Sverker is always prepared. He motions toward the exit, and two guards dressed in gray jumpsuits nod at him on their way out.

"I'm so glad you've returned," Dr. Santan says, his pupils shrinking in the light. "Tell me. How is Pradeep doing? How is his headache?"

"You'd better get used to peeing in there," Trey says. "Pradeep won't be coming back."

"That pleases me. We didn't get along, him and I."

"The message efficacy you've given us is not what we'd hoped for. We need more."

"You mean more hooks?"

"What? No. Messages."

"Call them what they are. They're hooks. You're trying to catch people like fish, but to what end? What do you want from them?"

"They're just *messages*. And all I want from them is to make the world a better place."

"How so? What do you want them to do, exactly? If I don't know, I can't give you the best hooks."

Trey glances at Sverker.

Sverker shakes his head. "You might as well tell him. It's not going to matter when I'm finished with him."

"Listen carefully, Doctor. Your research found people resisted being persuaded to commit acts of destruction, especially if it involved physically hurting each other. But, it also found that it wasn't impossible. I don't want them to hurt each other. I just want them to destroy the internet. That's all."

"You're mad."

"No. They are."

"I already gave your friend there every technique I had during his last visit." He gently touches the cut on his forehead. "He seemed pleased with himself when we were finished."

"We got a lot of clicks," Trey says, "but that's where it ended. We tested your messages—"

"Hooks." Dr. Santan grins.

"Whatever," Trey says. "Hooks. Fine, let's call them hooks. We beta tested 'the hooks' on a few users, and that's where it ended. No one did what we wanted after that. We need better messages—hooks—that will go beyond first sight and naturally pass from person to person. We need the hooks to be viral."

"You want to use word-of-mouth to recruit your terrorists."

"Exactly." Trey reaches into his pocket and comes up empty-handed. He forgot about losing his cell phone again. "Dammit. Sverker, give me your phone."

Sverker unlocks his phone and hands it over.

"Do you have a recording app on here?" Trey asks. "Never mind, I found it." He taps the *start recording* button. "Speak loudly, and give me something that will spread. Also, explain the structure of the phrases so I can have them replicated."

"I can't help you unless you help me. How are you distributing the message? Does everyone receive the message simultaneously, the way a congregation would listen to a priest, or do they receive it sporadically?"

"Sporadically, and that's all I'm telling you."

Dr. Santan squints at him. "Why is this so important to

you? Did the internet hurt you somehow?"

Trey grips the cage. "Sverker. I believe it's time for you to give the good doctor another session."

Sverker opens the cabinet below the microwave and retrieves a measuring cup. He uses it to measure and pour cleansers into a pitcher.

Dr. Santan glances at Sverker's pitcher, then returns his stare to Trey. "I could use a shower."

"Don't worry. We'll give you one if you don't cooperate, but you won't like it."

Sverker spills some bleach on the floor and wipes it with a towel.

"Again," Dr. Santan says, "what did the internet ever do to you? Be honest, and I'll help you."

"Shut up about the internet." Trey closes his eyes. "I'm going to make the world a better place." His throat constricts again, and he looks up at the ceiling to relieve the tension. "To do that, I need the world to listen."

"It hurts when they don't listen, doesn't it? Just like your dad never listened."

"Shut up. You don't know him." The cage's metal wires dig into Trey's fingers, but he squeezes anyway. He meets Dr. Santan's gaze. "My dad didn't listen because he lacked vision."

"It hurts, doesn't it?"

"Not anymore. Not since he died."

Sverker puts the pitcher in the microwave, sets the timer, and presses the start button.

The light comes on, the machine hums, and the pitcher spins slowly.

"Do you think if you can convince the world to listen to you," Dr. Santan says, "your father will finally hear you? Do you think he will finally be proud of you?"

"Give me some persuasive rhetoric." Trey shakes the cage. "Hooks. Do it. Do it, now."

"Do you think he will love you from heaven?"

"Heaven doesn't exist. Besides, I sent him to Hell."

Dr. Santan stands abruptly and crosses the floor as if gliding on ice. He comes face-to-face with Trey, the cage wires keeping their noses from touching. "Today, you let me into the world, and I made it a better place. Your father loves you now."

The microwave beeps. Sverker opens the door, pulls the pitcher out, and sets it on the card table.

Dr. Santan shouts, "Today, you let me into the world, and I made it a better place. Your father loves you now." Spittle from the doctor's lips hits Trey in the face. He closes his eyes and backs away from the cage. "Today, you let me into the world, and I made it a better place. Your father loves you now."

"Sverker." Trey's throat tightens. He struggles to get the words out. "Unlock the cage."

"Yes, sir." Sverker pulls out his gun and aims it at Dr. Santan's head. "On your knees."

"Today, you let me into the world, and I made it a better place." Dr. Santan lowers himself to the floor and raises his hands. He doesn't take his eyes off Trey. "Your father loves you now."

Trey puts his hands over his ears. "Open the door. Let him go."

"What?" Sverker asks.

"No. Wait." Trey closes his eyes and shakes his head. "Give me that." He takes the gun from Sverker. Points it at Dr. Santan's head. "Sverker. Open the door."

Sverker unlocks the cage, and the door swings open. It

creaks. He picks up the pitcher. "Shall I?"

"Today, you let me into the world—"

"Shut up," Trey yells. He struggles to hold the gun steady.

Dr. Santan stares at Trey in silence, his eyes unblinking. Trey nods in Sverker's direction.

Dr. Santan can't hide the pain when the burning hot chemicals hit his scalp and run over his face. He screams. Red welts rise like bubbling lava. He chokes, gasps, wipes his cheeks repeatedly, then tries to shake the chemicals off his reddening hands.

"Do you want that shower now?" Trey asks.

Sverker puts the pitcher down and picks up the water bucket.

"It sure would feel good, wouldn't it?" Trey steps forward, keeping the gun pointed at the doctor's head. "Give me a message for the masses. One that will spread. One that will make them listen to me."

"You mean"—Dr. Santan gasps and falls forward. Places his hands on the floor—"a hook." He chokes. "A fishhook."

"Sverker. Put the bucket down. He wants more of what's in the pitcher."

"No," Dr. Santan screams. "I'll help you. I'll give you all the messages you want."

"They have to be good this time. They have to work."

"For the love of God, they will. They will work."

CHAPTER FORTY-FOUR

EMMA

"I thought I could do this, but I don't want to be here," Malcolm says. "I'm going back to the car."

"But, I need your help asking questions." I try to see what he sees, looking down the long hall of the UBalt computer science department. It's between classes, so students hustle their way past each other, leaving little space to breathe.

"I don't like crowded places." Malcolm turns around and heads out of the building.

I'll have to do this myself. There's more to Malcolm's departure than simple enochlophobia. He started acting funny the moment we stepped foot on campus.

After hours of searching for photos of computer science majors online and on UBalt's internal systems, Malcolm still couldn't recognize the person he'd replaced on Trey's project back in the nineties. Instead, he did his best to describe the student, and Alyssa pretended to be a forensic sketch artist. The drawing in my hand isn't more than a short stick figure with a long beard. It resembles a malnourished dwarf with fumes coming off its shoulders. Malcolm said the apartment they shared stunk because the dwarf never showered. That part, Malcolm remembered clearly.

I duck in and out of the classrooms, looking for professors who might have been at the university for a long time. The first three are all too young, but the woman in the fourth room fits the bill. I recognize her from the alumni records. "Excuse me. Do you recognize this person? He would have gone to school here in 1998 or '99."

She takes a look at the drawing and almost laughs. I don't blame her. Alyssa has never taken an art class in her life.

"No, I don't think so."

"Are you sure? Were you here then?"

"Yes, I graduated in 2001, but that drawing . . ." She cracks a smile.

Students file into the room, chatting noisily.

"He was a computer science major here," I say. "I'm not sure if he ever graduated, but he was only about five foot, two inches tall, super skinny, and had an odor problem."

She gazes harder at the drawing. "That looks like—no, it can't be." Her eyes spark with recognition. "If you take the beard away . . . wait. This looks more like him now than back then, if it's him at all."

"Who?"

"How tall did you say he was?"

"Not tall. Under five foot three, I believe."

"The only man that short that I ever knew in the C.S. department was Dr. Atkinson. He got his undergraduate degree here around the same time as I did, so this could be him."

"Where is he now?"

She tips her head back and to the side. "Is he in some kind of trouble?"

"No, I'm trying to reunite him with an old classmate. They lost touch years ago."

"Everyone lost touch with Kevin. He was a professor here one day, and the next, he was gone." She diverts her attention to the class. "Everyone. Could you quiet down? We'll get started in a minute."

"Why did he leave?"

She leans in closer. "He snapped. It's only a rumor, but I remember hearing that he went screaming out of his office one day. Something about how the Devil had returned to make the world a better place. It didn't make any sense, but neither did he." She put her hand on my shoulder. "If he's a family member of yours, I'm sorry. He went completely insane."

I step back. "It's okay. He's not a family member. Do you know where he went?"

"The last time I saw him, he looked like your drawing. Sketchy. He was downtown near Market Place, selling stuff on the street. He ran when he saw me." She straightens her back. "Now, if you'll kindly leave, I have a class to teach."

I call Alyssa on my way to the car and tell her to meet Malcolm and me at Lombard and Market downtown.

She does.

One after another, she rushes up to strangers on the street and shows them her drawing. One after another, they shake their heads. We walk the distance, heading several blocks away from the harbor, then traveling back, winding our way through the streets. No luck. We zig. We zag. Alyssa becomes anxious. Desperate to help us, she left Vivian with her neighbor, but now she's desperate to go back. She has almost never left Vivian with a babysitter before.

Malcolm doesn't want to stop searching for Kevin, and

neither do I.

"I promised to pick her up before five o'clock," Alyssa says.

"It's close to that now," I say.

"Wait." Malcolm points toward the pier. A man—a very short man—carefully unfurls a blanket on the ground. Various odd things tumble out of the blanket. Picture frames and ceramics. He sits and arranges them. "That's him."

Alyssa pulls out her cell phone and takes a picture.

"Why'd you do that?"

"I don't know. It just seemed like we should get a good picture of him."

Malcolm marches toward the man.

"Wait," I say. "Are you sure it's him?"

He doesn't hear me.

The man resembles Alyssa's drawing, which is not only a great insult, but a testament to his rough life. He's a homeless street vendor selling random wares. His beard has fuzzy clumps, and he appears emaciated.

Alyssa and I catch up with Malcolm.

"Do you remember me?" Malcolm asks.

The man stops arranging his inventory and looks up at us.

"Are you Kevin Atkinson?" I ask.

"I'm known by many names." His ethereal eyes look like he knows a secret about the universe. He scoots his items into the center of the blanket.

"Is Kevin one of them?" I ask.

He doesn't answer.

"You remember me, right?" Malcolm says. "From college?"

The man folds the blanket's corners over his art pieces and picks everything up. He stands. He stares at Malcolm. He knows him. I can see it.

"Please," I say. "We need your help."

"The Hawk and the Devil." The man's head twitches. His eyes dart around like he just woke up in a strange land. "Where is he? Where's the Devil?"

"That's right." Malcolm holds out his hand. "They used to call me The Hawk."

"The Devil is back." The man turns away. "He's back. He's coming after me." He runs.

"Wait," Alyssa calls out.

Malcolm takes off after him.

"Kevin, freeze." Alyssa puts her hands together, forming a pretend gun. "Don't make us have to hurt you."

"What are you doing?" I grasp her arm. "Why'd you say that?"

"It's what detectives on TV always say when someone runs. I thought it might work to stop him." Kevin and Malcolm vanish around a corner. She lowers her arms. "I guess not."

CHAPTER FORTY-FIVE

EMMA

Flanked by looming brick walls, Alyssa and I find Malcolm standing in an alley near a basement window. He's holding a broken loading pallet with the words KEEP OUT painted in red. The window has no glass. It's a concrete opening into the bowels of a mid-century apartment building.

Malcolm sees us coming and puts the pallet down. "He went in there. He was using this to cover the hole."

We stop, and I peer into the opening. It's pitch black inside.

"Why didn't you go after him?" Alyssa asks.

Malcolm takes a step back. "I don't like closed-in spaces."

"Kevin?" I yell.

Nothing.

"Come out," Alyssa says. "We won't hurt you. We just want to talk."

"You sound like a cop," I say. "Stop it, or you'll scare him more."

"He's not coming out," Malcolm says. "He remembered me."

"What was that Devil stuff about?" Alyssa asks.

"I'm not sure, but I know I'm not the Devil. I'm the Hawk. It was my nickname in college. He thinks I know the Devil."

"Kevin," I call into the dark. "Can we come in?"

Still nothing.

"What are we going to do?" Alyssa asks.

"If you can hear me, Kevin, we're on your side." I get an idea. "We're trying to find the Devil so we can stop him. We need your help."

Something shuffles inside. Now I know he's in there. Or . . . *someone* is in there.

"You were right," Alyssa says. "The Devil is coming for you. We're the only ones who can help you now."

"Stop it." I lean forward and listen. The shuffling noises stop. "Let's not wait. We should go inside."

Malcolm raises his hands in protest. "No way."

"Why not?"

"Uh, I'll never fit."

"Yes, you will."

Kevin's decrepit voice reverberates through the concrete opening. "And he became Satan, yea, even the Devil, the father of all lies, to deceive and to blind men, and to lead them captive at his will. The Hawk works for the Devil. Go away."

"Kevin," I say, "the Devil's not here, and the Hawk wants to stop the Devil. We're all here to stop the Devil. Can you hear me?" I wait for him to respond, but he doesn't. "We're here to stop Trey."

"Trey," he moans. "Trey. It *was* Trey."

"We're coming in, Kevin. It's going to be all right." I turn around. "Malcolm, you first."

"No."

"What did you say will happen if we don't stop Trey? A virus unlike the world has ever seen?"

Malcolm turns away. His neck burns red. "Fine. You're right. But it had better not be cramped in there."

"You'll be all right."

His broad shoulders catch on the concrete and tear at his overcoat's gray fibers as he disappears into the hole.

I go next. The concrete is cold to the touch, and I bang my knee as I drop inside. Malcolm stands in a narrow passage lit by a dim light at the far end.

Alyssa drops inside, stands, and brushes her slacks off. "Hm. This reminds me of a blind date I once had, but nicer."

"Can we go?" Malcolm asks.

The passage opens into a room lit by desk lamps situated haphazardly throughout. Wires run everywhere. Some lamps are on the floor, others on cardboard boxes. My eye is drawn to a computer monitor on a makeshift desk. More wires—wires of all kinds—run from the desk, across the floor, and into the wall. In the center of the room, an abandoned chess game sits centered on a woven Indian blanket. White padding sticks out of a brown couch along the wall. Kevin's bed, no doubt. The boxes overflow with junk. More wires. Ceramic figurines. Old magazines and newspapers.

"Kevin," I say, "it's okay."

He steps out of a shadow. "Trey is the Devil."

"We know."

"How?" he asks. "How do you know?"

"He deceived us. Mostly me."

"Me, too," Malcolm adds.

"The Devil is the great deceiver," I say, "and so is Trey Wilkes."

Kevin's got to believe we're on his side. He's just got to.

We've got nowhere to go without his help.

He points at Malcolm. "You're the Hawk. You deceived me. You ruined my life."

"It was Trey. I didn't know you were living with him. I didn't know he would kick you out if I fixed the code."

"The code," Kevin yells. "You fixed it, but Trey—he wanted more." Kevin covers his ears. Begins pacing.

"I stopped working with him." Malcolm holds his hands out. "Please, believe me. He lied to me too. He tried to ruin my life, too. He *is* the Devil."

"He came back to me." Kevin stops pacing near the computer. "You fixed the code, but he wanted more. My life—it was good. I was a professor, but Trey—he wanted me to make the code handle more. Why? Oh, why did I do it?"

"It's not your fault," I assure him. "Trey is a master manipulator." I take a step toward him. He smells like burnt sugar. "What did he make you do?"

"I used the university's computer network to test a new version of the application. It was a virus. I know that now. Now. Now. Now—the code." His eyes flare. "I fixed your code, Hawk. Or—I made it bigger. Better."

"That's not good," Malcolm says.

"I know. They fired me, and once he got his hands on it, Trey disappeared. Like Keyser Soze, poof. He was gone."

"When was that?" Alyssa asks.

"A long time ago. Years."

"When was the last time you saw him, exactly?" I ask.

"Last night when I slept. I see him all the time. I resisted him the first time, the first time after graduation. It was, it had to be 2007, then again in—was it 2012? Yes, December 2012. The end of the Mayan calendar. Nothing happened. Nothing happened on New Year's Eve in 1999, either. Both times, the world was supposed to end, but it didn't."

"Calm down," I say. "We need to find Trey so we can stop him."

I take another step forward and almost fall, tripping over a cable. He's a hoarder. Aside from a mound of clothes in one corner, everything is in boxes. It looks like he's been collecting junk for years. Mostly computer equipment, but he has old paint cans and two car tires stacked in another corner.

Alyssa notices my fascination with Kevin's collection. "Show him the phone, Emma. Maybe he's seen something like it before."

I pull Trey's weirdo phone out of my pocket. "Here. We stole the Devil's phone." I carefully hand it over. "It's dead."

Kevin looks at the back of the phone. The screen. The bottom. "I can charge it." He slides a box away from the wall and rifles through the contents.

"Charge it, sure," Malcolm says, "but don't turn it on. He'll be able to trace us if you do. We don't want that."

"What good is it if we can't turn it on?" Alyssa asks.

"We'll turn it on when we want to lure him out. We'll do it somewhere safe later."

"That's a good plan," I say. "We can trap him."

Kevin sticks one end of a wire in the phone and the other in a power strip. "I want to help. I want to trap the Devil." He holds the back of his hand up. The ethereal, crazy look in his eyes dissipates. Fades away for a moment. "The Devil gave me this. It was the only way I could escape his mind games." A horrific scar with three prongs stretches over the back of his hand, rising from his wrist and dying at the base of his fingers. It's purple, pink, and greenish-blue, like a chemical burn. "We can't let him use the code. He almost destroyed the university with it. He says he wants to make the world a better place, but now . . ."

"Now, what?" I ask.

"Now, he wants to destroy it."

"I hope we're not too late," Alyssa says. "But . . . look, I get that he's a madman. A Devil, or whatever. But how could a computer virus destroy the world? Browser pop-ups are super annoying, but they're not the end of the world."

"I don't know if it's possible for him to take control of every computer," Malcolm says, "but with the way the code can crawl across the internet, he has a chance. If he can take control, he could shut every computer off. It would be like what we thought would happen on the eve of Y2K."

"Or the end of the Mayan calendar," Kevin adds.

Malcolm disregards his comment. "If Trey can control the right computers, he might be able to shut off the world's major power stations. I just don't know."

"And so it was," Kevin says under his breath, "cast out from the light of heaven, the Devil sought his revenge by casting the world into darkness."

"I had no idea computer geeks were so dramatic," Alyssa says. "A virus unlike anything the world has ever seen. Casting the world into darkness. Oh, man."

"Darkness," Kevin yells. "Darkness. Doug. I've got to warn my dog, Doug." He presses the button on the side of Trey's phone.

Malcolm lunges forward and rips the phone out of Kevin's hand.

The screen comes on. It glows.

"Kevin," I say. "What have you done?"

"I'll tell you what he's done." Malcolm faces the phone toward us. All four data connection bars light up. "He's doomed us all."

CHAPTER FORTY-SIX

TREY

Trey uses his remote control to switch off the floor-to-ceiling wall monitor, then he turns his attention to Sverker, seated on the other side of his massive desk. Trey slides his finger over the black marble top. He leans forward in his seat, and his knee brushes up against the mahogany drawers. He rests his elbows on the spotless surface. His office is an inspiration. Strip lights race across the ceiling, giving off a gentle blue glow not to be outdone by the light shimmering around the saltwater fish tank behind Sverker.

And then there's Sverker. The miracle man.

"Your chemical dousing was effective on the doctor," Trey says. "Why'd you wait so long to use it?"

"It's messy."

Trey smiles. "But it works."

"It wears off. If I use it too many times, they stop cooperating. They give up on life and refuse to talk."

"You're right." Trey leans back. "I've seen that happen. What will you do next?"

"Didn't you see the latest email from Lessard? We might

not need anything else from the doctor."

Trey flicks the wall monitor back on, destroying the peaceful blue ambiance of the room. He navigates to his email and reads the latest from Lessard. "This is great." He stands. "It's wonderful. They're reacting to the message."

"Yes," Sverker says. "It's spreading on its own."

"We're approaching twenty-percent conversion in Kandour, according to this." Trey eyes Sverker. "Have they . . . you know?"

"It's difficult to tell if it's related, but there has been an increase in news stories coming out of that region. Vandalism. Looting. I'm concerned we might attract unwanted attention from our test."

Trey thinks back to the beginning of this phase of the project. When the team targeted Kandour, Lessard brilliantly took a baseline measuring the number of daily Kandour news stories published locally versus the number with international exposure. Having fewer than ten thousand residents, the rural Indian village had almost zero mention in the world. Trey hadn't wanted to take the time to set up the news monitoring, but now he's glad he did. It's a great metric. "Do you think we should back off?"

"Maybe. Some of the news reports are troubling. There have been injuries, but again, it's hard to tell if it's related to us. More research is needed."

"Okay. We'll let it run for now."

The room buzzes, and the wall monitor shows Rasmus standing in the hallway, waiting to be let in. Trey has an open-door policy for all his employees, but only when he chooses to open the door. Rasmus presses the buzzer again. Sverker's right-hand man is holding a tablet, which is odd because he's not exactly computer savvy. He's a slimy beast. "What do you think he wants?"

"Let him in," Sverker says. "It must be important."

Trey uses his remote to unlock the door.

Rasmus slithers into the room and places the tablet in front of Trey. "They found your phone. It's the red thingy."

The tablet screen shows a map with a red indicator pointing at a building in downtown Baltimore. "I know this area," Trey says. "Hold on." He switches to his laptop and navigates to a folder titled *Keep Your Enemies Close*.

He opens a document, and it displays on the wall monitor. "The address matches, see?"

"I see," Sverker says.

Rasmus stares at the screen. His wormy lips grin like he's a good dog, and he is. He brought his master a bone.

"It's the last known location I have for Kevin Atkinson," Trey says, "but it doesn't make any sense."

Now, Sverker grins. "It's been a while, but if I remember right, the chemical dousing was effective on him as well."

"I haven't been anywhere near that place since losing my phone." Trey stands. Rubs his chin and paces. "How could he have it? This is too much of a coincidence."

"Do you want Rasmus to retrieve it?" Sverker asks.

"No." He scratches his chin. "Maybe. Kevin is harmless, or he *was* harmless. Completely insane, but harmless."

"He thought you were the Devil," Sverker says.

"No, he thought you were the Devil."

Rasmus laughs. "The Devil. That's funny. Let me go get your phone. I'll show him the Devil."

"I have a really bad feeling about this," Trey says. "I take it there hasn't been word on Malcolm Schmidt's location, since you haven't reported any to me, right?"

"That's right. We haven't detected him anywhere in

weeks. Do you think there's a connection?"

"Probably not. I don't know. They barely knew each other in college, and it was so long ago. I can't imagine how they'd find each other now."

"It could still be a coincidence." Sverker stands. "It might not be Kevin. Someone else could have lifted your cell phone and taken it to that building. You have plenty of files in your enemies folder."

"We can't take any chances. Whether it's Kevin or not, I'll have to talk to him to find out. If he's got nothing to do with it, I guess I'll start knocking on doors." He opens a drawer and pulls out a pistol.

"I want to talk to him, too," Rasmus says. "I want to meet him. He sounds like fun. The Devil—ha."

"Take Rasmus with you," Sverker says. He puts his hand on Rasmus's shoulder. "You might need backup."

"No offense," Trey says, "but your rabid dog can stay here. I just want my phone back. I'm not afraid of Kevin." The last thing he wants is to share a ride across town with Rasmus. The man has a one-track mind and reeks of fish. Trey doesn't know what Sverker sees in him other than a cold-blooded killer who enjoys his work. "I'll be all right."

"Rabid dog," Rasmus says under his breath. "I like that."

Sverker cracks his knuckles. "My job is to protect you. If you go it alone, I'll have Rasmus follow you, so you might as well save some gas and take him with you."

"Fine. I guess it isn't that far. It should only take a few minutes to get there, anyway." Trey stows his gun behind his back and picks up the tablet. "But he does what I tell him when I tell him. Got it?"

"Yes, of course," Sverker says.

Rasmus rubs his hands together. "With pleasure."

CHAPTER FORTY-SEVEN

EMMA

As fast as I can, I rip Trey's weirdo phone from Malcolm's hand and hold the power button down until the screen goes black.

Kevin runs to his desk. "I'm sorry. I'm sorry, but—"

"Who's Doug?" Alyssa asks.

Kevin's entire body twitches. He turns his computer on. "He was my dog growing up. I don't know why I turned on the phone." He sniffs.

I turn toward Malcolm. "Do you think the phone was on long enough for Trey to trace us?"

"I don't know," Malcolm says. "It's definitely possible. We should go."

Kevin sits down and types on his keyboard.

"This is great," Alyssa says. "We don't need to find a safer place to trap Trey. Look at all this stuff in Kevin's apartment." She opens a box marked VIDEO. "Do any of these cameras work? If Trey comes here, we can record him, then hand it over to the police. We just need to trick him into talking about Dr. Santan."

"No," Kevin says. "No, no, no."

"They don't work?" Alyssa holds up an old camcorder.

Kevin turns around. "No. They work. Some do, but the Devil—he might be on his way."

"I don't think we should stay here," Malcolm says.

"Alyssa's right," I say. "There are plenty of places to hide in here." I point at a pile of boxes. "Kevin, could you handle talking to Trey if he came? We'll protect you."

Kevin taps the keyboard, and the computer monitor shows a grainy gray image. It's a fishbowl view of a stoop and a street.

The three of us gather around him.

"Is that outside here?" Alyssa asks.

Kevin taps the keyboard again, and the image changes to an alley.

Malcolm points at the screen. "There's the KEEP OUT pallet. That's the way we came in. And there's the opening."

Kevin taps the keyboard once more, and the screen displays a stairwell leading up to a lobby.

"We need to stay here," Alyssa says. "This is the perfect place to trap him. We can see him coming."

"Kevin, are you okay with this?" I put my hand on his shoulder, and he shrinks away.

"Yes." He taps the keyboard again, and the view returns to the street. He lowers his head. "It's too late to run. The Devil will track us down if we try."

"Do you think you could talk to Trey? Get him to say he kidnapped someone?" I quickly explain D'Angelo's disappearance. Kevin doesn't lift his head. When I finish, I assume he listened to me, but I'm not sure. In the meantime, Alyssa has plugged one of the camcorders into a power strip and found a place to hide it between the boxes.

"Look," Malcolm says. "He's here."

Trey's golden Acura appears on the computer screen and parks across the street.

Kevin lifts his head. "No."

"He's not alone," Malcolm says.

Trey and a sinuous man wearing a tight black turtleneck and black slacks cross the street.

Kevin stands and runs toward the far side of the room, tripping over the chess set. The black and white pieces fly.

As Trey approaches the stoop, the sinuous man pulls out a gun, holds it to his chest, and glances back toward the street.

My heart sinks.

Kevin picks up a galvanized plumbing pipe with his free hand and pulls wires out of the walls with the other.

"What are you doing?" Alyssa screeches.

One by one, the desk lamps go dark until the entire apartment is black. Pitch black.

I attempt to feel my way to the front door, but someone hits me from behind, and I fall.

The door opens, light floods in, and Kevin runs down the concrete corridor, pipe in hand. I yell for him to stop, but he doesn't. Malcolm helps me to my feet, and we rush after him. "Kevin, wait."

He reaches the end of the hallway, turns left, and looks up. "Hurry, they're not here yet. We can still take the stairs."

Malcolm and I come to a stop mid-hall, and Alyssa barrels into us from behind. I stumble forward and fall. When I look up, a gunshot rings out, and blood springs from Kevin's back. He goes down. His pipe bounces off the concrete and almost hits me in the head.

I scramble backward, and again, Malcolm picks me up.

"I got him," yells someone with a thick Swedish accent.

It's a cheerful-sounding accent until I see the blood pooling around Kevin, and reality takes me by the throat. I try, but I can't scream.

"Rasmus, you bastard." It's Trey. He must be around the corner at the top of the stairs with the sinuous man. "I told you to wait."

Malcolm charges forward. Picks up the pipe mid-stride.

Alyssa yells for him to stop.

He peers around the corner. A gun goes off, and he jerks back. Then, he rounds the corner and disappears up the stairs.

"Stop," I shout.

Yelling comes from the stairs.

Wailing. Grunting.

The sound of flesh pounding.

The pipe bounces down the steps and comes to rest on Kevin's blood-soaked chest.

Alyssa wraps her arms around me from behind.

"Let go," I tell her.

The gun goes off again, and a door slams.

I break free from her and run to Kevin.

The sinuous man slides down the stairs like a bag of laundry. I step aside to keep from getting hit by his body. He has a cut on his head, a gun in his hand, and his eyes are closed. Blood gushes from his hip. He must have shot himself in the scuffle with Malcolm.

Alyssa runs to me.

There's no one at the top of the stairs. Malcolm is gone.

We kneel. The man is still breathing, but Kevin isn't. I brush his bloodied beard aside and see the bullet hole. It hit him in the heart. His ethereal eyes stare blankly at the ceiling, and I consider closing them, but there's no time. Malcolm needs my help.

I pry the gun from the sinuous man's hand, sprint up the stairs, and burst through the door into the lobby in time to see Trey land a punch. Malcolm's head rocks back. He stumbles. Trey points a gun at Malcolm. "Don't move."

The lobby is empty. There's no one here to help us. Outside, on the other side of the revolving doors, a car passes by, oblivious to the carnage in here.

Malcolm glances at me.

I take aim at Trey.

"Shoot him," Malcolm shouts.

I've never shot a gun before. My hands tremble. This can't be happening.

"Shoot him." Blood trickles out of Malcolm's nose.

Trey steps forward and presses the muzzle against Malcolm's chest. Then, he eyes me.

Alyssa appears at the top of the stairs and lets out a hair-raising scream.

Malcolm slaps the gun out of Trey's hand. It flies behind Trey, coming to rest at the base of the revolving doors.

Malcolm runs to Alyssa and me.

Trey runs to the doors. To the gun.

"Shoot him," Malcolm says. "Do it, now!"

I can't.

Trey bends over to pick the gun up.

I flex my trigger finger, but I can't do it. I can't shoot him in the back.

He turns around and takes aim at me. "I get it now. I must have left my phone at your place last night."

"Don't move," I say. I can't keep my voice from shaking. "Put the gun down."

"Where'd you get your gun, Emma?" Trey glances at the door to the stairs. "Did you take it from my friend?"

"Don't answer him," Alyssa says.

"You know, that's not a real gun." Trey speaks smoothly. "It's a toy. My friend was on his way to his nephew's birthday party. That gun was the birthday present."

"Don't listen to him," Malcolm says. "He's gaslighting you."

Trey puts on his amazing smile. The one I fell in love with when I first saw him at the awards banquet. "It's not a real gun, Emma. It's a toy."

"It *is* a real gun," I shout. "It's heavy."

Trey steps backward. "No, it's a *realistic* gun, but it's not a real gun. It's a toy."

"Shoot him," Malcolm shouts. "If you don't, he'll destroy the world."

"It's not a real gun, Emma. It's a toy." Trey presses his back against the revolving door. "It's not a real gun. It's a toy."

The door begins to revolve.

Police sirens sing in the distance.

Trey slips out of the building and races across the street to his car.

We chase after him.

He gets inside and cranks the engine.

People stop to watch him, then they look at us.

The Acura's starter whines, but the engine doesn't start. Trey watches us as he slides across to the passenger side and opens the door.

A car goes by, momentarily blocking my view.

When it's gone, so is Trey. He must have run around the corner.

I examine the gun.

It *is* a real gun.

It's not a toy.

CHAPTER FORTY-EIGHT

EMMA

The parking garage ramp leading up to Malcolm's forest green Ford Explorer taxes my knees. I was already out of breath from almost taking Trey's life, and now painful pinpricks sting my kneecaps from the inside. I'm not used to running uphill.

I'm not used to any of this.

I carry the gun I took off Trey's Swedish goon like a criminal. That's how it feels. The garage's darkness and solitude are both ominous and comforting.

Malcolm reaches the car first and jumps inside. He motions from the driver's seat for me to hurry.

"Front seat dibs," Alyssa calls out.

I check over my shoulder. No one is coming after us. No goons. No police.

She takes the front seat, and I open the back door on Malcolm's side. He's left a shoe box and a pile of mail on the seat. I shove everything over and hop in.

"Are you okay, Malcolm?" I ask.

He starts the engine. "I'm fine. He didn't hurt me. I just got a bloody nose, is all."

We cruise down the ramp and around the corner. Then again, down and around. And again. He pays the fee, and we're out.

"Where are we going?" Alyssa asks. "I need to get back to Vivian."

"I can't take you back there," he says.

"I have to."

"It won't be safe for you at your house."

"Take me to my car." She raises her voice.

"Trey might send someone to come for you." Malcolm takes the next right turn at a red light, barely slowing down. A police cruiser appears in the oncoming lane. He hits the brakes. "Or, the police."

Alyssa pulls her phone out. "Then I've got to call the babysitter."

The police cruiser passes, and Malcolm jerks the phone out of her hand.

"Hey," she says.

He shuts her phone off. "Emma?"

"Yes."

"If your phone is on, turn it off now."

"Okay."

"You're scaring me," Alyssa says. "What am I going to do?"

I realize I'm practically cradling the gun. I toss it beside Malcolm's mail on the seat. An insurance advertisement, an electric bill—a reminder to get his oil changed.

Alyssa turns in her seat to face me. "Emma, what are we going to do?"

Words don't come. I nearly took a man's life, and he nearly deserved it. No. He did deserve it, but I'm not a killer. If everything Malcolm and Kevin have said is true, the future of civilization is at stake. I should have pulled the trigger. "I'm sorry."

"Why?" she asks.

"I should have shot him. I had a chance."

"No," she says, "you would have gone to jail."

"Emma's right," Malcolm stops at a red light. The gun slides off the seat and tumbles to the floor. "She should have shot him."

"I need to pick up my daughter. My neighbor was only watching her as a favor."

"Isn't there somewhere else she can stay?" Malcolm asks.

"Her father could come to get her, but you turned my phone off."

The light changes, and Malcolm guns it. The dashboard has several deep cracks, and the Explorer's frame vibrates wildly when he accelerates. Alyssa grabs onto the dashboard when he spins the wheel. We lunge into the convenience store parking lot and screech to a stop.

"Wait here. I'm going to get us some burners." Malcolm jumps out. "You can call your daughter's father from a burner phone safely. Just be patient." He glances around the lot, then heads for the store.

"Do you trust him?" Alyssa asks.

"Do I have a choice?"

"We could run."

I gaze down at the gun. "I'm sorry I didn't shoot Trey. This would all be over right now if I had."

"Stop it. You'd be on your way to jail right now. That'd be worse."

"I'm not so sure."

"It was cool the way you scared him off, though. He totally backed down and ran away."

"Yeah, but Malcolm's right. He's going to come after us again."

Inside the store, Malcolm is already at the counter. The clerk slides a bag toward him, and he hands over a wad of cash.

"I think we should do whatever Malcolm says. I think we have to trust him. He seems very smart."

"Jeremy is going to kill me. His turn with Vivian ended this morning, and I think he planned on going out tonight."

"It's going to be okay."

Malcolm rushes past the gas pumps. He moves fast for a large man. "Here." He slams his door shut and holds the bag of phones open for us.

I feel like I'm choosing a piece of candy on Halloween.

Malcolm writes down our phone numbers.

Alyssa wastes no time powering hers on and calling Jeremy. She makes up a story about leaving Vivian with the neighbor, falling ill while out, and going to the hospital. She tells him she won't be able to come to get Vivian until tomorrow. Then, she spends the next ten minutes convincing him he doesn't need to visit her in the hospital. She deflects and doesn't tell him which hospital she checked into. In the end, it sounds like he buys her lie.

"Everything good?" I ask.

"Yes. Jeremy's on his way to get her now."

Malcolm wiggles, trying to straighten his leg out. He pulls a thick wallet out of his pants pocket and hands it to Alyssa. "Here. See if there's anything useful in there."

Alyssa opens the wallet. "There's almost a thousand dollars. That's useful." She turns toward Malcolm. "You sneaky bastard. You stole Trey's wallet."

"I know," he says. "Is there anything other than money

and business cards in it?"

Malcolm Schmidt, you amazing man.

Alyssa pulls out a stack of business cards, turns them over, fans them out, and tosses them on the floor. She pulls out a stack of credit cards. "For a rich guy, he sure has a lot of credit."

"He's never been as rich as he's claimed." Malcolm takes an on-ramp to the interstate highway.

"Found it," Alyssa says, unfolding a cocktail napkin. "Someone wrote all over the back of this."

Malcolm takes it from her and holds it above the steering wheel while he drives.

"Is it anything?" I ask.

"Yes." He shoves it into his pocket. "Part of it is a design for some system with IP addresses and URLs on it, but there's also a list that looks like passwords. I need to see if I can use it to hack into Trey's network."

"What about us?" I ask.

"We're going with him," Alyssa says. "We can hide out at your place, right?"

Malcolm flips on the turn signal and takes the next exit. "No chance. Now that Trey has seen me, he knows I'm trying to stop him. He doesn't know where I live, but it is only a matter of time. I'm going grab my laptop and go from Starbucks to Starbucks, using their wifi so he can't tell where I'm at when I hack into his network."

"Will that work?" Alyssa says. "I want to watch."

Malcolm takes a right at the off-ramp light. We're not far from the airport.

"You can't watch," he says. "It's too dangerous for you two to be with me." He whips into the Motel 6 parking lot and parks.

293

I pick the gun up off the floor and attempt to hide it under my shirt. It's cold and bulky.

"You can't leave us here," Alyssa says.

"Yes, I can." He reaches across her and opens the door. "Take Trey's cash and use it to pay for the room."

"No," she says.

I open my door. "It's all right, Alyssa. Let's go." I get out of the car. The three-story, blue-and-white motel has dirt streaks running down the walls. A flower pot filled with dead geraniums sits outside the lobby door. "It's going to be okay."

She gets out and walks around to my side.

Malcolm rolls his window down. "Don't use your personal phones. I'll call you on one of your burners by noon tomorrow. I hope to have hacked into Trey's network by then. Don't answer the door, and don't go anywhere."

"Anything else?" Alyssa asks, putting her hands on her hips. "May I go to the bathroom if the mood strikes me?"

Malcolm cocks his head.

"Thanks, Malcolm." I adjust the gun beneath my shirt. "We'll wait for your call."

CHAPTER FORTY-NINE

TREY

Trey limps up the alleyway, favoring his left leg. Somewhere in the scuffle with Malcolm, he'd twisted his ankle, and the pain came on with a vengeance. His black leather dress shoes are scuffed. His pant leg is torn. He's lost track of how far he's walked since leaving Kevin's apartment building. The descending sun paints the alleyway in a rusty-orange light, and a lattice of fire escapes hangs over the dumpsters. Dirt-caked cardboard boxes lay mashed and torn next to the sodden brick walls. A stench—an acrid mix of sulfur and raw animal feces—hangs in the air.

Someone like Trey doesn't belong here. He already paid his dues living on the streets years ago. If it weren't for the chance the police were looking for him right now, he'd have called Sverker sooner. But he's waited long enough. He needs to get out of here. He dials Sverker's cell.

"Can you hear me?" Trey asks, raising his voice so his cheap replacement phone can pick it up better. "Where's my car? Where's Rasmus?"

"I can hear you now." Sverker sounds like he's

underwater. "We towed your car an hour ago, and Rasmus made it out before the police came. We have someone attending to his bullet wound now. He took one in the hip."

"You should let him die. He killed Kevin for no reason." Trey's ankle smarts. He stops and leans against a dumpster. "He shot the skinny little bastard on sight for no reason."

"I'm sorry for that, sir."

"You promised you'd keep him under control."

"He'll be disciplined for this, I assure you."

"Has there been any sign the police know we were involved?"

"No. None at all. The bullet in your friend will be traced to a pawn shop in Richmond. We are in the clear."

A strange noise comes from the alleyway.

Trey glances back the way he came.

A black dog with bulging eyes and yellow teeth emerges from behind a dumpster. The sun reflects off the animal's eyes, burning red. He looks hungry. The best way to deal with him is to ignore him. Show no fear. Trey ambles away from the dumpster and the dog. It most likely won't follow him when he reaches the next intersection.

"Good," Trey says. "Then our big problem is Malcolm. He's back in the picture, and he's working with Emma Petranova. They ambushed us." He drags his left foot over a pothole filled with stagnant water. The pain is getting worse. "I think they were trying to trap me. Tell me you know where Malcolm is."

"We don't know where you are. We need to come to get you."

"Don't change the subject. Where's Malcolm?"

"We're looking but haven't found any trace of him yet."

"Your top priority is Malcolm. Find him and take care of

him immediately. This cannot wait any longer."

Click, click, click.

Trey turns around.

The menacing beast is following him, its toenails clicking on the pavement. It stops, snarls, and gnashes its teeth. Saliva foams over its jaw.

Trey looks around for a weapon. The words FREE MANDELA are painted in red on the dumpster across from him. Wet newspapers, bits of broken glass, mounds of discarded fast food—there's nothing here he can use. He's so close to getting away from the whole scene at Kevin's apartment. Using his gun now would be moronic. Someone behind any window above would hear it and call the police.

He turns his back on the animal and quickens his pace. His ankle screams in pain.

"Is everything okay?" Sverker asks.

"Give me a minute, and I'll tell you the cross streets. You can send a car to pick me up."

Click, click, click.

Trey glances over his shoulder.

The dog flattens his ears back over his skull.

Trey breaks into a hobbled run. He spies a broken tennis racquet propped against the building on his right and goes for it.

The dog bounds toward him.

He drops the phone, grabs the racquet, turns, and swings it into the dog's head. Unfazed, the animal's front paws hit Trey's chest, forcing Trey's back against the wall. He shields his face from the snapping teeth with the racquet and kicks the dog between the hind legs.

A terrific *yelp* escapes the animal's lips, and he backs off. Trey threatens him with the racquet.

The dog lowers one shoulder and turns away, keeping his eyes on Trey as he slowly meanders down the alley.

"That's it. Go on. Get out of here." Trey throws the racquet at him. Drops to one knee. Grasps his aching ankle.

None of this should be happening to him.

He leans forward and picks up the phone.

The screen is cracked, and it won't turn on.

It's okay. He'll buy a new one at the nearest convenience store.

He stands, reaches into his back pocket for his wallet, and comes up empty-handed.

CHAPTER FIFTY

EMMA

"How did I miss this?"

Alyssa rolls over, cradling her pillow. She has sleep in her eyes. "What?"

"There's a text from Malcolm. He sent it in the middle of the night." I throw my feet off my bed and sit up.

"What's it say?" she asks.

"He's made progress. He's been able to intercept and block some of the network traffic coming from Trey's company, but he still has no idea where Trey is located."

"That mostly sounds like good news."

"It is, except he had to go to his house to do it. Apparently, Starbucks' wifi wasn't stable enough."

"That makes sense, I guess."

"And there's something else." I hold the screen so she can see the strange text at the end of the message.

GmabflCTruck89

"That looks like a password."

"Uh huh."

Alyssa glances at the digital clock on the dresser. "How'd

it get so late?"

"Don't you sleep in like this every day? I've been up for hours."

"Are you calling me lazy?" She smiles. "You'd sleep in too, if you could."

"Never." I go to the sink and use my fingers to brush my hair in the mirror. We have soap and shampoo, but not much else. This Motel 6 is light on the amenities. "I hope he calls soon."

"What are we going to do if he doesn't?"

"Let's cross that bridge when we come to it."

The sun rose hours ago. Malcolm said he'd call by noon. We didn't have time to talk to him about what we'd do if he didn't. One thing's for sure. I won't stay here if he doesn't. I can't stand waiting. Besides that, Vivian is with Alyssa's ex, but she can't stay with him forever. He's only watching her because he thinks Alyssa was hospitalized yesterday.

"Want to watch a movie?" Alyssa asks.

"Sure, but how long will Jeremy watch Vivian without getting worried?"

"I don't know, but I think we have time. Don't worry. Malcolm is going to call. Let's just watch a movie and decompress, okay?"

"Okay."

We settle on *Something About Mary*. A classic. Something light-hearted ought to lift my spirits, but it doesn't. I keep checking the clock and my phone. Malcolm doesn't call. It's maddening. When I'm not trying to make time go faster by focusing on *Mary*, I'm replaying yesterday in my head. That poor man, Kevin, lying in the hallway. Dead. What a miserable life he had. Suffering from mental illness is no joke, and he had to spend part of his life dealing with Trey Wilkes. A natural born psychological predator.

"Any messages from Malcolm?" Alyssa asks.

The credits roll on the TV.

"No. Nothing."

"We've got to do something. I have a bad feeling. It's almost noon."

"I hear you." I get up. Pull my pants on. "Let's go."

"Yay," she exclaims. Jumps out of bed. "We're going to hit the streets and find out where the evil villain's lair is located. We'll stop at nothing. I knew you wouldn't let me down."

"No, we're going to find Malcolm and find out why he didn't call." Despite my initial trepidations, Malcolm has been nothing but reliable until now. I'm worried something has happened to him.

"How are you going to do that?"

"Get your coat. I'll explain on the way."

We head out the door. A brisk breeze hits us, and I pull my jacket tight. Clouds hang over the city to the north, and that's the direction I take.

"Why are we going this way?" Alyssa asks.

"Because of this." I pull an envelope out of my pocket. "You're going to be proud of me."

She takes it. "Oh, congratulations. Fifteen minutes could save you fifteen percent or more on your car insurance. I *am* proud of you. Woo, hoo."

"Not me, Malcolm. I swiped it from his car. It has his address on it."

"Emma." She puts her hand on my shoulder, and we stop walking. Her eyes meet mine. "I am proud of you. You're coming along very nicely."

"Thank you." I put my hand on hers. "This way. I don't

think it's far."

"Wait." She holds up the insurance letter. "We're completely on the wrong side of the city."

"What do you mean?"

"This says North Myerson Ave, not South. We're miles from there."

"Oh, no." The next street up is Wrigley Boulevard. It sounds familiar. I glance around this neighborhood, and the whole place seems familiar.

"Can we get an Uber or something?"

"Not with these flip phones. I don't think you can do it without installing their app."

"Well, taxis don't come out this far on their own. We could call one?"

"I'd rather not. We don't have time to wait." I head for Wrigley Boulevard. I know where I'm at now. "Do you see those townhomes way over there?"

"Yes."

"Wilson and his partner, Travis, live over there. We can kill two birds with one stone."

"You had to say kill, didn't you?"

She didn't mean to bring me down. There's pain in her eyes. I can still see Kevin's blood-soaked beard and his dead eyes staring up at me. Trey's man killed him right in front of us. He just killed him. "I'm sorry."

"It's okay. I—what were you saying?

"I said Wilson's partner lives over there. We can ask him for a ride to Malcolm's and find out if the police have told him anything about Wilson's disappearance."

"Right. Do you think Trey kidnapped Wilson, too?"

"His mistake if he did. Wilson knows the least about the project."

We cross into the townhome complex. The breeze lets up, and the mild warmth feels good.

"Could Wilson have been working with Trey all this time?" Alyssa asks. "You always talk about how he never shows up and how he never helps. Maybe he's always been an impostor. Maybe he doesn't know how to help, only how to steal information."

"I've had that thought. Especially after Trey told me about corporate spies." We round a corner. "There it is. He lives in that one." Travis and Wilson's townhome is sandwiched between two other units. The entryway is set back next to a one-car garage, shaded by a second-floor balcony.

Alyssa grasps my elbow. "Wait. This could be dangerous. What if Wilson is working with Trey? He could tell him where we're at if he's here."

"Don't worry. He's still gone. I don't see his stupid little sports car anywhere."

"I'm not sure." She tips her head to one side and glances up at the balcony.

"What happened to, 'We'll stop at nothing to find the villain'?"

"You're right, it's just that after yesterday . . . I don't know. Watching true crime documentaries on TV is one thing, but when I saw it for real . . ."

"I understand. I'm sorry I got you into this."

"It's okay. Let's get out of it." She presses the doorbell.

The curtains in the front window move, but not enough to see who moved them.

The door opens.

"Hi, Emma," Wilson says with pompous grin . "Let me guess. You were in the neighborhood and decided to stop by and see how I was doing. Am I right, or am I right?"

CHAPTER FIFTY-ONE

EMMA

I'd enjoy nothing more than slapping that stupid smile off Wilson's face. He stands in the doorway of his sub-par townhome, a lie because he always hinted he had a lot of money. I thought he lived in a mansion. His eyes twinkle, hiding more truths, like where the hell he's been this past week. His trademark turtleneck sweater squeezes his neck, and his black slacks taper at the bottom, choking his ankles. He looks me up and down, grinning.

"Who is it?" Travis yells from inside the home.

"No one," Wilson says. "Quite literally, no one."

"Hey." Alyssa raises her oh-no-you-didn't hand.

I grasp her wrist.

"Just kidding," Wilson says. "You know I like to kid."

"Where have you been?" I ask.

"With D'Angelo missing," he lowers his voice, "I decided I needed a stress reliever, so I went to Mexico. Cabo. Got back earlier this morning."

Something slams inside the townhome. "Tell them to go away," Travis calls. "I'm not finished talking to you."

"Really?" I say to Wilson. "You went on one of your 'trips'?" I make air quotes with my fingers. "You know the police are looking for you."

"No, they're not. They found out where I was a few days ago. They thought I had gone missing too when Travis didn't know where I was." He glances over his shoulder into the townhome. "They really messed everything up."

Detective Galen never told me Wilson was in the clear. He could have, when he came to warn me about Trey, but he acted as if Wilson's disappearance didn't matter. I guess it didn't, because here is Wilson, as egocentric as ever.

"Get *in* here!"

"Travis sounds upset," I say.

Wilson takes a step forward, and Alyssa and I both step back. "He's okay. Just a little feisty today."

"You lied to him, didn't you?"

"No. I forgot to tell him where I was going this time."

"You mean, you forgot to lie to him and tell him you were going to visit your mother."

The smile leaves his face. "How do you know about her?"

I love it. "You and D'Angelo went missing, and I was trying to find you, so Travis and I had a little talk the other day. There's a lot of things I know about you now."

"Yeah," Alyssa says. "We're investigating you, so don't leave town again."

Before Wilson can respond, the curtains in the front window slide open, and Travis steps into view. He's holding a trash can in one hand and a food container in the other. After Wilson turns and faces him, he pours the food into the can without breaking eye contact with us. It resembles leftover lasagna.

"What's he doing?" I ask.

"Uh, when he gets mad, he likes to throw my food away. He knows I won't eat his food."

"Why?" Alyssa asks.

"Because he's a vegetarian. I don't like all that eggy stuff."

"No," she says, "why does he throw your food away?"

Travis closes the curtains, obviously disappointed at Wilson's non-reaction.

"It doesn't matter," I say. "We need your help. Can we borrow your car?" I look around. "Where is it, anyway?"

Wilson rears his head back and howls with laughter.

It really wasn't that funny. "Seriously, we need your car."

"It's in the garage, but you're not getting it," he says. "Not unless someone is bleeding and needs to go to the hospital." He looks at Alyssa. "Are you bleeding?"

"No, but you will be soon if you don't—"

"Oh, you're feisty too." Another slam comes from inside the townhome. This one makes Wilson jump, but he quickly regains his composure. "Why do you want my car so bad?"

Without saying too much, I tell Wilson about Trey and Malcolm. He remembers Trey from the awards banquet. When I describe the supposed millionaire entrepreneur, I watch Wilson's eyes, looking for any changes in dilation. Any indicator he already knew Trey from before. He passes the test. I leave out Kevin and yesterday's tragic events. No reason to scare him. "So, if you want D'Angelo back, you'll loan us your car so we can check on Malcolm."

Travis appears in the doorway behind Wilson wearing a kimono and flip-flops. "Hi, Emma. I see you're back." He folds his arms. "Look, Wilson can't play right now."

Wilson turns. "Go back inside. I'll be there in a minute."

"No. You come in now."

Wilson steps forward, backing Travis into the doorway.

"Stop it," Travis says.

When Travis clears the threshold, Wilson pulls the door closed and holds the handle.

The door shakes.

"I've got to get out of here," he says. "I'll take you to your friend's house as long as we can stop and get something to eat on the way. I'm starving."

"Open this door, mister, or I'm going to—"

"I'll be there in a minute," Wilson yells.

I turn to Alyssa. "What do you think?"

She walks away, motioning for me to follow.

"What is it?" I ask.

"Do you trust him?" she whispers.

"I trust him to be him. He's a liar, but I'm convinced he's not working with Trey. I've known him too long, and he's just not smart enough. He had no reaction when I brought up Trey, like he'd never heard of him before the banquet. I also don't think someone like Trey would ever put up with someone like him for very long."

"Okay." Alyssa nods. "I agree."

The front door stops shaking. "You can say goodbye to that omelet I made you this morning, mister."

"Wilson," I say, "you can take us, but we've got to go straight to Malcolm's house. We'll get something to eat afterward, okay?"

A loud crash comes from inside the home.

"It sounds like he's trying to throw the refrigerator away," Alyssa says. "Is he always this mental?"

Wilson pulls a set of keys out of his pocket and presses a button.

The garage door opens, revealing his Audi TT sports car.

"Okay," he says. "Let's go."

CHAPTER FIFTY-TWO

TREY

Trey sits by the window with the curtains closed and his foot propped up on a chair with a bag of ice from the machine down the hall cooling his ankle. It's a cheap hotel, The Radmore Inn. He's surprised they can afford to print their logo on the paper and pens. A stale cigarette stench emanates from the yellow walls, and if he's not mistaken, the discoloration in the carpet by the bathroom is dried blood. He didn't notice it when he checked in last night, but now he can't stop looking at it occasionally, wondering what happened.

He flips the pad of paper to the next page and continues to review his new plan. There's something peaceful about creating a plan by putting pen to paper instead of fingertips to keyboard. Being here is like life before the internet—calm, detached, and gradual.

But when Trey thinks of Malcolm, he's the opposite of calm.

Within a single day, Malcolm Schmidt put events in motion that could undermine everything. Trey could have avoided this. He tried to avoid it. He knew Malcolm would return to stop him someday, but he never thought Malcolm would work with Kevin. At least Trey never needs to worry about Kevin again.

Poor, dead Kevin.

The new plan's first milestone deals with Malcolm. It's Sverker's top priority, and when Sverker's has a top priority, it gets done.

Light permeates the carrot-colored curtains, and two black flies take turns bouncing off the window pane. The buzzing distracts Trey from reviewing the plan. This is not the sort of place he would ever choose to stay in, but that's exactly why he's here. The police—especially Detective Galen—would never think to look for Trey in a place like this. Though, in the early years, Trey slept in much worse places.

He adjusts the ice bag on his ankle. It's swollen so much he can't tell where his leg ends and his foot begins. After that rabid dog broke his flip phone yesterday, he limped his way here. It was for the best. It gave him time to contemplate the situation. Create a new plan. Despite what Sverker had said— *We're in the clear*—Trey has come too far with *Thought*Fluence to take on any risk. If he'd been able to tell Sverker his location and return to the office, he might have been ambushed for a second time in one day. The police might have been waiting for him, hiding under the desks like ninjas. As he limped his way to the hotel, he saw more police cars than he'd ever seen in his life. It could have been paranoia.

Furthermore, it would not have looked good for his employees to see him unable to walk with authority. His torn pant legs and scuffed shoes. Unacceptable. No one will follow his orders if he doesn't project an impenetrable sense of success at all times.

He chuckles to himself.

No one will follow his orders.

It's not quite true.

The weak-minded desk clerk fell for Trey's salesman smile when he checked in. Trey lost his wallet somewhere along the way, but it wasn't hard to gaslight the clerk into thinking Trey had already paid for two nights.

The police probably have his wallet. They might have everything they need to shut him down. It's all Malcolm's fault for finding Emma, finding Trey's phone, and then luring him to Kevin's apartment. It's Rasmus's fault for killing Kevin.

It's Trey's fault for not being more careful.

This all could have been avoided if he'd had the balls to take care of Malcolm years ago.

A black fly escapes the curtain and circles Trey's head. He swats at it and unintentionally bends his leg. Pain courses up his calf. The ice bag falls to the floor, and the fly ascends to the ceiling. Trey leans forward and picks up the bag. When he sits back, he realizes, for the sake of mankind, that maybe he should start everything over.

Malcolm won't stop until *Thought*Fluence is destroyed, but he can't do that if Trey destroys it first.

He flips to the third page of his new plan. It'll be a lot of work to execute the tasks on these pages. If the police come after him now, he may never get this far. The smartest move might be to vanish. Sitting in this hellhole, he's already got a head start. No one knows he came here. Not even Sverker. He could leave tomorrow, go to a new city, start a new *Thought*Fluence, and—the other fly bursts from the curtain and careens into his eye. He digs it out with his finger and flicks it onto the table.

He's getting too old to put up with places like this.

He's also getting too old to go to jail for a long time.

But the thought of returning to the streets and rebuilding everything—that chills him to the bone. It's worse than the thought of sharing a jail cell with a sordid stranger. Yesterday morning, his message had crawled over the web and caused the citizens of Kandour to react. Some had posted online how they planned to disconnect their phones from the internet, then disconnect their family's phones. Then their neighbors'. For the first time, after years of failing, his vision had finally started to take hold.

He can't give up now.

The people of this world are finally listening to him.

They're starting to take the internet apart, piece by piece.

The buzzing is incessant. The fly beats his body against the ceiling as if it's the only way out.

Trey can't give up now, but his father would have.

No, that's not true.

His short-sighted father never had anything to give up because he never took any risks. That's why Trey did what he had to do. He did it so he could make the world a better place. It's a justification—a complex rationalization—he knows, but it's true. It's got to be true. Against his father's wishes, he built *Thought*Fluence on the back of someone else's money. His father's money.

No.

It was *his* money. *His* inheritance.

In a way, he complied with his father's long-standing edict. And he earned it. Sicking Sverker's man on his father was the hardest thing Trey ever had to do.

Walking away from *Thought*Fluence, away from his chance to save the world from itself, would dishonor his father's memory. His father's sacrifice. He can't give up. He won't give up. If he's been discovered by the police, then so be it. At least he went down fighting. With any luck, Sverker is right, and they're in the clear. The solitude of this place—minus his black fly friends—has just made him paranoid.

He needs to let things play out.

He goes to the phone and punches in the number to his office. He needs to talk to Sverker. Now. The police, the FBI, the Indian government—any one of them might listen in, but it's okay. After Kandour succumbs, he'll skip the intermediate beta test cities and go for the throat. Sure, it's not fair to those cities. They won't get to experience the freedom of an unplugged life like the residents of Kandour, but they'll get their turn. By staying one step ahead of the authorities, he can skip to the major metropolitan areas and finish what he started sooner. When he reaches his last milestone, the authorities will have much bigger problems than arresting him. They'll be too busy adjusting to the new world order.

Or is it the *old* world order?

It will be like the eighties. People will leave their homes to watch movies. To see each other in the flesh. To be with each other. No Netflix. No Zoom. Actual, real, in-person socialization.

Not social media.

It's what the world needs.

"This is Trey Wilkes. Can you put Mr. Sohlmann on?"

"Absolutely. One moment."

Trey turns, opens his hand, sweeps it through the air, and catches a fly. The vibration of the tiny beast tickles his palm.

"Where are you?" Sverker asks.

"Where is Malcolm Schmidt?" Trey counters.

"He's right where you wanted him. Next to a bucket of water and a microwave."

Trey squeezes his fist until the fly stops buzzing. "Good."

CHAPTER FIFTY-THREE

EMMA

There's a hole where the doorknob used to be. The brass knob lies bent and broken on Malcolm's porch. I whip around and scan the neighborhood. We're too late. We didn't see any suspicious cars or characters when Wilson parked his Audi, but I was distracted the entire way here, listening to Alyssa complain about the cramped backseat. The upscale ranch homes sprawl across their oversized lots, situated away from the road by turnaround driveways and shrubs, concealing their inhabitants behind shuttered windows.

There's no one within sight.

"I guess we don't need to knock." Alyssa pushes the door open and marches inside.

Wilson follows close behind.

"Be careful," I say. "They might still be here."

The foyer empties into a living room with dark wood flooring and muted gray walls. Black trim. A spotless gas fireplace. Two couches, a coffee table, an over-stuffed chair— all perfectly spaced, like a furniture store showroom. Everything is pristine and clean except for the red smears on the wall in the hallway.

"They got him," Alyssa says. "They murdered him."

The red smears look like blood, but the hallway isn't well-lit. I scrape some off with my fingernail and bring it to my nose.

It smells a little like rust.

It's got to be blood.

"What are we going to do?" Alyssa asks.

"I don't think anyone is here."

"What about Malcolm? His body might be here?"

"We don't know he's dead, but we need to find out."

She glances down the hallway. "Okay."

"I'll check the kitchen," Wilson says.

Alyssa and I walk down the hall, then separate to check the rooms. "Malcolm?" There's no sign of him anywhere.

"In here," Alyssa yells.

I find her in Malcolm's office. Well, it was an office. Now it's a devastated wasteland of broken monitors, cables, books, and papers. An overturned bookshelf blocks my way to the desk. Alyssa steps around it and gazes down at a computer tower. The metal casing is bashed in like someone knocked it over and stomped on it.

"Do you think we can get it to work?" I ask.

"It's worth a try." She plugs a monitor cable into the back, and I hand her a keyboard. She hands me the business end of a power cable, and I find an outlet.

The moment of truth.

I plug the cable into the wall, and . . . nothing.

She rocks the computer tower, wiggles the power cable, then stands. "It's no use."

"Let's see if Wilson found anything," I say.

We find him rummaging through the refrigerator.

"There's nothing good in here to eat." He faces us. "Is this guy a bachelor or something?"

"What the hell are you doing?" Alyssa asks. "A man has died."

"We don't know that," I say.

"And I'm going to die if I don't get something to eat." Wilson opens the freezer drawer. "Frozen waffles? Disgusting." He throws the box on the floor.

"Get out of there." Alyssa reaches for his arm. "You're tampering with evidence."

I look at the blood under my fingernail. "It's too late. Our prints are already everywhere."

"Should we call the police?" Alyssa asks. "This is serious."

Wilson pulls a frozen pizza out of the freezer and puts it on the counter.

"No," I say. "They'll arrest us."

"Should we go?" she asks. "Are they coming?"

"I doubt it. If the neighbors saw anything, they would have called 911 by now. The police would have already been here, and there'd be yellow tape everywhere." I rub my thumb and forefinger together. "The blood has had time to dry."

Wilson opens the pizza box. "What the hell is this?" He pulls a laptop out of the box. "There's no pizza in here."

Alyssa grabs the laptop out of his hand. "Looks like you'll have to find something else to eat."

"What kind of nut job is your friend?" Wilson asks.

"A brilliant one," I say. "He must have seen Trey's men coming and hid it in the freezer."

Alyssa puts the laptop on the kitchen table and flips the lid open. Malcolm left a few sticky notes on the keyboard. She glances at the illegible scribblings, then brushes them aside.

Please Enter Your Password

I pull my phone out and read the strange word Malcolm sent in his text last night.

GmabflCTruck89

It works. We're in.

I sit next to Alyssa and take over the computer.

Wilson searches the cabinets. It's hard to feel sorry for him, but I'd be hungry too if my boyfriend threw out my food.

The laptop asks if I want it to restore the windows, and I click YES. A map program appears with a red circle hovering over a building. I zoom in and determine the address.

"That's the same as this one." Alyssa holds up a sticky note. "And it has the word 'thoughtfluence' on it."

"That's the name of Trey's company," I say.

"Can you click on that?" she asks.

I double-click on the building, and a new window appears. It shows a floor plan, but some passages end abruptly, like someone didn't finish mapping it out.

Wilson opens a box of crackers and stands over us. "That looks like my Roomba app."

"What?"

"My Roomba." Crumbs fall from his lips. "My robot vacuum cleaner. It has an app on my phone that shows me where it's cleaned the floor."

My eye is drawn to the camera embedded in the laptop's lid. "We should get out of here."

"No." Alyssa puts her hand on my wrist. I wasn't aware that I'd started shaking. "You need to call the police. This has gone too far."

"I can't do that. They'll arrest us."

"No, they won't." Wilson pops another cracker into his mouth.

"They'll arrest me. That detective has wanted to arrest me

ever since D'Angelo went missing. Now he can get me on murder charges."

"Don't be paranoid," Alyssa says. "We'll vouch for you. I've been with you since yesterday."

I hate it when she's right. But is she? None of this would have happened if I'd listened to my paranoia about Trey. I'd never have gotten involved with him. When it came to Detective Galen, I listened to my paranoia. He made it easy by telling me not to leave town, but he only did that until he learned about Trey's past. He tried to warn me about Trey. But—he also implied I was working with Trey.

"C'mon, Emma," she says. "You need to call."

I pull out my personal phone, switch it on, and put it in airplane mode as quick as I can so my location can't be traced. "Put this number in your phone in case they do arrest me. It's the number for the detective I've been talking to."

Alyssa types Galen's phone number into her burner phone, and I do the same on mine.

I stand.

A glass sliding door leads to the backyard. Ash trees line the fence, their leaves fluttering, casting ballerina shadows across the lawn. I feel the cold air seep through the door.

This could be one of those moments I remember forever, like the first time I watched the Twin Towers fall on TV. I swore it had been faked. The second time they showed it, I recorded it on VHS. I replayed the video several times before going to school as if nothing had happened. The teachers sent me home immediately, instructing me to stay inside my house for the rest of the day.

If I'm to be arrested, then I want to spend as much time outside as possible while I still can. I open the glass sliding door, phone in hand, and step into the future.

CHAPTER FIFTY-FOUR

EMMA

I read somewhere once that you should beat up the biggest person in Gen Pop on your first day in prison, then become a gang leader.

Prison. That is not where I wanted my career to go. My mother wanted me to marry someone and have children, and I wanted to be recognized in the world of psychology, but now, a giant named Malcolm is missing, a madman named Trey is trying to take over the world for God only knows what purpose, and a two-faced demon named Detective Galen would love nothing more than to lock me up.

I wish my dad were here. He'd know what to do, but I don't dare endanger him. I've caused too much harm to Alyssa's and Wilson's futures already. I wish I had my mom's magnifying glass with me. I'm not sure I'm seeing things clearly. I'm not sure making this phone call is the right decision.

Malcolm's backyard is bounded by a tall fence and ash trees, stretching toward a shed barely visible behind a cluster of overgrown rose bushes. The vibrant green lawn has no blemishes and rivals that of any golf course I've ever seen, though I haven't seen many.

I pull Detective Galen's number up on my burner phone and hit the call button.

"Who is this?" he says.

"It's me, Emma Petranova. I need your help."

"Where are you? I've been trying to reach you."

"If I tell you, I want you to promise not to arrest me. I need your help." I walk toward the shed. I have an empty feeling in the pit of my stomach.

"Emma, you know I can't promise you that. It depends on what you have to tell me. Have you been in contact with Trey Wilkes since we spoke last?"

"No."

"Are you lying?"

I stop mid-lawn and turn toward the house. "I think this was a mistake. I'm sorry for calling you."

"Wait. No, it's me who's sorry. I didn't mean to accuse you like that. Just answer some questions, and I'll help you. Promise."

"I don't want to answer your questions. I want you to find Malcolm Schmidt. He's gone missing, and I know who took him."

"Trey Wilkes?"

"Before you say it," my voice rises, "I am not working with Trey Wilkes. I haven't seen him since before you came to my apartment."

"It's okay, Emma. I believe you."

"You do?"

"Yes. I initially suspected you, but now, given what we know about Trey Wilkes, you're most likely just another gullible target in a long line of victims."

"Gullible?" Sprinklers suddenly pop out of the ground and spray me. I run toward the shed. "You think I'm—"

"Sorry. No. I didn't mean it like that."

I escape the water. A rainbow forms in the ambient mist between me and the house.

"Emma? Are you still there?"

"Yes."

"How do you know Malcolm is missing?"

"It doesn't matter. He's in trouble, and I need you to find him. If you find him, you'll find Dr. Santan. I know for a fact Trey kidnapped Dr. Santan."

"How do you know that?"

"If I tell you where I think he took them, do you promise not to arrest me?" I picture the map on Malcolm's laptop and re-commit it to my memory.

"How do you know Trey kidnapped Malcolm? Couldn't they be working together?"

"No. They're mortal enemies. You've got to believe me."

He pauses.

There's clicking and paper shuffling in the background. Someone says, "We have the location."

"Emma," Galen says, "stay right where you are. We're going to sort this out. You're safe, I promise."

"So you won't have me arrested?"

"I'm going to come to help you. Stay where you are, okay?"

"Okay." I hit the end-call button and shove the phone in my pocket.

The breeze blows through my wet clothes like an air conditioner, crisp and cold. The sprinklers really did a number on me. I edge my way along the fence, avoiding the spray. Detective Galen isn't going to help me. I can't trust him. It dawns on me—if Trey is as powerful as Malcolm said, he could have the detective in his pocket. Trey said he'd talked to Galen the same day I met each of them for the first time at the harbor. The first time Trey *coincidentally* ran into me.

I can't believe Galen accused Malcolm of working with Trey. There's no way. After watching Malcolm go toe-to-toe with Trey yesterday, I believe he's innocent. Trey may be the world's best con man, but they didn't fake that fight. Malcolm's nose was bleeding for real.

What am I doing, inching my way along the fence? I'm not a witch. I won't melt if I get wetter.

I burst across the lawn, sprinklers be damned, shouting for Alyssa.

She opens the sliding door to the kitchen.

"Grab the laptop," I shout. "We've got to get out of here."

Moments later, we're in Wilson's car, racing down the street. This time, I'm the one crammed into the back of his sports car. I've got Malcolm's laptop, and I hold onto it like my life depends on it. Maybe my life doesn't depend on it, but my freedom does.

"Where to?" Wilson asks.

"We're staying at a hotel near your place," I say. "I think we'll still be safe there."

"I can't go back." Alyssa bites her lip. "I need to see Vivian." Her eyes begin to water.

I've never seen her like this. "Vivian's okay. Don't worry."

"I know she is, but—I lied to Jeremy and told him I was sick in the hospital yesterday so he'd take her. He's going to wonder what's going on if I don't come to pick her up. He'll think I'm seriously ill, leading to more lies."

"You're right."

"Take a left up here," she says.

Wilson puts his turn signal on.

"Will you come to the hotel later?" I ask.

"I don't think I can take much more of this." She covers her face. "It was fun when we were investigating the crime, but now I'm afraid to go home."

"Where are you going to go?"

"I don't know. I—oh, I know of somewhere."

"Where?"

She turns to face me. "I'm not going to tell you. It's best if you don't know in case they find you. They already did something to Malcolm." She puts her hand on mine. "You're probably next."

"I understand."

"How far do I go on this street?" Wilson asks.

Alyssa squints to read the next sign. "Two more blocks, then take a right."

"I think you can slow down now," I say.

"Never." Wilson guns the engine to beat a red light.

"Are you going to be okay?" I ask Alyssa.

"Yes." She wipes her face. "I'm fine. Promise me you'll call from the hotel before you do anything else, okay?"

"Okay. I promise."

"I still want to help."

Wilson takes the next right.

"This is good," she says. "Drop me off here."

I hop in the front and tell Wilson where to take me. He promises not to speak a word about Malcolm to anyone, especially the police. I believe him. I don't really have a choice, but I threaten him anyway just to be safe. I tell him he'll go down with me if I'm arrested, and he should hide out like

Alyssa. I tell him I know he's been lying to me for years about his extravagant trips. He seems sincere and honest when I bring up his mother. His story lines up with what Travis had said. Wilson's mother does have dementia, and most of the time, he was visiting her, not Cabo.

He drops me off several blocks from the hotel.

I walk, ponder, and check over my shoulder for anything strange every few steps.

In my hotel room, I sit in the dark with the curtains closed.

I open Malcolm's laptop and start poking around, hoping to find more information about Trey and *Thought*Fluence.

I pray Malcolm is still alive.

CHAPTER FIFTY-FIVE

TREY

The Great Hawk of the University of Baltimore's Computer Science Department graduating class of 2002 sits humbled in the corner of Sverker's interrogation cage across from Dr. Santan. Malcolm has changed a lot since Trey saw him last. He finally abandoned those ludicrous concert T-shirts and lost some weight. He also lost his hair. The shadow cradling the lower half of his scalp hints he is shaving it now, which shows he cares about his appearance. If only he'd cared in college, things could have been different. We could have stayed in business together if his appearance hadn't scared away all the big investors.

Now the big guy is half-naked in Trey's cage. It's his own fault. He should never have blocked the transmission of *Thought*Fluence's messages to Kandour. Trey is not sure it was Malcolm, but there's no one else he can think of who could do it.

"What's it going to be?" Trey asks Sverker.

"I'm feeling nostalgic today. I think I'll go with an old classic." Sverker peruses his card table of conversation starters and picks up the brass knuckles. He slips them on his right hand. His punching hand.

Malcolm didn't only lose weight. He's clearly been working out. His chest and arms bulge with muscles. His abdomen is cut. But he's not a picture of health right now. Sverker said Malcolm didn't lose much blood when they extracted him from his house yesterday, but his pale body says otherwise.

Malcolm's cellmate resembles The Toxic Avenger, a character from one of Trey's favorite eighties movies. His face has almost melted away from Sverker's chemical facials. His left eye is permanently swollen shut. Trey tilts his head and decides Dr. Santan also resembles the mutant from *The Goonies*. He had never thought about how similar those two eighties characters looked before now.

"Cover me," Sverker says.

Trey pulls his gun out.

Sverker unlocks the cage door, and they approach Malcolm.

Trey takes aim at the big guy's wounded arm. "How'd you do it?"

Malcolm sits on the floor, slumped forward. He opens his eyes. Stares at his feet. Says nothing.

Trey kicks him in the calf. "How are you blocking the messages?"

"I'm not doing anything."

"Don't lie to me. The second you popped up on our radar, we began receiving delivery failures. I know it's you."

"Are you still getting the failures?" He glances up at Trey. He has a lovely gash on his forehead.

"Yes."

"Good."

Trey kicks him again. "Tell me how to stop it."

"I'm not doing anything. I'm locked in here. You must have a bug in your code."

"Sverker," Trey says.

The Swede winds up and delivers a crushing blow. Blood flies from Malcolm's nose. His head rocks backward, slamming against the cage wires.

"Tell me how to stop it," Trey demands.

"Nope." Blood trickles over Malcolm's jaw.

Sverker winds up again and swings, but this time, Malcolm reacts. He seizes Sverker's arm and yanks him down to the floor. The Swede's face smashes into the concrete, and Malcolm lies down next to him, pinning his arm to the floor.

Trey can't get a clear shot without blowing Malcolm's head off.

"Do something," Sverker yells.

Dr. Santan makes a sudden movement and catches Trey's eye.

Trey swings his gun and points it at the doctor.

Malcolm rolls on top of Sverker.

Dr. Santan reaches up and attempts to grasp the cage wires but fails to stand and falls back onto the floor.

Trey rushes to Malcolm and presses the muzzle against his back. "Get off him."

Malcolm reaches for Trey's leg and misses.

Trey kicks him in the head, and Sverker scrambles out from beneath the behemoth.

"Not smart, Malcolm," Trey says. "Try it again, and I *will* shoot you."

Sverker stands and straightens his suit jacket. Rebuttons the bottom button and smooths his hair. Makes a fist with his punching hand and steps toward Malcolm. The fury in his eyes lacks any reasonable control.

"Wait." Trey holds his hand up to Sverker. "Don't kill him. We need him to stop blocking the messages."

Malcolm sits up and puts his back against the cage wall. "I'll never do that. I'd rather die."

"You'll wish you were dead." Sverker takes his brass knuckles off and returns them to the card table. He gazes at his torture toolset like a kid in a video game store.

"Leave him be," Dr. Santan moans.

"Shut up, old man." Trey has had enough of this. "You're not out of the woods yet. I want more from you, too."

"I gave you the hooks. Good ones. They worked, right?"

"They are messages. Not hooks."

"Yes. Of course. Messages. People began spreading the messages on their own, right?"

"Yes, but the transmissions will eventually wear out. We need to be able to create our own messages for when you finally die. I want to understand the power behind them."

Sverker opens the cabinet beneath the microwave and pulls out a butane torch.

Malcolm sees it and shakes his head.

"Leave him alone," Dr. Santan yells. "I'll tell you what you want."

Trey has never seen Sverker this fired up. He keeps his gun trained on Malcolm as Sverker charges back into the cage. Dr. Santan isn't a threat. Beaten, bruised, and old—he can't even stand on his own.

Sverker presses the ignite button, and the tip of the torch comes to life with a brilliant blue flame. He positions it over Malcolm's chest.

"Last chance," Trey says. "How are you blocking the messages?"

"Go 'F' yourself," Malcolm says.

Sverker applies the torch, running it from Malcolm's belly button to his left nipple.

The big guy's howl shakes the cage.

"Stop it." Dr. Santan's voice is so ragged Trey barely hears him. "Listen to me. Listen."

Sverker makes another pass with the torch, this time searing a path from Malcolm's belly button to his other nipple.

Malcolm lets out another wailing howl.

"That's enough," Trey says.

Sverker backs off.

Dr. Santan attempts to open his swollen eye before speaking but fails. "To create effective messages of mass persuasion, you must always do three things." He pauses. Gasps.

"Go on," Trey says. "I'm listening."

"First, the message must change the cognitive structure of each person who reads it. It must convince them the message is the truth. Second, the message must change each person's motivational structure. It must alter their will." He gasps for air again. "Finally, the message must suggest the new form of behavior and the rationale for social participation."

"What are you telling him?" Malcolm asks.

Trey thinks for a moment. "Okay, I think I understand, but that doesn't help. I don't want to know what the messages must do. I want to know how they do it. How do I make the messages do those things?"

Dr. Santan tries to speak, but his gasping turns his words to dust.

Trey gets closer to him, keeping his gun trained on Malcolm. "Speak up."

"I'll try." He clears his throat and takes an exhaustive

breath. "To promote cognitive change, the sense organs must receive the messages frequently, and the messages must be compatible with each person's belief system. Culturally applicable. If the messages are too devious, they will be distorted or rejected by everyone. The messages must convince each person the requested action will not only benefit them but will have no effect unless others agree and propagate them." He gasps again. Licks his dry lips. "The messages must convey a sense of unity. Whether a cohort of believers exists yet or not, tell your virus victims they belong to a special group, and ask them to spread the word to others." His head drops to his chest. He breathes heavily.

"What else?" Trey asks.

The doctor does not respond.

Trey returns to Malcolm. "Your turn. How are you blocking the signal?"

Blood oozes from the crevasses Sverker burnt into Malcolm's body. Sverker holds the torch near Malcolm's belly button. He twists the nozzle, and the flame doubles in size. "Do you want another one?"

"No," Malcolm says. "I'll—it's no use. Please, don't."

Trey puts his hand on Sverker's shoulder.

The Swede backs off.

"I left a back door in the code a long time ago," Malcolm says. "It listens on a rarely used port." He adjusts his position. "Ouch. It stings. Oh, it stings so bad."

"Continue." Trey waves his gun.

"You really should update your firewall. I got through it with no problem. I connected to some of your servers and uploaded a filter that returns the delivery failures."

"I told you, Sverker. If we redeploy the code and restart everything, the problem should go away. It would clear his filters."

Sverker eyes Malcolm. Waves the torch. "Is that true? Will that work?"

"No," Malcolm says. "My code modifies hidden configuration files. They're read on startup."

"Where are the files?" Trey asks. "How do we fix this?"

"If I tell you, will you let us go?" Malcolm glances at Dr. Santan. "Is he still alive?"

Sverker runs the torch up the center of Malcolm's body, dividing the last two burn lines. He leans back to admire his work. The three burns begin at Malcolm's belly button and sprawl across his chest like a pitchfork. It's a trademark of sorts.

Malcolm's howling has reached a new level. His bald head burns bright red. Trey hadn't noticed before, but Malcolm also had dental work done since their last meeting. His teeth are straight and exceptionally white. He really has tried to get himself together. What a shame things have to end like this.

"Where are the configuration files?" Trey asks.

Sverker holds the torch near Malcolm's forehead. "Ever been to India? How would you like a third eye?"

"The files are compiled in a linked library called 'utils_92.'" His face scrunches. "Now, please. Stop this."

Sverker turns to Trey. "Should I continue?"

"Go ahead, give him that eye. I want him to reflect inwardly on what he has done by blocking our message. I'll give Lessard the new information so he can create a new message and redeploy the application."

"No," Malcolm yells.

Trey leans over him. "All we're doing is trying to make the world a better place. You, of all people, should know that, Malcolm. Now, meditate on it."

CHAPTER FIFTY-SIX

EMMA

They say home is where the heart is. That may be true, but it's also where all my stuff is. When Malcolm dropped Alyssa and me off at this Motel 6 after the carnage at Kevin's apartment building, we only had the clothes on our backs. Now, I don't even have Alyssa. I hope she picked up Vivian without alerting her ex-husband to our investigation and found somewhere safe to stay.

I've stayed out of sight so Trey's contingent of goons won't find me, but I can't do it forever. I don't smell very good. What's the point in taking a shower when all I have to wear is the same dirty clothes I have on now?

I go to the heater and crank it on high. I wish I had my coat. The temperature outside dropped last night. Why does every hotel room heater blow cold air no matter what setting it's on?

Sitting at the desk with Malcolm's laptop, I spend hours combing through files, most of which have nothing to do with Trey. I view the floor plan and location of *Thought*Fluence at least one hundred times. The files in related folders look generated by the computer based on their esoteric filenames, but one stands out.

high-volume-traffic-location.log.

This file contains thousands of lines, all with the same text labeled "geographic location code." A search on Google for the code—a-ii-up-kndr—returns nothing that makes any sense. The top-listed search result offers a luxury hand balm on eBay. Not my thing.

Examining every file on his laptop is exhausting.

My erratic sleep doesn't help, either. My brain spends the night debating whether to look for Malcolm by myself or wait for Alyssa. It could be days before Jeremy watches their daughter again, but she could find a babysitter. It's times like this when Mom's magnifying glass helps. Just holding it in my hands clears my brain and sets me on the right path. But the glass is in my apartment, along with my coat and everything else I own.

They may have left the light on for me here at Motel 6, but this place is far from being home.

Thinking. Debating.

I'm driving myself crazy.

Time after time, I arrive at the same conclusion. No matter what I do, it's safest to stay here. Trey's goons may already have broken into my apartment and trashed it like they did Malcolm's. Or, Galen and his blue-suited goons could have obtained a warrant and done the same. Or, the worst possibility, they're both staking out my apartment, waiting for me to stick my head out.

Either way, I can't stay here. I've got to do something before I go mad.

I'm leaving.

I promised I'd call Alyssa's burner phone when I decided

what to do. I promised Wilson the same, but he can wait. The chill air wraps around my core the moment I step outside.

"Emma," Alyssa answers. "Is everything okay?"

"Yes. How about you? Did you pick up Vivian?"

"We're great. We're safe. Any word on Malcolm, or—"

"Nothing. He still hasn't called."

"I didn't think he would. Not after what we saw at his house . . ."

"I searched his laptop for more clues but only found a strange code. Do you know anything about 'geographic codes'?"

"Is it latitude longitude?"

"No. It's a series of letters and dashes."

"I don't have any idea."

The wind blows orange and black leaves across the sidewalk. They scuttle into my path. I step through them briskly, keeping one hand in my pocket for warmth. My other hand freezes, holding the phone to my ear. "Ah, it's so cold out here."

"Where are you?"

"I left my room to call, just in case. No one should be able to trace these phones, but I'm paranoid."

"Me, too."

Around the next corner, one of my favorite stores anchors a strip mall. Goodwill. On my pitiful stipend from the university, this chain of retail donation centers has saved me hundreds over the years. I check the parking lot and neighboring street for anything suspicious, then head inside.

"Hey, when is Jeremy watching Vivian again?"

"Not for a while. Why?"

"I need your help. I've decided to go back to my apartment to get a few things, but I don't want to do it alone in case it's being watched."

"I can't, Emma."

"What do you mean?"

"I can't be a part of this anymore." Vivian shouts something in the background, then it sounds like she's laughing. "I'm sitting here, watching Vivian, and I can't leave her again. She's watching TV and dancing along with the cartoon characters."

"At some point, it will be Jeremy's turn to watch her again, right?"

"He's gone on an extended vacation. It will be a couple of weeks."

"What about a babysitter? Your neighbor?"

"No. You don't understand. I'm not leaving her again. I can't ask my neighbor—I can't even go home." She sniffs. "I'm so sorry. I really wanted to help."

"You did help. I'm the sorry one." I stop near a coat rack. "I should never have dragged you into this."

"You didn't. I forced my way in. I—what are you going to do now?"

That is the million-dollar question. I'm afraid to go to my apartment alone, and the thought of storming into Trey's office building in search of Malcolm by myself is terrifying. But, despite what Alyssa says, I let her get involved, and now she's in danger. Maybe I *should* go Rambo on Trey.

I grab the ugliest but warmest coat off the rack. Fuzzy white with green stripes. "I'm going to find Malcolm and end this mess, one way or another."

"Be careful."

"I'm not sure there's time for that. I've wasted too much already. You stay safe, and I'll call you when it's over."

"Thank you."

I grab a paisley scarf large enough to wrap around my head on my way to the checkout counter. A black-rimmed pair of sunglasses with amber swirls and green speckles dwarfs the others on the rack. I put it on the counter with my coat and scarf, pay, and head for the hotel.

I don't have to storm into Trey's office building.

I can sneak inside.

The new-to-me coat thwarts the wind. I wrap the scarf around my head as I walk. That feels even better. Talking with Alyssa has me all fired up, but she's right. I need to be careful.

I leave the sidewalk and hide behind a tree near the motel. There's no one in the parking lot. No golden Acura slinking down the street. No dark, undercover police cars anywhere in sight. It's safe to go inside, but an overwhelming sense of dread washes over me. The scarf flutters in the wind, and I suddenly feel ridiculous in this disguise. If I were to sneak into Trey's office building, I'd stick out like crazy. It's highly doubtful anyone there dresses like this. They certainly don't wear sunglasses indoors.

I need help. I can't do this alone.

But I don't want to endanger anyone else's life by asking for help. I'd know what to do if I had my mom's magnifying glass. My next steps would become clear. I've got to go back to my apartment and get it.

Mom. I need your help.

My pocket buzzes.

I pull out the burner phone, and there's a text message.

It's more than a virus. You must stop him. He's attacking cities. People will die.

a-ii-up-kndr

The geographic code from Malcolm's laptop.

It's him. It must be him. Only he could know that code

and the number to my phone. I didn't read it off to Alyssa.

I text, *Where are you?*

Phone in hand, I race to my room and turn on his laptop. I've already searched for the code on the internet, and I've already searched the laptop for everything on Trey and *Thought*Fluence, but maybe with Malcolm's help now, I can find something new.

I wait.

Stare at my phone.

Nothing.

I resend the text.

Where are you?

Three dots bounce inside the message box, telling me he's about to respond.

I'm in 2B.

CHAPTER FIFTY-SEVEN

EMMA

Sweat trickles down the center of my back. My disgusting shirt clings to my body beneath my Goodwill coat like a second skin. The hotel room heater did its job while I was shopping for my disguise. It's hotter than hell in here.

I stare at my phone. When I asked where Malcolm was texting me from, he responded with "2B."

I type, *Where is 2B?*

I wait for the three dots to bounce, indicating he's responding, but they don't move.

I wait. And, wait.

He doesn't respond.

Something must have happened.

I shake the phone, as if that will do anything, then scroll up and re-read the location code he'd sent before. I can't keep waiting, so I type the code into the global search box on his laptop, hoping to find something new. Nil.

Glancing back at my phone, the dots bounce, and a message appears.

Trey's virus is for their heads, not their computers. Dr. Santan is here. He helped him. I helped him. He doesn't need us anymo—

And that's it.

Cut off.

I wait, hoping Malcolm will finish typing, but the dots stop bouncing.

I take off my coat—sweat running down my arms—and throw it on the bed.

Malcolm's messages meld in my brain. It's not a computer virus intended to take over computers. It's a "people" virus. Our work on mass persuasion—D'Angelo helped Trey. He must have helped him persuade people to do something. Malcolm had texted, *he's attacking cities, people will die.*

No. He can't be persuading people to kill each other. It's impossible. Even under hypnosis—which on a mass scale is almost completely ineffective—ninety-nine percent of people will not violate their core moral belief system. But if this isn't Trey's plan, why would Malcolm text the warning?

I stand.

There's got to be more to this. Convincing people to kill each other doesn't sound right. There's nothing in that for Trey. Yet, whatever the details are, the situation is worse than I could have imagined. Malcolm's final message—*he doesn't need us anymore . . .*

D'Angelo and Malcolm might be dead by now. Trey's goon had no hesitation when he killed Kevin. Now, Trey attacks cities? The location code Malcolm sent me matched the code I found in a file titled *high-volume-traffic-location.log.* The code must represent a city somewhere. The letters and dashes mean nothing to me. Alyssa didn't recognize the code either. Malcolm's text begged me to stop Trey, but how?

It's too late.

I should have shot Trey when I had the chance. I had him

at gunpoint, and I didn't pull the trigger. I couldn't do it, and now people are dead. More will die. I could have kept all of this from happening.

My ridiculous disguise—the coat, scarf, sunglasses—lays on the bed. Who was I kidding? Save Malcolm? I'm not cut out for this. I'm never getting my life back.

The hot air here makes it hard to breathe. I go to open the window, but it's not the kind that opens. Outside, the wind blows leaves and papers across the parking lot. Taking a right turn on the road out of here leads to the airport. From the airport, I could go anywhere. It wouldn't be the life I had, but it could be a better life.

My mom and dad always wanted to go to Costa Rica. See the sloths. I could do that.

But I couldn't leave my dad here, could I? He's not safe as long as I'm a threat to Trey. Detective Galen considers me a threat to society. Vanishing from Baltimore might be the best thing I could do. I wish I knew whether or not Trey has truly gotten what he wanted from Malcolm and D'Angelo. If he has, he might not even still be after me. He might be too focused on spreading his mental virus. While there's still a chance of that, I can't run away. I should have shot Trey when I had the chance, but it's not too late.

I take my shirt off and hang it, hoping the sweat will dry.

If Trey has killed Malcolm and D'Angelo, then he has moved on. He won't be staking out my apartment. If he's actually attacking cities, then I'll be of little concern to him. The best thing I can do is let my clothes dry and go to sleep. Things will be clearer in the morning.

In bed, I meditate on the magnifying glass. The rusted metal frame. The scratched glass. The distorted image flipping upside down when I hold it too far away from the truth.

CHAPTER FIFTY-EIGHT

TREY

Eight computer monitors stretch across the wall above a central workstation, displaying crucial data on Kandour. Lessard sits at the workstation with his head buried in his laptop. Software developers, system reliability engineers, and data analysts work away at nearby desks, facing the wall monitors. Trey checks the time. It's late, but everyone is still here, working from the command center to make the world a better place.

"How are we looking, Lessard?" Trey gazes over the lead geek's shoulder, watching green text stream down a black background.

"A few data points short of great. In some ways, it's working too well."

Sverker steps next to Trey. "It's getting late, sir. Some of the developers have started complaining."

"Let's see where we're at," Trey says. "If we're in a good place, they can go home." The monitors on the wall all show upward trends. "What do you mean by 'too good,' Lessard?"

The geek types something quickly and punches the

ENTER key. The scrolling text stops. He turns and looks up at Trey. "After redeploying the code with the new messages, the response rate doubled in less than an hour. Look over there." He points to a monitor on the left. "The biggest hotspot is near the center of Kandour, the downtown area, but there are also pockets of influence on the edges, and smaller ones in other cities are forming. Places we haven't sent the message."

"That's good," Trey says. "It's not *too* good. It's great. It's what we wanted."

"I'm concerned it's spreading too fast. We run the risk of affecting too many citizens in too little time. Our previous research shows that a certain percentage of the population will react quickly and with great vigor. It might draw unwanted attention from world authorities."

"Are you suggesting we slow things down?" Trey asks.

"No." He averts his eye. "Maybe." He glances at Sverker. "Let me put this in simpler terms. If we don't slow it down, citizens prone to anger may act out violently. They could start tearing the city down, trying to honor the messages. On the other hand, the messages could burn too hot and become ineffective overnight, putting us back where we started, but that doesn't seem likely."

"Are all the messages being sent full force now?"

"Yes. You were right about that 'utils_92' file. The bug that was blocking us was in there."

Trey scratches his chin. Begins to pace. Malcolm set the project back several days with his interference, but he is taken care of now. If the police investigating Kevin's murder thought Trey or anyone at *ThoughtFluence* had anything to do with Kandour, they would have stormed the office complex days ago. They still could.

And, somewhere out there, Emma Petranova is on the loose. Working with that detective. It's only a matter of time before they come calling.

"We have to let it run," Trey says.

"But—"

"We'll revisit the data in the morning and see where we're at. Sverker, tell everyone they can go home."

"Yes, sir."

Lessard stands. Picks his laptop up, leaving the lid open. "This is dangerous. People could get hurt."

Trey puts his hand on Lessard's shoulder. "You've got a kind heart, Jack, but it doesn't become you. Stick to what you're good at and prepare to launch in the next city."

"Tell everyone on the floor they can go home," Sverker says into his cell phone.

Trey raises his hands. "Thank you so much for your work today, everyone. Let's call it a night."

It's time for a little celebration. Trey exits the command center, goes to his office, and mixes a drink. He sits in front of his laptop, viewing the polling page. The number of respondents climbs over fifty at a time with each refresh. The "F5" key is his best friend. He laughs out loud. The test in Kandour is succeeding far better and faster than he thought possible.

He makes another drink.

Without a doubt, he can have Lessard move on to the next test city in the morning.

He refreshes the screen. The number of members in his new world order jumps by over one hundred this time. A percentage of them might cause excessive damage, as Lessard warned, but it's a small percentage. You can't make an omelet without breaking a few eggs.

He refreshes the screen again.

More and more people are joining. He switches to the map view. People in surrounding areas of Kandour are signing up on their own. It's spreading person-to-person like a virus. The small village of Anlish appears to be completely consumed. There's no need to move to another test city tomorrow.

This is no longer a test.

He pulls up the master plan. There are five cities listed ahead of Carlsbad, U.S.A.

There's no point in messing around. When the burner's hot, and you have bigger eggs to break, the world is your omelet.

He goes to the wet bar and pours his drink down the sink.

This is why he usually avoids alcohol. It makes him have crazy thoughts.

The world isn't an omelet.

It's a piece of cake.

CHAPTER FIFTY-NINE

EMMA

The convenience store coffee tastes like a metallic swamp. It's somehow both weak, yet overly strong, and has clearly suffered inside the tank for hours. Maybe days. Maybe as many days as I have been wearing these clothes. I don't smell great, but that's about to change.

I'm going home, and the first thing I'm going to do is take a shower and put on a fresh set of clothes.

I convince the clerk to call a taxi for me, claiming my phone is dead. She must do it because I'm buying the coffee and a charger. She owes me. I always buy something if I use the bathroom or ask for anything extra. That way, I don't feel guilty for being a freeloader.

The taxi arrives, and I give the driver my address. It won't be long, and I'll know whether the police or Trey are watching my place. Even better, it won't be long before I hold my magnifying glass, close my eyes, and intuit what I will do next. I'd love to take the magnifying glass to the farmhouse and visit Mom like usual, but the taxi ride there would cost a fortune.

"Are you going to a business meeting?" the driver asks.

It's an odd question, considering how I'm dressed. I'm sweating underneath this ugly coat and scarf. Peering at him from the backseat through my oversized sunglasses, I wonder why he thinks a businesswoman would dress this way. His credentials are stuck to the dashboard. He's in his early sixties, and his gray curls have won the war with his black ones. His name is Xavier. "No. Why did you think that?"

"Just a guess." Xavier spins the steering wheel. "I picked you up at a hotel, but you didn't bring any luggage. Instead, you're carrying that laptop like a businesswoman on her way to a meeting."

Unsure I'd return to the hotel, I brought Malcolm's laptop with me to be safe. "Are you a part-time detective or something?"

"No." He chuckles. "I've been driving for a long time, and I'll be honest. I'm trying to find out if you'll need a ride back to your hotel later. Since you left your luggage behind, chances are you will. This far from downtown, I'd rather stay out here and wait than drive back with an empty cab."

"I understand, but I don't know if I'll need a ride back. Sorry."

A picture of a young woman swings from a yellowed piece of tape stuck to the rearview mirror. "Is that your daughter?"

"Yes, that's her." Our eyes meet in the mirror. He gazes at me like an airport security agent matching my face to my identification. I pass the test. His crow's feet deepen when he smiles, and his eyes light up. "She's a veterinarian now."

"That's impressive. How long ago did she become one?"

A car cuts into our lane. "Out of the way, you." He hits the horn hard. Slows down. "Crank yanker."

I pull out my phone. My real phone. I haven't checked messages in a long time. If I'm quick and do it while on the move, I don't think Trey will be able to trace me.

"Beg my pardon, but these people." He punches the accelerator and tailgates the car in front of us. "What did you ask me?"

"I asked how long ago your daughter became a veterinarian."

"It's been too long. Years. A few more payments and I'll be done. Then I'm retiring. No more dealing with these crank yankers." He honks his horn again.

"You paid for her school?"

He gazes at me in the mirror again, his speckled brown eyes filling with pride. "And I'm still paying, but it's worth it. She's my everything."

"That's very noble of you."

He focuses on the road. "I'd do anything for her. Do you have children?"

The empty cradle in my brain rocks. My mom speaks to me from the weeping cherry tree. *You'd make me so happy if you would settle down and have children.*

"No," I say. "But I plan to someday."

"You should."

I have five messages from my father on my phone. We've never gone this long without speaking since Mom died. He must be worried. I don't have time to listen to all these messages, so I call him.

"Hey, stranger," he says.

"Hi, Dad. Sorry I haven't called you back 'til now, and I don't really have time to talk. I just wanted you to know everything is okay."

"Of course it is, now that you've called. What have you

been doing? Did you decide whether you're staying on Jerk Face's project?"

They might have killed Jerk Face by now. Painful emotions surface, and I close my eyes. So much has changed since I talked to Dad last. "No, I haven't decided, but that's where I've been. I thought some time away from everything would help. I'm sorry I didn't tell you."

"It's okay. You sound upset. Do you need help?"

"I'm fine. Don't worry about me." I should get off the phone now, but I feel horrible letting him go. He sounds lonely. "Anything new with you?"

"No, just this crazy world. Have you seen the news? Wait, don't answer that. I know you don't watch it. They're attacking each other in India for no reason, fighting over oil as always in the Middle East, and your government is out of control."

I picture him sitting in front of his giant flat-screen TV, wearing his shorts and sandals, shaking his head. He could go on about the news forever. I've got to cut him loose. "I'm sorry, Dad. I really don't have time to talk now. I'll call or come by as soon as I can."

"Okay. I love you."

"I love you, too."

Before I can press the power button, my phone rings. It's Nimisha.

I glance out the window. We're about halfway to my apartment and still moving. I'm suddenly desperate to know if Detective Galen has talked to her more about me. I want to know if he's still on the hunt.

"Hi Nimisha, I'm glad you called, but we have to make this quick."

"I've been trying to reach you. Why didn't you answer any

of my calls?"

"It's a long story. Has that detective talked to you lately?"

"No, not since Dr. Santan went missing. Why?"

"I've been trying to find D'Angelo myself, and I was hoping the detective might have said something that would help."

"Nope. Haven't seen him, but *I* want to help you."

I hadn't thought of reaching out to Nimisha. She's so young and bright, and I need help . . . oh, it's bad to think this way, but maybe I should let her. It wouldn't be like bringing a close friend or my father into this mess. I endangered Alyssa already, but because I don't know Nimisha as well . . . how bad would I feel if something happened to her?

Ugh.

I'm losing it.

I don't believe desperate times justify desperate measures—not if it could hurt someone.

"I can't let you get involved," I say. "Just let me know if the detective comes back."

"But, I can help. Really. I talked to everyone who met with that rich guy before the banquet. I got a good description and found out he chose to learn about our project because of the mass persuasion aspect."

"Are you talking about Trey Wilkes?"

"Yes. I know he kidnapped Dr. Santan."

"How do you know that?" My throat tightens. "You shouldn't know that."

"Don't be mad at him, but Wilson told me."

Wilson.

He promised he wouldn't speak a word to anyone. I'd like to say I should have known better, but I *did* know better. I knew Wilson would be Wilson. Once a liar, always a liar. "Is he there now?"

"No. You know how he is. In and out. He didn't come in at all today. So, can I help? Can we meet somewhere?"

"The best thing you can do is keep working on the project and text me if the detective comes back."

"But—"

"And do your best to forget everything Wilson told you."

"Are you sure?"

"Yes."

"Okay, but I'm worried about you. Do you have anyone helping you? How about your friend, Alyssa? What if the detective comes back, and you don't answer my calls again? Can I call her to make sure you're okay?"

"Over there," Xavier says, pointing at a gray office building. "My daughter went to school over there."

I ignore him. "Alyssa's not helping me anymore. Wilson shouldn't have told you about her."

"Over there." Xavier mashes his finger into the side window, pointing.

"I see it," I say. "It looks like a very nice school."

"Where did Alyssa go?" Nimisha asks. "In case I need to find her."

The taxi swerves to the right, knocking me against the door. Xavier wasn't paying attention when another car cut him off.

"Uh, she might have gone to her ex-husband's house or maybe his condo. I don't know. She has an aunt in Virginia, but listen. Don't worry. Nothing is going to happen to me, and I won't wait so long to call you back next time."

"Can I have her number? I'm not letting you go unless you tell me her number."

Alyssa won't answer her real phone anyway, and I need

Nimisha to trust me. I need her to call if Galen comes back. I pull up Alyssa's phone number and read it off.

"Thanks, Emma. I feel much better now."

"I've got to go now. I'll be in touch."

We're getting close to my apartment. I scan the road ahead, looking for any suspicious vehicles. When we stop at the last intersection before my building, I look down the side street, and a black SUV with a chrome license plate holder is parked three cars back. It's tall, broad, and new. I've never seen a car like that in my neighborhood before.

Xavier presses on the gas, but before we exit the intersection, the SUV's headlights come on, and it pulls away from the sidewalk.

"We're here." Xavier flips his turn signal on and slows down.

"No, no, no." My ridiculous disguise didn't work. I grasp the back of his seat. "Don't stop."

"What?"

"Keep going." I look out the back window. The SUV hasn't made it to the intersection yet. "Turn left." I push his shoulder.

We round the corner.

"What's wrong?" he asks.

"Just go. "

"Where?"

"Go faster."

"What's happening?" He hits the accelerator.

"You were right. I need a ride back to the hotel, and I need it now."

CHAPTER SIXTY

EMMA

My neck hurts from twisting to see out the taxi's back window. I haven't seen the black SUV since Xavier drove away from my neighborhood. He must think I'm crazy. I refused to tell him why I'd changed my mind and insisted we return to the hotel. He never saw the SUV. The less he knows, the less he'll have to say if Detective Galen or any other cops ever talk to him.

"Here we are." He pulls into the Motel 6 parking lot. "Right where we started. You know, just because you didn't really go anywhere, it doesn't mean you don't have to pay the fare."

I stare at the entrance to the lot.

I count to ten.

No SUV.

"Hey," he says. "Did you hear me?"

"Yes. Let me get your money."

I look down to open my wallet, and when I raise my head, the black SUV is cruising down the street toward the motel. The chrome license plate cover gleams in the sunlight. I lower my head. The SUV slowly passes the parking lot entrance. I'm not close enough to recognize the driver, but I can see him turn toward me.

He sees me.

He slams on the brakes and spins the steering to make the turn into the lot.

"I changed my mind," I say. "We need to leave. Now."

"What? Again?"

"Yes. Go, go, go."

He puts the car in drive.

"Not that way," I shout. "Go out the exit on the other side of the hotel." I pat his shoulder and point.

The SUV pulls into the lot and stops, blocking the entrance we came in.

"Hurry."

"Where are we going?" Xavier asks. "Back to where we were?"

"Anywhere. Just go."

We begin to move, then he hits the brakes. "No. I'm not doing this again. You can get out here."

"No, I can't."

A gunshot rings out.

Xavier looks in horror as the passenger side mirror explodes.

"Go," I shout.

He hits the gas.

We race around the side of the hotel.

The SUV follows.

"What do they want?" he asks.

"Just lose them."

He takes a right onto the street, and at the first light, he follows a sign to Baltimore Washington International

"There's security at the airport. They can help us."

"No. We can't go to the police."

He accelerates. "What kind of trouble are you in?"

"All kinds. You don't want to know."

The highway is cluttered with people trying to make their early morning flights. Xavier deftly threads the needle, swerving and passing cars until the pack is too tight. The SUV gets stuck behind a delivery truck three cars behind. When the time comes, Xavier exits the main road and takes the service entrance for ground transportation, flashing a public transportation badge to open the gate.

"They'll have trouble following us in here," he says.

The SUV passes the delivery truck and exits the main road as we enter the parking garage.

Xavier finds a dark corner and parks. He shuts the engine off. He shuts the lights off.

We watch for the SUV, but it doesn't come.

"You can get out now," he says. "I don't want any more trouble."

I'm afraid of being seen before I can find another ride. Then, it occurs to me: there is always Costa Rica. I could go back to plan B and run away. An absurd thought, but the universe did bring me to the airport for a reason.

But, running away isn't it.

I'm not giving up. "Can't we just wait a while and sneak out?"

"Please, leave. I don't need this."

"You said you'd do anything for your daughter."

He glances at her photo hanging from the glove box. "Yes. I would."

"I'm someone's daughter. Please help me."

He sighs. "But they might spot us again. You're better off

getting in a different car. I can't believe I'm saying this, but you should take an Uber."

"They'll catch me if they see me walking around or waiting for a ride. Can't we blend in with the other taxis and leave? You heard that gun. They want to kill me."

He glances at his daughter's photo again.

"If I was your daughter," I say, "what would you want the taxi driver to do?"

"I'd want him to bring her to me."

"Good. Then do that. Take me to my father's house."

"Okay, but when we get there, if you change your mind again, I'm calling the police."

CHAPTER SIXTY-ONE

EMMA

Dad opens the door with a huge grin. "When you said you'd call or come by soon, I didn't expect you'd be here today."

I hug him.

He tentatively returns the embrace, senses my need, and squeezes me hard. His television blares from within the house. He doesn't admit to having some hearing loss, but he always plays the news loud.

"What's with the laptop?" he asks. "And that scarf?"

"Oh, it's nothing." I remove my sunglasses. "I thought I might want to do some research."

"From here?"

"No, I—"

He looks past me, squinting at the street. "Where's your car?"

I turn around in time to see Xavier pulling away and do a quick check. There are no black SUVs in sight. No cop cars. No cars resembling undercover cop cars. "Let's go inside." I slide past him and head down the hall to the living room.

As expected, the news is blaring on his giant screen TV.

The typical *Breaking News* banner—white letters on a red background—spans the bottom of the screen. It's part of why I rarely watch the news. Everything is always "breaking news."

"You can turn that off if you want," he says.

I pick his remote up off the arm of his leather EZ chair, aim it at the screen, and—

What do we know about the latest in Kandour, James? asks a studio news correspondent dressed in a blue suit and tie.

The on-location correspondent stands on a busy urban street, microphone in hand. He's surrounded by rustic terracotta shops, some with broken windows. *The unexplained violence and looting in the small town of Kandour, India, has continued to escalate in recent days. We estimate the death toll has reached well over twenty, and many businesses have been broken into and vandalized.*

A separate video plays in the upper right corner as the correspondents discuss the situation. The video shows people breaking into stores, punching and pushing each other, starting fires.

"What's going on there?" I ask.

"I already told you on the phone." Dad sits down in his chair. "They're attacking each other for no reason anyone can figure out."

I turn the volume down so I can hear him better. "It looks like they're attacking businesses."

"Yeah, you're right. Earlier, they said people were taking businesses hostage, but they weren't asking for a ransom. They're a bunch of nuts. You can turn it off."

Malcolm's text messages crowd into my consciousness. *He's attacking cities. People will die.*

It couldn't be. The carnage I'm witnessing on the screen—Trey? Is he behind this? It fits with Malcolm's warning, but it has progressed much faster than I'd imagined it could. It still doesn't seem possible Trey could convince this many people to harm each other using our research, but maybe Dr. Santan gave him information from research I'm not aware of. The video in the upper corner shows a man falling in the middle of the street. His body disappears beneath the pounding feet of a motley mob, his screams drowned out by their shouting. The camera quickly pans away from the scene.

But why? How could Trey's company possibly benefit from this?

"Shut it off and tell me why you're here. I know something's up."

"Hold on." I'm captivated by the news story. It must be Trey's work. The caption above the red and white breaking news alert reads, *Kandour, India - A City Under Siege.*

Kandour.

Kandour.

I sit on the couch, flip open the laptop, and pull up the file with the location code.

a-ii-up-kndr

That last part—kndr. It's the word Kandour with the vowels removed.

"What's wrong?" Dad raises his voice.

"I'm sorry, I—" I point at the screen. "This is all so horrible."

"I didn't know you cared so much about India."

"I don't. I mean—I do, and I don't." I switch the TV off. He stares at me like I'm an alien. I've got to tell him something. "Dr. Santan disappeared, and I've been trying to find him. It's been a rough couple of weeks. I'm sorry I didn't tell you sooner, but it's been one thing after another."

"What do you mean, disappeared?"

"After the awards banquet, he never went home. His wife filed a missing persons report, the police have interrogated me and everyone at work, and the project is falling apart." I put my face in my hands.

"I'm so sorry." He leans forward in his chair. "How can I help?"

The image of the man being trampled overloads my mind. He might have lived had I pulled the trigger and taken Trey down when I had the chance.

I know the purpose of guilt.

Guilt tells us when we've done something wrong so we can change our behavior to better ourselves and others, but it also burns like a red-hot poker, reigniting ashes of the past. Based on the news, it appears Trey doesn't need Dr. Santan and Malcolm anymore. He's probably killed them by now.

And more people will die if I don't do something.

"I need to borrow your car, Dad."

"Where's yours?"

"Would you believe it broke down?"

He smiles bitterly. "No. I would not."

"I can't tell you, but I need it."

"I need it, too. Tell me why you need it, and I'll give you the keys."

"How about your utility truck?" His ancient, white Ford sits idle next to the driveway, rusting in the sun. It's always there. "You don't need it, right? You only ever drive it when you have to haul something."

"I want to help you. Please tell me what's going on."

"I'd love to tell you, but . . ." I go to him. He stands. "But, it's highly confidential. If the people I'm dealing with knew I'd told you anything, you could lose everything." I wave my hand through the air, ending near his TV.

"What? Why can't you tell me?"

"I'm in danger, Dad, but don't worry. They're leading me to Dr. Santan, and I'm meeting with one of them later today. It's a safe meeting, and it will be over soon." My insides tighten. I hate lying to him so much, even if these are only half-lies. "I promise. Everything will be okay."

I hold out an open palm.

He pulls his keyring from his pocket, removes a Ford key, and hands it to me. "Promise you'll call if you need anything?"

"I promise."

"I hate to say this." He wrinkles his nose. "But you don't smell good."

"I know. Can I take a quick shower? I just need some clothes."

"Oh, let me see what I have in the garage. I still have a few boxes of your mom's things I was planning to take to Goodwill."

In minutes, I'm showered and dressed in the smallest blouse and slacks my mother owned. It's not bad. The scarf matches her blouse. I put on the sunglasses, tell my father goodbye, and step outside with Malcolm's laptop in hand.

There's no one around.

Dad's Ford Ranger is marred with rusty dents up and down its sides. I hope it still runs well enough to take me where I'm going. A tire iron, a toolbox, a shovel, a rake— these things are going to sound lovely when I hit the speed bumps getting out of here.

Before I can put the truck in reverse and back down the driveway, my pocket buzzes. It's Alyssa calling my burner phone.

"I don't know how," she says, "but that detective you told me about found me."

"Oh, no. Detective Galen?"

"Yeah, him. He's looking for you, but don't worry. I didn't tell him anything. I know how these things work. I know my rights."

"Thank you."

"Wherever you are, you should leave."

"I am. Did anyone else contact you?"

"No. Why?"

"One of the people on my project, Nimisha, insisted on helping me find Dr. Santan. She's the intern. I think I told you about her before."

"I kind of remember her."

"I gave her your number to call in case she couldn't reach me." Something in the rearview mirror catches my eye, and I look out the back window. A police cruiser drives slowly past the driveway.

"Emma? What's going on? What are you doing?"

I watch the police cruiser leave the cul-de-sac. "I'm going to stop Trey."

"Alone?"

"No. Not alone. There's one person whose life is already in danger because of all this, and I don't care if he goes down with me." I plunk the transmission into reverse. "I'm on my way to his house now. He owes me."

CHAPTER SIXTY-TWO

TREY

Trey stops by the command center on his way to the meeting. He's late. Sverker and Lessard are probably waiting for him in the hall outside his office. He doesn't care. He wants to see the statistics on Kandour one more time before discussing the next steps.

He stands in front of the central workstation facing the wall monitors. He spreads his arms out wide. Tips his head back. The wall monitors bask his face in a green glow. Every status indicator is green. It's a go. His father said he'd never succeed, but the data disagrees. Trey's long-held dream is on a precipice. He's only days away from reality.

His new cell phone vibrates and plays the chorus to Europe's song, "The Final Countdown".

Sverker is calling. The rigid Swede loves to adhere to schedules and possesses little tolerance for anyone's tardiness. Even his boss's.

Trey finds Sverker and Lessard waiting outside his office, as expected. "Greetings, gentlemen." He moves past them and opens the door. "Let's go over the numbers." It's everything Trey can do to keep from bursting with joy. He wants to dance, shout, jump, and scream to the world.

I did it!

Lessard and Sverker take their usual seats between the fish tank and Trey's desk.

Trey tells Lessard to cast his laptop screen onto the wall monitor so everyone can see it.

Green.

Every bar on the chart is green.

The main chart indicates the number of people responding to the *Thought*Fluence messages in Kandour plus eight other cities. The message continues to spread on its own. The green bars mean they have surpassed the number of believers needed for organic mass persuasion. It's unbelievably good.

"As you can see," Lessard says, "we're ahead of schedule. I could show you more, but we don't have any issues to discuss."

"So, we're okay to move ahead of schedule?" Trey asks.

"No. I suggest we hold off. We should stick to the original plan."

"I agree." Sverker's voice is gruffer than usual.

"Why wouldn't we want to move on?" Trey asks. "What's there to gain by waiting?"

Lessard minimizes the graph. "Have you seen the news today?"

"No." A grin snakes its way onto Trey's face. "I've been too busy *making* news to waste time *watching* news."

"We're going to have issues." Lessard pulls up a live news stream. The banner across the bottom reads *Breaking News*, and the caption above the red and white alert reads, *Kandour, India - A City Under Siege.*

362

"So a few crazies are acting out," Trey says. "Maybe this type of thing happens in that town all the time."

"It doesn't," Lessard says. "In fact, Kandour was a sleepy little place until we unleashed our campaign to destroy the internet. They're taking it too far. It's driving them mad. It won't be long before the Indian CBI, the CIA, the FBI, and others trace the mess back to us."

"All the more reason to accelerate our timelines." Trey stands. Faces the monitor. "We need to accomplish our goals before they come after us. If we do, it will be too late for them. In fact, if we succeed, the people serving those agencies will be on our side. They will have received the message and won't want to arrest us."

"I see what you're saying." Sverker rises from his chair. "They will be assimilated."

"Exactly."

Lessard also stands, laptop in hand. "To do that, we'd need to start targeting U.S. cities, but we're weeks away from safely doing that."

"No." Trey leans over, places his palms on his desk, and lifts his head to address Lessard. "We hit the first U.S. city tonight. Carlsbad, California."

"Are you insane?" Lessard takes one hand off his laptop to point at the screen and fumbles. His computer crashes onto the floor. "Don't you see what they're doing?"

A herd of shouting citizens trample a man lying in the street before the camera can pan away.

Trey pulls his laptop near and takes over the monitor. "I've taken the liberty of creating a new schedule. We'll launch in Carlsbad next, then bounce between European, Russian, and U.S. cities. Baltimore, of course, is still last. We've proven the effectiveness, so there's no reason not to focus on the most technologically advanced areas first."

"What about China?" Sverker asks.

"The preliminary tests proved China was the most difficult to penetrate. They blocked almost everything. We'll have to rely on word-of-mouth from the countries near there. Isn't that right, Jack?"

"I want no part of this." Lessard picks up his laptop. The screen didn't survive the fall. "They weren't supposed to harm each other. If we don't take the time to alter the message and reduce this carnage, more will die."

"I thought you were a numbers man, Lessard. Isn't that what a data scientist does? Statistics and numbers? There is something like eight billion people in the world. Less than one hundred people have died on the news there. That's a drop in the bucket, wouldn't you agree?"

Sverker unbuttons his suit jacket.

"It's a small percentage, yes," Lessard says, "but the loss of a single life is no less tragic than a hundred." He turns toward the door.

Sverker steps in his path.

"Being a numbers guy," Trey says, "don't you want to know how the application performs in other countries?"

Sverker lifts his jacket and rests his hand on the butt of the gun tucked into his belt.

Lessard's face turns pale. "Yes, I have wondered." He stops trying to get around Sverker. "Aside from mistakes made translating the messages to other languages, I'm interested in knowing how the differences in cultures might affect the conversion rate."

"Great." Trey shuts the lid to his laptop. "Then, you'll begin with Carlsbad, right?"

Lessard bows his head. Rubs his templates. "I'll need to

get a new laptop from IT and set it up, but yes. I'll get it started."

"In that case," Sverker says, taking his hand off his gun, "I suggest you go straight to the IT department."

Lessard steps around Sverker and leaves unimpeded.

"Do you think he'll do it?" Trey asks.

Sverker smiles. "He'll do it. He lacks the vision for the greater good, but he's not stupid."

"It is for the greater good, isn't it?"

"Yes, sir. It's like you always tell me. Sometimes you have to break a few eggs to make an omelet."

"That's right." A fire burns inside Trey. It feels so good to be saving the world from itself. Returning to the time before the internet enslaved everyone's eyes to computer screens.

"And speaking of eggs, what should I do with our guests in 2B?"

"We don't need them anymore. Eggs are eggs. You should go ahead and break them."

It feels good to laugh.

CHAPTER SIXTY-THREE

EMMA

It's hard to believe it's come to this.

I warned Wilson.

I told him if he said a word about Malcolm's disappearance—the blood smeared down Malcolm's hallway, what we found on Malcolm's laptop—I would take him down with me.

And what did he do?

He told Nimisha.

He might have told the police by now.

Fortunately, it was clear sailing all the way to Wilson's townhome. Almost. I saw two police cruisers on the way, but they ignored the thirty-something woman in the giant, clown-like glasses and paisley scarf driving the forty-something Ford truck. No black SUVs or other suspicious cars crossed my path.

Wilson left his Audi sports car in front of his garage for the world to see.

I press the doorbell and wait.

It's hard to believe it's come to this.

Me, asking Wilson for help.

Travis answers the door wearing the same robe and slippers from when I came here a few days ago. It makes me wonder if he ever leaves. His puffy black beard hugs his face, and his eyes turn into warriors. "Wilson's not here." He tightens the cloth belt around his robe.

I turn and gaze at the Audi. "Are you sure?"

"Yes." He puts his shoulder back and lifts his chin. "I kicked his ass to the curb."

"Why is his car here? Wait. Don't tell me. That's not his car, is it? He lied about that, too."

"No, that's his car. He'll be back for it and the rest of his things in a while. Hey, I'd love to sell it before he returns. Are you interested?"

"No. Are you saying he moved out?"

"Yes. I kicked him out. I'm done messing around with you academic types. You're all so dry and boring and full of lies. Tell him I hope it works out with that hideous Nimisha. I don't care anymore." He begins to close the door.

"Wait."

"Unless you want to buy his car, we have nothing else to discuss."

I grab the door handle and hold the door open. "Can you tell me where he went?"

"Promise to never come back?"

"Yes."

"I overheard him renting a storage unit off Liberty Heights by the zoo. Goodbye." He pulls the door from my hand and slams it.

Minutes later, I pull up to the storage facility. The entrance is blocked by a crossbar that only opens for customers with access codes. I park along the street, grab

Malcolm's laptop, and walk to the complex. The storage units reside in four long buildings that stand too close to each other. There's only enough room for one car to drive between them at a time, and their roofs sag. The place was built in the sixties. I find Wilson unloading a U-Haul truck in the fourth row.

He walks out of the unit empty-handed and greets me with a smile. "Well, look who's still alive."

"No thanks to you. Why did you tell Nimisha about Malcolm?"

He strides up the ramp into the back of the U-Haul truck. It's almost empty. "I like her. We're friends." He turns around. "Nice outfit. I see you've been hitting the donation boxes at the homeless shelters pretty hard."

"And you're clever as ever." The sight of him always infuriates me. I've got to calm down. Swallow what little pride I have left. "I need your help."

"Is that so?" He picks up a box and heads toward the unit. "What are you going to do for me?" He nods over his shoulder toward the truck.

"Okay. I'll help you unload, but only because we've got to go as soon as we can." I lay the laptop beside the storage unit where it won't be stepped on and head for the truck.

"Where do you think we need to go? I'm kind of busy. I don't know if you noticed, but I'm in the middle of moving."

Our paths cross, carrying boxes to the storage unit. "You were thrown out for lying."

"Is that what Travis told you?"

"I'm sorry," I say. "It doesn't matter why you're here. I need your help to stop Trey."

"I'd like to say I'm flattered." He puts a box down on the floor, starting a new stack. "But, it only makes sense you'd come to me. I'm always bailing you out."

"What?"

"Get real, Emma. Don't you realize how many meetings and proposals I've had to step in and save at the last minute? You're not good under pressure."

"That's not true. I spend months doing the work, then you show up at the last minute and take the credit."

He shakes his head, grinning slyly. "Without me, you'd never get anything over the line. You always choke. It's why D'Angelo thinks you and I make such a great team. Didn't you know that?"

His perspective is preposterous. I don't choke. "You don't add anything. You're almost never there, and when you are, you—you're just a blowhard."

"No, I'm a communicator. I put our work into simple terms businesses and government agencies can understand. Without me, the project would have died years ago."

Be kind, Emma. You need him.

"So," he continues, "it only makes sense you would come to me when the going gets tough outside of work. I'm surprised it's taken this long."

"Are you going to help me or not?" I ask.

"Like I said. I'm busy at the moment."

I carry the last box into the storage unit and sit on it. "The project will die if you don't help. We need D'Angelo back, and if we hurry, there's a chance he's still alive. If you help me stop Trey and save D'Angelo—you can save the project. You'll be a hero."

He sits down on a box across from me.

"Will you please wipe that smug grin off your face?" I ask.

"You need me."

"Yes. Fine. I need you."

"What's your plan?"

I pick up the laptop and open the maps application we first saw at Malcolm's house. "Remember this? It looks like an office building. I think it's where Trey's company is located. I don't have much of a plan, but we need to find out if this *is* Trey's office building, go inside, and see what we find. We'll have to play it by ear after that."

"What do you want me to do?"

"I can't go in there. Trey or one of his goons will recognize me. I need you to do it."

"Goons? I don't know."

"It'll be safe. There should be plenty of people working there. Here." I double-click on the map to zoom into the building. The laptop displays a floor plan. "This is the layout of the first floor." I click on an up-arrow. "And this is the second floor. After we left Malcolm's house, he found a way to text me. When I asked where he was, he wrote, '2B.' I think the *two* means he's on the second floor."

"Okay, so you want me to waltz in there and ask them where 2B is?"

"No. It's best you talk to no one except for me when you're inside. I can guide you."

"How?"

I reach into my pocket and pull out the white earbud Trey left in my apartment. "With this. Connect it to your phone, and I'll call you before you go inside."

He takes the earbud and turns it over in his hand, examining it. "I suppose that will work, but like I said, I can't just waltz in there. I'm sure they have some sort of security."

"You're right."

He stands. Pockets the earbud. "I have an idea." He walks to the back of the unit and returns with a box marked HALLOWEEN. "A few years ago, I went as a Ghostbuster."

He pulls out a dingy white jumpsuit. "Maybe I can get inside if I pretend to be a repairman."

"I have tools in the back of my truck. You can carry them in with you."

He steps to the entrance of the storage unit, looks both ways, then up to the sky. "What do you think would happen if I got caught?"

I don't want to scare him. He's the only way I have of stopping Trey, and if he backs out now, I don't know what I'll do. We've got to stop the attack on that Indian city before more people are trampled to death. "They will probably call the police or something. I'm sure you'll be able to talk your way out of it. You're a communicator, right?"

CHAPTER SIXTY-FOUR

EMMA

The tools in the back of Dad's truck clang and clatter as I hit the speed bump leading into the Monroe office complex. My nerves are already on high alert, and they will only get worse when Wilson sneaks inside.

It's difficult to tell how many buildings are here because they're all so tall, blocking each other. There are at least three. Maybe four. I drive around until Wilson spots one in the shape of an "L," like on the maps application. Sure enough, the closest parking spot to the entrance harbors Trey's golden Acura.

I park on the other side of the lot as far away as possible.

The black buildings have narrow windows outlined with silver trim. They reflect the afternoon sun in a kaleidoscope of dark blues and oranges. Tall shrubs—spires—separated by thick, leafy bushes surround the buildings. Somewhere in there, inside the L-shaped effigy of first-world success, a psychological virus is sending copies of itself to India, and people are killing each other.

"Are you ready for this?" I ask.

"Let's look at the floor plan one more time."

I pull up the first floor on the laptop. "The elevator is here. Take it to the second floor." I click on the up arrow. The second-floor loads. "You're looking for anything that will take you to 2B. I'm guessing it will be a smaller room, so we can rule out these larger areas."

"Right." Wilson points to the screen. "Do you think I should check out the cloudy, unmapped areas first?"

"I don't know. Maybe."

"It totally looks like the type of map my Roomba makes when it can't get into some places, like the closet."

"Yeah." I barely know what he's talking about. My apartment isn't big enough to warrant a robotic vacuum, and I don't make enough money to buy one anyway. "Let me call you."

Wilson puts the earbud in his ear and answers his phone.

"Can you hear me?" I ask.

"Yes."

He stares across the lot to the office complex. His ashen face stills.

"Are you okay?" I ask.

He grins. "Of course I am." He opens the door and gets out. "Piece of cake."

"Don't forget the tools."

He trudges across the lot in his Ghostbusters suit, carrying Dad's toolbox. The load pulls on his shoulder, and he walks with a stunted gait. It's so obvious to me that he's not a handyman, but he should be okay. If the employees inside are busy working, then they shouldn't give him more than a passing glance.

He waits by the door.

I speak into my phone. "Look at your watch if you can

hear me."

"I don't wear a watch."

"Shh."

A young man in a blue suede jacket approaches him.

"Excuse me," Wilson says. "I'm here to check the heater on the second floor, but I'm late. Do you think you could let me in?"

"Are you meeting someone?"

"Uh, yeah. One of the janitors. The head janitor. He didn't answer his phone."

Don't blow it, Wilson.

We should have practiced what he would say. Buildings like this don't have heaters. They have an HVAC system. Even I know that. And the chances there's a "head janitor"?

Ugh.

"Sure, buddy. I can show you where the utility closet is."

He's in.

I listen to their footsteps.

A door opens.

"There he is," the man says.

"Can I help you?" A gruff voice comes across the line.

"Yes," Wilson says. "I'm here to check out the heater on the second floor."

"The heater?"

"Yes."

"You mean the HVAC ducts?

"Sure. Yeah, right. The ducks."

There's a pause, then, "I didn't know anyone was coming."

"They called me in late this morning. It won't take me long."

The gruff guy sighs. "They don't tell me anything."

I listen.

The familiar *ding-dong* of an elevator and the swoosh of sliding doors sound.

"What company do you work for?"

"Sinclair Heating and Cooling."

Why did you tell him your last name, Wilson? You idiot.

Another elevator *dong*, a *swoosh*, and footsteps.

A door opens.

"Here you go. The HVAC system is back there."

"There aren't any windows."

"Of course not." The gruff voice sounds indignant. "It's a utility closet, not a luxury suite."

"Right, right."

There's a long pause, and then, "I'll be downstairs if you need me."

"Sure."

I examine the second-floor plan on the laptop. "Can you hear me?"

"Yes," Wilson whispers.

"Do you know what side of the building you're on?"

"No. There aren't any windows in here. It's not very nice."

"Never mind. Wait a while, then move out and try to orient yourself."

"Hey, I was right. There's a vacuum like mine in here."

"Don't touch anything."

A song plays, and a female computer voice says, "Ready to clean."

"What did you—" I hold my tongue. A window pops up on the laptop. It's a crude version of the second-floor plan with a red dot flickering inside a small room. Four buttons with arrows like a game controller appear in the lower right corner.

"What did you say, Emma? You're breaking up."

"Don't say my name out loud," I shout.

"Ouch. Don't yell at me."

"Are you holding that vacuum cleaner?"

"Yes."

"Go to the door."

The red dot on the map moves toward the hallway. I can't believe it. Malcolm must have hacked into the vacuum and used it to map the office. I picture the robot roaming the halls every night, sucking up dirt, and playing its little song. Malcolm was brilliant.

Is brilliant. He's not dead. He *is* brilliant.

"I can see where you are now," I say. "Just keep the vacuum with you."

"I don't understand."

"I can see where the vacuum is on the map. Don't worry about it. I want you to explore one of the unmapped areas. Remember, you're looking for 2B. Take a right turn down the hallway."

"Okay," he whispers.

The dot moves.

He passes what looks like an open office area on his right. "Keep going."

I hear the upbeat sounds of an active workplace. Fingers tapping keyboards. Conversations blending. Squeaky office chairs squeaking.

He nears the end of the hall, and the noises die away.

"The first unmapped area is on the other side of the wall to your right. Do you see a door?"

"It's not really a door. There's no handle on it. Just a keycard reader."

"Can you open it?"

"Let me try."

There's a *clanging* like he's rummaging through the toolbox. Then, a scratching and a scraping.

"Excuse me, can I help you?" A man's voice, thick and rich, booms over the line.

"Oh, hello, officer." Wilson's voice shakes. "No. I'm fine. I'm here to fix your heater."

"There's no heater in that room."

"There's not?"

"No. We don't have any heaters. We have an HVAC system. Who are you?"

CHAPTER SIXTY-FIVE

TREY

Trey sits back in his chair with his feet on his desk. He has his hands behind his head and his eyes on the Carlsbad penetration map. It's the perfect place to strike next. Small, but close to Los Angeles and San Diego. With momentum, when the message spreads to those larger cities, it will be unstoppable.

He glances at the fish swimming in the tank beside the large screen monitor. Like so many people in the world right now, they haven't a clue.

Sverker appears on the monitor. He's outside the office door.

"Come on in." Trey presses a button on his remote, and the door unlatches.

Sverker bursts into the room. "We might have a problem."

"I'd say so." Trey points at the screen. "The people of Carlsbad don't seem to be cooperating yet. Has Lessard started the campaign?"

"It's only been a couple of hours," Sverker says. "He said

it will take longer in the U.S. because the population density doesn't compare to India's."

Trey swings his feet off the desk. "We need to move fast. Isn't there something more he can do?"

"No. Maybe. It—we might have a bigger problem."

"What's that?"

"One of my men found someone trying to break into the interrogation room."

Trey stands. This is horrible. It could be the police. Undercover. "Did you take care of our guests like I asked?"

Sverker's face tightens. "No. They're still in 2B."

"Why didn't you do it?"

"I—"

"Well? Why?"

"I'm an information extraction specialist." He puts his shoulders back. "I have a one-hundred percent success rate. I've never had to kill anyone before. They've always talked before it's come to that."

"Are you saying you're afraid?"

"No, I'm saying, when I went to take care of them, I wanted to make sure to do it in a way that would make disposing of their bodies easy and untraceable in case the interrogation room was ever discovered. And now, it's been discovered."

"And they're still in there. What happened?"

"Please calm down. Everything is okay. Someone posing as a repairman tried to get into the room. One of my security guards has him in the break room."

"Is he a cop?"

"I don't think so. He doesn't seem smart enough to be a cop. For some weird reason, he was carrying a robotic vacuum cleaner. He refuses to let go of it."

Trey breathes a sigh of relief. It's probably a mentally deranged subject from the fifth-floor test lab. Occasionally, a test volunteer reacts poorly to receiving messages. They flip out. It's nothing sedation and Xanax, followed by a trip to the North Virginia wilderness, hasn't handled.

The numbers on the bottom of the wall monitor begin rising. Fast.

"You didn't schedule to have the heat fixed without telling me, did you?" Sverker asks.

"No . . . no, I didn't." He can't take his eyes off the screen. It's happening. Carlsbad is assimilating. "Look. It's working."

"Yes, sir. I see that."

"Get Lessard in here. We need to get started on Europe and Russia."

Sverker pulls out his phone and taps on the screen. "What about the intruder?"

Suddenly, the wall monitor goes black.

Trey hits the refresh button on his laptop.

Nothing happens.

He hits it again, and this time, the screen comes on, but—horror of all horrors . . .

500 - Internal Server Error

No. Not now.

Trey is thrust back to the first time he ever saw this error. The prototype demonstration Malcolm botched in front of the first serious venture capitalists. It marked the beginning of two hellish decades for Trey. The pain and suffering he endured to get this far, and—

"It could be a scaling problem," Sverker says. "Lessard warned us about that."

Scaling. That was the problem back then, too.

Lessard appears outside the office door, and Trey lets him in. "Lessard, look."

As usual, the geek is walking around with his laptop open, looking at the screen. He glances up at the monitor, then sits.

"Fix it. Fix it. Fix it." Trey feels himself losing control.

Lessard types something, and the status page returns to the monitor.

The bars on the graph turn green.

Trey puts his hand over his heart. Gasps.

"Are you okay, sir?" Sverker asks.

"Yes, of course. I'm fine." The numbers at the bottom of the screen have increased two-fold. "I'm better than fine."

"What about the intruder?" Sverker asks.

"What about him?"

"Should I put him in with the others?"

"Show me."

"Just a moment." Sverker swipes his phone and steps near Trey. He holds it so Trey can see the screen. "Here's a visual on the break room."

The grainy image shows a man in a jumpsuit sitting at a table. He's clutching a vacuum cleaner and watching the guard by the door. He's somewhat familiar, but it's hard to see his face from the security camera's angle. "When did we start making the test subjects wear white suits?"

"We didn't. Do you think he escaped from the fifth floor?"

"I do," Trey says. "He looks like a wacko."

"I'll need to verify that."

"There's no one better for the job. Let's find out if he actually knows anything. Better safe than sorry."

Sverker pockets his phone. Cracks his knuckles.

"Will do."

CHAPTER SIXTY-SIX

EMMA

I quickly scan the *Thought*Fluence parking lot, looking for anything unusual, then return my eyes to the laptop. The red dot on the map stopped moving a while ago. Wilson might have the vacuum cleaner with him still, but it's hard to know. I do know he's still wearing the earbud because I hear him talking to the man with the deep voice. He referred to him as "officer," but I don't think the police are in there. The man is probably a security guard. Either way, this is not good. He's holding Wilson against his will in a small room.

"How long are you going to keep me here?" Wilson asks. "I need to fix the air conditioning."

"Hold on," the guard says.

He's having a muffled conversation in the background. I don't know if he's talking to Wilson or someone else.

"Well?" Wilson asks.

"I thought you said you were here to fix the heater," the guard says.

"It is. I am. It's both. The heat and the air conditioning."

"Mr. Sohlmann says the heater isn't broken. He's on his

way."

"He just doesn't know about it. Come on, buddy. Let me go. I didn't do anything wrong. If I don't fix it, I could lose my job."

"Sit back down."

"Okay, okay. You don't have to do that."

"Don't move."

"I won't. You can put that thing away.'

"Wilson," I whisper. "Good job. Keep him there as long as you can. I'm coming in."

I jump out of the truck and look in the back. There's a clawed tire iron beneath the rear window. I take it and glance at the laptop inside the cab. Without it, I won't be able to track Wilson's location anymore, but I don't dare take it with me. If Trey got hold of Malcolm's machine, things would get a whole lot worse.

My trek across the parking lot is a blur. I wait and tailgate someone into the building, then head for the stairwell. A few people in the lobby give me strange looks, but no one says a word. With all the adrenaline, I don't feel the weight of the tire iron in my hand. I take a right at the top of the stairs and run to the door Wilson said had no handle. I look up and down the hall, scanning for trouble.

So far, so good.

I bash the key card reader with the tire iron, but the door doesn't open. I thrust the claw end into the door seam and pull, using all my weight. The door makes a harsh *crack* and pops open. I quietly close it behind me and pull my phone out. Fortunately, there aren't any security cameras in here.

A voice I hadn't heard before, one with a Swedish accent, says, "Wait here. Don't let him leave."

"Yes sir," says the guard.

Tall metal containers, like high-school lockers, line the walls. They're labeled—2E to 2H on my left and 2A to 2D on my right. When I open the one marked 2B, the back of the container slides open, revealing a hidden corridor.

Very sneaky, Trey.

A bloody, salty odor fills the passage. I don't want to go down there, but I have to. When I reach the end, I see where the smell is coming from.

D'Angelo is barely recognizable, lying on a sanguine-stained floor, his head cradled in Malcolm's lap. They're locked in a cage on the left side of the room. A microwave sits on a cart outside the cage on the right side. D'Angelo's face has been obliterated, and Malcolm's doesn't look much better. He has a giant mark between his eyes, and his cheeks resemble burnt lunch meat.

"Emma," Malcolm says.

"Quiet." I ram the tire into the cage door and pry it open.

Malcolm stands. Helps D'Angelo to his feet.

"Can he walk?" I whisper.

"Oh." D'Angelo opens his good eye. "It's you." He hangs from Malcolm's arms like a sack of wet mice.

"I can carry him," Malcolm says.

"Okay, come on."

The sound of a door slamming in the hallway breaks the silence.

We exit the cage.

Malcolm drags D'Angelo across the floor and lays him next to the microwave cart.

I stand to the right of the hall entrance, and Malcolm stands to the left.

Footsteps come down the corridor fast, but we're out of sight.

A gun extends into the room, and I swing the tire iron.

The iron misses the gun but connects with a man's shoulder.

Malcolm tackles him to the floor, and the gun goes flying.

I race over and pick the weapon up. It's exactly like the one they used to kill Kevin.

Malcolm puts all his weight on the man and holds him down.

"Get off me, you oaf."

"Hold him there," I say.

The man struggles, and Malcolm pops him in the nose. "I ought to kill you."

I reach under D'Angelo's arm and pull him up. "Can you walk?"

"I think so."

We cross the floor. When we near the hallway entrance, the man reaches for my foot, and Malcolm pops him another one.

I drag D'Angelo down the corridor to the metal containers and lean him up against the one marked 2E. "Stay put."

What a stupid thing to say. He isn't in any shape to go anywhere on his own.

As I stride back to the cage room, I raise the gun and promise myself I'll shoot it if I have to.

I'll kill that man if I have to.

I won't make that mistake again.

"Over there." Malcolm nods toward the microwave cart. "There are zip ties in the cabinet under the microwave."

I keep the gun trained on the man while Malcolm fastens his hands behind his back. The man says nothing. He stares at me, unblinking. Malcolm uses another zip tie to fasten his ankles together and another to hitch his arm to the cage.

"He won't be going anywhere anytime soon," Malcolm says, then punches him in the face one last time. The man's eyes close for only an instant before returning to their cold stare.

He says nothing.

"Let's go," I say.

At the end of the hall, Malcolm hands me the tire iron and throws D'Angelo over his shoulder. I stow the gun in my waistband, and we sprint toward the stairwell. Malcolm's lumbering footsteps thunder down the hall. Workers steer clear of us, putting their backs against the walls. Some scream when they see my gun.

The door to the stairwell opens before we reach it, and two guards draw their weapons. "Freeze!"

We change course and rush to a window. I bash it with the tire iron and step onto the ledge. A black and white striped canvas awning stretches over a concrete patio below. I toss the iron to the ground and turn around.

"Don't move, or we'll shoot." The guards have stopped halfway down the hall. One has striking blond hair, and they're both young. Their uniforms make them look more like rent-a-cops than Trey's goons.

Malcolm eases D'Angelo over the broken glass into my arms. I set him down on the canvas awning and let him slide. He comes to rest near the bottom edge.

When I look back at Malcolm, the window next to him shatters. I shield my face from the flying shards of glass.

"Stop," a guard shouts. "I won't miss next time."

Malcolm steps onto the ledge and shuffles to the corner of the building without stepping on the awning. He moves fast for a big man.

The guards appear in the window, weapons drawn.

Malcolm bends down, grasps the awning, and drops his feet over the edge. He lets go, and his body makes a *thwump* when it hits the ground.

"Don't shoot," I say. "This man is hurt. We're only trying to take him to a hospital."

The blond guard leans forward, squints, then cocks his head. "What do you think, Steve?"

"What the hell happened to him?" the other guard asks.

"Emma," Malcolm shouts. "Let him down. I'm ready."

My chest swells. I can't see Malcolm from here, but there's no time. The guards could shoot at any moment. I shove D'Angelo off the awning, hoping Malcolm has the strength to catch him. Hoping Malcolm is standing in the right spot.

"Freeze," the blond guard yells.

I shake my head. Like Malcolm, I drop my feet over the edge, swing out, and let go of the awning. The ground hits my right side the hardest, sending throngs of pain up my thigh. I roll as carefully as I can, but it still annihilates my side.

Malcolm is already carrying D'Angelo across the parking lot.

Limping, I force myself to run after him. "Wait. It's that way."

Malcolm turns his head.

"The white truck up there."

He nods.

I make a mental note to buy my dad a new tire iron when this is over.

Malcolm loads D'Angelo into the truck's bed and climbs in after him.

I hop in the cab and open the rear window so Malcolm

can hear me. "How's he doing?"

"He's still breathing."

I grab the laptop. The red dot on the maps application hasn't moved.

"Wilson, can you hear me?"

His voice sounds like an old modem making a call. "Yes."

"Are you alone?"

"Yes."

"Get out of there. Now."

"I—there were gunshots."

"Just run." I start the engine. "I'll drive by the front door and pick you up."

"But—I can't."

Between the bad connection, the truck's engine, and my thumping heart, I can barely hear him.

"Oh my God," he says. "It's you."

I hear another voice, but I can't understand a word.

"Go on without me, Emma," Wilson says. "It's going to be okay. I have help."

"Don't say my name."

Malcolm pounds his fist against the cab. "Let's go. He's starting to bleed a lot. We need to get him to the hospital now!"

CHAPTER SIXTY-SEVEN

TREY

Trey can control nearly every aspect of his office with his custom remote control. The lighting. The heating. The cooling. Access to the safe behind the fish tank. Security cameras throughout *Thought*Fluence and, of course, the large wall monitor. He can send it straight to Netflix at the touch of a button. He could use an app on his phone to control these things, but he prefers the solid feel of his remote control. He doesn't have to input a username and password like he would if it were an app. It's real. It's control.

He has control.

Lessard and Sverker sit across from him, side by side.

He presses a button, and the lights dim.

Lessard has his laptop on his lap. The glow upon his face intensifies when Trey dims the lights a little more.

Sverker has his head bowed. His hands clasped on his lap.

"I cornered your dog in the hallway a little while ago," Trey says. "Rasmus said he found you tied up in the interrogation room."

Sverker nods. Stares at his hands.

"How did this happen?" Trey asks. "You let them get away."

"It may not matter," Lessard says. "Our influence has spread well beyond Carlsbad."

"Oh, it matters," Trey says. "Malcolm will stop at nothing to destroy me, and he's back out there." Trey slams his hand on his desk. "Sverker."

"I have every available man searching for him," Sverker says. "At last report, he hadn't returned to his house."

"And he won't." Trey stands. Wipes his forehead. "It's impossible to find him now. He won't let us do it again." Sverker sits motionless. Eyes cast down. "I can't believe you let this happen. I don't understand. What were you doing?"

"We were short-handed today. Rasmus was having his hip looked at by a doctor, and two others were on vacation. I was interrogating the intruder when that woman broke into 2B. I couldn't be in two places at once."

"The intruder?"

"Yes. The heating and cooling repairman."

"Hmm." Trey paces. "He must have been sent to distract us, and you fell for it. Where are we holding him?"

Sverker shifts in his seat. Says nothing.

Trey approaches the Swede. "Sverker, look at me."

He lifts his head. "He escaped as well."

"You've got to be kidding me."

"After they tied me up—after they escaped from the interrogation room—the guard saw them on a monitor. He left the intruder alone in the break room to try and stop them. Like I said, we were short-handed today."

The shame in Sverker's eyes does nothing to lessen Trey's rage. It won't bring Malcolm back.

"Dammit!" Trey turns his back on the two men. Walks to

the fish tank. "Why didn't the guard lock the door to the break room?"

"He said he did."

"Have you reviewed the security footage? Was your man lying?"

"There was no footage. The security cameras stopped recording right before the guard left the break room."

Trey thinks for a moment. "We have a mole. Someone shut the cameras off and helped him escape."

"That is a possibility, sir." Sverker wavers. Trey has never seen him this shaken.

Lessard types on his keyboard as if he's at his desk.

"What about the others?" Trey asks. "Was there footage of the parking lot?"

"Only from before their escape. Malcolm and the woman arrived in a white truck. It was gone after they ran away. My men are looking for it now."

"Are you tracking the license plate number? Emma doesn't own a truck."

"No."

"Why the hell not?"

"It was parked too far away for the cameras to catch it."

"It may not matter," Lessard says. "You should look at the latest on the campaign."

"Fine." Trey marches to his desk and uses his remote to give Lessard's laptop access to the wall monitor. "Go ahead."

The status map appears on the screen. Lessard pans the map to Southern California. An amorphous red blob centered on Carlsbad has spread north and south, reaching Los Angeles and consuming San Diego.

Trey gasps. "I don't believe it. We're overtaking Los Angeles. You might be right, Jack. It might not matter." It's happening. It's really happening. "Change it to the news. How is the world responding?"

"Wait," Sverker says. "What is that?"

"Where?" Lessard asks.

"Near Carlsbad. There's a hole."

Trey steps closer to the monitor.

Lessard zooms in. Sverker's right. Several areas to the south are returning to normal.

The influence is receding.

"I was concerned this would happen," Lessard says. "We hit it too hard, too fast. People are rejecting the message."

The breaks in the red coverage grow. The conversion rate number at the bottom of the screen slows down. "No." Trey turns away from the screen. Eyes Lessard. "It's not that. It's Malcolm." Sverker bows his head. "Malcolm is blocking the signal again."

Lessard's fingers fly over his keyboard. "You're right. Something is stopping the follow-on maintenance messages."

"My men will find him," Sverker says. "We're scanning every mobile phone tower in the Baltimore area looking for a bead. Eventually, he'll pop his head up, and we'll nab him. It's only a matter of time."

"We don't have time," Trey says. "Malcolm isn't going to 'pop his head up' again. He's too smart. And, now that Emma has the professor, she might go to the police."

"I would have taken him to the hospital if were her." Lessard hits a button, and the status page disappears.

"We're circling the police stations and the major hospitals, watching for that truck."

"You'd better be," Trey says. "What about the repairman? Do you have any idea who he was?"

"No."

Sverker has never failed like this before. If only he'd killed Dr. Santan and Malcolm when Trey had asked him to. Sverker's inexperience in that department has put the entire project at risk. "What else are you doing? Anything?"

Sverker looks up from his lap. "Yes. Rasmus reminded me of the other woman at the apartment where Malcolm shot him. The blonde with the curly hair. You saw her, right? Do you remember her?"

"Yes, vaguely."

"Her name is Alyssa Brown. She's a longtime friend of Emma Petranova's."

"Okay," Trey says. "I think Emma mentioned her to me once or twice. Where is she now?"

"We don't know. We thought she might have been a part of today's rescue, but she didn't appear on any cameras."

"Find her," Trey says. "I have an idea."

"We're already working on it, but like I said"—Sverker raises his hands—"we're short-handed."

"Pull your men off the search for Malcolm and Emma. It's a waste of time. I want you to put everyone on this Alyssa person. I want to know everything about her. Who she spends her time with. Where she is. What she is doing. Let me know when it's done."

"How will that stop Malcolm from blocking the signal?" Lessard asks.

"You need to think more like a human once in a while, you know that?"

Lessard looks up from his laptop. Cocks his head.

"We can't stop Malcolm directly because we can't find him. He's probably still with Emma, so he won't let us find her either. But, if we find her friend—this Alyssa Brown—we can make them come to us."

CHAPTER SIXTY-EIGHT

EMMA

The pain in my hip wakes me, but I'm not ready to get up. I keep my eyes closed, hoping for sleep to return, but it doesn't. The cold air flowing in and out of my nostrils keeps me awake. The entire right side of my body aches. When I attempt to straighten my legs, they hit something. I'm cramped. Slowly, I realize if I rolled over, I'd fall onto the floor of Dad's truck.

Yesterday rushes into my mind.

I labor to a sitting position and open the glove compartment. Good. The gun is still there.

I swipe a path through the condensation on the windshield, and the weeping cherry tree on my mother's childhood home sways in the wind. I don't know where Malcolm went to. He must have slept in the farmhouse, if he slept at all. After leaving D'Angelo at a Walgreens pharmacy and asking an employee to call an ambulance, we went to a convenience store and purchased more burner phones with data. Malcolm spent the trip up here using one to connect his laptop to the internet and block Trey's messages.

For several minutes, I lost my mind when Malcolm told

me Trey had attacked a city in the U.S.

I almost stopped breathing, panicking.

Halfway here, I remembered the gun I'd left between the mattresses at Motel 6. Malcolm is probably still mad at me for turning around and going back. For a while after that, he thought a red mini-SUV was following us, but it turned off the road before we pulled up to the farmhouse.

I had to have the gun. Malcolm thinks he can stop Trey using his laptop alone, but he won't be able to if Trey's goons find us and take it away from him.

If they do find us, I will be ready.

The door to the truck creaks when I close it. I step into the morning sun, its rays shooting through the weeping cherry tree's branches. Malcolm wouldn't let me retrieve the magnifying glass from my apartment yesterday, and he was right. It's not safe there. Still, it's awkward being here without it.

The wooded hills loom over the farmhouse. The weather-worn front door doesn't latch anymore. "Malcolm? Are you in here?" I go inside. He's not in the living room or kitchen. The bedroom is also empty.

I step onto the porch. "Malcolm?"

"Up here."

Around the side of the farmhouse, I find him sitting on a granite rock halfway up the hill. He's perched there like a gargoyle, hunched over his laptop.

My hip hurts as I trudge up the steep incline.

"I had to come up here to get a signal," he says.

"How's it going?" I sit on the ground next to his rock.

"Really well, actually."

"How's your face?"

"I've never had good skin, so not much has changed." He

keeps his eyes on his screen. "Maybe now I'll finally do something about it and have surgery. I found some Ibuprofen in the truck. It feels better now."

When this is all over, I'm going to pay for him to have the scars fixed. I'll take out a loan if I have to. "Were you able to find Wilson?"

"No. The vacuum cleaner hasn't moved. I check it every once in a while. I've been spending all my time trying to stop Trey."

"And?"

"And it's working. I installed a new filter. He started sending his messages to machines in Carlsbad, California, so that's where I started. My blocker is coming in behind his transmissions, but it's not enough yet. His messages have already spread to Colorado."

"Oh, no. Are we too late?"

"Wait. What's this?"

"What?"

"There's a new file here." He jerks his head back. "Someone just uploaded a file to my computer."

I stand. Look over his shoulder.

OPEN-ME-MALCOLM.readme

"Are you sure it wasn't there before?"

"Yes. The timestamp is one minute ago."

He highlights the file, copies and pastes the name into another program, and a box pops up, displaying a green check mark. "It's clear. It's not a virus."

"Are you going to open it?"

He does.

Malcolm, stop what your doing and come to the address below by 4 p.m. today. Bring Emma. In exchange for you, we will give the little girl to her. Tell her Vivian wants to see her auntie Emma. We'll know when you have read this file. Confirm the exchange by renaming it to 'CONFIRMED.readme.'

Malcolm picks up a burner phone and smashes it against the rock.

I stand too quickly and almost tumble forward down the incline. "Do they know where we are?"

"They found my laptop's IP address, but I doubt they could geo-locate the nearest cell tower." He glances at the smashed phone. "They won't be able to now. Besides, they want us to come to them, so they've probably given up trying to find us."

I read the message again. "Do it."

"What?"

"Rename the file. We have to meet them."

"No, we don't. We've got to shut him down. Look." He switches to a different window. "Tiny pockets are showing in Texas now. It's still spreading."

"Have you read the news?" I ask. "Is it as bad in California as it was in India? Are people killing each other?"

"No, it's not as bad, but that's not the problem."

"How is people killing each other not a problem?"

"It's not about that. He has convinced everyone to destroy the internet. They're attacking cell towers. Cutting internet coax cables. Digging up fiber optics. Ripping old ethernet cables out of walls. Police have surrounded electrical stations in some places to protect the cable companies' power supply, but there aren't enough cops to go around."

"Why would he do this?"

Malcolm pulls a new burner phone out of a plastic shopping bag and switches it on. "Because—"

"Wait. Never mind. We've got to save Vivian. We should go now."

"No. We need to stay here and save the world."

"Can't you do that from the car?"

If Alyssa were here, she'd accuse him of being overly dramatic.

Alyssa.

The gravity of the message sets in.

They've kidnapped her daughter. They probably have her, too. Vivian is somewhere in the hands of Trey's goons, and it's all my fault for not—no. Guilt is self-serving. It helps no one. Blame isn't much better, but Alyssa promised me they were in a safe place.

No.

I can't place the blame on her. It's all Trey. How did he find her?

"On the way up here last night"—Malcolm puts the burner phone down—"I couldn't make much progress from the car. The signal kept going in and out. It was miserable. I've got to stay put if I'm going to stop him."

"If you do that, he'll kill Vivian."

"Who's Vivian?" He begins typing frantically.

I tell him about her. The sweet child of divorce. Her innocent chestnut eyes. We have to do both: save her *and* save the world.

I rip the laptop out from under his hands and run down the hill.

My right leg screams in pain.

He calls after me.

Inside the farmhouse, I barricade myself in the bathroom and rename the file.

CONFIRMED.readme.

CHAPTER SIXTY-NINE

TREY

She's not an ugly kid. Vivian. In the short time Trey has been around her, she's grown on him. She reminds him of his niece when she was little. It's been years. Katie must be in college by now. He wishes he'd spent more time with his family, but the world needed him, and his sister disowned him after their dad died. She blamed him for their father's death.

Witch.

Everything Trey has done, he's done for the greater good. The world needs him to finish what he started.

"Take this." He hands Vivian an iPad and a pair of headphones. "You can watch a movie during our trip." Vivian's smile warms his heart. "Go on, get in." She climbs into the rear bench seat of a *Thought*Fluence fleet vehicle. One of many black SUV behemoths.

Sverker is already sitting on the other side of the girl. "What do you have there?" He raises his devilish eyebrows.

"I'm going to watch a movie," Vivian says, putting the headphones on.

"Let me get you started." Trey climbs in next to her and

opens up Netflix. "You can choose from any of these."

She chooses one, and it begins to play.

Having kids of his own someday isn't out of the question. It always was before, but now that he's on the verge of success, raising a child in the new world would be a blessing. Trey Wilkes—entrepreneur, savior. Father. He imagines how things will be when Emma sees the light. She was so beautiful when he first saw her at that awards banquet. Knowing he could never hurt her, he'd originally wanted to get close only to keep her from finding Dr. Santan. That hadn't worked. He still loved her. If it hadn't been for that detective, they would have kept dating.

He had fallen in love.

Real love.

But it's okay now. The future is bright.

Once Emma adapts to his new world, they will be together. She'll come around.

"Are we ready?" the driver asks.

"Yes," Trey says. "Let's go."

"Punch it, Nils." Rasmus sits in the front passenger seat. He's been giddy since Sverker convinced Trey to let him come to the exchange. He wants revenge for being shot in the hip.

Nils puts the SUV in drive, and they head for the storage lot.

"When we arrive," Trey says, "we stick to the plan. You're absolutely certain they're meeting us, right?"

"Lessard said he received the confirmation file from Malcolm," Sverker says.

"Okay, then we stick to the plan."

"Absolutely."

"Did you hear that, Rasmus?" Trey asks. "The plan?"

"I'll follow the plan, but if they try anything, I'm killing them all."

Trey glances at Vivian. She doesn't react to his comment. Headphones in place, she's focused on a cartoon bear in a big red hat.

"We stick to the plan," Sverker says, raising his voice.

Trey lowers his. "You said you had him under control."

"For Rasmus, this *is* under control."

"How's the hip, Rasmus?" Trey raises his voice over the engine.

"Don't worry about me," Rasmus says. He racks the slide on his handgun. "Worry about the big bastard who shot me."

"Just hold off until after we have him subdued." Trey has a bad feeling. "You'll get your revenge. We can't risk letting him get away again."

"Patience, Rasmus." Sverker reaches over the seat and puts his hand on the dubious sociopath's shoulder. "Remember what we talked about."

"I remember." Rasmus stows his weapon in his jacket. "I just don't like it."

Sverker leans over Vivian's head and whispers to Trey, "What about the woman?"

"What about her?"

"I still don't think we can let her live. She's seen the interrogation room. She knows everything."

"Unlike Malcolm, she can't stop the campaigns. Once it's all over, she'll come around. You need to have patience, too."

Vivian giggles at something she sees on the screen. The bear has his head stuck in a bucket.

As planned, they arrive early. Rasmus jumps out and unlocks the chain holding the gate closed. The sign reads SAGE STORAGE CENTER. Barbed-wire spirals run along the top of the chain-link fence surrounding the container yard.

Nils guides the SUV through the gate, then stops to wait for Rasmus.

Trey lowers his window. "Leave the gate open so they can get in."

Rasmus ambles back to the SUV, favoring his right leg, and reclaims his seat. He's definitely not one hundred percent.

Beyond the vacant mud field ahead, the yard is a chaotic jungle of forty-foot steel shipping containers stacked haphazardly throughout. Streaked with rust, the once brightly colored containers—solid blue, red, orange, yellow—are now faded monstrosities taking up space. Nils positions them on the far side of the dirt area, swinging the SUV around so they can see when Emma arrives. Though at least a mile away, the harbor's briny scent wafts in through Trey's window. He pictures himself lying on a beach in the sun somewhere far away with nothing but his mind for entertainment. No computers. No phones.

He'll get there. Someday. Someday soon.

Nils picks up a pair of binoculars and puts them to his eyes. "They're here."

The white Ford truck from the surveillance footage cruises through the gate.

"There are two people in the vehicle," Nils says.

The truck stops in the middle of the clearing, keeping a safe distance.

Nils exits the SUV with his gun drawn.

Malcolm and Emma get out of the truck across the clearing. They appear to be unarmed.

Trey pulls the headphones off Vivian. "We're here. I'm going to hang onto your arm and not let go until it's time, like we talked about, okay?"

She nods.

Nils motions for everyone to join him and they climb out.

Trey can see that Malcolm brought his laptop with him. That's a good thing.

"Tell him to put his gun down," Emma shouts. "We not going to cause any problems."

"It's just a precaution," Trey says.

Malcolm steps closer to them. "Don't worry, Emma. He's not going to hurt us. He needs me to help him with his project, just like old times. He's still trying to be the next Bill Gates. He thinks he's going to be a billionaire."

"That's not true," Trey says. "I want to make the world a better place." He glances down at Vivian, her arm held tight in his grasp. "I want to do it for the children."

"How will destroying the internet make it a better place?" Emma asks.

"It's not," Malcolm says. "He's just doing this so he can hold the world ransom. He's a greedy businessman. He's evil. He's Dr. Evil. He wants one *million* dollars."

"This is why things didn't work out between us, Malcolm. You were always too short-sighted. Emma's too young to remember, but you know how things were before 1994. You used to wear all those concert T-shirts from the eighties for a reason. It was a golden time, then the internet ruined our lives. People like you and your Facebook friends ruined our lives. Don't you remember?"

"You're insane," Emma yells.

"No," Trey says, flashing his salesman smile. "We're all insane. Can you remember a day when you didn't look at your cell phone? The beginning of this millennium is rife with mental disorders. Everyone has anxiety, depression, ADHD, suicidal thoughts—it's not a coincidence. It's the internet. I ought to know. Dementia killed my father."

Malcolm shakes his head. "No. You killed your father."

Trey keeps the smile on his face, but his insides begin to burn.

"Are we going to do this or not?" Rasmus pulls out his gun and aims it at Malcolm.

Malcolm puts the laptop down and raises his hands.

"Come over here, Mr. Schmidt, and we'll release the girl," Sverker says.

"How do we know you're not going to kill him?" Emma asks.

"Emma." Trey tightens his grip on Vivian. "You know me. I'm not a murderer. Let's say Malcolm's right for a moment. I'm a greedy businessman, not a murderer."

"I'm not a businessman," Rasmus says. He closes one eye and aims at Malcolm, holding his gun with both hands. His forearms flex.

Emma reaches behind her back and pulls out her weapon. Aims it at Rasmus.

"I see you brought your toy," Trey says. "That's not a real gun. It's a toy."

"Shut up," she screams. "That's not going to work. Let Vivian go."

Sverker pulls his gun out.

Vivian yells, "Run. Run. Run. I heard them talking. They're going to kill you." She breaks free of Trey's grasp.

He lunges forward, trying to stop her, but misses. His hands skid across the ground. He looks up and sees her running toward Malcolm. Malcolm opens his arms as Trey attempts to stand, but Rasmus fires his gun, and Trey drops back to the ground, covering his head. When he looks up again, Malcolm is lying on his back beneath a fountain of blood, and Rasmus is running toward the fountain.

"Everyone, calm down," Trey shouts.

Sverker runs toward Emma.

She ignores him and fires her weapon at Rasmus, missing wildly. Her bullet pings off a salmon-colored storage container, and Trey ducks down, covering his head for the second time. Damn her. "Everyone, calm down!"

Vivian changes course and heads for the jumble of steel containers at the back of the yard.

"Nils," Sverker shouts. "Go after her." He stops short of Emma and points his gun at her.

Vivian disappears behind a red container, and Nils follows.

Trey stands. Puts his hands in the air. "Everyone, please. Calm down." He begins walking toward Emma.

Rasmus stands over Malcolm, pointing his gun at the big guy's head.

Emma and Sverker are in a stand-off.

Malcolm has both hands on his thigh, but he can't keep the blood from spraying into the air with each heartbeat. Trey hopes he doesn't bleed out before they can shove him into the SUV. It's not too late to stick to the plan.

"Drop your weapon, Emma," Sverker says.

"No."

"Rasmus?" Sverker sneaks a glance at him.

"Yes."

"How badly do you want to blow that man's head off?"

Rasmus licks his wormy lips.

Emma lowers her gun, kneels, and puts it on the ground.

Before she can stand, Sverker steps forward, puts his foot on her outside shoulder, and shoves her sideways. She flails and lands in a mud puddle.

Despite everything, she still looks great.

CHAPTER SEVENTY

EMMA

The one they call Sverker blocks out the sun. He stands over me, pointing his gun at my face. I'm lying on my back—muddy water seeping into my hair, my right leg shaking in pain, my heart hoping Vivian escaped, my soul hurting for the people of Carlsbad, California.

I turn my head and see that sinuous man, the one they call Rasmus, blocking out Malcolm's sun. Malcolm is in a similar predicament, except instead of lying in a mud puddle, he's lying in a pool of blood, holding his leg. "Malcolm. Are you all right?"

"Shut up," Sverker says.

He's on my right side. My gun is to my left.

It's not far away, but I can't reach it without moving my entire body.

"Don't even think about it," he says.

Trey appears over me. Stands next to Sverker. His perfect genetics are skewed by the misguided philanthropy burning inside him. If I could spit in his face from here, I would, but my mouth is dry, and my jaw is tight.

"Can I do it?" Rasmus asks. "Can I? Can I put one in that hole between his eyes?"

"Wait," Trey says.

"But," Rasmus protests, "he's subdued. You said I could kill him when he was subdued. Look at him."

I focus my attention on Rasmus. He clearly tortured animals as a child. Behind his zeal lives an infant no one ever loved. He was a mistake. "How's your head, Rasmus? The last time I saw you, you were unconscious in my friend's basement. I'm glad you're okay."

He looks at me. Tilts his head like a dog hearing a high-pitched whistle. "You are?"

"Don't listen to her," Trey says.

"I saw you limping," I say. "That was Malcolm's fault. He shouldn't have shot you. You have every right to be angry with him."

"Can I shoot him now?" Rasmus asks. "She wants me to do it."

"No," Trey says. "We can still stick to the plan. Make a tourniquet for his leg."

"Stop telling me what to do." Rasmus shakes his head violently. "Stop it."

"Did they tell you who they're going to kill after Malcolm?" I ask. "Did they tell you that part of the plan?"

"Shut up." Sverker kicks my shoulder, knocking me closer to my gun.

"We were going to kill you next." Rasmus licks his lips. "But Mr. Wilkes didn't want to."

Trey smiles at me. "That's right, Emma. No one's going to hurt you."

"After you kill Malcolm," I shout, "they're going to kill you, Rasmus. They never loved you."

"What?"

"Don't listen to her," Trey repeats.

"Don't tell me what to do." Rasmus bends his knees, bouncing.

"Your parents never loved you," I shout. "Why would Trey let you live? You're nothing but a burden to him, just like you were to them."

That strikes a chord.

Rasmus turns. Points his gun at Trey. "Is that true?" he growls.

Sverker aims his weapon at Rasmus—a good dog instinctively protecting his owner.

I roll over, grasp my gun, and begin firing. I pull the trigger again and again, aiming at Sverker. The blasts hurt my ears, and my eyes close involuntarily, and Sverker yells. My gun stops shooting and starts clicking each time I pull the trigger. I roll over again, and something *whizzes* past my head. I look up to see Rasmus aiming at me. He pulls the trigger, and a clump of mud explodes in my face.

I push myself up, and I run.

He fires again.

He misses again.

I look over my shoulder. Sverker is lying on his back, motionless, and Trey is running the other way. He's halfway back to his SUV.

Rasmus lumbers after me, favoring his right leg.

I sprint behind a storage container.

He lets off another shot, pinging my barricade.

"You didn't know my parents," he says. "I wasn't a burden. I was their good boy."

Sandwiched between two rows of storage containers, there's only one way to go. I run to the other end and turn right. Another bullet flies past me, and I glimpse Rasmus back where I started running. With that leg, he has no chance of keeping up with me. I sprint through the steel jungle, changing direction whenever there is a break between containers, generally heading in one direction. The storage yard goes on forever.

"Vivian," I call out. "Where are you?"

My legs stop listening to me. I slow down and catch my breath. A car horn honks, and I head in that direction. A chain-link fence separates me from the rest of the world— what's left of the rest of the world.

On the other side, a sizable patch of grass extends to a street. Cars stream by in both directions.

I grasp the fence and shake it. Flakes of rust fly into the air. The barbed wire running along the top of the fence wiggles.

Then, I see her.

Vivian runs into the street.

A Jeep slams on its brakes to keep from running her over.

"Stop," I scream. "Vivian. Over here."

She makes it across, turns around, and sees me. The wind blows her curly locks to one side, and she waves.

"Wait there," I shout.

A black SUV with tinted windows screeches to a halt in front of her. It blocks my view.

I shake the fence. "Don't get in. Run!"

When the SUV takes off, she is gone.

CHAPTER SEVENTY-ONE

TREY

Crouched in the backseat of the SUV, Trey waits for the gunfire to stop. He hasn't heard any in a while, but that doesn't mean it won't start again. It's fifty-fifty whether Emma got the upper hand or not. She started the gunfight, but Rasmus likely ended it.

Sverker was shot in the chest. He's out of it.

Trey waits a minute, then peers out the windshield.

Rasmus has Sverker by both feet, walking backward, dragging him across the muddy flat. He takes a step, stops, rests, then takes another step.

Trey looks around for Emma. She's not there.

Neither is Malcolm.

That man always could move fast.

Trey reaches into the front seat, grabs the binoculars, and exits the SUV. He doesn't see Malcolm anywhere. The big guy was bleeding profusely, but he didn't die.

He got away.

In the worst possible outcome of all, Malcolm got away.

This is all Rasmus's fault for not sticking to the plan.

Trey slips his hand inside his chest pocket and grips his gun.

Rasmus approaches the SUV, still dragging Sverker.

"Is he still alive?" Trey asks.

"Yes." Rasmus grunts. Pulls Sverker closer. "But not for long."

Nils emerges between two storage containers and sprints up to Trey.

"Where's the girl?" Trey asks. He lets go of his gun and takes his hand out of his jacket. Rasmus looks broken. He's not going to try anything.

"She found a hole in the fence," Nils says, gasping for air. "I couldn't fit through it."

"Damn." Trey slams his hand on the SUV's hood. Rasmus drops Sverker's feet. He gives Trey a cold stare. Blood pours from Sverker's chest, but the Swede still breathes. "Don't just stand there. Take him to the hospital. Drop him off outside." Trey shakes his head. "Help him, Nils."

The two men lift Sverker, and Trey takes off running. He's got to find Malcolm. He's got to make sure Malcolm crawled away and died before causing more damage to the campaign. Trey would love to know the progress. The last he saw, the messages had spread into Texas and the Midwest. The West Coast had been liberated. Internet-free. He wants to celebrate with his followers, but first—where's Malcolm?

He sprints to the place where Malcolm was shot. A trail of blood leads toward the storage containers. Trey follows it. Malcolm must be hiding in one of them. He draws his gun. Is Malcolm in the red one? The blue one? As he gets closer, the bloody trail thins out.

He opens the door to the blue container.

Empty.

The red one.

Also empty.

Malcolm couldn't have made it much farther.

Trey heads for the next container—dark yellow, not unlike his car—and notices scuff marks in the mud next to a large plywood sheet. *Clever, Malcolm.* Slowly, he kneels and pushes the sheet aside. It appears Sage Storage had planned on building something here and dug a deep hole for a foundation or something. Malcolm lies on his back at the bottom, his laptop on his chest, illuminating his face. He's shirtless. Sverker did a wonderful job scarring his belly. His shirt is tied around his leg, and he's no longer bleeding, but he's as pale as parchment. He types quickly. It reminds Trey of the first time he saw Malcolm in the UBalt student center. Geeks love to work in the dark.

Trey takes aim. "Stop blocking the signal, Malcolm. It's over."

"There." Malcolm raises his hand, extends his index finger, then forcefully hits a key on the keyboard.

"What did you do?" Trey asks. "Are you blocking my messages?"

"No." He chokes, and blood runs out of the corner of his mouth. "The opposite."

Trey lowers himself into the hole.

Malcolm closes his eyes.

Trey lays his gun down and picks up the laptop. He sits back against the dirt wall and looks at the screen. Malcolm wasn't lying. From what he can tell, Malcolm opened the transmission up to more cities. The East Coast, starting with Florida. There is a pocket of influence in Virginia. That's only two hundred miles away.

Malcolm was sending messages to all these places.

Why did he do this?

Trey switches to a UNIX window and lists the files. The timestamps show each file was modified within the last twenty minutes. He opens one and reads it.

His world unravels.

His new world retreats into a dream.

The file contains his name, the address of *Thought*Fluence, an explanation of his plan to make the world a better place, and his last known location. Sage Storage.

No.

No. No. No.

This can't be happening.

This file, and the others Malcolm modified, are being sent to millions of people on the East Coast right now. He begins to rewrite the messages, typing as fast as he can.

"Drop the laptop," Emma says. She stands over him, aiming her gun down. "Don't touch another key."

"Emma." He puts on his salesman smile. "Join me down here. It's not what you think."

Malcolm convulses. Red spittle runs down his chin.

"Drop it," she says.

"I can't do that, but it's okay. Once the world starts over, so can we. We had some good times, remember? We can start over."

She shakes her head. "Drop it."

"We had some good times, remember? We started over."

"Shut up."

"We had some good times, remember? We started over."

"Say it again and die."

"You won't shoot me." He pauses. "Do you know why you won't shoot me?"

"I should have shot you at Kevin's apartment when I had

the chance. I won't make that mistake again."

"You won't shoot me because we had some good times, remember? We started over."

Her muzzle flashes, and the laptop explodes. Trey shields his face, but shrapnel rips into his cheek anyway. He pushes his back against the dirt wall and rises, keeping his face covered. "Why? Why would you do this to us, Emma?"

"You're a murderer. Do you know how many people have died?"

"I only wanted to make the world a better place. Sometimes, to make an omelet, people have to—"

"Over one hundred thousand are dead because of you— fathers, mothers, children."

The air leaves his chest. "Lessard said it would only be a small percentage."

"You infected millions with your lies."

"I didn't mean for them to die. I only wanted to make— "

"Don't say it again. I swear to God—if you say that one more time . . ."

A chopper's shadow covers the ground, its mighty blades slicing through the air. *Womp, womp, womp.*

"Emma, help me. We can make this right."

"This is the police," an impossibly loud voice thunders from above. "Put your weapons down. We have you—"

A cacophony of sirens attacks the sky. Trey covers his ears. He pictures black trucks with the word SWAT painted on the side breaking through the chain-link fence. Police cruisers with giant front bumpers. Specialists in black masks and bulletproof vests wielding automatic rifles.

Emma looks over her shoulder and shouts, "It's over, Trey. They're here for you."

CHAPTER SEVENTY-TWO

EMMA - *Two Months Later*

For me, there's something soothing about ice cream. I suppose this is true for most people, but lately, it's meant the world to me. It's meant sitting in a Baskin-Robbins booth across from Alyssa and Vivian on a lazy Sunday afternoon, watching the world return to normal.

"Vivian, what time does she make you go to bed?" I ask.

"Eight o'clock." She dabs at her ice cream sundae. Whipped cream, chocolate chips, and cherries.

"Do you go to sleep at that time, or do you sneak out of bed and play for a while?"

Alyssa raises her eyebrows.

Vivian grins at her mom. "Sometimes I go to sleep."

"Do you have dessert before bed?" I ask.

"Yes."

"What's your favorite?"

"Ice cream."

"I thought it was cookies," Alyssa says.

"It is." She spoons a dollop of the creamy goodness into her mouth. "It's both."

"What happens when you get in trouble? Does she send you to bed without dessert?"

"Why are you asking her all these questions?" Alyssa tries to see through me.

"I don't know." I lick my cone. "Curious about mom-life, I guess."

Vivian pushes a cherry aside with her spoon. She's been through so much. Her therapist says she's doing great dealing with the kidnapping. Her post-traumatic stress disorder symptoms have decreased dramatically over the last month, but she's not out of the woods yet. She'll carry it with her for the rest of her life.

I wish I knew who picked her up in the SUV the day they arrested Trey. Vivian said they wore masks. The driver had a man's voice, and the person in the back was a woman, but other than that, she couldn't provide any details. For a time, we hoped she had suppressed something useful. We hoped her therapy would help her remember, but it didn't happen. Whoever it was, they knew where to take her. They dropped her off outside Jeremy's condo, where Alyssa had been hiding.

I'm forever grateful to them for saving her, whoever they are.

"That's it?" Alyssa wrinkles her nose. "You want to know about mom-life? Let me tell you about *mom-life*. It's a nonstop thrill ride." She rolls her eyes. "Nothing but snacks and laundry. Sometimes all at once. You haven't lived until you've picked granola bar pieces out of the washing machine filter."

I laugh. "Okay. Maybe I just want to be a good aunt." I put my hand on Vivian's wrist. "And if that means no dessert when you've misbehaved, then—"

"Hey," Vivian protests.

"What's the real reason you're asking these questions?"

Alyssa narrows her eyes.

"Someday, I might have a little Vivian of my own."

"What's his name?" Alyssa asks.

"Nobody." I sit back. "His name is *nobody* because I'm not seeing anybody. But who knows . . ."

As much as I've meditated, exercised, and distracted myself reading journals and literary fiction for the last two months, I still can't keep Trey from popping into my head. I'm still embarrassed by his power over me. I marvel at the fact we only went on one date. His perfect looks and charisma hid his damage. He was an Adonis on the outside and a Kraken on the inside. Now, all of his sides are serving multiple life sentences. The authorities seized *Thought*Fluence, and the government put new laws in place regulating the use of the internet to disseminate harmful messages. Lies and half-truths. So far, it has mostly affected social media companies. Ironically, I think it will eventually make the world a better place.

I picture Trey sitting in his prison cell, and I have to laugh, thinking I could become one of those women who fall in love and marries an inmate. That's a psychosis I've never researched and, therefore, never understood.

My ice cream cone suddenly tastes sour. What am I thinking? I'd never date Trey again.

My stomach churns just thinking about it.

Because of him, Malcolm died.

"So, you're getting back in the game?" Alyssa asks.

"You could say that. I'm told I should wait a year, but I think I'm ready. I'm returning to the university next week."

"That soon?"

"It's been two months. I'm not sure if I'm going to stay, though. I'm only going for a meeting to discuss the future of the project."

"Is it going to be hard for you, going back? Seeing Dr. Santan and everyone again?"

"I don't think so."

"What about Wilson? You never liked him. I don't really like him. Is he still a conceited know-it-all?"

"I don't even know if he's still there. If so, I hope he's changed." I glance out the window. "We've all changed."

"I hear that," she says.

"The project will have a ton of scrutiny now if it continues. I'm not sure if that's a blessing or a curse."

"How so?"

"Trey proved the viability of our work to the world, but the new social media laws might wrap us up in so much red tape we might not be able to make progress. Granting institutions might avoid us because of the publicity. There are a lot of factors. I just don't know."

"I don't know either, but—sorry. I wasn't listening." She smirks. "You lost me at 'viability.' *Boring*. Anyway, it doesn't matter. I know you'll make the right decision."

"Thanks."

"Can I have another one?" Vivian asks.

"You haven't finished that one yet," Alyssa says.

"What do you want?" I pull out my wallet. "The same?"

"Yes."

"But you didn't eat the cherries?"

"I still want them. I like the way they look." She uses her spoon to roll one around the bowl. "They're funny."

CHAPTER SEVENTY-THREE

EMMA

McConnell Hall hasn't changed during my two-month sabbatical, but nothing here is familiar. The same tile flooring runs down the corridor, separating our offices. D'Angelo's name plate is still hanging on his door. The windows—those have changed. Eight-by-eight, frosted glass squares adjoined by white mortar. They let light in and keep prying eyes out. I heard the news vans and reporters caused tons of chaos when the *Thought*Fluence story broke.

I stop near the break room.

I'm wrong.

The windows haven't changed. I just never looked at them before. I was always too busy working to concern myself with the outside world. The clock on the wall tells me I'm ten minutes late for the go-no-go meeting. I never liked that clock.

I hang here a minute longer.

Someone hung our award plaque on the wall. It was in D'Angelo's office before. Seeing it in the smelly break room is off-putting, but who cares. My name isn't on it anyway.

I open the door to the conference room, and Dr. Halsford waves me inside. As the department chair, he's running the meeting. He stands at the head of the table, and the only seat left is immediately to his right. I hate sitting in front of the class. Wilson has always loved it. He sits directly across from me, next to Dr. Judith Aimes and a very young woman, presumably her intern. D'Angelo's intern, Tory, sits to my right.

D'Angelo isn't here.

I double check the room.

Neither is Nimisha.

Stranger than that, Wilson has his laptop open, *and* he's looking at it. I've never seen him do that unless he was presenting. The last time I saw him, he was in a Ghostbusters suit. When I went on sabbatical, I *went* on sabbatical. I haven't seen anyone since they hauled Trey away. It's been great. No TV. No social media. Almost no internet. Nothing other than a few visits with Alyssa, Vivian, and my father.

The thought of going on Facebook makes me want to stab my eyes out.

"Sorry I'm late," I say.

"That's quite all right." Dr. Halsford picks up a stack of papers and levels them by banging the edges against the table. "We waited for you. Now if you give me a minute, we'll get started."

I lean to my right and whisper, "It's good to see you, Tory. How have things been around here?"

"Oh, things are—"

Wilson peers at me over his laptop and says, "I'm so glad you're here, Emma. How have you been?"

"Great, Wilson. Really great." Like McConnell Hall, I recognize him, but he's not familiar. He's never been glad to see me before.

"Let's get on with this," Dr. Halsford says. "You can all have your little chat session when we're done discussing the project." He picks up the first page from the stack of papers. "I want to start with a brief history of the project from the beginning for those of us who weren't a part of it. We all know how it ended." He glances at me.

I smile in return.

As he reads, I remember the hours I spent toiling under D'Angelo. The late nights. The stale coffee. The non-existent recognition and the minuscule pay.

"And that brings us to today," Dr. Halsford says.

"Excuse me," I say. "But where is Dr. Santan?"

"I'll get to that."

He continues to talk about the project. The effect Trey's misuse of our research had on the world. The promise and the threat. "And that is why I believe Dr. Santan decided to leave the project. In fact, he left the university. He's retiring."

No one appears particularly surprised. I visited D'Angelo in the hospital once shortly after everything went down. It was a nightmare. He couldn't speak, but his wife could. Marjorie gave me a tongue-lashing like none I'd ever had. She blamed me for unleashing Trey on the world. I thought I'd see D'Angelo today, but I guess not.

"It's sad how Dr. Santan cracked," Dr. Aimes says. "He couldn't take the guilt. He never dreamed his work would hurt so many people."

Dr. Halsford flashes her a disconcerting look.

"What about Nimisha?" I ask.

"You didn't hear?" Wilson says.

"No, I don't know anything."

"She left the country. She toured Africa, then found a

place in Italy. We had a small going away party for her. I tried to invite you, but you didn't return my calls."

"I'm sorry. I was unplugged."

"It's okay." Wilson lowers his head and sighs. "I miss her." When he looks up, everyone is staring at him. "We all miss her, right?"

I nod to give him some comfort. "Whoa. Italy. Are you and Travis still—"

"We're working on things," he says. "We have trust issues."

"Ahem." Dr. Halsford shakes his papers. "We're here to discuss the future of the project, not gossip. The College would like the work to continue, which is why we have Dr. Aimes and Courtney here. Without intending to sound unsympathetic, we're suggesting they step in and replace Dr. Santan and Nimisha."

"Not a replacement," Dr. Aimes says. "I could never fill D'Angelo's shoes."

"I never met Nimisha," Courtney says.

Dr. Halsford nods at Dr. Aimes. "Of course not, Judith. But it's not due to a lack of experience. You're very well respected. It's only for lack of knowledge on the project itself." He rears his head toward me. "That's why it can't continue without you, Emma."

That familiar anvil of responsibility materializes over my head, ready to crush me.

"That's right," Dr. Aimes says to me. "I already have too much on my plate. But I'd help you navigate the university's bureaucracy. Anything you need, I'd get it for you. Courtney here would support you as much as possible, and Tory would be your intern." The two young women grin ear-to-ear.

"Emma," Dr. Halsford says, "we want you to take over

Dr. Santan's work. It will all be yours."

I gaze at Wilson until he stops taking notes and lifts his eyes to me.

"Don't look at me," he says. "You know I don't know anything about the project. At least, not as much as you do. I have a ton to learn, but if you'll have me, I promise to catch up. I've spent the last month studying nothing but mass persuasion." I can't believe my ears. Did he just admit to slacking off for the last several years? "I know how this looks, but my heart wasn't in it before. You were the only one who ever called me on it. But now, after everything that happened . . . I promise I'll work day and night to help you finish this thing."

Everything that happened . . .

I know what happened to me. I can only hope Wilson has stopped lying. I found peace, serenity, and security away from work. I found a future where my mother's wish could at least have a chance of coming true—fall in love, marry someone, have the experience of being a mother.

Avoid loneliness.

I don't know what happened to Wilson, but it must have been significant. This sort of psychic change rarely happens to anyone, let alone someone as flawed as he was. Something inside urges me to help him.

"Everything going forward on the project," Dr. Halsford says, "would be in your hands, Emma. We'd like additions and revisions made to the work based on results from the tragic events of these past few months, and we'd like your experience to drive us forward. All the work would go in your name—representing the psychology department, of course."

"That's correct," Dr. Aimes says. "I'd only be an adviser."

"So?" Dr. Halsford puts his papers down. "What's it

going to be?"

Without D'Angelo here, pushing me to work nights and weekends, I could set my own schedule. Create a balance. I have always loved my work. Looking around the room— expectant, hopeful eyes—I feel truly needed. This has never happened to me in McConnell Hall before. I wonder if I could have the windows replaced with clear glass.

"Emma?" Dr. Halsford says. "Did you hear my question?"

"Yes, I heard you."

"Well?"

Usually, given the chance, I'd make everyone wait until I could hold my magnifying glass beneath the weeping cherry tree and ask Mom for guidance.

I don't need to do that anymore.

"Wilson, Tory, Courtney—meet me in my office in an hour," I say. "We have a lot of work ahead of us."

CHAPTER SEVENTY-FOUR

EMMA

My breath hangs in the air like whispers from my ancestors. The clouds hang low, pressing down on the tops of the mid-morning mountains. The damp ground cradles my knees before the weeping cherry tree. I raise my magnifying glass and gaze at the bark, but it exposes nothing new.

Yet, everything has changed.

"Hi, Mom. You'll be happy to know I've decided to start dating. And I mean, *seriously* start dating. I'm also not giving up on my psychology work. I can do both." I bow my head. "I miss you."

The wind blows my hair into my eyes. Goosebumps form on the back of my neck. I aim the magnifying glass at the farmhouse. It's blurry from this distance, like the past. My mom grew up here. She used to tell me warm stories about her childhood—time spent with her family, sitting by the fire at Christmas, playing checkers on the porch in summer. But now, the cold wind whistles through the broken windows. The farmhouse watches me like a hermit who hasn't seen another face in years. I'm not going to end up like that.

I'm going to have a family of my own.

A raindrop lands on the magnifying glass. Another one hits me in the eye. I stand, and the wind gusts and the rain comes. I'm not ready to leave, but the deluge drenches my body within seconds. I race to the farmhouse and burst through the front door. Vainly, I try to brush the water off my pants, but it's no use. I'm a sponge.

The wind sucks the front door open wide, then slams it shut with a *bang*. The latch is broken, so I wedge a stick into the door frame to keep it from happening again.

The wind howls at me.

The rain beats on the roof.

The shadow from the kitchen table reaches across the floor into the living room and dies at my feet.

"Hello, Emma. Let me bring you a towel."

"Who's there?" I creep toward the kitchen. No one's seated at the table. There's a microwave on the counter and an electric generator on the floor. White paper plates and plastic cutlery. "Who's here?"

A blonde woman with dark skin appears in the bedroom doorway holding a Hello Kitty beach towel. The dim light obscures her features.

"Nimisha?" I ask. "Is that you?"

She crosses the room and hands me the towel.

"It's good to see you, Emma." The downpour relaxes its attack on the roof. She takes a seat at the table and gazes out the window. "Wow. It's really coming down out there."

She looks like a different person, but it's her. She must have dyed her hair blonde and cut it short herself because it's jagged on one side. Her cheeks have lost their youthful glow.

There's a sadness in her eyes.

I try to dry myself off, but the towel doesn't absorb much.

"What are you doing here?"

"You're alone, right?" she asks.

"Yes." I put the towel down and sit across from her at the table. "How long have you been here?"

"Long enough to know I can't stay forever."

"*Why* are you here? Wilson said you went to Italy." Once a liar, always a liar.

"Oh, Emma." She puts her face in her hands and sobs. "I'm so sorry."

"For what?"

"For believing in him."

"Wilson? What did he do?"

"No. Trey Wilkes. I—I helped him." She raises her head. Tears stream down her cheeks. "He said he loved me. We started dating the day after I joined you at the university. I'm so sorry."

I reach over and put my hand on hers. "It's okay. He's locked up."

"You don't understand. I helped him destroy the world. I hurt all those people. I hurt you."

"How?"

She collects herself. Looks out the window. "All my life, my parents made fun of Kandour. They were both originally from Anlish, so they always told Kandour jokes and laughed at how stupid the people who lived there were. When Trey asked me if I knew of a place gullible enough for his first campaign—it's my fault those people died."

"No, it's not."

"Then it spread to Anlish."

"It's not your fault. Believe me. I fell for Trey's lies, too. You didn't make him attack those places."

"No, but I made it possible. I stole Dr. Santan's research

and gave it to him." She raises her voice. "I stole from you, Emma, and when I couldn't get everything, I helped him kidnap Dr. Santan. I made sure Trey knew about the awards banquet. I showed him where Dr. Santan lived. I—"

"Calm down. It's going to be okay. It's all over now."

"No, it's not." She stands and turns toward the bedroom. "There's more."

I stand. Water escapes my hair and runs down my face. "What?"

"When I called you and asked if you would return to work, we were going to kidnap you. I swear, I didn't know what Trey had done to Dr. Santan at the time. Really. When you rescued Dr. Santan and that other guy, I saw their faces on the security camera—oh, my God." She chokes. Puts her hand on her stomach and coughs.

"It was you," I say. "You were the one who saved Wilson."

She nods. "I turned the security cameras off and went to the break room. We left before you did. It was only luck that we saw you later that day."

"What do you mean?"

"Wilson and I were trying to decide what to do when we saw you in that truck. We followed you to a Motel 6, then up here."

"What kind of car do you have? Is it red?"

"Yes." She sniffs. "It's a little SUV. I hid it in the woods."

Malcolm was right. We had been followed. "You did the right thing, rescuing Wilson."

"It doesn't make up for everything. I tried—we tried to make up for everything, but . . ." Her forefinger taps against her thumb relentlessly. "You'll never forgive me," she says.

"For what? What is it?"

"Vivian."

"What?"

"I lied to you. I told you I wanted to help you. I told you I wanted to help your friend, and to do that, I needed to know where she was. I tricked you into giving me Alyssa's phone number and telling me about her ex's condo." My heart sinks. "I didn't only help Trey kidnap Dr. Santan. I helped him kidnap that little girl."

"Nimisha . . ." I'm at a loss for words. Vivian could have been killed at the exchange. Trey's influence over Nimisha, blinded by love or not—is it excusable? Couldn't she have done something? Said no?

She turns. Looks me in the eye. "I didn't know he was going to take her, I swear. And—Wilson and I. We tried to make it right, but what she went through before we picked her up. That poor little girl." She wipes the tears from her face. "How is she doing?"

"You picked her up?" Of course. The black SUV outside the storage container yard. Nimisha had access to *Thought*Fluence's vehicles.

"We wore masks so she couldn't identify us, but she was so terrified when we pulled her into the car. I had to hold her down while Wilson drove. She thought she was being kidnapped again, and in a way, she was."

It's never been colder in the farmhouse than it is right now.

"How is she doing?" Nimisha asks.

"She's damaged, but she's okay." I reach into my pocket and pull out my car keys. "She will be okay."

"What are you going to do?" Nimisha asks, staring at my keys.

I have to get out of here. This is all too much. Most of

the time, self-serving guilt is punishment enough for someone who's made mistakes, but I want to blame her for everything. I want her punished. I want her punished for falling for Trey. Believing his lies.

I turn to go.

"Emma? Please."

I stop.

The truth hits me like a hammer.

I fell for Trey, too. I believed his lies—too. If there's blame to be had, it belongs to both of us. I could have stopped him before he started if I'd only trusted Detective Galen. If I hadn't been so paranoid about the police.

"Emma, what are you going to do?" she asks.

I put my keys back in my pocket and pull out my magnifying glass. "You took Vivian back to her mom's. You rescued Wilson. You did the right things when you weren't under Trey's spell."

"The police won't see it that way. I'm an accomplice. Are you going to turn me in?"

I glance at the generator. Her blonde hair.

Water drips from the ceiling.

She can't stay here forever.

"Emma?"

"I can't blame you for being brainwashed. If I did that, I'd have to blame everyone who ever believed something they read on the internet."

"So?"

"So, no. I'm not going to turn you in."

The air outside is fresh.

Clean.

The clouds clear, and I drive home.

Alone.

ENJOYED THE DELUSION?

If so, I'd love to hear from you. Please send me an email at topaine@topaine.com and let me know your thoughts. If you'd like to hear about upcoming releases from me, follow me on Amazon, BookBub, or sign up for my newsletter at:

https://topaine.com

You can also connect with me on:
    Facebook – https://facebook.com/topaineauthor
    Instagram - https://instagram.com/t.o.paine
    Twitter (X) - https://twitter.com/topaine

A review on Amazon, Goodreads, or BookBub would mean the world to me. Reviews are the single most important factor in an author's success and longevity. If you enjoyed this novel, please consider leaving a review, even if it is only a line or two. I would very much appreciate it.

ACKNOWLEDGMENTS

Thank you!
Dear Fearless Reader, thank you so much for sharing your time with Emma, Malcolm, Trey, and the others. Readers like you make the world of fiction a wonderful place.

I also want to thank my editor, David Downing, my awesome ITW critique group, my pre-release review team, and most of all, my beloved first reader, Kim. She always helps me see the truth through the magnifying glass.

GET AN EXCLUSIVE BONUS STORY

There is always a FREE short story, novella, or full-length novel available on my website. Come on over to:

https://topaine.com/free

ENTER TO WIN A GIVEAWAY

Several times a year, my publisher and I sponsor giveaways as a thank you for reading. Past giveaways included Kindle Paperwhites, Amazon Gift Cards, Headphones, my novels, and novels by other authors. Check out the current giveaway at:

https://topaine.com/giveaway

ALSO BY T.O. PAINE

THE DELUSION

"Don't believe everything you read on the internet. It'll drive you crazy. Literally."

This year's Psychological Research Award winner, Emma, ponders the years she's spent meeting her professor's demands. Then he goes missing and her work is to blame. Now, she must rescue him before the world destroys itself.

THE EXCURSION

"Escape was never an option."

Charly Highsmith is a survivor, but when a blizzard traps her neurodivergent brother with a murderous hunter high in the Colorado Rockies, survival takes on an entirely new meaning. It's not about what God gave you. It's about your ability to adapt.

ALSO BY T.O. PAINE

THE RESENTMENT
"A Wickedly Sharp Suspense Thriller"

They killed her husband. Now, they're going to kill her son. The Resentment is an emotionally charged thriller about anger, addiction, and redemption with more twists than a night on the town. You're only as sick as your secrets . . .

THE TEACHING
"A thriller based on the author's experience living in a cult."

They had her life planned, but when a mysterious girl goes missing, the search just might end her life. The Teaching is a suspense thriller set in a cult where there is no death, and there is no dying. Or is there?

ABOUT THE AUTHOR

T.O. Paine is an award-winning author of fast-paced thriller suspense novels. He is a member of International Thriller Writers and holds a master's degree in computer information systems. When he is not writing, you can find him running and cycling through the mountains of Colorado, USA. T.O. has run fifty marathons in fifty states, ridden his road bike over 10,000 miles up 10,000-foot mountains, and completed an IRONMAN.

T.O. resides with his wife, two children, and two Boston terriers: Fiona the Ogre and Rudy the Trickster.